Demons of Solomon

FLASH FICTION FROM HELL

A Hydra Productions Anthology

Published by

Hydra Productions Online LLC

CONTENTS

BA'AL: A TRUE CONVERSION
J. BECK

July 14, 1951- "Oh hear our cries, lord above all!"
Their chanting concluded this fourth round, and it would begin
anew, louder, as it had before. I was hired to investigate this cult,
just a group of local boys with nothing better to do, they said. Scare
them off and they'll move on to something else. I don't think that
option remains to me. This is much greater than a group of kids
wanting to have fun outside their parents' control. Worshipping a
false god is a sin. I must bring this to my Bishop's attention.

24 July, 1951- The Bishop's response came in the mail today. While
he does share my concerns, he believes that wayward youths make
the best Catholics, as they have the experience in life to understand
that this is the true faith. He released me to continue my
investigation if I thought it relevant, but that I had fulfilled my
duties to investigate and can tell the local parish that it's not a major
concern, and that they'll grow out of it. I will do as he asks, but my
investigation will continue. It was a little too real for me to say that
nothing is going on.

11 August, 1951- I believe they noticed me tonight. It didn't seem to
interrupt their ritual, but one of them gestured in passing for me to
join them. I didn't, of course, as I am true to my faith, but that they
are welcoming of complete strangers into their midst surprises me.
How do they know they aren't inviting a policeman or other official
into their midst? This could cause significant problems in the parish,
as many in the congregation have an outstanding reputation in our
community. I will have to take steps to remove this cult from our
community without taking direct action.

13 August, 1951- How did they find out where I live? I came home
from work today and saw a note in my door. It just read "24 August,

big feast, you are welcome to attend". No other information. This is getting odd, but if they are inviting me, then there is nothing to risk in attending. I suppose it will be at the same place and time as their previous meetings. At worst, I'll have to get the police involved to help straighten these boys out.

25 August, 1951- I was right, and it was a feast. I don't know how they came up with so much food. There were a few strange things that occurred on the way there and during it though. First, when I was walking to the area, a man appeared out of thin air, head turned aside, offering me a long black cloak and a mask. He bid me to wear these over my clothes, as all attendees tonight are to remain anonymous. I took them and put them on, after which he turned and bid me to make myself welcome. I was encouraged to come up with a different name to help with my anonymity. My name amongst them is Michael. I hope that invoking the archangel protects me should this be more than it seems. When I arrived at the site of the feast, I was the only one standing in the area for a few seconds, then others started to arrive, trickling in through the trees, all in black, all silent. All of us took a place behind a chair and waiting for something. Fortunately, I was not kept waiting long. A man appeared in the chair at the head of the table, invisible until then my illusion. I will admit it was a clever one, as I saw nothing to indicate anything was present in the chair until he appeared. He bid us all sit, then said an invocation to this Ba'al while tracing a strange shape in the air in front of him. I didn't hear any of what was said, as I was mentally invoking St. Michael to protect me, but when it was done, a sense of calm came over the group. He said that there was a visitor amongst them, that he should introduce himself as the night goes on, and that all should welcome him with open arms. He then called for food and drinks to be brought. I need to stop writing for today, as pressing matters are at hand in my home, but this is burned so vividly in my mind I doubt I'll forget any of it.

26 August, 1951- I forgot a little of it, specifically how I got home. The food and drinks were brought by women, wearing little clothing to cover themselves. As I was sweating profusely under the cloak and my clothes, I could understand why, yet it still is outrageous to think that women will dress in so little. The food and drink were excellent, all home cooked. The wine had been diluted down, as this group views drunkenness the same as we do. The man who was in the chair came around and asked if I had any questions about the group. I don't know how he knew I was the visitor, given the cloak

and mask, and he said he noted me when I walked in before everyone else. He gave a brief lesson on what Ba'al was and meant. I was surprised to learn that the Israelites knew my own God as Ba'al for a long time. My surprise must have registered under the mask, as he went on to say that Ba'al as a word simply meant "lord". He said that they still worshipped the same God as the parish, just in a different way, and that he hoped the police would not be involved. How did he know I was considering this? I'm writing another letter to the Bishop.

14 September, 1951- I found another note in my door, inviting me to a ceremony for remembrance on Hollow's Eve, and requested I leave my reply in the door where I found the note. The Bishop's letter also returned, and he said simply to live as a Christian among them and they will return to the fold. I think I'll go to this Hollow's Eve ceremony.

17 September, 1951- A package was at my door, with a cloak and instructions on how to make my own mask, as well as a depiction of the sigil of Ba'al. I think I'll put Michael and Gabriel on my mask as protection.

12 October, 1951- A revelation came to me today. If Ba'al is the term for "lord", and our Lord can be called as "Ba'al", why were others killed for worshipping Ba'al? Is the history of my faith a lie? Ba'al is God, God is Ba'al, or so they would teach. I cannot let this go unchallenged.

01 November, 1951. Ba'al is God, God is Ba'al. Ba'al is God, God is Ba'al. Ba'al is God, God is Ba'al. I know the truth of his power. The police arrived as I requested, and I watched the entire ceremony vanish before my eyes. The police ridiculed me and left, leaving me with my own embarrassment. I threw off my cloak and mask in shame, and started to leave, but bumped into someone who I could not see. He simply asked if I now believed what he said was true. I nodded, words refusing to come to my lips. All of them reappeared in front of me, seeing me for who I truly was. The ceremony ended as a result of the disruption, but I will no longer be attending the parish. I will tell the parents that it's nothing for them to be worried about, as they are still worshipping the one true God. That the Bishop himself leads them I will keep to myself.

About the Author
J. Beck is a new author with a passion for history, music, and fantasy gaming.

2

AGARES: THE QUAKES HE MAKES
CHANDRA TRULOVE FRY

He sat upon his most cherished pet, waiting for the earthquake to end. It happened every time he made his appearance on Earth. Almost as if the earth was just too fragile to handle his presence. Still, he was summoned and so he must appear. Well, he didn't have to really, but he always chose to. It gave him something more exciting to do than see over his thirty-one legions of spirits. Eternity could be so mundane. This at least gave him a chance to stretch his limbs and do something different.

He road Timseh slowly down the deserted street to make his way towards the home that he was summoned too. Soon his trusted hawk, Teyre, landed on his arm to join him. The crocodile he rode was a fierce looking creature. Larger than most crocodiles with a deep green skin and bright beady read eyes. Formidable indeed. The hawk was large and black with sharp eyes and a beak to kill. He loved his pets dearly and never went anywhere without them. He supposed in this day and age where there were cars, trains, and planes, that it would be an odd sight to see a fair man as he is riding upon a large demonic crocodile while carrying a hawk. He could have caught up with the times and changed things up a bit, but he was set in his ways and chose to stick with tradition.

Closing in on the house he wondered what the man that summoned him wanted. Probably another human that wanted sound financial advice or one of those earth lovers that wanted the perfect garden, usually it was a pot garden these days. Maybe he wanted someone in power to be removed. Agares liked that idea. It would be fun to destroy yet another dignitary. He continued down the street looking for his seal upon the door of the house that he was summoned to. He could just appear at the door in a flash but where was the fun in that? This slow approach was much more fun. Life could be so dull so why hurry?

Just when he thought that he would not have to chase any spirits this day he caught one darting off out of the corner of his eye. He had no choice but to pause his journey and go off in pursuit of this runaway. He spoke a word to Timseh and soon the crocodile was off on the hunt. The spirit picked up its pace when he saw he was being pursued. All spirits knew that Agares would come for them should they manage to escape Hell. If caught they would face dire consequences, as if Hell were not bad enough. The spirit was wise to run but it would be to no avail. Agares always caught them. He told Teyre to fetch. The hawk bobbed its head in excitement as it flew off after the fleeing spirit. Agares laughed as he watched the goshawk dig its talons deep into the spirit and pin him down. The spirit squirmed trying to break free but once Teyre's talons were sunk in there was absolutely no escape.

"You may as well stop. There is no escape now. You will be returned back to Hell where you belong." Agares stated.

"Please, god no!" The spirit begged. Agares broke out into hysterical laughter,

"Your chances to make appeals to God are over. You should have done that while you still breathed. Now, you belong to Hell!"

"No! I beg of you, let me go. I'll do anything! Anything!" The spirit begged.

"You really don't get it do you. There is no bargaining. No get out of jail free card. Nothing! You are sealed to Hell for eternity!" Agares spat as he leaned down over the spirit. He placed two fingers on the spirit's forehead and said,

"Tkun marret lura għall-infern li inti ħarbtu!" The spirit let out a wail that could wake the dead. Agares looked around and saw many spirits dancing about. He never did understand that. Maybe they rejoiced that they would not be pursued and sent to Hell like the poor soul he just caught. The spirit vanished from the earthly realms, descending down to Hell where he belonged. Agares brushed his hands off and turned his crocodile back towards the town and on to the house that he had been summoned to. He bowed his heads to the dancing spirits as he rode onward. Teyre landed on his shoulder, licking her talons while joining him once again. He smiled, knowing that Teyre loved being a part of his entourage.

They came to a halt in front of a small house on the outskirts of the town. His sigil stood out on the door, beckoning him to enter. He moved right through the door, causing a young man to cry out in fear.

"Relax, it's me. You must be the one who summoned me?" Agares knew that he was since his sigil burned brightly on the man's forearm. The man had on some ridiculous long black hooded robe and wore an upside down cross. All manner of occultish items cluttered the living room. This made Agares chuckle. Humans knew so little of the spirit realm. Yet, every once in a while they got something right, hence why he was there.

"You are Agares?" the man's voice faltered. He had to be around nineteen. He was tall and lean with bright green eyes and sandy blonde hair. He prostrated himself on the ground in front of Agares. False worship was still a form of worship, right? He let the man grovel before him for a bit before responding,

"Yes, yes. I'm Agares. Rise boy. Why have you summoned me?" He watched the boy's excitement grown.

"I can't believe it's you. It's truly you! I'm just so overwhelmed that the summons worked!" The boy's elation was starting to irritate Agares.

"It's really me. Now, what do you want?" He demanded.

"Oh, of course. You must be very busy. I mean, you lead legions. That must be a lot of work." The man's praise was annoying.

"So, stop prattling and tell me what you want or I'm leaving." He rarely lost his temper but humans had a way of riling a demon up.

"I'm sorry. Ok, my name is Shane. I would like to learn every language that exists, including spiritual ones." Shane gained a sudden boldness that Agares rarely saw in humans these days. Still, he was a bit disappointed in the request,

"Languages? You summon me to learn languages? The era you live in has every language known to man at your fingertips and yet you ask this of me?" Agares shook his head and muttered under his breath, 'I had hoped it was the death of a dignitary.'

"You said it though, every language known to man. I want to learn those that even man does not know. Also, computers don't always get things right. Things get lost in interpretation. I believe that with you I can learn them properly and with better clarity." Shane smiled as he held his hands out in supplication.

"Hmmm... you make valid points there. Why do you want to learn these languages so badly?" Agares grew curious. The man's cheeks grew bright red and his eyes shifted away from the demon. Agares waited.

"I want to impress Megan." He stated simply. A woman. Of course. It was always a woman or a man. Humans made simple things so complicated. Agares sat back on his crocodile and stroked his beard.

"Of course. Very well then. Let's get started shall we?" He offered.

"Really? You'll teach me?" The man's voice grew in excitement.

"Silly man. You summoned me therefore I must abide by the summons. You must know however, that it does come with a price. You will owe me in the future. So, if you feel that it is worth it then let's proceed." Agares was a fair demon. He always allowed them to back out. They never did.

"I agree! It's so worth it!" Shane cried out. They always thought it was worth it until the end when he came to collect his dues. Then they regretted it all. Agares shook his head. Would humans ever learn? He supposed not. He pulled out his language book and lay it on Shane's coffee table,

"Let us begin." The eager man fell on his knees and stared at the magical book that was displayed before him. Agares delved in teaching him. He would take his time since he had no idea when his next summons would come. It became rarer as time moved on and thus he learned to treasure these moments.

About the Author

Chandra Trulove Fry is a multi-genre author who longs to try her hand at every genre at least once throughout her author career. She resides in Northern California with her wonderful husband and kids.

https://www.facebook.com/ChandrasAuthorPage/

VASSAGO: TO TRAP A DAEMON
PHILIPP J. KESSLER

***Rob carved a "V" into the chest of the young man
on the table.*** He giggled to himself as he watched the blood well
up and flow along the naked skin. This was victim number twelve in
his campaign of terror. The man had done nothing to deserve his
fate. Just in the wrong place at the wrong time. Or, as Rob "Vassago"
Cameron would say, the wrong place at the right time. One more of
those wrong place, right time scenarios and he would be ready to
perform the ritual.

Each of the murders had been a part of the ritual, building up to
the big bang. He'd been cautious with his plans. First one, then
another, and another. Slowly working his way around the calendar.
He'd read an article on a Satanic site that said a year-long ritual
could be sped up and done over the course of weeks as long as
proper adaptions were made.

He had taken a ritual from the Lesser Key of Solomon and
combined it with something he'd found in the Necronomicon. The
result was an accelerated ritual to bring the Devil himself into a
human body. One more victim, one more sacrifice and his ritual
would be complete!

So far the authorities had not been able to connect the bodies to
him or his mission. The only connection they had made, according
to the media, was the connection he had given them. The letter "V"
carved into each of the victims. Ironically, the media said it was the
Roman numeral for "five", an idea that should have been blown out
of the water as soon as the sixth victim was found.

"Buffoons," Rob said to himself as he admired his handing work.
"They'll not figure it out before it is too late." He smothered the
bleeding man with a plastic bag. Bloodletting was one thing, getting
it all over himself was another. Suffocation was a much cleaner way
to finish them off.

DING! DING! DING! His phone started going off as soon as he
left the abandoned garage. 'I knew I should've turned that thing off,'
he thought to himself as he looked at the screen.

WHERE U AT BRAH? The message was from his friend Alex Case. WE WAITIN 4 U AT BREWS. WANT US TO ORDER?

"Shit," he said aloud as he stared at the screen. "I nearly forgot..." he tapped out a response letting Alex know that he would be there in fifteen minutes or so. He stuffed the phone into his pocket again and hopped into his Impala.

*****

After dinner and drinks with Alex and the guys from work, Rob returned to his small apartment near downtown. One of the guys had asked about a spot of blood on his shirt. He dismissed it as being from a nosebleed. He hurried into the bathroom and checked to see if he had missed any other blood stains. Satisfied that he had only gotten one drop of blood on him, he stripped down and took a shower. He'd have to dispose of that t-shirt somewhere.

"I really should be more careful," he said aloud. "I've managed so far not to be connected, but if I get careless now it is over."

He finished toweling off and climbed into bed. He was so tired that he was asleep soon after he closed his eyes...

..."What do you think you are doing, Rob?" a voice asked him in the darkness.

"Wh-what? Who is that?" he was confused. He couldn't see.

"You know who it is," the voice said, Rob could actually hear the smile behind that voice.

"No," Rob shook his head. "No, I don't."

"Think, man!" the voice taunted him.

"I really don't," Rob shook himself. Or tried to. He found that he couldn't move more than his head. "Hey! What's going on here!"

"I thought you'd appreciate a taste of your own medicine," the voice said, the taunting tone had turned sinister. "Should feel familiar if you think about it."

"You keep telling me to think. Think about what?" The casualness to the conversation clued him that he was dreaming. It was too surreal not to be a dream. He squinted and peered into the darkness. "Who are you!?"

"I am that which you seek," the voice chuckled. "Riddle me this: What do you desire most in the world but is not of this world?"

"Power over Hell," Rob gave the simple answer. He didn't know why he said that. It was a dream. So, he decided it didn't matter.

"I think it is more than that, young man," the voice in the darkness countered. "There is something more than just power, in Hell or on Earth, that you desire. What is it?"

He just laid there. He couldn't move, so why not? His thoughts were racing. He closed his eyes and tried to wake himself up. 'This is only a dream, this is only a dream.'

"Keep telling yourself that, Robert," the voice startled him. "Yes, I can hear your thoughts. I can do a lot of things."

"Who are you!" Rob demanded. He thrashed his head about, still unable to move anything else.

"You do know. You've been invoking my name for the last... Let's see here, going on twelve weeks now."

"No. Impossible," Rob protested.

"If you don't believe, then why are you doing what you are doing? Why have you killed twelve innocent men?" The voice in the darkness had grown cold, no longer a hint of sinister humor.

"To control you and hell," he said simply.

"You have no idea what you are doing," the mysterious voice. "You will learn, soon enough."

▲▲▲▲▲

A week later Rob was stalking again. He'd been watching this particular man the whole ritual. He learned a lot about the stranger in those twelve weeks. Alex was a retail manager, no one really all that important. He was single, no children, and no pets. He was a high school dropout, but you wouldn't know by the books he chose to read. Every Friday, like clockwork.

This Friday was going to be different. Rob was ready with his knockout shot in the syringe and an extra dose in reserve to be on the safe side. He followed Alex down the street and around the corner of an alley. The alley was not well lit, but no one really seemed to mind. The neighborhood was quiet and had been for several years. He smiled when Alex paused for a moment to look at the motion activated yard light that didn't come on as he approached. That was the first time that had ever happened in all his years on the block. He shrugged and continued down the alley in the dark.

Rob snuck up from behind and jabbed the syringe's needle into Alex's neck. The other man smacked at his neck like he would if he were bitten by a mosquito. He kept going, his steps started to falter and his sight got blurry. Rob waited patiently for the other man to stagger against the wall of a garage butted up against the dark alley.

When Alex leaned against the wall Rob came up to him, "You okay?" he asked

"Yeah, I'm fine. Just a bit wooshy," Alex answered, his words had begun to slur. Alex took that as the good sign it was.

"Need any help?" he offered helpfully. People in the area were often kind and helpful, that made this part of the evening much easier for Rob.

"Nah, I sshhould be fine. Just need to rest for a second," his speech was getting worse. "On second thought, hold thish," he held the quart of soda out. "Hate to looshe that."

"Of course," Rob smiled warmly and took the soda. He stood there and waited for Alex to slide down the wall and plunk his backside onto the cobblestone alleyway. "Uppsie daisy," he chuckled as he stood the man up. The food and drink were forgotten on the ground.

For this final step in his ritual, Rob took Alex to an abandoned church on the edge of the city. It was run down and boarded up, well off the beaten path. It was just close enough to the nearest residential area that the body would be discovered in short order. Maybe even before it began to smell the ramshackle building up too much.

He had his victim stripped to his underwear and tied to the cracked altar on the dais. A dozen or so shattered wooden pews faced the front and Rob with his doomed companion. He felt like he had an audience for this one and smiled at the thought of it.

"You, my friend, are going to be the final step in this," he stroked the man's hair back from his face. "Vassago will be born into the world again tonight."

Rob lit a candle with his electric lighter and used it to light the rest of the candles around the space. The flickering flames added to the ambiance of what was to come. He set one of the candles at the man's feet and another at his head, the rest he left where they were.

Taking up a black marker, he uncapped it and began to draw a series of strange symbols on Alex's naked chest. A four-tongued tool with a rounded end came from the center of a square that had two arms. From the four corners of this square, Rob drew lines that ended in circles. A pair of horns came from the bottom side of the square. He drew a double circle around the piece and admired his handy work for a moment.

As he drew the knife from his belt to move to the next and final step of the ritual a cold air filled the chapel and the candles were blown out. He growled in the back of his throat and fished in his pockets for the electric lighter. A sound at the foot of the altar caught his attention.

"Who's there?" he asked.

"The one you wish to summon," the voice from his dream answered him.

"You are early," Rob said nervously.

"I can come and go as a wish," it said.

"Then why all this ritual? Why all these deaths?" Rob asked curiously. His nervousness was increasing as his eyes adjusted to the darkness.

"To prove to me that you are worthy," it answered him. "You have proven yourself satisfactorily."

"I'm pleased you approve," Rob said to the daemonic visage that had taken form from the shadows.

"I wouldn't be here otherwise. You could kill a hundred men in my name, I still would not come to you if you were not worthy," it took a step around the altar and took the dagger from Rob's hand. "There is no need to shed this one's blood."

"Why not? He'll wake up here and then everything will go to hell," he protested as the daemon used the knife to cut Alex's bonds.

"The final sacrifice is yours, not his," Vassago plunged the blade deep into Rob's chest, burying it to the hilt above his heart. Rob could not make a single sound as the shock of his fate settled upon him.

Vassago smiled and pulled out the blade. The silly human fell to the floor in a heap, his last breath escaping in a dull rattle. He ran his tongue over the blade, licking every last drop of blood. Rob's spirit rose from its corpse then and glared at the daemon.

"What?" Vassage asked. "You summoned me."

"To rule over you and hell!" Rob's transparent form spat.

"In your jeweled hell," Vassago said as he pulled a gemstone out of his own body and drew Rob's spirit into it. "To hell we go!" He cackled, waking Alex with the echoes as he disappeared from the old church.

About the Author

Philipp J. Kessler is a multi-genre author, editor, and publisher with a flair for paranormal and LGBTQIA stories. Search him on your favorite social media site under RevKess.
https://www.facebook.com/RevKessPMPC/

SAMIGINA AND THE DESPERATE MAN
CHANNIE COCKER

If you were to look at Kyle Warren you would think he was your typical average young adult male. About five seven and weighing around one eighty, he had sandy blonde hair and dark brown eyes with sun kissed skin. He kept a tight muscled figure by working out and ate like any other person. If you knew him you would think he was pretty normal. He mainly kept to himself and didn't go out much. He was an introvert by nature. What most didn't see or know about Kyle was that he could see ghosts. Ever since he was a young boy of five he was able to see and interact with the afterlife. As he got older he would learn why they never crossed over and through a lot of research he learned how to help them. During his teen years he helped many spirits move on and it felt good to help them. Knowing this would make most people uncomfortable and not wanting to be thrown into an insane asylum, Kyle learned how to hide his special gift.

Kyle never had a problem helping spirits cross over until he met Mera. She was the most beautiful young woman he had ever met even if she was dead. Mera had been murdered back in the 1920's by a drunk abusive husband. For a time Mera pursued revenge until the man had been murdered himself due to a drug deal gone bad. After that Mera simply roamed the earth without any direction or purpose. She happened upon Kyle when he entered her old home which had once been a mansion but now turned museum. The sparks flew between them right away and Kyle swore he was in love. The idea of dating a ghost was a bit bizarre and he had no idea how it would be accomplished.

The one thing he did know was that he could not keep coming to the museum to visit her. After several visits the owners were becoming highly suspicious. Wanting to keep Mera in his life he did the one thing that he knew would work. He found a personal object of Mera's. It was a locket she used to wear often. Mera had guided him to it. It was a precious heirloom of hers that she treasured dearly. Kyle took the locket and hid it in his jacket when Mera created a distraction by making a ghostly appearance in one of her paintings. People were mesmerized and excited that they got the rare treat of seeing a haunting.

Kyle managed to get the locket to his home without incident and was elated when Mera appeared before him in his living room.

"It worked! We did it!" Mera cried out.

"Yes!" Kyle wanted to hug her so badly, "What now though?"

"I don't know. I've never done this before," Mera shrugged. Kyle looked Mera up and down, admiring her sexy curves even if they were covered by a dress.

"Can you get naked?" He asked boldly. He admired the lovely blush that his question had brought on.

"I've never tried before," she replied shyly.

"I have a plan if you are up for it," he winked as he started taking off his clothes.

"Oh! Are you sure?" Mera watched him as he undressed and sat on the couch. His large erection giving her chills.

"I'm very sure. Your turn," Kyle smiled as he began to stroke himself. Mera disappeared for a moment but when she returned she was fully nude. Kyle motioned for her to lay on the couch. Once she was on the couch he leaned over above her as if he were on top of her, "Now, spread your legs wide and lift your arms up above your head." She did as he told her. He found her so damn sexy in that pose and more than anything he wanted to have her. Instead he began to masturbate as he stared at her nude body. She closed her eyes and moaned as if they were copulating. Then the most erotic thing Kyle had ever experienced happened to him. Mera possessed his body and finished the job for him. It was the closest thing to sex they could have. Mera left his body and lay next to him on the couch. He lay there for some time, enjoying her company before going to clean up.

*****

Five months later Kyle sat at his kitchen table. He and Mera had tried several ways to make it work between them but they soon grew old or just didn't work. Kyle researched many things to help them, even resurrection. They both wanted it so badly. That's when he read about the demon Samigina. A demon known to help with the afterlife.

Kyle set things up to summon the demon and did as the book suggested. He and Mera waited to see if the summons would work as they stared at the center of the kitchen table. A cough from behind them startled them out of their chairs.

"Whoa!" Kyle cried out when he saw the being before him. Mera simply stared in silence. "Are you Samigina?" Kyle asked.

"In the flesh. You can call me Sami. My full name makes most people think vagina and well I'm just not in the mood for those jokes right now," Sami explained.

"I honestly tried not to think that way. Sorry," Kyle apologized as he stared at the beautiful being before him. "You are so beautiful!" Sami laughed,

"Well thank you."

"Are you an angel?" Kyle asked, slightly confused as he continued to stare at the creature with wings.

"Not in the sense that you are thinking. Let's get to the meat of it though. Why have you summoned me?" Sami changed the subject.

"Oh! Well, I hear that you help with the afterlife?" Kyle questioned.

"I can help you find a loved one that has crossed over or let you know if they wound up in Heaven or Hell. Who do you want me to find?" Sami asked.

"There is no one to find. I found her. I was hoping you could help me find a way for us to be an actual couple." Kyle explained.

"I'm not sure I fully understand." Sami raised her brow.

"Mera, show yourself please." Kyle called out. Mera appeared by Kyle's side. She attempted to hold Kyle's hand but it went right through him. "Can you make her more solid or bring her back to life? Something like that?" Kyle pleaded.

"That's a bit unorthodox and I must say in all my life I don't think I've ever had someone summon me for such a purpose. I am afraid that that is something not within my expertise. I am not able to do as you ask." Sami gave him a half smile.

"There has to be a way though! I really want to be with her." Kyle whined. Sami closed her eyes and pinched her nose. Humans could be so odd at times.

"There is a way but not what I think you want to hear.

"Please! Anything." Kyle begged.

"Are you sure you are ready for it?" Sami bore into him with her deep black eyes.

"More than anything else in my life." Kyle replied proudly.

"Alright, here it is. You have to kill yourself. Only as a ghost can you be with her." Sami explained.

All of the blood drained from Kyle's face as he stumbled and nearly fainted,

"Uh...there really is no other way?"

"I'm sorry but no." Sami was growing impatient, "I can assist you if you like."

"How?" Kyle found a chair to sit in before he passed out. Sami pulled out a vial from her pocket and handed it to Kyle.

"All you have to do is drink that." She informed. Kyle held the vial up to see its contents then opened it to smell. He gagged at the smell of it and was not so sure he could drink it. Then he saw the pleading eyes of Mera who wanted nothing more than to be with him. Would it be so bad as all that? He tipped the vial at Mera and said,

"Bottoms up!" He downed it before thinking. The poison was instantaneous as it coursed through his veins. He doubled over, falling to the floor and clutching at his heart. He was dead in minutes. Mera watched as Kyle's spirit left his body. As soon as he spotted her, she was in his arms with him kissing her, passionately. Sami stood back silently and watched. She perked up when she saw a portal open up and a few of her fellow brethren came in straight from Hell. They walked up to Kyle and tapped him on the shoulder.

Kyle's eyes grew wide when he saw the demons standing there waiting for him. He noticed the portal and the inferno inside it. Turning to Sami he cried out, "I don't understand. What's going on?"

"You humans make it so easy. See you in Hell, Kyle." Sami laughed. Kyle screamed and begged as the demons drug him to Hell's gates. He reached out to Mera in desperation. Mera's heart broke as she watched them drag him away. She turned and glared at Sami with a fuming hatred. Sami motioned to the portal,

"No one is stopping you from joining him. Definitely a for sure way to stay together." She watched as Mera stood tall and with a firm determination she followed Kyle into the portal. The portal vanished, leaving Sami alone. She examined her nails as she said,

"A two for one special. Not bad. Not bad at all."

About the Author

Channie Cocker is a steamy romance/erotica author who loves to explore the naughty realms of writing.

5

MARBAS AND THE SECRET
CYNTHIA STATON

Melanie was a now a young woman who sought the deeper things of life. It seemed she always had a thirst to learn the hidden secrets of things. No one could understand this unquenchable thirst of hers and for the most part she didn't really understand it herself. There were times when she would discover something and a secret would be revealed. In her mind she thought that once this happened her thirst would be quenched and she could go on with life. Sadly, it had the opposite effect upon her. The more she learned the more she wanted to know.

Now she stood before a dark door that had been hidden until she exposed it with the moon's light. Rumor had it that the demon of secrets lived behind this door. She had done a lot of research that had led her to find this entrance and even then it was not easy to find. Mel grew ecstatic when she discovered it but she didn't quite have the guts to knock upon the door. A sudden fear had crept up on her and kept her frozen in place. Her heart beat faster and she started to sweat, leaving her feeling alone and vulnerable.

Marbas' sigil was carved into the door, confirming to Mel that this was the right place. She closed her eyes and started to hum, in hopes that it would break her from this fear and give her courage to pursue the thing she longed for the most. She had so many questions and longed to know so much but she was not sure that Marbas would be willing to answer her questions or give her the knowledge that she sought. Mel focused on her breathing and was able to clear her mind and allow herself to drift away to a safe place where she could find peace.

The fear dissipated, giving her the ability to focus. She opened her eyes and took in a deep breath before reaching out and knocking on the heavy metal door. It echoed loudly through the rock that the door was hinged in, causing Mel to cover her ears. She had given it three hard knocks and hoped that that would be enough. Mel stood there and waited, hoping that someone would open the door. Just when she was about to turn and walk away the door creaked open just a tad, exposing an eerie blue light. Mel pushed the door further in and peeked inside. A long hallway illuminated by that strange light was all that she could see.

She tiptoed into the hallway and followed it around a bend then went straight again for what seemed like forever. Mel wasn't entirely sure why she was being so careful or painstakingly quiet but she continued to do so regardless. The corridor finally came to an end and opened up to a large wide cavern. Looking up she was met with pure darkness. The eerie blue light came from a bowl in the center of the cavern. It cast its light within the whole room but oddly did not reach the ceiling. Mesmerized by this light, Mel walked up to it and peered inside.

"Young maiden, what is it that you seek?" A gravelly voice greeted her from above. Startled Mel looked up and watched as a huge lion's head appeared out of the darkness. Then the full form of a lion dropped to the ground with ease. He sat and watched Mel with soulful eyes.

"Are...are...are you Marbas?" Mel stuttered.

"Indeed, I am," Marbas did a slight bow, causing his mane to tussle about. "What can I do for you?" He asked.

"I heard that you are the one to go to if we wish to learn secrets," Mel stated, "I wish to learn." She suddenly grew shy as she confessed this to him. Deep down she feared that even he would reject her.

"You have come to the right person. What secrets do you wish to learn?" Marbas sounded like a seasoned professor teaching a slow student.

"I wish to know the deepest darkest secrets there are. Ever since I can remember I have wanted nothing more. There is just something inside me that desires this more than anything else! I have tried all my life to discover secrets but I just can't seem to get enough and I honestly do not know what more I can do. That is why I have sought you out. I was hoping that you would be willing to share some secrets with me?" Mel blurted nervously. Marbas stood on all fours and moved closer to her. His muzzle was in her face and she could feel his hot breath on her skin. A part of her feared that he was going to eat her.

"You are young and eager, that much is for sure. However, what you ask is not a light matter. Most who have sought the darker secrets have regretted it instantly and were never the same again.

Are you sure you want this?" Marbas warned. His sincerity touched her and gave her the courage to keep on.

"I have to. I just can't go on living life the way that I have. If I wind up a miserable wretch after knowing then so be it! I have to know!" Mel declared.

"Very well. Close your eyes," Marbas commanded. She closed her eyes as he asked. Marbas leaned in and licked her face, leaving warm saliva to drip down her chin and neck.

Mel fell to the ground as a piercing light invaded her mind. She fell back and lay on the ground as the dark and deep secrets of life came to her like a flood. Tears flowed freely down the sides of her face and regret set in. Despair filled her mind and Misery claimed her heart. Marbas looked down upon her with sad knowing eyes and said,

"So be it."

About the Author

Cynthia Staton is an inspirational speaker and author. Her first book is called Life Lived Not Lost a journey of hope.

Cynthia has also jumped feet first into down the rabbit hole into the anthology world, but also plan to have her next novel out this year.

6

VELEFOR: SOUL THEFT
JOSEF KASTLE

The rattling of dice and the noise of spinning roulette wheels filled Vele's ears as he strolled through the illegal gambling den. Smoke, both from cigarettes and marijuana, filled the air along with the fumes of alcohol. He inhaled deeply, getting intoxicated off the vapors of humanity falling to their lust, greed, and debauchery. He loved it! These humans reeked of the Seven Deadlies!

"Olivia," he said softly to the young demoness who tended the bar. "Make sure that Mr. Haviland gets more gin than tonic in his drinks tonight."

"Of course, Mr. Velefor," she replied. "Anything for you." She winked at him and started making another GnT for the bank manager.

"None of that from you, my dear," he smiled at her. "He's for me and you might get to take Mr. Clifford over there." He pointed to the young man leaning against the end of the bar. He'd already had a few more to drink than he should, but Velefor wasn't going to ask Olivia to cut him off. She deserved a little fun.

"I appreciate the offer, my lord," she smiled at him. "I do wish you'd take me up on my offer some night."

"I may do that yet, but not tonight." He looked over to the blackjack table where Haviland was winning yet another hand. "Tonight, I think I will take Haviland down a notch or two. And enjoy him in the process."

"Of course, sir. Shall I?" she made to come around the bar to deliver the drink herself.

"Oh, no, my dear," Vele took the glass from her. "It is my pleasure."

Vele dodged smoothly through the crowded room, nodding and greeting the regulars as he went. Everyone in the room knew him, none other than the staff knew what he was. He and all the staff were demons of some level another. He was one of the princes of hell and general of his own army. An army that he chose to use by stroking the egos and darker urges of the humans around them.

"Roger!" he exclaimed as he approached the banker. "So good to see you again tonight!"

"Mr. Velefor," the man replied with a warm smile. His dark hair was combed back from his forehead accenting his widow's peak. "Very glad to be here," he rolled the dice again. "Eleven! Another win for me!"

"So it is, my friend!" Velefor clapped him on the back. "Have another GnT, on the house."

"Why thank you, sir!" Haviland took the drink and downed half of it in one gulp. "Potent! You know how to show your clients a good time!"

"There're more good times to be had," Vele hinted coyly. "The game room is just part of what we have on offer. As you well know."

"Oh, no. None of that for me tonight!" the man said with a laugh. "I'm on a roll."

"On the house, I assure you." The demon winked at the gregarious human. "I've got something special you might enjoy. I think it will be right up your alley."

"Tempting, tempting..." Haviland replied with a smirk.

"More than you know," Vele smirked back at the man. "Clarence," he said to the box man. "Tally Mr. Haviland's winnings and make sure they are on account. I'm going to steal him away from the table for a while."

"Right away, sir," the lesser demon said dutifully as he made notes in his ledger. "$5,455 on account, sir."

"You have done well tonight, Roger!" Vele said, he shot a dark look at the box man that told him he would pay for that with a strong whip before the night was out.

"Like I said, on a roll," Roger smiled again. "Now, what's this special something you have for me?"

"As you know," he began as he led the man through to the private rooms beyond the game floor, "we cater to all kinds of tastes and fancies around here. You could say we cater to all the vices."

"Just what do you have in mind?" Haviland asked curiously.

"Oh, I've seen how you've been eyeing some of my staff the last few weeks. I think I know what you are looking for..." he trailed off as they went into the hallway off the game room. A series of dark doors lined both sides. "Each one of these rooms holds a secret delight for our customers. Most, of course, are not legal in this country. That is why we keep them... How should I say it? 'Under wraps.'"

"Oh," he moaned slightly at the thought of what could be hidden behind the closed doors.

"The special treat I have for you is something I am sure you will enjoy." Velefor led the human to a door on the far left, almost at the end of the hall. "This one is from my private collection," he opened the door to reveal a youth barely old enough to serve in the military. The young man was slender and nearly hairless. He was chained to the wall, naked as the day he was born.

"Well, how do you do?" Haviland asked with a leer on his face. "You do know what I like!"

"I told you, Roger. We aim to please." Vele closed the door behind them. "Hank is all yours with one condition."

"What is that?" Roger asked him suspiciously.

"No worries, my friend. I am not going to do anything untoward," Vele smiled back at the man. "I just want to watch."

"You dirty old man!" Roger shot back with a laugh. "You have similar tastes?"

"Depends on my mood. To be honest, I'm more interested to see what you have under that banker's suit."

"Ah-ha!" Haviland laughed harder. "Just a look, I prefer my men to be boys."

"Don't I know it," Vele laughed along with him. "Hank just turned eighteen last week. I allow most every vice, but I draw the line at pedophilia."

"It will have to do, then," Roger sighed half-heartedly. "He does look the part, doesn't he?" Roger walked forward and stroked the young man's chest. "Not a single hair on his delicious chest." He let his hand trail down to the boy's navel. "And just a light dusting along his happy trail."

"I'm glad you approve," Vele smiled as he pulled a chair out from the shadows along the wall and took a seat. "Pretend I'm not even here..."

"That shouldn't be too hard... to do..." Roger walked his fingers down from Hank's navel to the root of his semi-erect penis and circled his index and thumb around the base. He was rewarded with a sharp intake of breath and more blood rushing to the tube of flesh.

"Please, mister," the young man begged, "be gentle."

Roger tightened his grip on the flesh in his hand and smacked the youth with his other hand. "You will speak only when spoken to!" Hank gritted his teeth and stifled a retort.

"Good boy," he gripped his chin and forced a kiss on the firm lips. He bit the boy's lower lip. "Is this what you want?" he asked. He'd not made a move to stroke the penis in his hands nor to make himself more comfortable.

"Yes, sir!" Hank replied. The look in his eyes told the older man that he was sincere in his consent. He was playing a role, one that Roger hoped he was well suited to. His lust had not been satisfied in this manner for some time.

Haviland looked down at the engorged member he held in his hand and smiled. "Lovely, my boy!" The cock he held was long and slender. A perfect fit for his own tight ass. "We won't be using it for that... Not this first time around..." he said as if his thoughts were obvious. He spoke to the boy as if he owned him.

Haviland unbuttoned his shirt and pulled the tie away from his chest. Leaving both on, he tossed his suit jacket to the side and knelt before the youth chained to the wall. He took a moment to admire the narrow hips and pale skin of the boy's body before he dove in for a taste of the boy's navel. He licked and kissed from the trail of light-colored hair up to the now hard nipples on the hairless chest.

"Yes, this is just the withdrawal I needed," he whispered as he slowly rose to his feet and pulled the youth into a hot embrace. The coarse hairs on his own chest rubbed painfully against Hank's nipples causing him to hiss in that tone that combines pleasure with pain. "You can make all the noise you want, little boy, just don't talk!"

Vele watched quietly from his ringside seat. The smile on his face was almost painful. Just you wait, Roger, he thought with venom, you'll get your rocks off and then I will have my fun! He glanced over his shoulder to make sure the hidden camera was not blocked. The quiet click of the shutter was just audible to his demon ears.

He watched the banker have his way with the boy. The sounds of slapping flesh and grunts filled the room, turning him on as well. He fought the urge to take matters into his own hands. The show was much more entertaining without that release. At least for now. When Haviland was done he would have his.

All too soon for Vele's taste Haviland was finished with Hank and straightening his clothes. The man had never taken his pants off, but he made sure that there were no visible signs of what he had done as he tucked his dress shirt back in and tightened his tie. Hank, on the other hand, showed signs of use and abuse. His now flaccid dick was nestled in a wet mass of blond curls, bite marks all of his chest and stomach.

"Done already?" Vele asked.

"For now, Mr. Velefor," Haviland answered as he slipped his coat back on. "Thank you. I truly enjoyed that."

"Good, I'm glad," Vele smirked at the human.

"Would I be able to arrange for Hank again soon?" Haviland nearly drooled at the thought. "He's got quite the tool on him."

"That can be arranged, Roger," the demon kept the sneer out of his voice. "Payment is negotiable..." he let that hang in the air.

"Negotiable?" Haviland squared his shoulders. "I already told you, I prefer them young. You, my friend, are not young."

"You have no idea," Vele laughed. "Nothing like that, I had something else in mind."

"Like what?" the banker shot him an untrusting look.

"You'll see," Velefor said mysteriously. "For now, cash out and go home. I'm sure Mrs. Haviland would enjoy your company tonight!"

"Quite right, Mr. Velefor. Quite right," the banker checked himself in the mirror before exiting the room and returning the game floor.

Vele opened the door the mirror concealed and checked the negatives from the hidden camera. He was very pleased to see the shimmering form of Roger Haviland hovering off to one side of the man and his youthful toy chained to the wall.

"Excellent," he said to himself. "A few more visits and he will be all mine..." Vele shrugged his shoulders and his own suit disappeared in a puff of smoke. It was then that he took pleasure in what he had seen and what the camera contained.

About the Author

Josef Kastle is an MM erotica and romance author. Look for his upcoming solo release Faeries Do Where Boots out late in 2019.
https://www.facebook.com/JosefKastle/

AMON: WHOM TO BE RECONCILED?
CHANDRA TRULOVE FRY

The demon watched as the two men fought over something trivial. Why did they think it was worth fighting over? He never understood these finicky humans and their ways. Nevertheless, he was drawn to those who quarreled like a moth was to a light. He never jumped in without being invited but oh how he wished he could. The two men walked away from each other. One sat on his couch while the other slammed the door behind him on his way out.

"Now that wasn't quite how you had hoped was it?" Amon snickered as he came into full view. Not his original appearance. Humans could not handle his natural form that consisted of a wolf's body, the tail of a snake, and a raven's head. Sure, they could handle all those by themselves but when you put it together well that just messed with their fragile minds. So, Amon chose to put on his magician's hat and took on the form of a blue human with a raven's head and sharp teeth. It was the closest he could come to their own human form. Even then they would still freak out. Just as this man did as he came into the light.

"Holy crap! You scared me." The man yelled.

"My apologies young man. I was drawn to your quarrel as is my way." Amon sighed.

"Drawn to my quarrel? What the hell are you?" The man sunk into the couch trying desperately to meld into it.

"Angel, demon, myth, god. I've been called many things. What you should be most interested in is why I am here." Amon put his hands on his hips with a gesture of annoyance.

"Uh, okay. So, why are you here then?"

"I've been known to help settle disputes among friends. I would be more than willing to do so for you if you like. I've been so bored these days that I'd do it for a mere pittance. Just some favor you'd owe me soon. I think that seems fair. Don't you?" The demon smiled, exposing his pointed sharp teeth.

"I'm not sure it's even worth the effort at this point. What's your name anyways?" The man asked.

"Oh, how rude of me. I'm Amon, at your service." He bowed.

"I'm Kyle. Nice to meet you, I guess." Kyle whimpered. Amon cocked his head sideways at Kyle, silently observing him.

"Your quarrel was quite interesting. I'm used to much bigger disputes if you will. Did you actually steal his girlfriend?" Amon inquired.

"Seriously? How much of it did you hear man?" Kyle cried.

"Why all of it of course. I can't see why the two of you couldn't just share the woman. I mean, it does seem that she is into both of you. Makes sense to me." Amon watched the man turn red in the face.

"I didn't steal his girlfriend man. He broke up with her two days ago. That's the whole point! She didn't belong to him any longer. So yeah, I jumped at the chance. Who wouldn't? Delilah is smoking hot!" Kyle was growing furious now. He was making fists with his hands and his breathing grew more labored.

"Relax Kyle. I'm on your side. Don't you think that Delilah should have a say in all of this? I mean, maybe we should bring her and the other guy in. What's his name?" Amon asked.

"Jeff, his name is Jeff. And I suppose. If anything, you could smite them dead or something right?" Kyle bore into him with eyes like daggers.

"That's not typically how I handle things. Sorry. I'd much rather the three of you come to an agreement and things are set right." Amon offered.

"Yeah, sure. Why the hell not?" Kyle scoffed sarcastically. Amon sat on a chair across from Kyle and templed his fingers. He waited until Kyle calmed down before asking,

"Can you invite them both over then? I'd like to get this done and over with if you don't mind. I have to get back to Hell and deal with my legions. If I'm gone too long, they tend to get out of hand." Amon was eager to see this deed done. Just another notch on his success belt.

"I don't know if Jeff will talk to me right now." Kyle shrugged.

"Then invite Delilah and have her invite him. I guarantee that he'll come over then." Amon suggested calmly.

"Pfft... yeah, I'm sure." Kyle whine as he did what Amon suggested.

An hour later both Delilah and Jeff arrived. They all sat in the living room in an awkward silence. Delilah didn't freak out over Amon. This wasn't her first encounter with a demon. Jeff, however, nearly peed himself. Once everyone had gained some sort of composure Amon chimed in,

"Delilah, my dear, why do you keep messing with these poor boys' hearts?"

"What do you mean? I haven't done anything wrong." Delilah grew defensive.

"Come now, darling. You want both of them, don't you?" Amon could see the desire rising in her at the very thought of having them both.

"Yes! Okay. I want them both. Is that such a bad thing?" She pouted.

"I don't think so. Jeff, would you be willing to share Delilah with Kyle?" Amon watched as Jeff reacted to his question.

"I don't know that I could man. She was my woman then Kyle went and took her."

"Or did she take him?" Amon asked. Jeff looked perplexed while Kyle appeared more intrigued. "Kyle, would you be willing to share Delilah with Jeff?" Amon treated all three of them with a fatherly patience.

"Yeah, I think I could do that. Why not? I mean, Jeff, we've been best friends for years. We've shared everything! So, why not a woman too?" Amon could tell that Kyle was warming up to the idea. Jeff was still a bit hesitant. His possessive nature held him back from the proposal.

"I just don't know if I could man. I never did anything like that."

"We could give it a try?" Delilah offered as she batted her lashes at Jeff. That woman knew how to get what she wanted.

"Well... uh..." Amon noticed his sudden arousal at Delilah's words. "You really want this?" Jeff questioned.

"I sure do!" Delilah smiled wickedly.

"Well then I guess we could give it a try." Jeff conceded. Amon became invisible. Such was the way things went when his job was done. He watched as Delilah got up and straddled Kyle on the couch then motioned for Jeff to come up behind her. Sandwiched in-between the two young men she guided them step by step into the threesome she had longed for oh so long.

Amon smiled as he disappeared from their house. He took a knife and placed another nick on his belt. He was pleased to have another successful dispute solved. Now he would go back to the pits of Hell and watch over his legions until another dispute called to him. He looked forward to those moments. He didn't always get called to disputes. Goodness, there were too many. The call came randomly from time to time. He could look for them but that would take too much effort. Instead, he allowed those random calls to summon him. It made it more fun and exciting and it helped with the mundane day to day leading of his hordes in Hell. Now in Hell he sat back in his divan and began barking orders to his legions that had grown lazy in his absence. He let out a loud yawn and said to himself,

"Just another day in Hell."

About the Author

Chandra Trulove Fry is a multi-genre author who longs to try her hand at every genre at least once throughout her author career. She resides in Northern California with her wonderful husband and kids.

https://www.facebook.com/ChandrasAuthorPage/

BARBATOS AND THE HUNTSMAN
MAGGIE LOWE

The sun shone high up in the sky with rays splashing throughout the woods and illuminating the shadowed places. It was the perfect time to hunt game and Jasper was ready. A white stag stood in the midst of a clearing with not a care in the world. It munched on the grass with a grace befitting its stature. Jasper often envied his prey, but food was food. He couldn't go feeling sorry for an animal that was built to feed a family. It was better to put such thoughts aside and just focus on the job at hand.

Jasper had heard that white stags were magical and that it was bad luck to kill one. He believed in magic but not in luck whether it be good or bad. He reasoned that if it were a magical creature then eating of its flesh would bring magical qualities to he and his family. Besides, it wasn't as if there were anything else in the forest at the time. The urge to claim this creature's life became stronger.

He pulled back his arrow with the patient ease of an expert and waited for the perfect opportunity. The arrow let loose with his release of breath just as the stag looked up and the arrow pierced him right in the heart. The stag fell to the ground instantly as it let out a mewling cry. It was a good shot, but he feared that cry would alert the other animals that he was on the hunt. At least the stag was a good size and would feed his family of three for a week if done right.

He shouldered his bow and walked silently over to the dying stag. He stood above it solemnly for a moment as if giving up a silent prayer. Just as he was pulling out his dagger to end the stag's suffering an odd-looking man came out from behind a tree. He had four horns hovering in the air around him as if in readiness to sound off that the hunt was on. He had bones protruding out of his forehead and was dressed for the hunt. Jasper wondered if he were going to try and steal his kill.

"Good evening, sir," the man bowed politely.

"Good evening. Good day for a hunt," Jasper greeted.

"Indeed, it is, and I see that you have made a kill. Such a majestic beast, the white stag is. And said to have amazing magical abilities. It is a pity you chose to kill him," the man lamented.

"I merely saw an animal and hunted it. My family needs to eat," Jasper grumbled.

"Hmm...yes, I can see that. Would you like to know what this beast is saying?" the man queried.

"Beasts do not talk," Jasper huffed.

"Oh, but they do! And I can make it so you can understand him," the man sang.

"Very well then, do it," Jasper challenged. He did not believe this odd magical man.

The man seemed to disappear then reappear right in front of him. He leaned in and whispered some strange words into Jasper's ear. It sent an odd sensation throughout his body and caused him to shiver in fear. He looked upon the white stag with fresh eyes as the stag's innocent eyes peered into his own. Jasper saw the majestic beast for what it was. A magical creature who would have given him great blessings. Instead he would be cursed for all eternity.

"You have taken my life needlessly and now I curse you. You will never be able to hunt again. You will only ever feel the fear and shame of what you have done to me. Had you shown me the slightest respect I would have guided your bow and given you many kills. Instead, you killed a magical beast without a care. This curse will be sealed as I breathed my last breath," the white stag stated emphatically to the huntsman.

It lay its head on the ground and closed its eyes. Jasper could tell that it did not have much longer to live. He turned to the horned man with pleading eyes.

"Please, don't let the stag die," he begged

"It is an interesting request. I wonder that I should grant it," the man said as if he were conversing with others beside him. "Yes, it would be fun wouldn't it? Very well, I shall do this thing."

The horned man walked over to the stag and lay his hand upon its heart. He spoke a few odd words over the stag before backing away and waiting. The wound sealed up completely as the arrow disappeared. After a few minutes went by the stag jumped up, bowed to the horned man, and leaped off into the woods as though nothing had happened.

Jasper turned to the man in relief and cried out, "Thank you! You have saved my life and I am forever in your debt!"

"Did you hear that? He says he is in our debt. I like the sound of that," the man exclaimed. "You are right, young man. You will be forever in my debt. I am Barbatos and you will be my pirate. I'll help you seek out treasures untold and you will do whatever I command!"

"That seems an amazing life. I am honored," Jasper bowed.

"Oh, trust me when I say it comes with a price. You will lose everything you hold dear in this world. And in the very end your soul will be forever mine!" Barbatos declared.

Jasper fell to his knees in despair. He had been saved from the curse of the stag only to be cursed by the demon before him. He was not sure which curse was worse but as things now stood, he would have nothing of his own ever again. This was his life now. So be it.

9

PAIMON: LOOKING FOR
FORGIVENESS
JEFF DUCKER

I know everyone already knows that demons are evil. They are associated with basically everything evil. Even at the sound of the word demon, most people freeze. They get chills as their blood runs cold. But what if there was a demon that wanted forgiveness. He wanted to change his ways before it was too late, before the end of time. I suppose most people would say that`s impossible, no demon wants forgiveness. Many would even say it is too late. And all that may very well be true. Still, be that as it may, in this story, a demon has that very hope.

Paimon had been watching this family being tormented for many months now. Demonic presences were always making trouble. It didn't seem that they actually wanted to harm the family. Just scare them as much as they possibly could. Normally Paimon would join in on such evil activity. He would be all about getting his excitement at the expense of human's terror. But with the end of the days coming, he had changed his mind. He desperately wanted to change his ways. He wanted to be erased of his sins and wrong doings. But of course, he was concerned that it may not happen. However, he was still determined to try. Some way or another he was going to stop these entities from terrorizing this family. Then he would personally protect them until the end. And if it didn't work then at least he did something for the better.

Paimon spent each day and night in the little boy's room; or otherwise following him around. He got the worse of it. They tried to scare him awake each night. As far as the entities were concerned this house belonged to them. They scared away everyone that moved in. The landlord didn't believe all the stories. He just thought all the tenants didn't want to pay him rent anymore. He called all the stories and claims `nothing but garbage`. He was on the verge of just finding a different use for the house. The family currently living there now had been there longer than anyone else. They had asked him if anything bad had happened in the house, or if anyone else had complained of "strange things" happening in there. He just told them nobody had said anything. To him everyone just had over active imaginations. He had been inside the house too many times, and nothing out of the ordinary or unexplainable had ever happened. Sure, once he found a note that said `Nobody Else Moves In`, but he had no doubt that was a joke that the tenants that had just left, tried to pull on him. Probably to try to scare him into boarding it up or something.

Paimon was also in the process of recruiting a dog to help him. To explain better, about a month earlier a dog was hit by a car during the night, he took the carcass and gave it life. He had been training it to do good deeds, ever since. He figured, worst case scenario, if the dog turned evil, he would just put it back to sleep. Right now, he stood watching the little boy play with his toys. He never tried to talk to the boy or appear to him. In fact, he never tried to talk or appear to any of the family. He didn't want to scare them. After all that would defeat his purpose. He was a nice little boy, he never bothered anyone. Paimon tried very hard to keep the entities' trouble making to as much of a minimum as he possibly could. When they moved or hid stuff, he tried to put everything back where it was. He was prepared to whatever took to keep this family safe. He spent many hours trying to figure out a way to trap the entities. The family had even spoken of calling paranormal investigators and other people that might be able to help, but the landlord would not allow it. In his words, he did not want this house to be made into a mockery. He did not want it to become a source of entertainment. He did not want books or movies made about it. To him it was all unnecessary. He knew it could and more than likely would hurt the value of the house. When he was ready to retire, he would not be able to sell it. Or if it did sell, it would only go for a fraction of what he wanted. Needless to say, he expected the future selling of the house to help pay for his retirement. He was also strict about it being kept clean and rent bent being paid on time.

One night, just a couple weeks ago, although Paimon was not sure how, he stopped one of the entities from bothering the little boy as he slept. He saw the entity by the bed. Somehow, something about Paimon's presence scared it away. He certainly was not trying to be like a superior to them. As mentioned before, he wanted nothing do with them or their shenanigans. Actually, since that night they seemed to be almost scared to bother the little boy very much. But he knew stopping them completely would be a much more difficult task. He would stop at nothing to accomplish it.

Little did he know, Paimon was soon about to find out something else about himself. He was about to find out he had another ability. An ability that would help him very much. This ability would end up saving the life of the man of the house. And then it happened. One day the man stood at the stop of the stairs speaking on his cell phone. The entities came up behind him ready to push him down the stairs. Paimon came up and stared into the eyes of one of the entities. The next thing Paimon new was this entity seemed to freeze solid. The others fled to another part of the house. Paimon then grabbed the frozen entity and took it far out into the middle of the ocean and dropped it in the water. Since them some of the activity has slowed up, but he is not willing to take any chances. He would need to know that the threat is over one-hundred percent. All he knew was that he could keep on doing everything he could, for even just a fraction of a chance at redemption.

So, did Paimon get redemption? Well, he is still here on earth. Nobody knows when the end of days will come. Nobody knows the day or the hour. It is not believed that such a thing will happen. So, therefore we may never know.

About the Author

Jeff lives in Georgia and has been writing anthologies before he wrote his First novel, but he has a poetry book out called : Beside Still Waters. Jeff want to write his first novel this year.

10

BUER: THE FOREST OF DARKNESS
P.S. HARRIS

Buer stood on two of his five goat legs, nervously waiting for his name to be called. He had no idea who had summoned him, he had never seen this place before. The room was stark white and empty except for him. He didn't see any door, but that was no concern as doors were useless in the realm he occupied.

Relatively neutral, as far as the ever-raging battle between Heaven and Hell, he preferred to keep to himself in the forests of earth unless summoned. His life was spent in the wilds, that was his comfort zone. Irritated at being interrupted in his never- ending search for the cures to human diseases, he started rolling around the room in frustration.

He didn't like this. The last time he had been summoned like this he had been forced to destroy. Hades had used his knowledge of the plants of the earth to help create a powerful, addictive drug to let loose on the humans. Controlling humans in this way was a game for Hades. Buer would rather use his knowledge to help human kind. They were after all the whole reason for his existence.

He noticed the first flicker of light when he turned around, then then whole room was full of them. He didn't think the room could get any whiter, but it did.

"Buer," The voices blended in harmony. "We are here on behalf of the special council." The lights twinkled as they spoke, creating a rhythmic lightshow. "The earth is in grave danger, time is running short."

This didn't feel like one of Hades jobs. Buer was still a bit skeptical though. He had never heard of a fallen angel being summoned by anyone from Heaven. "Look, whoever you are, I'm not going to get caught up in your Good and Evil politics. I just want to be left alone!"

"Please, Buer, this is life or death. If you don't help us none of us will exist. The lights twinkled fiercely for a moment, and then settled back into soothing rhythm of tranquil. We cannot go into Hell, we need you."

"I don't like going there. It's an evil place." Buer growled. "You can't trust any of them, plotting their own demise if you ask me. I don't really care what happens. This constant fighting and plotting, all of you can disappear."

"What about earth? The humans?" The voices whispered, echoing. "Everything will disappear..." fading out into silence, the lights stopped twinkling, leaving the white room eerily dark.

"OK, OK, why don't you tell me what you need and then I will decide." Buer couldn't stand the sadness that had filled the room. Besides it couldn't hurt to listen to what they needed. Maybe I'll even earn my way back to Heaven.

"Hades has trapped one of our angels in the Forest of Darkness, we need you to find her and help her to safety. This is of up most importance. She is to save the world and we cannot lose her." The voices in unison as they continued. "We cannot enter Hell, but you can. You know your way around the Forest of Darkness and can lead her out of harm's way."

"Wait just a minute," Buer interrupted, "I have never been in that forest and I don't plan on ever going in there. I've heard terrible stories about that place and besides I'm not about to go against anything Hades has done. No way. I've worked hard to stay off his radar and this sounds like something that would piss the big guy off."

The voices started twittering fiercely, their lights flashing on and off in chaos. Arguing amongst themselves on how to convince him to accept the mission. Buer could hear bits and pieces of their conversations as he stood there pondering his decision.

"What's in it for me?" Buer spoke up causing the twittering to stop. "If I decide to do this, I could be in danger. Are you going to protect me? Do I get back into Heaven?"

"We will protect you as much as we can, and we do have allies in Hell that will help, but we do not have the authority to allow you back to Heaven." The voices were in unity again.

"Well get the authority here and I'll make a deal." Buer decided if he was going to risk his like he might as well be promised eternal life in Heaven.

"That is not possible" The voices were saying "You must take this on faith that you will be rewarded and know that you play an important role in our salvation. We do this not only for Heaven and earth, but also for Hell. There will be nothing if this earth is destroyed. The angel we are sending you to save is vital in keeping that from happening. Hades knows that. You are the only one that has the skills to help this one. We know you can do this. You MUST do this." The lights were blinding and fierce.

Buer shut his eyes against the sudden brightness. Take it on faith? Could he trust that? That wasn't a word he heard in his world. They seemed earnest and were obviously desperate. To summon a demon, they had to be worried. He didn't know what to do. I should check into this story. Make sure there really is an angel stuck in the Forest. "Ok, tell you what. I'll go ahead and investigate this, see if I can even get into the Forest of Darkness. I'll get back to you when I decide."

"I'm sorry," the voices were firm and strong. "We cannot allow you to leave this room until we have a decision. This is your moment of reckoning. You can continue, living without making choices or you can take a leap of faith and turn your existence into something meaningful for all. We leave you now. The decision is yours, when you have decided you will return to where you were taken from."

*****

Buer took the first step into the Forest of Darkness and felt the evil surround him.

About the Author

P.S. Harris is a sci/fi fantasy writer with her first novel out now. Watch for the sequel coming 2019. Author page

https://www.facebook.com/psharrisauthor/

11

GUSION: THE CURSED DEMON
CYNTHIA STATON

Here I will you the story of a once powerful demon. So powerful he at the time ruled over at least forty-five legions of demons. He was said to be able to tell everything about the past, the present, and the future. But, unfortunately, he must not have been able to see his own future. If he had then he would know of the curse that was about to be cast over him. His name was Gusion. As I said he was very powerful and feared. He caused a lot of havoc. He ruined a lot of lives. He even caused relationships to end. Yes, friendships too.

Gusion made a mistake one day when he failed a task and set his master into a fury. So, his master set this curse on him. He was cursed that he not only, no longer had power but also that nobody, earth being or other would ever be afraid of him. However, he underestimated his master, because he did not believe for a second that nobody would ever fear him. So, he decided to prove his master wrong. He set out for earth, because he knew obviously that earth beings were the easiest to scare. He would end up putting himself in different scenarios and places to try to prove his master wrong. Would any of them work? We will soon find out.

The first scenario he put himself in was the obvious. He was going to haunt a house. He chose a nice two-story suburban house. He began trying everything he could to scare the occupants. He stated moving tables and chairs. He turned water faucets on and off. He even turned the stove on. But the occupants got excited and brought out cameras and recorders. Gusion could not believe that they were so amused. Then he attempted to leave threatening messages at night for them to see when they woke up the next morning. He tried to write 'GET OUT OR I WILL KILL YOU', but the next morning it read 'STAY HERE I WILL NOT HURT YOU'. They laughed so hard as they took pictures of the wall. That could not possibly be part of the curse, he thought. He even tried to push one of them down the stairs, but instead he went right though them and he felt every step as he bounced all the way down. He could not believe it. He had never felt pain. This just couldn't be happening. Nonetheless, he gave up on the haunting and left the house and the family for good.

Next he decided to try to take over a school. Definitely students would be scared out of their wits. Right? Well, at first they were startled, but then they soon realized all the activity was harmless. He tried to throw a garbage can, but instead it went up in the air above him, the contents covering only him. On a chalkboard, he tried to write 'IT IS COOL, TO DROP OUT OF SCHOOL', but instead it came out 'IT IS COOL, TO STAY IN SCHOOL'. This just made no sense to him. He tried to start a fire before remembering that he had no power left. He started yelling threats and obscenities at them, but they didn't seem to be able to hear a word he said. He was done with this school. It was no use, he had failed here too.

After that he figured he would go to a church. He could surely wreak havoc there. There was just no doubt about it. But the second he entered, the sound of hymns being sung was already burning his ears. The prayer added to it. He left unable to try anything. The church had won too.

Walking away from the church, he spotted a hospital. His excitement suddenly recharged. He could not possibly fail here. A lot of people there were sick or fighting for their lives. What could possibly go wrong. He went in and tried to hit a nurse, but slipped on a wet floor. He could not understand how he actually slipped. He wasn't even clumsy. He tried to mess with the machines in the rooms, but each time he did he got electrocuted. After that he wandered into an elevator and it shut down. At least he could go through the wall, he thought. But instead he smacked his face on the wall. And it actually hurt. Sometime later, the elevator finally began to work again and he was able to leave. Where could he go now? Doubt was now beginning to consume him.

From there he just drifted all over the place. Aimlessly, from place to place he went. He was unsure what to do. It was looking like his master's curse had indeed worked. He was even feeling depressed. Something else he had never felt. It was like he was becoming a shell of his old self. What would he ever do? What could he do? For the first time ever, he was even feeling scared. He was so use to being the one that does the scaring. Where could he even go? No earth beings were scared of him, and back in Hell he would only be the subject of everyone's jokes. They would never let him live this down. No demon had ever angered their master to this point before. As he walked (he just realized that he could not even float or fly anymore) he kicked at a rock, and his foot just went through it. He felt ashamed and even worthless. Again, something that demons had never felt. What was happening to him? How far was the curse going? He could not possibly be turning human. Could he? He knew his master hated humans, well the ones that did not worship him anyway, but he would never go this far in the name of punishment. There was no way, and Gusion just knew it.

Suddenly, Gusion opened his eyes and he was back in Hell. He realized it must have all been a terrible dream. Yes, he decided, just a bad dream. But a horrible fact occurred to him. Demons do not sleep.

About the Author

Cynthia Staton is an inspirational speaker and author. Her first book is called Life Lived Not Lost a journey of hope.
Cynthia has also jumped feet first into down the rabbit hole into the anthology world, but also plan to have her next novel out this year.

12

SITRI: PASSION'S SURPRISE
AMANDA J. EVANS

In every demon's rule, the screams of torture no longer satisfy. They become nothing more than an endless buzzing noise. I no longer found joy in listening to piercing cries as skin was ripped from bone. Whips flew through the air tearing at flesh leaving gaping wounds that leaked blood onto my floors and yet it did nothing to stir my arousal. I'd grown bored after centuries of monotonous agony.

Dominique positioned herself above me. "What ails you Sitri?"

"Huh?"

She wriggled, shoving her tight ass into my groin. "You're not enjoying the show?"

She was aware of my lack of interest, the bulge that usually greeted her when she sat - missing. I shoved her off. "I grow tired of this incessant noise. These wretched souls are useless."

"Where are you going?" She shouted as I marched from the throne room.

I ignored her. I needed quiet, time to think.

The dark, dank tunnels that burrowed through hell called to me. Escape, mischief, tomfoolery – I craved excitement and destruction.

You've been dormant too long.

My inner demon knew only too well what had happened to me. Lording it over my minions, spending my days watching as they took their anger out on the unfortunate souls who'd spend their eternity here.

You need to have some fun. Like the old days.

A slow grin spread across my face and I shook my head. The old days before I became prince of 60 legions, before I became trapped in the misery of this existence. "I need a holiday," I mumbled as I pushed the doors to my private quarters open.

Even the soft furnishing of my room offered no comfort. I craved human flesh, the touch of delicate skin, and the look of pure and utter horror as my victims realized what they'd done. Oh yes, how I missed it.

"Dominique, I shall be gone for a week. You will be in charge."

"But..."

"No buts. Everything shall operate as normal."

"Where are you going?"

"That is for me to know," I grinned, as I pictured the small town of Castlevale, the one where Jonathan said the witches lived. He'd come to see me last week asking for my assistance in thwarting his brother's absurd notions. Little Flynn wanted to break the curse that binds them. Jonathan intrigued me and he's a demon even if he does possess an angelic shell. His appearance allows him entry where I cannot dwell and keeping him on side was useful. It's why I agreed to help him destroy the witch capable of removing his curse. Not that I was going to obliterate her. I was going to have my fun first and turn her to the dark side in the process.

"What if I need to contact you?"

I'd forgotten Dominique was still standing there. "Operate as normal until I return," I bellowed and dismissed her with the wave of my hand. She was getting too clingy for my liking. Yes, she excited my inner demon, allowed him to play in such vile ways, but I didn't belong to her. I belonged to no woman.

*****

Castlevale lay silent as I stood watching from the outskirts of the trees. A small hamlet protected by a thick forest on either side. Jonathan had informed me that one of the witches was a direct descendant of the witch who had cursed him. He thought he'd irradiated them all, but the children had been hidden the day he butchered the coven. Now it was my turn. I sniffed the air. Smoke mixed with burning herbs. There were witches close by. Changing into my human form, I stepped from the tree line and followed the scent that filled the air. The moon was high spilling light onto the path. Stars filled the sky. I never tired of seeing them. In the pits of hell stars became but a memory. They reminded me now of a time long ago when I roamed the earth. I shook my head. "Memories are for the weak. You are a prince of hell and you're about to have some fun."

The herb infused smoke led me to a small hut. It stood alone. The rest of the village huts were nestled together further down the pathway. "Perhaps this little witch has been shunned," I mumbled. "All the better for me, she'll be more than willing to enjoy my company." I stood at the door and listened. Soft chanting seeped under the gap. A conjuring spell. I listened closely. *A love spell, she conjures a man.*

I couldn't help the excitement that coursed through my veins as I raised my fist and let it fall against the wooden door. Hurried footsteps and a couple of crashes and bangs followed. *You've startled her. She's hiding the evidence.* I ignored my inner demon and knocked again, smile at the ready.

The door creaked as it peeled back, and a woman's head poked around the gap. "Can I help you?"

Her green eyes darting from side to side. I assumed she was checking to see if I was alone. Dark curls hung around her face and I wanted to lick my lips. *Control Sitri. Don't ruin this.* I sucked in a deep breath before exhaling. I knew the power of my pheromones. No woman or man could resist. I watched her inhale, and her demeanor changed instantly. She straightened and opened the door wide. "What can I do for you?" Her lips pursed as her tongue moved across them slowly. The slight blush to her cheeks and increased heart rate told me I had her.

"I need shelter for the night. My horse broke loose on the other side of the forest and I have no food or supplies to get me to the next town."

"Oh, you poor thing, come inside." She stepped back, and I walked inside making sure to brush off her. Her tremble a welcome response.

She ushered me to the chair at the side of the large open fire. "Have a seat, I'll get you a warm drink."

"Are you a witch?" I asked motioning to the cauldron and the table filled with herbs.

"Um, yes," she muttered as she returned with a cup of something steaming. "Here, drink this."

I smiled up at her as I took the cup from her hands. *Time to play.* "Are you a good witch or a bad one? I've heard stories of witches who work with dark magic and steal the souls of men lost in the forest."

She laughed. "Don't believe all you hear. I am of the Tree Coven. We are light witches and only work with natural magic."

"Oh," I said, nodding my head. "You don't have any real power then?"

"What makes you think that?"

She seemed irritated now which meant my plan was working wonders. "I just assumed that nature magic was less powerful. I've heard tell of witches who can see inside a man's soul, read his every thought..."

"All witches can do that," she snapped and then stopped. "Sorry, I'm being rude."

"It's okay," I said, gazing up at her, allowing my demon to do its work.

"No, it's not. I shouldn't have snapped at you. I meant to say that all witches can look into someone else's mind and read their thoughts, but it is against the laws, a breach of free will if you like. It can only be performed if requested by the person."

A slow smile crept across my face. "You really are beautiful, tell me, what spell were you performing before I knocked on your door?"

"I...I..."

Taking her hand in mine, I stood and looked right into her eyes. "You will tell me the truth."

"I was casting a spell for love, true love, to enter my life." Her gaze moved to the floor. "I don't know why I'm telling you this."

Cupping her chin, I forced her to look at me once more. "You conjured me, love. I'm here for you."

She gasped and moments later I had her right where I wanted her, naked and willing in front of the roaring fire. Her body willing to take everything I planned to dish out. My demon stirred as my human form reacted to her soft, plump flesh. "Tell me, love, what is it you fear?" I asked as I trailed kisses across her heaving chest.

"I fear being alone," she mumbled before moaning in pleasure.

She lies. I met her gaze and plunged deep into her mind to find her biggest fear. I saw the smoke, the flames, the hands and legs bound. *She's afraid of being burned alive.*

As I caressed her skin and thrust deep insider her, I put my plan in motion. She closed her eyes, shouting her pleasure. "Open your eyes, let me see your pleasure," I murmured. As she forced her eyes open, I conjured fire and allowed it to dance over my body. Terror filled her eyes as the fire stroked my body. "What's the matter, love?" I asked licking the side of her face.

"What are you going to do?" She tried to shove me off.

I didn't answer. I grinned. Let her reach inside my mind and find out.

She reached up and placed her hands on my temple. That's it, reach inside me. She paused and removed her hands. She struggled to break free, but I sent my fire dancing across her body. Her hands instinctively flew to my head and she plunged deep into my mind. She cried out, "It's you, you're..."

I laughed as I watched her piece the threads together. "You broke the rules. You invaded my mind little one."

"I...I..." The words stopped, and she writhed in pain as my flames licked her skin. "What have you done to me?"

"It's not me," I moaned as I thrust deep inside her once more.

Her head rolled back, ecstasy and pain at the same time. "Stop," she cried out as she gripped my buttocks and pulled me deeper into her.

"You want to stop?" I smirked as she moaned beneath me. "Let go, love, give in to it."

Panting, her body begging for release, she flung me to the side and mounted me. I knew what she was experiencing, a power like she'd never felt before was raging through her as she moved above me. Her dark locks touched my knees as she looked to the sky and let her body take over. My hands found her breasts and I squeezed. "Harder," she shouted. "More."

"I knew you couldn't resist, love. Welcome to the dark side. Are you ready to have the time of your life?"

"Oh yes," she cried. "Yes."

*****

Spent from the exertion, my demon rested, content. "How are you feeling?" I asked, stroking the soft skin of my newly turned witch.

"Alive, more alive than I've ever been."

"Good, there's a lot more to come."

"What do you mean?"

"Darkness courses through your veins now. A power like no other. You can control all of nature, all of darkness, anything you desire can be yours with just a thought, if you wish it so."

I watched her brow furrow. She had a choice to make and the struggle within her was evident. *Perhaps she needs a little push.* Placing a finger at the side of her temple, I let my thoughts caress hers, sent images of grandeur and worship into her mind. I knew that's what she wanted, why she resided away from her coven. She was considered weak by them.

"What if I don't want it?" she mumbled.

"What if you do?" I grinned knowing full well she couldn't resist me.

"I do," she whispered. "I want it all."

My lips devoured hers and my body ignited. I had a week to enjoy her flesh before returning to my palace and leaving her here to do my bidding. "Welcome to my world, little witch. You've much to learn," I whispered in her ear as the fun began again.

About the Author

Amanda J Evans is an award-winning Irish author of YA and Adult romance in paranormal and fantasy genres. Her stories centre on good versus evil with a splice of love and magic thrown in too. You can find out more on her website www.amandajevans.com.

13

BELETH AND THE WITCH
CHANNIE COCKER

Beleth felt the familiar pull of a summons tugging at him. He rubbed his hands together as he decided which form to take on that would determine the summoner's courage. In his mind's eye he saw the conjurer as she stood before the triangle etched in the floorboards. She struck her hazel wand in South, East, and North as she demanded that Beleth come to her. He noticed the silver ring on her middle left finger and smiled. This witch knew what she was doing. He decided he would take on the form of a grotesque zombie like being with entrails hanging out and everything. That should give her a good shock.

Beleth entered the triangle in a flash and bellowed, "Who dares to summon me?" His voice held that terrifying tone as his flesh appeared to peel and fall of his body.

"Shut up and do as I say!" The witch commanded as she flicked the hazel wand at him and held her left hand up to her heart. Much impressed by her courage he stood tall and transformed into his main image. A tall naked man with sharp Asian features stood before her. He was handsome and foreboding with eyes that spoke of death and pain.

"What do you want from me?" He asked in a gravelly voice.

"I command you to mate with me." She threw off her cloak revealing her long lean naked body to him. Her wavy red hair cascaded down her back as she stared daggers at him with piercing green eyes. Beleth admired her body as he took it in. From her full pouting lips to her small perky breasts down to her flat stomach and luscious shaven mound. She was firm and confident.

"Gladly!" He growled as he motioned for her to enter the triangle. She fell into his arms still holding the hazel wand and keeping the silver ring close to her heart. He pushed her to the ground roughly then mounted her. She cried out as he entered her but it did not stop him. He pulled her up to his large broad chest, reached down and bit her neck, leaving a trail of blood to flow down her body. She let loose the wand as she grabbed onto his chest with her nails once the throes of love took over her. She reached up with her left hand and grabbed him by the mane. He let out a loud roar as he came to fruition within her. Her cries mingled with his roar as her body rippled in ecstasy. They fell to the floor exhausted from their love making. He dipped his finger into the blood that pooled slowly on the floor from her neck then ran it down her body. She shivered at his touch with both pain and longing.

Did the witch want to go again? He could tell she barely survived the first round. She would die if he took her again. Her ring was no longer held up in homage and the wand lay off behind him somewhere. With a wicked smile he rolled her over face down then pulled her backside up against his fully erect member. She let out a weak moan but had no strength to stop him as he entered her again. He did not hold back this time as he gave her all he had. He knew she was building up to a climax, even though her body was being ripped apart from the inside out. He let flow his seed inside her in a full release. It was more than her small frame could take as bones snapped and ligaments were shredded. Blood filled her eyes and spilled out of her mouth and ears. He pulled out as she fell limp to the floor, barely breathing.

He watched as a smile slowly lit her face. Ecstasy and pain had mingled at the end, leaving her fully satisfied. Beleth smirked at her with admiration. She had gotten what she wanted even if it did kill her. He bent down and whispered in her ear,

"See you in Hell, dear witch." He returned back to his realm to take charge of his legions and waited.

*****

The witch lay there in her blood, her body torn and broken beyond repair. She could feel her life force fading quickly and knew that her time was drawing near. On the cusp of her last breath she watched as the demons of Hell came to retrieve her spirit and drag it down to hell. All went dark as she breathed her last and soon she was hovering above her own tattered shell. She turned to find the demons waiting for her, almost reverently.

"What is this? Not going to drag me down?" She mocked.

"King Beleth wishes you to not be harmed." One demon hissed.

"That so? Doesn't sound like him," she said with a pout.

"Oh, he wants you to be harmed, just not by our hand," the other demon cackled. The witch's eyes lit up at this revelation. So, there would be fun to be had after all. They took her through a mass of swirling blackness and on into the very pits of Hell itself. She followed them through the vapors of sulfur and brimstone, down a path, and onward towards a large palace atop a hill that looked over the vast hellish landscape.

Entering the palace was an entirely different scene. She found herself surrounded by black marble and onyx with grotesque scenes displayed throughout. They led her to a giant throne room. She saw him sitting there on his giant throne. A massive powerful god displaying everything she found appealing. He was much bigger in Hell and she knew it would be pleasurably torturous to be with him. They led her up to the throne itself and left her at the feet of Beleth, bowing as they exited backwards out of the room. The witch knelt before him and waited.

"Rise!" He commanded. She did as commanded and looked him boldly in the eye. This aroused him greatly. He flew out of his throne and grabbed her by the hair, "You are mine for all eternity!" He bent down and kissed her ferociously then let out a loud roar, much louder than the one sounded in earthly realms. He ran a long talon down her naked body sending shivers of delight through her body.

"Thank you." She murmured. He slapped her hard across the face.

"You will not speak unless I say you speak," He grabbed her forcefully by the arm and dragged her to a device with chains attached to it. He had pulled her arm out of socket, sending shocks of pain waving through her body. Beleth held her up onto the device as he locked her arms, legs, and neck up to it. Her arms and legs were spread out and her body was exposed from both front and back. The device was held up by a chain that hung from the endless ceiling above. The witch's eyes grew wide and her mouth parted as she watched Beleth's member grow five times bigger than it's already large size. He smiled at her wickedly.

"I am going to tear you apart day after day after day. You are mine and mine alone to do with as I please." He had hoped to find fear in her eyes but instead he found nothing but lust and desire. Oddly this spurred him on to thrust her with his overly large member. One thrust ripped her body right in half but everything held together by the chains. Her screams echoed throughout the chambers as her body melded back together.

"More! Give me more!" She begged. Beleth looked at her with a baffled expression.

"Witch! What is your name?" He demanded.

"Lilith, my name is Lilith." The witch smiled evilly.

About the Author

Channie Cocker is a Steamy Romance/Erotica author who loves to explore the naughty realms of writing.

LERAJE: FESTERING WOUNDS
AMANDA J. EVANS

Anger curled in the pit of my stomach as Robert slipped his hand into Sandra's back pocket. "That filthy, rotten toad. Thinks he can cheat on me, does he? Well I'll show him." I crouched low as I passed the window of Hon's Takeaway. Robert said he'd be working late, a last-minute business meeting scheduled for the morning that he had to prepare for. I thought I'd surprise him with his favorite meal. More you fool, I thought as I rounded the corner and back to our little apartment. Tears threatened to fall, but I held them back. He wasn't getting them. He wasn't getting anything ever again. He'd made a fool out of me for the last time.

The door slammed behind me and my purse hit the hall table with a thud. "I'll show him what happens when you mess with Marnie Jacobs." The apartment was stuffy, the evening sun streaming in through the windows, light beams and dust dancing in the air. I shoved the windows open as I made my way to the spare room. The latest consignment of books arrived yesterday for the shop and I had yet to sort through them. Robert didn't approve of my *hobby*, as he liked to call it. "It's all hocus pocus nonsense. When are you going to get a real job?" I let him away with it, laughing at his jokes, when inside I resented them. But I'd show him what my hobby could do. The image of Sandra cozying up to him, him with his hand dipping into her back pocket as he squeezed her ass. Too right, I'd show him what a witch could do.

The box of books sat just inside the door and I grabbed the small knife off the desk to cut the seal. The smell of old parchment hit me, and I inhaled deeply. I loved this part of my job – breathing in the scent of old-world tomes, inhaling the history in the pages – but not this evening. The first book was a collection of Gaelic myths; the second Irish fairies and their influences on the land; the third herbs and infusions for healing; none of these would do. The pile beside me grew as I searched for something that would help. A small black, leather-bound journal was shoved into the side of the box. It looked promising. Inside the cover a pentagram and the words 'Summoning Demons'. *This is it.*

The living room had cooled slightly. I curled up on the sofa with a glass of wine and the journal. A quick glance at the clock told me I had at least another hour before Robert would be home. The wine tasted bitter, but I knew that was more to do with my sour mood than anything else. How could he betray me like that, and with Sandra Dickens of all people? Her and her tight... "Stop it Marnie."

I placed the wine on the table and concentrated on the book. The first page was an index of all the demons, but their names meant nothing to me. I turned the pages quickly. Each demon, listed along with a brief description and then the summoning spell. My eyes scanned them one by one until I found what I was looking for. Leraje. She sounded perfect. She was strongest at the end of May and could be summoned in daylight hours. She was for love and war and could put an end to love affairs. "Perfect," I said as I scanned the rest of the page to see exactly what I'd need. According to the summoning spell all I needed was red candles. The spell itself was easy enough too. A drop of my blood and a short incantation.

With everything ready, I gulped back the last of my glass of wine and set to work. The red candles placed in a pentagon on the table, a small bowl with a photograph of Robert and me – taken last month as we celebrated our five-year anniversary – and a piece of paper with my intention – to end his love affair and bring him back to me - written in black ink. The candles burned brightly as I read the incantation. I paused at the part that called for my blood to fall on the photograph. I hated blood spells and flinched as the needle pierced the tip of my finger. Blood pooled under the skin and I squeezed tightly and let three drops fall on the picture. It sizzled, the plastic covering bubbling as the faces disappeared. The final line of the incantation was to be repeated three times and as the last word left my lips the candles flickered and extinguished themselves as a gust of wind swept through the room.

"Who summons me?"

The voice boomed and reverberated off the walls. I swallowed and composed myself before turning. Leraje stood, draped in a cloak of green, a bow and arrows held in her hands.

"I did," I said, trying to keep the tremble out of my voice. "I need your assistance in destroying a love affair."

Her lips curled as she looked me up and down. "Your heart has been broken and you seek revenge?"

"Yes."

She tossed her cloak over her shoulders and it disappeared to reveal a petite, Egyptian princess-like woman. So young and beautiful. "Tell me of the betrayal so I may determine the punishment."

I told her what Robert had done, what I'd seen. She didn't speak, merely nodded her head and tapped a long-sculpted nail against her chin. She stalked around the living room her eyes taking in everything. "This is him?" She asked as she tapped the glass on the photo frame that sat above the mantle.

"Yes, it was taken..."

"I do not need details." She ran her finger over the picture before placing it inside her mouth and popping it back out. "Festering wounds. A fitting punishment for this..." She didn't finish her sentence. Her lips curled in disgust and she motioned for me to stand beside her. "My arrows are tipped with poisonous pestilence. Strike him with one and the wound will fester and cause great pain. Pain that equals your heartbreak."

She placed an arrow in my hand and bowed. "Strike fast for once sunlight fades so too will its power."

My fist closed around the arrow. "How am I going to shoot him with an arrow?"

She smiled. "You'll see."

I looked down at the wooden rod, its tip a silver metal glinting in the sunlight. "But..." She was gone. I spun on my heels, but the room was empty. The arrow in my hand started to burn and I dropped it. It transformed into a glove. I picked it up and slipped my hand inside. It immediately blended with my skin. *An invisible glove. Now all you have to do is hit him. That shouldn't be difficult.*

The clock struck seven and I braced myself for Roberts return home. He was exactly on time and as I heard his keys rattle in the hallway, I stood ready.

"What a nightmare," he huffed as he pushed the door open. "I'm sick of them organizing meetings at the last minute. They think I've nothing better to do than spend a Thursday evening working late."

"Liar," I shouted as I lashed out and struck his cheek. My hand tingled, the glove shimmering.

"Marnie, what the..."

"Don't even think about it. I saw you Robert. You and Sandra, all cozy in Hon's. Do you think I'm stupid? Well you'll pay for it, now won't you?"

He stumbled, his hand gripping his cheek. My handprint, red and raw, bloomed on his skin and blood trickled through his fingers. He pulled his hand away and raced to the mirror. "You stupid..." He turned to face me, his eyes wild. "I have an important meeting in the morning, Marnie. What did you hit me with?" He wiped a hand across his cheek and it turned red. Blood poured from the wound.

I ran to the kitchen and fetched a cloth. When I returned Robert was on the floor groaning and gripping his head. "Robert! Oh god, what have I done?" I bent down beside him. The wound on his cheek was oozing green and yellow puss.

"I wasn't with Sandra. I didn't cheat on your Marnie. I promise." He was struggling to breathe, and his eyes rolled his head.

"I saw you Robert. You put your hand in her back pocket."

"She took my money," he gasped. "Put it in her back pocket, said I had to get it myself. You know what she's like, Marnie." He sucked in a breath. "She's always teasing, but I love you. I went to Hons because I had to work late and I was starving." He started coughing.

What have I done? I heard the truth in his voice. I had to fix this, and the only way was to summon Leraje again.

Robert had passed out by the time I'd finished the ritual and Leraje appeared in my living room once more. "You need to heal the wound. I was wrong. He didn't cheat."

"Festering wounds can't be healed," she said.

"What? But I command you to undo it," I gasped.

Leraje laughed. "You do not command me. I helped you because I wanted to and now you decide you don't want it." She walked over to Robert and poked him with her foot. "His wound festers well but don't worry it will all be over soon."

"Over! What do you mean? You need to stop this now. I don't want him punished anymore. I was wrong. Take it back, please."

Leraje shifted her gaze to mine. "What are you willing to offer me?"

"Anything, I'll give you anything you want. Please save him."

"I can save him, but you must give me your love."

I looked down at Robert, my heart clenching, before answering. "I will give you whatever you want if you promise to heal him."

"So be it," she said as she waved a hand over him.

Robert's face began to heal, and his eyes opened. "Marnie, love, what happened?"

"Robert..."

I didn't get to finish. Leraje placed her hand on my chest and a thousand blades ripped at my skin. "What are you doing?" I screamed.

"Taking what you owe me."

My chest ached and as she pulled her hand away, blue tendrils followed. She directed them to her lips sucking in deeply. The blue energy disappeared inside her. The pain stopped.

"Marnie are you okay?"

I looked down at Robert. I felt nothing. He meant nothing to me. I turned back to Leraje. "What have you done?"

She licked her lips. "I took what was mine." She tossed her cloak and disappeared.

Robert got to his feet. "Are you okay, Marnie?"

His wound had healed, he was okay, but my heart was empty. I felt nothing for the man that stood in front of me, his hands in mine. I looked away as a tear fell. The demon had tricked me. The festering wound was now inside me burrowing deeper and deeper, oozing black hatred into my being.

About the Author

Amanda J Evans is an award-winning Irish author of YA and Adult romance in paranormal and fantasy genres. Her stories centre on good versus evil with a splice of love and magic thrown in too. You can find out more on her website www.amandajevans.com.

15

ELIGOS : BATTLE PLANS

AMANDA J. EVANS

Severed limbs scattered the battlefield. A river of blood soaked the ground and after weeks of holding, King Ivor was down to one hundred men. He paced back and forth as his advisors cowered in the corner of the battle tent. "We need more men," he fumed.

"But sire, there are no more. We've taken all that could be taken from the kingdom, all that remains are women and children."

"Lower the age then, boys of ten can hold a sword. Get them here."

"But sire..."

"Do it," he shouted and moved towards the table in the centre of the tent. Unraveled maps of the kingdoms covered the surface, carved figurines marking the battles being fought. "Get Eldridge in here. We need to strategize."

He spoke to no one in particular. The king knew the battle was lost but he would never surrender, not to Tyran. He would fight till no one remained.

Someone cleared their throat and he turned.

"A mage to see you sire, says he can help turn the war to your advantage."

Ivor spat on the floor. The word mage left a bitter taste in his mouth. His father's face floated to the front of his mind. "Send him away. I do not need help from vermin."

"Sire," the man said and bowed before taking his leave.

"Mage, indeed," Ivor mumbled. "Blasphemy."

Mages had been banished from the kingdom after his father had been tricked into using their magic to heal his mother. She had been healed, but her heart no longer belonged to his father. Her only desire was to bed the demon the mage had summoned.

Ivor shook his head. He wouldn't think on that. He had more important matters at hand. His eyes scanned the battle maps as he rubbed his temples to try and relive the headache that pounded inside his skull.

The pieces scattered as an icy wind swept through the tent. Ivor turned and gasped. "You."

"Yes, Ivor. I've come to help, make amends, help you win this war."

"Get out," Ivor shouted lunging towards the black cloaked figured that stood inside the flap.

The mage shrugged. "I will be in the forest if you change your mind or perhaps I will offer my services to Tyran."

Ivor stopped dead. Tyran would allow the mage to help. He would do anything to take the kingdom. "Wait. I will hear what you have to say."

The mage stepped inside and bowed slightly before making his way to the table. "Your maps are wrong, Ivor. Tyran's soldiers hold more than you think."

Ivor watched as the mage repositioned the figurines. "Tyran's forces are strongest here," he said as he placed pieces behind the forest. "His men move swiftly, and they will surround you."

"What? That can't be true. I have men in the forest. They have not reported this."

The mage smirked. "You have many traitors in your camp, Ivor, and many that would see Tyran rule."

Ivor slammed his fist on the table scattering everything. "You lie, mage. My men are faithful."

The mage held his hand out and circled it in the air while chanting. The air solidified, and Ivor saw, Garrison, his second in command standing beside Tyran. "What trickery is this?"

"I show only the truth. It is you who does not see it. He has betrayed you. Watch."

Ivor watched as the image played out. Garrison and Tyran moved inside a tent, a map spread along a table. He watched as Garrison positioned figurines showing Tyran the location of his soldiers.

When the image faded he turned to the mage. "Is it true?"

"Yes."

"And you can help, show me how to defeat him, save the kingdom?"

"I can, but it will cost you."

Ivor thought of his father and his mother, of the magic that destroyed them. He should say no, should send the mage away, but if there was a chance to save the kingdom, to defeat Tyran, he must take it. His father would understand. The kingdom comes first. His shoulders sagged. "What will it cost me?"

"You will lift the ban on mages and appoint me as chief advisor."

Ivor scowled. "I will lift the ban, but you will never set foot inside the palace. I remember what you did, Margon." It was the first time he allowed the mage's name to leave his lips and he did so with disdain.

"You must agree to both, Ivor, or I will not help you."

Ivor gritted his teeth. He was down to one hundred soldiers. They wouldn't last another day. He had no choice. "I will agree to your terms if the battle is won."

Margon bowed and turned to leave.

"Where are you going?"

"There is much to prepare. I will send a crow at sunset. Follow it."

Ivor remained in his tent for the rest of the evening. He spoke of his meeting with Margon to no one. When Garrison returned from scouting, Ivor pretended his headache was so severe that he couldn't see anyone. He had just fallen asleep when a cawing woke him. A crow perched on his chest, pecking at his tunic. He brushed it away and stumbled to his feet. He followed the crow out of the encampment and to the forest where Margon waited.

"Were you seen?" Margon asked.

"No."

"Good, we will begin."

"What are you going to do?" A sweat had broken out on the back of Ivor's neck. He knew the consequences of magic, dark magic, and he knew that was exactly what Margon would use.

"I will summon Eligos, demon of war. He understands strategies and he has the ability to foresee the enemy's position and tactics ahead of the battle. With his help you can defeat Tyran and secure your kingdom."

"And the consequences?" Ivor asked stepping forward into the circle Margon had created in the dirt.

"There will be no consequences as long as you adhere to our bargain. Your kingdom will flourish, I guarantee it."

Ivor consented and Margon began the ritual and summoning of the demon. He appeared in the form of a knight carrying a lance and a similar of a snake. He didn't appear to be evil or demonic and Ivor relaxed as the demon listened to his battle strategies.

"You cannot win a war that way," he said when Ivor finished. "War requires knowledge and men. I will supply you with men and you will attack under the cover of darkness. While the enemy sleeps you shall destroy."

Ivor stepped back. "That is not how it is done. The battle commences with the dawn, to attack under darkness is cowardice."

Margon, placed a hand on Ivor's shoulder and shook his head. "Do not anger him, he can destroy you in an instance," he whispered.

Ivor swallowed and muttered an apology.

"My men wait in the forest. Take this." He handed Ivor a medallion with the sigil of a snake. "Show them this and they will fight for you."

Ivor took the medallion and hung it around his neck. He listened carefully as Eligos detailed the attack plan. Tyran and his army were camped to the right of the forest – the opposite direction to the information Ivor's scouts had brought him – and they slept soundly under the influence of a sleeping spell Margon had cast.

The forest shrieked and howled as Ivor fumbled his way through, branches reaching for him like demonic hands. He found the men where Eligos had said they would be. He held the medallion aloft and they followed. Tyran's men slept soundly as Ivor and his demon league slaughtered and ravished their way through the encampment. It was over swiftly, and Ivor, soaked in the blood of his enemies, crept back into his tent as dawn was breaking. When his general lifted the flap and entered, he ordered that Garrison be brought before him.

The traitors were rounded up and executed and the kingdom rejoiced.

Ivor paraded through the streets to rapturous applause and fanfare and when he finally settled in the comfort of his chambers after weeks on the battlefield he let out a sigh of relief. He'd won, ensured Tyran would never be a threat to his kingdom again. He fell back on his bed and smiled. The weight of the medallion on his chest reminded him of the bargain he had struck and the dark magic he'd used. He knew he'd regret his decision, but for now he would celebrate the victory. Margon was human after all and an accident could be arranged before he had to lift the ban on mages. As soon as he'd thought it the medallion's surface heated. He whipped it over his head and threw it across the room. It was too late; the snake sigil was burned into his chest. His bargain with magic sealed.

About the Author

Amanda J Evans is an award-winning Irish author of YA and Adult romance in paranormal and fantasy genres. Her stories centre on good versus evil with a splice of love and magic thrown in too. You can find out more on her website www.amandajevans.com.

16

ZEPARAR: BARREN
JOSEF KASTLE

"Janice, are you sure about this?" Ralph asked his wife of ten years.

"It is the only thing we haven't tried," she reminded him. "We've been trying since before our honeymoon. Still no kids."

"But a demon, sweetheart? Must we resort to that?" he shook his head adamantly. "God forgive me for even considering it!"

"It is God keeping me from having a baby!" she said, choking back tears. "What have I done that God won't give me a child!"

"Baby, baby," he soothed. "God will provide, I promise."

"He hasn't yet!" she buried her face in her hands. "I. Want. A. Baby."

"I know you do, darling. But why a demon?" Ralph was not happy about his wife's plan to summon a demon to conceive a child. He wasn't a diehard Christian, but he certainly wasn't going to take that risk with his soul. If he even had a soul.

"It is the only way!" she pleaded. "Please, my love, do this for me."

"How do you even know it is going to work?" he asked her.

"We don't, but what do we have to lose?" she returned.

"Our souls?" he queried lamely.

"You don't even believe you have a soul!" she fired at him.

"Doesn't matter, I'm scared," he admitted.

"And there we have it, ladies and gentlemen," she addressed the empty bedroom. "Big Bad Ralph is afraid!"

"Dammit, woman!" he roared. "Fine. Fuck it! Summon this demon and let's get it over with!" Janice knew what buttons to push, not just to piss her husband off, but to get what she wanted. She needed him angry in order for this to work.

"Good, we can do this now," she remarked. She crossed the room grabbed a couple of candles off the mantel and a book of matches.

"Do what?" he asked lamely.

"Summon Zeparar," was her simple answer.

"Now?"

"Of course, now!" she snapped. She wanted to keep him angry.

"Just like that?" he barked.

"Just like this..." she set the candles on the side table by their bed and lit them. Without any preamble," Zeparar, I summon you! Zeparar, make me full with child! Take my sacrifice!"

"Sacrifice?" Ralph asked from his side of the bed. "What sacrifice?"

"This," came a gruff voice from behind him. The owner of the voice smacked Ralph on the ass.

"What the fuck!" he yelped as he scrambled across the bed. "What the hell are you?"

"Zeparar," was his one-word response. The man was just over average height, but lean. His red hair was plastered to his head making his skull's shape clearly visible under the nearly translucent skin. A small pair of black horns protruded from his forehead just below the hairline.

"What the fuck are you?!" Ralph shouted as he stood from the bed sheltering his wife from the strange man.

"Zeparar," he rumbled from deep in his throat. "She called me."

"Yes!" Janice gasped from behind her husband. "I did summon you."

"See, Ralph, she knows what is going on."

"How do you know my name?" he asked dumbly.

"I know lots of things, my sweet," Zeparar responded. He moved up onto the bed, kneeling on the edge. His clothes had disappeared. Ralph stared at the man's naked chest and tried not to look down any further. "Like I know you want to look down."

"I do not!" Ralph protested.

"Honey, it is the only way," his wife said from behind him. "Just let it happen. You've wanted a threesome..."

"With another woman!" he protested weakly.

"You know that isn't true, dear," she said as she placed a hand on his shoulder. He realized that his t-shirt was gone. He glanced down and saw that he was naked.

"What the fuck?" he grabbed a pillow and hid behind it.

"I've already seen what you have to offer, Ralphie," Zeparar said seductively. "Just as I can see what your wife has to offer."

He looked over his shoulder and saw that Janice had let her nightgown drop off her shoulders and puddle at her feet. "Honey!" he stepped between Zeparar and his wife's naked body. "Put that back on!"

"Ralph, please, stop being like this. He can help me have a baby."

"How?" he asked her.

"Just let him guide the way," she answered and kissed him on the back of the neck. "This is supposed to work the first time."

"I don't even know what the hell you mean," he pleaded to her with his eyes as he turned to embrace her. He wasn't entirely sure why he was holding her. He was pissed at her. The pillow fell from his grasp as he pulled her into his arms.

"There, sweetheart," she cooed to him and kissed him on the lips. "You are letting it happen."

"I am?" he was bewildered. His every instinct told him to fight Zeparar and get the fucking monster out of his house, but his body was reacting differently. He was strangely aroused. He wasn't sure if it was the stranger in the room or the excitement of something different. He'd not felt this way before.

"You are, Ralphie," Zepar said as he reached across the bed offering his hands to both of them. "Come, join me." His raging erection was pointing straight at the two of them. "I can help you have a child. All I need is to use your body to transfer the seed."

"Transfer the what?" Ralph asked as he allowed himself to be pulled into the bed by the naked demon. His wife was right there with him, smiling at them both.

"The seed. My seed." Zepar answered him soothingly. "You are why your wife is childless. It is not her body. It is yours. And I can fix that."

"What the hell?!" Ralph tried to protest but his voice betrayed him as it broke on the last word. He was more than just aroused. A wetness had begun to leak from his enflamed member.

"I have to implant my seed in you for you to implant in her," Zepar explained. "The details don't matter. What matters is that you both want it."

"Yes, we want it," Janice answered.

"No, my sweet lady, he has to answer for himself."

"Ralph," she pulled his face towards hers and kissed him again. "You want this, don't you?"

"I want a baby, yes," he agreed.

"Then tell Zeparar you want this," she said, her eyes pleading for him to consent.

"I want this," Ralph said to the strange creature that held them under a spell of lust. "I want to have a baby and want your seed."

"There, was that so hard?" Zepar asked as he looked down at Ralph's crotch. "I guess maybe it is."

Zepar reached for Ralph and pulled him to the center of the bed. His own nakedness was burgeoning between his glistening thighs. He gently pushed the human male onto his side facing away from him and motioned for Janice to lay down facing them both. She complied with a smile, lust in her eyes. Was the lust for Ralph or was it for Zepar? She didn't know where her feelings were coming from, but she was so hot her sweet spot was damp with anticipation.

"I'll be gentle," he whispered into Ralph's ear as he clamped his teeth down on the man's shoulder. Janice moved in for a deep kiss when her husband gasped in pain and pleasure. As Ralph was distracted by the bite and the kiss, Zepar spread the man's cheeks with his fingers and plunged inside of him.

Ralph bucked forward, trying to escape the sudden invasion of his nether regions and his own manhood found its home inside of his wife. Several long minutes of rhythmic motion ensued. The human couple was locked into a passionate embrace, their breath coming in gasps as they neared their own release.

Zepar kept time with them both, his spike planted deep inside of Ralph. He met each thrust of their hips with a thrust of his own. He kept a hold of Ralph with his teeth. The man's hot blood seeping through his lips and staining the pillow tasted so good. The man was far from a virgin, but he was to what they were doing. That made it worth Zepar's while. He had stolen this man's ability to procreate and he was returning that to him by taking his pride.

Janice screamed in ecstasy as she came. Ralph grunted with the sudden wash of wetness and he quickened his pace. He screamed with something between pain and pleasure as Zepar let loose his own seed into the man. With the sudden flow of hot into his innards, Ralph let loose and pounded one final time into his wife and gasped for breath buried deep inside her.

Ralph woke to the morning light and rolled over on top of the sheets. He had fallen asleep inside his wife and the stickiness of their love had dried just enough to cause discomfort as he popped out of her. She slept through it, her hands thrown up over her head making her breasts flatten across her ribcage. There was a smile of contentment on her lips he hadn't seen in years.

"What the...?" he whispered. He wasn't exactly sure what had happened, but he felt exhausted. He swung his legs over the edge of the bed and sat up, wincing at a pain deep within that seemed to send a surge of pleasure to his crotch. Glancing down, he saw a dried drop of blood on the tip of his member. Thinking it must have come from Janice he stood and started his day. She just rolled over and inhaled deeply of his pillow, her covering the dark red stain of his blood.

Two weeks later Janice squealed with excitement as the pregnancy test she'd picked up at the drug store read positive. They hadn't shared another night of passion since Zeparar's visit, but she didn't care. She was pregnant. She didn't seem to care that Ralph had lost all interest in her sexually, preferring to go out to the bars on weekends. He came home smiling, but she never smelled perfume or saw lipstick on his collar. She did smell cologne that wasn't his brand.

17

BOTIS AND THE REVELATION
CYNTHIA STATON

Botis sat cross legged on a large royal blue cushion with gold fringe. Before him was a giant crystal ball inlaid with gold filigree. He was peering into the ball and watching events of past, present, and future unfold before his eyes. Not that he needed the crystal ball to see these things but it helped him to focus more. It also gave his customers a way to see the predictions he made of their lives. Most were fascinated by the images no matter how gruesome they might get. Many were blown away by the amazing display and clarity it gave them. Botis enjoyed giving out predictions and seeing how humans reacted to them.

He waited patiently for the next person to enter. Today he had chosen his human form because it scared the humans less if he did so, though many of them still feared him due to his large teeth and the horns on his head. Still, it was less unsettling than a large Viper talking to them. Occasionally, when he was feeling especially naughty, he would sit there in his Viper form and see what happened. Most of the time the human would simply turn tail and run. It always gave him a good laugh.

Botis waited patiently for the next customer to arrive. He had already foreseen who was coming to see him and knew exactly how things were going to play out. It intrigued him to know these things and he was very much looking forward to the arrival of this particular man. This man had a mysterious past, a mundane present, and a future that was going to change the world as everyone knew it. He watched as the man entered exactly as he had seen him do in his mind. The man sat down before him on the cushion opposite the crystal ball on its pedestal.

"Hello Tyler," Botis greeted. Tyler caught Botis eyes with an intense gaze.

"Hello, Botis," Tyler aptly greeted in return.

"What can I do for you?" Botis asked with a yawn.

"You know what I want and what I need." Tyler replied with a sly grin.

"Yes, I know. Just thought I'd let you feel like you were in control." Botis shot back. Tyler leaned back in his chair and waited. Botis knew that Tyler wanted him to tell him everything without any promptings or outside sources. There were many frauds out there but not so him. He was one of the rare ones who actually spoke the truth. "Tyler, you are here today because you want to know what your past is hiding, why your present is so dull, and what your future holds for you."

"That is spot on!" Tyler exclaimed. Botis looked at him with sharp eyes.

"Alright, let's start with your past," Botis waved his hand over the crystal ball and whispered a few words in his demonic language. The ball came to life with images that soon became as clear as a 4k television. Tyler looked intently at the images on the ball. A woman was screaming during childbirth, begging for death. The man beside her was not fully human but he was soothing the woman and assuring her that the baby would be fine. When the baby was born all the electrical equipment had gone haywire and the baby's cry was more of a raspy growl. The mother had died right after giving birth to the baby boy. The father took the baby into his arms, laid his hand on the baby's forehead, and recited something in a foreign tongue. The baby stopped growling and looked up into the eyes of his father in silence. A nurse came over to them with her arms out and the otherworldly man handed the baby to the nurse then vanished before her eyes. The nurse seemed to be in a trance before coming to and declaring the baby an orphan.

"Your mysterious path has been revealed. You are half demon," Botis stated seriously.

"I always felt as if I were different somehow." Tyler whispered, completely mesmerized by the facts displayed before him. Botis ran his hand over the ball again and spoke another incantation. The ball sprung forth Tyler's present life. Showing him living the everyday life that most humans led. He had an ordinary job, lived in a studio apartment with a roommate, and had a plain girlfriend. None of it appealed to him and he felt listless, as if he were falling fast through a downward spiral and could not climb back up. Tyler began to cry,

"I hate my life man. Nothing feels right. It's so... so..."

"Boring?" Botis added.

"Yes! Life is so dull. I need something but just don't know what it is." Tyler admitted.

"Perhaps a glimpse of your future will give you a clue to what you need?" Botis offered. Once again he waved his hand over the ball and spoke another incantation. The ball covered in a fog and remained that way. Botis stared deeper into the ball, knowing full well what should be showing. He looked up to Tyler,

"The ball will not reveal your future unless you are a hundred percent sure you want to go down this path."

"I am sure! This life sucks! I'll do whatever it takes to change it." Tyler declared. Botis closed his eyes as he ran his hands over the ball only this time he remained silent. The ball cleared and displayed a scene of utter chaos. The apocalyptic scene before them was one straight out of nightmares. Tyler looked upon the destruction with utter fascination, his eyes lighting up with self-discovery. Botis watched him as the light bulb lit up in the man's mind. Tyler looked at him and said,

"I am the one that causes this?"

"Yes," was Botis simple reply.

"What do I need to do to begin on this path?" Tyler asked eagerly.

"You must find your father and unlock the demon inside you." Botis disclosed. Tyler clapped his hands as he jumped up, threw a few hundreds on the floor, then flew out the door without so much as a thank you. Botis shook his head. His part in the coming destruction was done. Now all he had to do was sit back and watch it all unfold.

About the Author

Cynthia Staton is an inspirational speaker and author. Her first book is called Life Lived Not Lost a journey of hope.

Cynthia has also jumped feet first into down the rabbit hole into the anthology world, but also plan to have her next novel out this year.

18

Bathin was a demon of the deep, waiting for his bidding above, in Hell below. He had under his command, thirty legions of lesser demons that did what his will was at all cost. He was the seer and knower of many things, including precious stones, and a great identifier of herbs and their uses.

His greatest gift however was that he could bring men from one place to another, helping them attain a state of being, called astral projection. Astral projection was an out of body experience that could take the soul of a person away from its body, so it could travel to another place entirely.

Men and women from far and wide came seeking Bathin for his services, but his specialties often came with a price...a hefty one. There hadn't been a soul that had asked him for herbs for a spell, stones for wealth, or an out of body experience for self-gain that had not been expected to pay handsomely.

Bathin was a strong humanoid being with the tail of a serpent. Everywhere he traveled, he was seen riding a pale horse. Bathin was mentioned in "The Lesser Key of Solomon" and was the eighteenth spirit of the seventy-two demons of Solomon.

He sat with a smirk on his great horse, flicking his tail like a whip to punish souls of the damned, waiting on his next big adventure topside.

*****

Sivan stood on a balcony through an open doorway, the cool wind was whipping through her white cotton night gown. She had tears rolling down her cheeks and blood pouring from her nostrils, but no noise was coming from her at all. Her blond hair fell like silken sheets down to her hips, and her eyes were the most interesting color of bright blue.

She was losing nearly everything and was feeling only sadness seep into her. Sivan was trembling uncontrollable at the situation she was in. The past week had been the worst one of her life, and no one knew what had happened to her.

She reached into the pocket of her gown and pulled out a bloody cloth she had used to dab her bleeding nose many times before. She sat it to her crimson drip again as more blood poured onto the cloth. She had learned less than a week before that she had an aggressive form of cancer and would only live another week or two.

She felt fine for the most part besides the atrocious pain and the infernal bloody faucet of a nose. She had even bled from her mouth a few times. Sivan tried to hold it all together, but in the end, she couldn't think of one person left that would miss her.

Her parents had died in an accident when she was eighteen, no other family to speak of had been around her whole life. She had friends, but she didn't want to burden any of them.

The moment the doctors diagnosed her, Sivan withdrew all her savings, packed a single bag, and took off in her Mini Couper to see things she had never seen.

There was no way she was going to get to all of it before she died, but the one thing she knew to be true, was the fact that she was going to die...and alone at that.

A trip into town in a city Sivan had not bothered to look at the name of, she found herself in a local shop scanning shelf after shelf of books, candles, and herbs. Deep down, she knew she was looking for a cure in the Wiccan book store, but also knew there was no such thing.

"Can I help you?" A beautiful gothic woman asked her.

"Got a cure for cancer?" Sivan joked, but felt guilty right after.

"Not yet," the woman answered a bit more somber, "but if you want to see the world before..."

"I die," Sivan interrupted her.

"I wasn't going to say that," the woman smiled weakly.

"It's alright," Sivan smiled. "I am going to die...and soon, but I don't have the money, nor time to travel the world."

"What I have for you doesn't require money," the woman spoke softly, as she searched for something on a shelf. "This one," she smiled, as she handed Sivan a book. "For you."

"Thank you," Sivan smiled back, then looked at the price of the book. "I can't afford this one...thank you though," she tried to hand the book back.

"It's a gift," the woman smiled again.

"Are you sure?"

"I am very sure, just do me a favor," the shop keeper whispered.

"What's that?" Sivan asked.

"Go to Paris," she smiled.

Sivan looked down to see the book once more, when she looked up, the woman was gone. There was not a soul in sight. Sivan walked out of the store and back to her hotel as another tirade of bloody snot dripped down her face.

Sivan felt a bit skeptical as she tossed the book down on her bed once she got back to her hotel. Immediately, the book flipped open to a page. The top of the page was labeled Bathin, but Sivan had never heard of anything or anyone that went by that name. She closed the book quickly as a chill ran down her spine.

She sat the book down on her side table, then went to take a shower. She needed to wash the grime off her body from such a loss of blood. When she returned from the shower, Sivan stopped dead in her tracks. There on the side table, was the book, but it was opened again to the page marked Bathin.

Curious as to the magic that might be in the book, Sivan sat cross-legged on the bed. She sat the book on her lap and read what was on the page.

Bathin the demon of the deep sits awaiting your call. He wishes to help you. He is the finder of precious stones, knower of herbs for spells and healing, and taker of souls to places unseen...if you have need of him, simply ask the words below.

Sivan knew nothing about Bathin, but she did know what a demon was. She didn't know if she wanted to deal with the devil, but was intrigued about the herbs for healing, or possible even seeing things unseen.

She put the book down on the bed in front of her and began to use the words to call Bathin forth. What felt like a small earthquake occurred in the room alone. A tall man with a tail like a snake appeared in front of the woman. The exertion from the conjure had caused her nose to drip red, wet with blood once again.

She couldn't believe she had asked for Bathin to come forth and there he was standing in front of her. He was not at all what she had expected as a shiver went down her spine and her heart fluttered all at once.

Bathin stood and looked at the woman as she dabbed at her bloody nose. Something about the woman struck fondly with him, and he didn't know why. A human had not made him feel that way before and he often enjoyed punishing them.

"The name is Bathin, how may I help you?" He grumbled in her direction.

"I am Sivan, and I am not sure," Sivan's voice trembled.

"Why would you call me if you did not know?" He asked as he whipped his tail back and forth.

"A woman from a book store downtown gave me this book," Sivan picked up the book and showed it to Bathin.

"Mylan," Bathing grumpled. "She is one of my legions, but one of the best you will ever meet."

"Your legion?"

"My servants," he half smiled. "Mylan is always good at sending souls my way, but I have never seen one like yours yet."

"Is this good?" Sivan asked.

"It is, but I can't figure out something yet."

"What's that?"

"Why is your nose bleeding?" He asked sounding a bit softer.

"I am dying," she smiled. "Cancer."

"Damn cancer," he grumbled. "You know, cancer is not something that Satan designed...neither did God...cancer is made by man."

"Damn man," she smiled at him, sending a shiver down his spine for a change, and hers as well.

Bathin walked up to the woman and ran his large hand through her wet hair. He looked at her like no one had ever looked at her before. She couldn't figure out how he wasn't some scary monster, serpent tail and all, but he wasn't.

"Do you want to go somewhere?" He asked.

"Mylan says I should see Paris," Sivan smiled.

"That doesn't surprise me," Bathin said. "That is Mylan's favorite place ever."

"Then I shall see Paris," Sivan coughed a little as splashes of blood fell on her hand. "But I cannot travel like this."

"I can take you anywhere Silvan."

Without another word, Bathin gently laid Silvan's weak body back on her bed. He placed his hands on either side of her ribcage as he looked down into her blue eyes.

"I'm ready," she sighed.

"You're beautiful," Bathin said.

Before she could answer, Bathin pulled Sivan's soul out of her body and sent it to Paris. He saw through her eyes as she saw the Eiffel Tower. He Astral Projected her from Paris to Rome, then to Italy, France, Mexico, and any place he had ever thought was beautiful for the beautiful woman.

He looked down and saw a steady stream of blood coming from Sivan's nose...he wanted to pull her from the projection, but she was smiling. He sent her to Japan, Africa, and many other places before the blood began to puddle around her head.

He removed his hands from her ribs. Her soul jolted back into her body as Sivan tried to sit up, gasping for air.

Sivan was barely breathing after her soul returned to her body. She smiled at Bathin.

"Thank you," she huffed through short breaths.

"Don't talk," Bathin said as he took her hand. "I can show you so much more."

"How?" She wheezed.

"Come with me?" Bathin asked rather than commanded. "I will make you my queen, and we will rule my dominion together."

"You want...me...to be...your queen?" Her words and breathing were labored.

"I do," Bathin said as a single tear fell down his face.

"I will," she spoke her last words.

Bathin leaned down, and kissed Sivan on the lips, soft and warm. Lightning struck her heart as parts of her went warm, while others were cold. A swirling wind whipped around her body as it caused her to rise off the bed. She smiled and then returned his kiss. Their eyes glowed with love.

Bathin took Sivan up in his arms. He carried her out of the hotel as he mounted his steed with her behind him. They strode together into the distance where they reigned over legions, and legions of legions.

Sivan chose not to die, but to live forever in and out of Hell with the man of her dreams, Bathin, the demon of the deep.

About the Author

Paige Clendenin is a spunky and vivacious author who takes pride in who she is...weird, corky, eclectic, or otherwise.
Facebook Author Page:
https://www.facebook.com/paigeclendeninauthor

19

The tall man with balding chestnut hair and brown/gray beard was looking at his wife with confusion.

"Jayne, please tell me you are joking...."

The middle-aged woman by his side, with curly blonde hair and flashing green eyes laughed nervously.

"Lynn, you know when I'm being serious...."

Lynn ran his hand through his beard, brows furrowed.

"I do. That's why I'm concerned, you can't seriously be talking about.....de-"He grunted at his foolish fear as the word got caught in his throat, he cleared it then barked roughly "demons!"

Jayne had to hold her hand over her mouth to hide the smile on her face at his false bravado.

"You know I've been doing research. I'm serious, what's the worst that can happen, no demon shows up and we feel like fools?"

Lynn was shaking his head,

"That's probably the BEST thing that could happen when trying to summon a demon Jayne!" He was waving his hands emphatically, then folded them sternly.

"Not that I believe it's a possibility, but still, it seems mighty stupid to mess with something like this Jayne; no matter what the reason."

"But I've been doing research! Demons aren't all that bad, they're much like humans, they run the gamut of evil to good! They have special powers we don't, and if you summon just right...you control them!" Jayne said with too much excitement for Lynn's taste.

"Look, I know you want what's best for Rose, but I am not convinced this is even worth our time to discuss!" Lynn yelled in frustration; this was getting ridiculous. Demon summoning to find their daughter a man, "It's poppycock! WE can find OTHER ways to introduce Rose to the right guy to....you know...."

"Lynn, honey..." Jayne took his face in her hands gently, and looked him in the eyes. "We HAVE already tried those ways. It's not working." Lynn's shoulders sagged, she was right, they had already tried everything.

"Do you...erm, have to do anything crazy for the demon?" He asked quietly, eyes on the floor.

"They often request something, it's usually really random and weird, but nothing dangerous or bad." Jayne answered, "I already know the demon we can summon!"

Lynn jumped, "Oh?" was all he could think to say in response.

"Sallos, one of the Demons captured by Solomon supposedly. He is a handsome aristocrat, a duke I believe, that brings love between men and women." Jayne's eyes were wide with hope, excitement, and despite her best efforts to hide it, a touch of fear.

Surprisingly the fear he saw seemed to melt away a good proportion of his worry; his wife didn't ever jump into anything without knowing everything she possibly could about it.

"He doesn't sound like a demon to me." Lynn answered.

"He rides a crocodile." Jayne smiled. Lynn rolled his eyes.

"Well fine, you can try and summon this Sallos with your candles and incantations. But don't get upset when it doesn't work OK?" He said with love, his hand on her shoulder.

Jayne nodded, then left the room quickly; already ready to get going. Lynn sighed nervously;

"What have I gotten myself into with this woman..." It was a phrase he had said many times in their marriage.

Lynn was pacing nervously outside his wife's altar room. He couldn't hear anything and it was making him nervous. Soon he saw the lights go out in the room. There were candles on, because he could still see a flickering glow coming from underneath the door. Next he heard his wife chanting,

"Oh Sallos, wise Duke of love,
I, Jayne, dedicated mother of Rose,
beseech thee to come to us.

Your powers in matchmaking
our young Rose needs,
Please hear my plea,
and come set my Rose free."

Lynn watched as the flickering glow under the door started to fade as candle after candle went out. Once it was dark he heard a strange humming tune. It sounded like Jayne, but it was as if she were on stereo all around the house. He didn't recognize the tune. Then it went dark and silent, everywhere. Lynn covered his ears, as if to drown out the deafening silence. He wasn't sure how long he stood there in that void of sound or light, but it ended as suddenly as it had started. Once he was sure things were back to normal he opened his eyes; but things weren't back to normal.

Standing in the middle of his living room was an ornately dressed gentleman, who had a lavish crown placed upon his long salt and pepper hair. And by his side? A humongous, grizzly crocodile on a gold leash; the crocodile was smirking at him.

"Ohhhhhhhh booyyyy...." he said in a big breath, and sat down quickly on the couch, white as the moon. He covered his eyes while trying to regain his composure. When he opened them, he skirted past the crocodile and man and settled on his wife.

She was grinning triumphantly from ear to ear, her eyes sparkling, cheeks flushed, her hair was flowing wildly around her. She looked beautiful, and powerful.

"Jayne?" he asked in a shaky voice.

"Everything is OK, Lynn." She answered in her normal voice, no fear or supernatural power did he sense in it.

"And, uh, this is...uh?"

"Duke Sallos, sir," the man said with a bow. "I understand your lovely lady and you are seeking my help for your daughter." He smiled, and it made Lynn take a liking to him, despite his unease.

"We are. Can you help?"

The Duke smiled with confidence,

"I can indeed. Where is the young lady?" He asked, looking around.

"She is at the park across the street, she enjoys walking there," Jayne answered.

"Well then with your permission, I will be off. Leave the rest to me." And with that he was out the door, crocodile in tow.

The Duke saw a young man walking around the gazebo in the middle of the park.

"Hello young sir!" He said in a raised voice. The lad didn't respond.

"Sir!" He tried again, louder. The boy turned around.

"Me?" he asked. The Duke jogged up to him, his crocodile sauntering behind. The lad's eyes grew wide.

"Yes! Do you know a Rose? I'm looking for her." The young man's face showed recognition when he heard the name. But he didn't say anything.

"Do you know her then?" The Duke asked patiently after a long pause.

"I...I do." He said hesitantly

"Do you know where she is?"

The boy scratched his head, and shifted on his feet, he seemed nervous and the Duke couldn't understand why. Finally, he said,

"I don't, but I can help you find her."

The Duke nodded, "Thank you, that would be swell. Your name lad?"

Again, the boy looked confused and out of sorts. After a short pause he answered shakily,

"R-Robin." Robin's cheeks flushed, and his eye twinkled. "Robin, it's Robin." He said more firmly.

"Aye, well Robin, lead the way! I'm sure you have a better handle on this park than I do!" He laughed jovially. Robin couldn't help but smile.

"OK, I can do that." He said. To himself he thought 'But what am I going to do when we don't find.....her?'

The Duke, crocodile and Robin had been walking around the park for a good thirty minutes. Robin's shyness wore off quickly; Sallos was a charming and engaging fellow and he always brought out the best, and truest parts of people. He was enjoying getting to know Robin. He was an incredible lad, sensitive, kind, but brave and engaged with his world. His mind was sharp, and his ideas unique.

"Politics huh? That's a tough one, are you sure you can handle it?" Sallos asked as Robin was talking about his goals.

"The tough part is not becoming corrupt I think. That would be always on my mind." He said seriously, his finger rubbing his upper lip as his mind wandered through a political daydream. The duke smiled. He loved this kid, they needed to find Rose, because he had a feeling he had found Robin for a reason.

"I think you could do it young sir." Sallos said smiling at the lad much like a proud father. "I hate to interrupt this scintillating conversation but...Rose?"

Robin grew shy and quite again. This time his face turned so red Sallos knew something was up.

"Robin...." Sallos pried.

He wrung his hands, sweat broke out on his forehead and upper lip, he looked close to tears.

"My name isn't Robin." He whispered.

"What?" Sallos asked

"My name isn't Robin." He said again a little louder.

Now it was Sallos" turn to look perplexed.

"OK." He said, unsure.

"It's...I'm.." he took a deep breath, and then finally blurted out, "I'm Rose!"

Sallos simply blinked, several times. He looked a little closer at Robin.

"Why didn't you just tell me?" The duke asked.

"I....well, my given name is Rose...and I'm told I'm a girl. But I feel like a boy, and Robin is the name I call myself."

They were blushing now ten times redder than they had previously, and this time there were actual tears.

"You saw me as myself, you called me sir, you talked to me like I was Robin, and it felt so good. I didn't want that to stop. Also...I don't want a man." Robin was looking down at the ground, tears streaming down his face. Sallos didn't know what to do. This was a first for him, his powers were making men and women fall in love...this felt outside his realm. But he couldn't stand there and just watch Robin cry. He didn't know what he was going to do or say, he just acted on instinct.

He wrapped his arms around the lad.

"Robin..." He said, shocking the boy, "I can't pretend to not being somewhat confused right now...but one thing I know, is that if you say you're a boy, and that your name is Robin...then that is who you are to me. And if you don't want a man, well, maybe I can help you find....a woman?"

Robin was ugly sobbing at this point, and it lasted, Sallos hugged him longer, then sat on a bench with him until he could regain himself.

"My-y parents...they sent you to fix me, to make me a girl. They think the right "man" will change me. But it won't. I don't want to be with anyone right now. I'm not ready, I barely know who I really am."

Sallos looked at Robin, and finally knew what it was he had to do.

"Come, it's time to go see your parents." Sallos said, offering him a hand. He looked at his crocodile next,

"We're going to help Robin; his parents need to see he doesn't need fixing. I may need backup."

The crocodile nodded it's head, then licked it's lips. "No, you aren't going to eat them, we don't do that anymore remember?" Sallos sighed. "Come, let's go."

"Jayne! The Demon and Rose are coming!" Lynn called from the living room, Jayne came quickly, face flushed with excitement.

The Duke and Robin walked in, and the two of them could tell something was going on; there was a very intense energy in the air, and Robin was avoiding eye contact.

"What's going on?" Jayne asked sharply.

"I went out to look for your daughter." Sallos started "I found this young man."

Jayne and Lynn's faces looked shocked, confused and angry.

"Rose is not a man."

"Yes, I am mom." Robin said quietly.

"His name is Robin, I talked with him for a good hour, I had no idea he was your son."

"OUR DAUGHTER!!" Lynn yelled.

"No! Your SON. You asked for my demon powers to help your child. Do you want to help your child or not??" Sallos asked, pulling himself up to his intimidating 7' of full height. "Accept him, he is an amazing lad, and he doesn't want any lover right now. He's smart. He needs to find himself. Finding the right "person" isn't going to fix him! It's going to trap him in a life that is a lie, and I've seen firsthand through many years how that ends. You want my power, I can see people for who they are, it's how I connect lovers. Your son is a man, and he needs to be acknowledged."

Jayne and Lynn stood in shocked silence. The room had gone dark and his voice was booming, and they couldn't ignore the significance of everything he said. Robin's breath hitched, and his parents saw that he was sobbing.

"P-please, I don't know why I don't fit my....mold, but my brain knows I'm a man. Please." He begged his parents.

Jayne was on her knees crying, Lynn was stunned.

"R-r-Robin." his mom sobbed, then Lynn said, "Robin...." And then they were all hugging, and sobbing, and they were calling Robin their son, and apologizing. Sallos was grinning, as was his crocodile, and slowly they faded into the distance with no warning. Their job was done.

About the Author

Koi Garfield is a Transgender man who served in the Navy where he wrote his first book. He has always been an avid writer and reader as well as lover of culture and language.

20

PUSON AND THE MAGIC EIGHT
BALL
CHANNIE COCKER

Nina sat on the park bench completely immersed in what she had in her hand. It had been given to her on her tenth birthday. She had been ecstatic when she opened the gift. Almost to the point her parents worried they had made a mistake in giving in to her constant begging. Now she held it in her hand on her seventeenth birthday, pondering if she should look into it and ask the one question that had been burning in her heart for nearly a year now. She had never asked it this question for fear of the answer it might provide. She drew in a deep breath and exhaled to help calm her nerves. Looking into the murky window she gathered the courage to ask,

"Magic Eight Ball, do you see a future for me, Nina Milton, and Jacob Lewiston?" she shook the black orb and looked in the window again. It read, 'More than Likely'. Growing excited she asked, "Will it be a good future?" It read, 'Difficult to Tell'. Sometimes that eight ball could be so vague. There had been many times she had wanted to just toss it but refrained because it had given her so much security. Her heart could only take so much. She just had to know the answer to this one question. Nina shook the ball again and asked, "Does Jacob Lewiston like me?" The orb said, 'It is decidedly so.' This made her very happy. The fates had spoken making Jacob and her an item. Hope grew in her heart as she stared out at the football field. There he was, the hunky quarterback, dressed in his football gear and practicing. To Nina he was a dark-skinned god and no mortal stood a chance against him.

Nina continued to watch Jacob play but was slightly distracted by the sudden sounds of trumpets playing. She wondered if the band were also practicing but that seemed odd since they usually chose a different day than the football team to practice. Still, she heard the trumpets loud and clear but could not pinpoint where they were coming from.

"You like that boy eh?" said a man beside her. She turned quickly to see who had chosen to sit right next to her when there were so many other places he could have sat. She almost screamed but curiosity got the best of her. The man next to her was no ordinary man. He had the body of a man but the head of a lion.

"Who are you? And what's with the lion's mask?" she asked bluntly.

"The name is Puson and this is no mask, dear," he growled.

"You can't be serious?" she rolled her eyes at him.

"Oh, trust me. It's real. Go ahead and examine it. I don't mind," Puson offered. Nina reached up and gave his mane a firm tug. When it didn't budge, she searched for any openings in the back or seams around the neck. Sure enough, his head was real.

"What are you?" she demanded.

"I'm a demon, naturally," Puson replied.

"Why the hell would a demon be talking to me?" Nina scoffed.

"Honestly? I'm jealous of that eight ball of yours. After all, it took my job." Puson whined.

"Jealous? What? Took your job? I don't get it man," Nina shrugged.

"Alright, so I have the ability to see the past, present, and future. You want to know if you and Jacob have a future? I can tell you in way more detail than that thing ever could. You want to know what that future is going to be like? I can offer that too," Puson smiled as he crossed his arms over his chiseled chest.

"Why would you do that for me?" Nina asked. The idea of getting clearer answers appealed to her greatly.

"It's what I do," Puson winked.

"What's the price? These things always come with a price," Nina glared at him.

"Yes, there is always a price. Your soul, of course." Puson looked at her with serious eyes.

"That's a steep price!" Nina exclaimed nervously.

"It's the price, nonetheless. You know it's totally up to you to make the deal or not. Either way, I don't care. I'm here and I made you an offer. I need to know if you are going to accept it." Puson purred. Nina sat quietly, giving his offer some serious thought. She really did need to know if she and Jacob were going to have a life together and what the future might hold for them and her eight ball was letting her down. Still, old habits die hard. Nina shook the eight ball and asked,

"Eight Ball, should I accept this demon's offer?"

Puson raised a bushy brow with a sly smile and whispered something right as she turned the ball to look at it. It read, 'Definitely So'.

"Eight Ball, is my soul worth it?" Nina still had reservations, but it was important to her. It read, 'Yes'. She looked at Puson and nodded.

"Hold your hand out," he demanded. She held her hand out as he asked. Puson ran his sharp talon across her palm and watched as her blood bubbled up in the palm of her hand. She let out a small gasp yet watched in total fascination. Puson placed his hand on top of hers, closed his eyes, and spoke an incantation in a language she did not know.

"Close your eyes child and your future will be known to you." Puson commanded.

As soon as she closed her eyes images began to invade her mind. They ran like a fast movie clip and at first it was difficult for her to focus. That is, until she saw Jacob holding her hand. They were together and seemed to have been together for a while. He knelt before her and revealed a box with the most beautiful ring she'd ever seen. Next it was on her hand then fast forward and they had a place as man and wife. She was pregnant then they had two, no, three kids. Nina had a smile from ear to ear as she watched these images fly by, but that smile was short lived when the next images came in. She and Jacob were maybe in their fifties and were having a serious fight. She threatened divorce which angered him greatly. He punched her in the face, knocking her over the banister that she had been leaning against. She fell to the first floor of their house and broke her neck. It was instant death and Jacob simply stared at her dead corpse with cold uncaring eyes. As if that were not horrible enough, she watched as Puson came up to her corpse and waited patiently for her spirit to leave its shell. As soon as it did, he placed chains upon her and drug her body straight to hell.

She came to with a jolt as fear coursed through her body. For the first time in her life she wished that she did not know what her future held. It took her some time to gain her composure as Puson waited by her side. Looking down at her palm she noticed a nasty scar where the demon had cut her and circling it was Puson's sigil.

"Is there a way to avoid that ending?" Nina managed to ask.

"You could 'not' get with him," Puson suggested.

"And that will change my future?" A gleam of hope shone in her eyes.

"It will change the series of events of your life, but our deal is sealed. No matter what future you fall into, your soul belongs to me." His calm demeanor unnerved her. She looked down at the eight ball and felt betrayed. Nina threw the ball as far as she could before running off to get as far away as she could from the demon that had stolen her soul. Puson watched her flee and shook his head as he got up, walked over, and picked up the eight ball she had tossed aside.

"You, my friend, have been a very good asset. I think I will keep you." He placed the eight ball inside a sack he kept by his side before vanishing from the earthly realms and entering his own dimension.

About the Author

Channie Cocker is a Steamy Romance/Erotica author who loves to explore the naughty realms of writing.

21

MARAX: PRESIDENT FROM HELL
JEFF DUCKER

It is near the end of October 2020, and the Presidential Elections are coming up. Everyone will be rushing to the nearest poll booth to vote. Everyone will have their opinions as to who is the best candidate to elect as President. Many will argue over their reasoning. As it's known, some friends and family members will turn their backs on each other. In some incidents, blood may even spill. Also, it's very possible that someone might try to rig the votes. But this year, nobody would be prepared for what was going to happen. This could even be the very last election. Ever.

A man by the name of Homer Miles, stands in a home in the Bellevue area of Washington D.C.. He is watching the political news channel. Now, Homer is not visible to the residents of the home. That's because Homer is not a real person. Actually, he is not human at all. Now, he used to be. The real Homer Miles was a homeless man, who had no friends, and was estranged from his family. He resided anywhere he could find a place to sleep. In fact, he was sleeping under a bridge one night, a few months ago, when without warning he was snatched up by an unknown being. This horrible looking, foul smelling being killed Homer on the spot. Well that's putting it little nicer, I suppose, because the truth is, this being mutilated Homer. The being kept only a portion of Homer's blood and DNA. The being can now take the form of Homer Miles in case he's ever seen. This being's real name is Marax. Just Marax. Marax had been keeping an eye on the political news ever since the first talk of the election term. He was very interested indeed. He had very sinister plans. These plans involved one of the popular candidates, Kennedy Richards. Marax was watching and waiting for his moment.

Marax left the family room of this house, he went back to the basement. He chose to dwell there until he would put his plans into action. You have probable guessed by now that Marax is demon being. He used to teach demon....students, I guess you could call them. He had a knack for Astronomy. But he had long decided he wanted to do something more. He didn't just want to teach forever. He wanted to lead. Or you might say he wanted to control. He wanted the entire planet earth for himself. Of course, once he was had earth in the palm of his hands, he would bring in the rest of his kind to aid him in his eternal reign of terror. As long as they agreed to obey him. There would be no second in command or anything of the like. Earth would belong to him. He decided the best way to go about this was one country at a time. Starting with the United States of America. I guess you might be wondering what he planned to do with the human beings, after he took over. Well, that would be for him to decide. I suppose he might let them live if they agreed to yield to him. Or he might just kill them off.

Down in the basement, Marax did the only thing he really could do while the old couple of the house didn't have the news on. He drifted around, muttering to himself about all the stuff stored down there. Of course, he could do other things if he wanted, but he didn't want to bring unnecessary attention to himself. He would make himself known when he was ready. Not a second before.

"Nothing but a load of worthless junk down here", he muttered to himself. Just like he always did. He did once get bored and set fire to the basement. But then the annoying alarms went off, waking the old couple. He was forced to terminate the fire and altar the old couple's memories. Or he could have just killed them. But he decided what's the point. They probably didn't have many years ahead. So just let them live while they could. As he looked round the basement for the millionth time, he saw a rat run across the floor. He caught it by its tail. He was about to rip it in half, when he got a better idea. An evil smile spread across his face. Now imagine that, an evil smile on a demon's face! Go figure! Right?

"I wonder if the old hag upstairs likes rats very much?", he asked out loud. "It won't hurt to have a little fun. He drifted back upstairs. The old lady was in the living room reading a book. The old man was sitting on the porch reading the newspaper. Marax sat the rat on the back of the old lady's chair. It ran down to her lap. She jumped up screaming.

"HAROLD! HAROLD! GET IN HERE! HURRY! HURRRRRRRYYYYYY!!!!!", she shrieked.

He scurried in the door. "What is tarnation, is going on Geneva?, he demanded.

"A RAT! A RAT!", she was still screaming.

"Oh, for cryin' out loud! The neighbors don't want to hear about it", he insisted. "Besides, I'm sure ya scared the dad-burned thing away by now!"

Unbeknownst to either of them, Marax was standing there laughing hysterically at his handiwork. He certainly enjoyed entertaining himself, but he knew he couldn't chance causing too much commotion. So, he went back down to the basement. He let out another evil laugh as he thought to himself, these human beings are nothing. He figured if the humans in the other counties were this simple then taking over the entire world would be a cinch. The next morning, Marax drifted upstairs again and watched the old couple stumble around the kitchen making their breakfast. The old woman was scrambling eggs and frying sausage.

"It sure smells good in here, Geneva!", Harold remarked. "It looks delicious."

Harold poured his coffee and sat at the table and picked up the morning paper. "Look at this, Geneva, Richards is gonna be signing autographs at the town hall today", he told her. "We ought to go."

"Aw, Harold, there will be too many people", she declared.

"Aw, shucks", he grunted in reply.

Speaking of Richards, thought Marax, I have to get moving it's nearly time to make my move. Later that night, Kennedy Richards was getting ready for dinner. Marax drifted in and watched him washing his hands in the bathroom. Marax used a toxic gas to cause Richards to pass out into a deep sleep. He would kill him later. Marax took blood and DNA, which he used to make himself able to transform in to Richards.

Now, I go win the election, Marax thought to himself with excitement. Then this country is mine. He laughed a sinister laugh that only he could hear.

A couple weeks later, with the polls finally closed, it was time for the winner to be announced. Kennedy Richards had triumphed. He had scored the majority of votes.

Marax, posing as President Richards, almost immediately ordered a city gathering. He wanted to make a public speech and he wanted aired on television throughout the entire country. He smiled as looked out at the sea of people. They had no idea about what he was about to do.

"Welcome, to one and all", Marax mimicked in Richards voice. "Thank you for being here." "I am eager to let you in on my plan for this country."

There was a mass of cheers and whistles from the crowd. As well as a loud chant of 'RICHARDS' going around. Marax was almost enjoying it. But he was on a mission and there was no time to waste.

"Now", he shouted, "for my first piece of business." Then without warning, Kennedy Richards vanished before the crowd`s very eyes as Marax took form. There were screams, shrieks and shouts. A lot of people fainted on the spots. Marax let out the most sinister laugh he ever had.

"Thank you, really, for all your votes", he roared. "This pathetic country is mine." He roared with more evil laughter. He laughed even more when he saw security guards try to move closer to him. With a wave of his hand he set them on fire.

Then he looked right directly into a television camera and said, "WELCOME TO YOUR NEW HELL!"

About the Author

Jeff lives in Georgia and has been writing anthologies before he wrote his First novel, but he has a poetry book out called : Beside Still Waters. Jeff want to write his first novel this year.

22

I P O S : THREE WISHES

J . BECK

The child stands before me, reasonably afraid. He
called my name into the circle, and yet seemed surprised that I
appeared. This will not do.

"Child, did you call me?"

"Yes" came the meek reply.

"Then stand up and speak up. You did not summon me without
purpose."

"I want to learn."

"Very well. What would you like to learn?"

"Everything."

"Can you give me a place to start? After all, you are mortal, and
I am not. You only have so much time in which to learn before you
must start using it."

"I want to learn that which will serve me best in my life."

The phrasing confused me for a moment. This child actually
thinks I will tell him his entire future. No, that wouldn't be fair to
him or others. He would only become entitled, as he would know
what he would have at the end.

"First, tell me what year it is."

"1892."

That helps a lot.

"I won't tell you everything, but I will give you lessons to which
the meaning should reveal itself when you need to know it. Is that
acceptable for this summons?"

"If you continue to teach, yes."

"Let us begin then. Tell me, which philosophers do you know
of?"

"My teacher told us about Confucius and Locke, but didn't go
into detail about what they taught. It was only a 'very important

Chinese philosopher' and 'one of the foundations of American beliefs'. "

I admit I chuckled a little at just how lacking his understanding of philosophy was. A simple lesson will do for him.

"Are you familiar with Aesop and his fables?"

"Yes. I didn't know he counted as a philosopher."

"Philosophy is simply the love of wisdom. His fables are a way of passing a lesson on. While his fables give the moral at the end, I will leave mine for you to discover. Are you familiar with Sparta?"

The child squints in concentration. "No. I don't think I've ever heard of them."

"They were a nation of great warriors, such that armies were glad to have them as allies. Their cities had no walls, relying instead upon their soldiers to protect them."

"What does this have to do with philosophy?"

"Patience. You may not grasp this lesson for some years yet. The King of Macedonia had sent for ambassadors from several of the Greek nations- Thespia, Athens, and Sparta were among them. When the Spartan ambassador arrived, he saw the many ambassadors talking with each other, and noted there were several ambassadors from each nation. The King of Macedonia began calling all the ambassadors forwards, with ea-"

"What's an ambassador?" the child interrupted.

"An ambassador is someone who represents a nation to another nation, such as between your country and its neighbor. As the King called them forwards, the ambassadors gave him wonderful gifts and great praise, saying that he was the greatest King Macedonia had ever had. The Spartan, however, only stated that Sparta sends its greetings and seeks to maintain peace. When the King heard this, he asked how Sparta could only send one ambassador to greet a King. The Spartan replied that Sparta sent one ambassador for one King. Heed this lesson, for it shall serve you well in your life."

"I don't understand." The child looked at me, seeking further answers.

"Remember it, and think on it. The meaning will become clear later in life. I have done as you agreed was satisfactory. Until you summon me again." With that, I departed back into my realm.

I am summoned into the same home. This time, a man greets me, bold of voice, confident.

"I understand your lesson from 10 years ago. I seek more knowledge to aid in my life."

"First, tell me what lesson you learned."

"Proportionality. To each as each deserves, and no more, but never any less. While Sparta would have fit in by sending more than one ambassador, by sending only one Sparta sent a very clear message to the King that they were only here to do business with him and no other nation. A King could not fail to understand that message, nor would the other ambassadors."

"Proportionality is one of the lessons to be learned from that, certainly, but there is one other you are missing. I will give another to you, as per our terms. There was a man named Kongming in China who gave some of the soundest military advice in a war, yet he was never a soldier. Can you tell me how he was able to do so?"

"Had he studied warfare in his life?"

"He had studied, but was no soldier."

"The he would have learned by reason to account for all matters of a battle."

"That is very possible. However, is there another way in which he could have done so? I will leave you to consider this. Know that I see all, and the next time you summon me shall be the last time we speak."

"Am I to die so soon?" Oh, mortal concerns. At least he didn't ask me that the first time he summoned me. It gets so tiring after the 5,000th time.

"I will not comment on how much longer you have to live, nor how long after we talk you die. Until you summon me again."

This last time I am summoned, I see him again. He is in his 50's, missing an arm, and there are two children in the room with him- a boy and a girl.

"Why are there others present? This was an agreement between the two of us."

"I understand the lessons, will tell you what they are, and ask that you continue this through my family so that we may prosper as I have. Under your lessons, I took my family from poverty to a stable life. I fought for my country and paid what it cost to defend my nation's allies. The lessons gave me an advantage and let myself and many others return alive from the trenches. I do not see a way for things to become worse under your influence. The other lesson from our first meeting was that of tact. Knowing how to politely call attention to a problem is invaluable, especially in this society. Kongming may have simply studied a diverse subject area. Being able to forecast weather is a surprising advantage, and the army with that ability may use it to leverage a victory. A Farmer's Almanac can be a wealth of knowledge."

"You have learned them well. You are certain you wish for me to teach your children similar lessons?"

"I am certain. They have served me well, and I would not deprive my children of this wisdom."

"Very well then."

"Grandpa, why are there sirens?"

I answer for him. "The sirens are because you are in London, and it is 1942." Having answered his question, I returned to my realm.

About the Author

J. Beck is a new author with a passion for history, music, and fantasy gaming.

23

AIM AND THE COP
P.S. HARRIS

Dan stumbled his way through the dark room looking for a light switch. He had no idea where he was or how he got here. The last thing he remembered was sitting in a bar waiting on his informant to show up. He had been working on this case for three months and was no closer to solving it now than when he first started.

Yesterday, out of the blue, he received a phone call from a long-time informant that he had some information that might be useful. He agreed to meet in their regular spot and had just gotten there when everything went black.

He woke up in this room and after a quick search realized not only was his badge and gun were missing, he also had no phone. Apparently, no lights in here either.

He had almost given up on this case. It was beginning to be a thorn in his side. He pursued every lead only to come up against dead end after dead end. Now this. This case will be the death of me. "Is anyone here?" Dan didn't know what else to do. "Hey, Mouse, you here?" He called out to his contact.

The room was quiet. The silence was deafening. Dan was beginning to feel a bit nervous.

"HELLO!" Dan yelled, his voice echoing around the room.

"You need information." A deep throaty voice came from, well everywhere.

"Hello, yes, who are you? Where's Mouse? Where are you?" Relieved to finally find out he was not in danger, the questions tumbled out. Dan turned around the room looking for the source of the voice.

"It's best you don't see me." The voice surrounded him. "Your friend is safe. I am Aim, I am here to make a deal with you. You need information and in return we need you to do something for us."

"What kind of information do you have? Is it going to help me solve this case?" Dan wasn't sure he trusted this Aim, whoever that was. What kind of name is Aim? I need information and unfortunately this is the first lead I've had in three months. "I'm not going to make any kind of deal with you, until you show yourself."

"I'm sorry," Aim replied. "You are going to have to take this on faith. We can help you, but we need you to give us your soul. Hades has big plans for you in Hell."

"My soul?" Dan began pacing around the room, peering into the darkness trying to find whom he was talking to. "I'm not giving up my soul for your information. I've been working this case for three months and I'm prepared to keep working on it without giving you my soul." Dan was getting agitated. Waving his arms in the air he pumped his fists and started punching at the air, in hopes to maybe hit Aim and cause him to show himself.

"We can give you the knowledge to solve this case and any other case you may have in the future. In return Hades will have your soul and you will live an eternal life in Hell where you will be treated like royalty, everything you've ever wished for will be yours. This is a great honor. You have been chosen." Aim's voice was soft and soothing, almost hypnotizing, caressing his mind, calming his fear.

Dan didn't answer. I can't believe I'm actually considering this. His career in law enforcement had been rocky at best. He barely passed the detective exam and had not closed a case in over a year. His boss had already warned him if he didn't step up his game, he would be stripped down to file clerk. I can't afford to fail this time. Ever since he could remember his family had expected him to become a cop. His father and grandfather had both been in law enforcement after their stints in the Army. It was ground into him from an early age that this was his life.

Aim was quiet. He already knew Dan would accept the offer. They had been watching him. Hades had decided that they could use this young detective in the future and he wasn't going to leave until they had what they came for. He watched as Dan paced the dark room, mumbling to himself. "Dan, we need your decision" Aim finally spoke up.

"I don't know," Dan stopped pacing and faced where he thought Aim might be standing. "I don't know how I could trust you."

"Let me show you your future, if you decide to help us, all this could be yours." Aim raised his fire stick and pointed to the wall in front of Dan.

Dan saw a movie screen on the wall in front of him. He was walking up on a stage and the commissioner of police was handing him an award. Everyone in the auditorium was clapping. "That's me? I'm getting an award?" Dan asked.

"Yes, you will receive many awards in your future. You will rise to the top of your profession and will be revered as an important person in this life." Aim replied, "After you have lived a long successful life here on this earth you shall be taken to Hell where you will be treated as royalty for your part in our Master's plan.

"So, what will I have to do for you?" Dan asked. He knew this would come with a price.

"Nothing right now, we will let you know in the future when we need you. You are important, but we cannot force you to work for us. This must be your choice. Aim was getting impatient now, he did have other things to do after all. "Dan, this isn't a hard decision, you are failing now. If you don't do something to help your career you will disappoint you and your family. You need to do this. Just say yes."

Dan knew that Aim was right, he had to do this. At least I get special treatment in Hell. Maybe it won't be so bad and besides I'm young, I won't be dying for a long time. I've seen my future and it looks good. "Ok, yes," Dan finally decided with a sigh a feeling of peace coming over him at making the decision.

*****

Sitting in the bar waiting on his informant, Dan was looking through his files on the case. Wait a minute! How did I not notice this before?

Dan jumped up from his chair. He didn't need the informant, he knew who the murderer was.

About the Author

P.S. Harris is a sci/fi fantasy writer with her first novel out now. Watch for the sequel coming 2019. Author page https://www.facebook.com/psharrisauthor/

24

NABERIUS AND THE RUNAWAY
MAGGIE LOWE

The young man was fast losing energy as his feet continued to propel him as fast as he could make them go. He could hear the hell hounds closing in on him and feared he would not make it in time. Many had told him that he could not out run Naberius' hell hounds but he feared hell more so than anything and was determined to escape. As he continued to run through the depths of hell, he looked for any means to get out of the place.

He had heard rumors of a portal that demons and other various beings of hell often went through to traverse to the earthly plains. This was what he was looking for. One never knew if a demon was telling the truth or not but in this case what did it matter? It was either get out of hell or face eternal damnation. What more could they do to him that they hadn't done already? He shivered at the very thought.

As he rounded the corner he came to a sudden halt. In the midst of all the molten lava and black rock was a swirling round portal just beckoning him to go through. He took in a deep drought of air and started to make a run to it but was quickly pulled down by the ankle. He screamed in agony as the sharp teeth of the hell hound dug into his ankle. He could hear the crunch of his bones as it continued to chomp down. The sudden action only caused him to be more determined than ever and he lunged forward with all his might.

He didn't think he was going to make it, especially with the hell hound still clamped tight on his foot. He felt his body lurch forward and stumbled into the portal with the hound. They landed with a thud inside the swirling mists. The hell hound let out a shriek as it disappeared back into hell. This gave the young man courage and he thought for sure he had won. He would not be able to walk or run now with a broken foot, but he could still crawl. Crawling was still better than not moving at all. He moved forward within the swirling mists and, though it felt like it was taking forever, he would rather spend eternity escaping hell than being in it.

"Oh, little Jimmy," a hoarse voice called out.

"What? Who's there?" Jimmy called out.

"I see you managed to get by the hell hounds. Did you really think you could get by me though?" the voice cackled.

"Naberius? Look, I had to try okay? I don't want to be in hell!" Jimmy pleaded.

"Most humans don't. Yet, they seem to love to make choices that lead them straight here anyways. I find it humorous," the demon laughed. "Look, I've been over your records, Jimmy. You definitely belong in Hell. Murder is one of the big ones. Though, I'm sure you'll engross me with reasons why you did it and how life isn't fair. So on, and so forth."

"Oh, I murdered that man. I won't deny that," Jimmy said defiantly. He pushed himself up into a sitting position and made himself as comfortable as he could.

"So, then you belong in hell," Naberius reasoned.

"No, the man I murdered belongs in hell. I watched him as he abused my mother and my sister. I took the hits myself. Even when he violated us, I still took it. There was only so much I could take, man, before something had to be done. So, I stopped the abuse once and for all."

"Murder is still murder," Naberius shrugged.

"You don't think my sister and I tried to reach out to others for help? We begged and pleaded with them but every one of them turned a deaf ear and blind eye. If I had not stepped in and killed my father, then my mother and sister would have died instead. I did what was right. I did what had to be done," Jimmy confessed.

Naberius appeared before him. All three of his dog-like heads stared down upon Jimmy with curious eyes. Snakes protruded out of various parts of his body as they wove in and around it. The center head spoke up as the other two continued to stare, "You make some valid points, Jimmy. It would seem you are here rather unfairly. I don't think I would ever do this again but I am going to let you go. You must understand though, Jimmy... that if you wind up in hell again you will never leave and the torments you will face then will make what you have already gone through seem like heaven."

Jimmy quaked in his skin, not only at the very sight of Naberius but at his foreboding words as well. He merely nodded as he whimpered quietly. He watched as Naberius pulled aside what looked like a gossamer curtain and motioned for Jimmy to go through. It took him a few minutes to catch his bearings before he quickly crawled through the curtain and found himself butt naked next to a grave. He turned to read the head stone and saw that it was his own name etched in it. Jimmy pushed himself away from the grave as fast as he could. He had attempted to get up but his ankle was still broken.

Jimmy managed to lean up against a stone wall of a catacomb and closed his eyes. The air he breathed was fresh and crisp. He could not be happier to be alive but needed to figure out what his next move was going to be. He couldn't steal and he could not face his mother and sister without causing a panic. No, he had to start a brand-new life without them in it. At least he could see them from afar. He hoped so anyways.

The only thing he could think to do was visit a church and hope that they had mercy on him. Maybe they would provide him with some clothes, food, and shelter for the night. Jimmy looked up to the sky and said a silent prayer of thanks to a God he had once cursed. Then he went off in search of a church nearby. He was bound and determined to make this second chance a good one and even more bound and determined to never go to hell again.

25

SUMMONING RIPPER WITH
GLASYA LABOLAS
CHASITY GAINES

Jack the Ripper became the name I am remembered by, however; my Christian name was Albert. Named for our matronly Queen Victoria's German husband and son. I came from an old aristocratic family who had lost much during the American Revolution. My father returned from the Americas in disgrace as he brought along his free Nubian mistress. Mother kept herself busy with court life to ignore the fact that Father was living openly with his whore. I overheard it said he found her plying her trade in the dirty dung filled streets of New York.

My mother, a fair-haired aristocratic beauty, was close to the Queen, traveling to Balmoral and riding horses with her Royal Highness. Mother was quick to bring me into their familiar fold with the Queen doting on me. Her bright eyes would shine so bright when I accompanied Mother to court. Her Highness would ruffle my dark hair as a smile showed her pearly teeth. I spent much of my childhood in the Royal nursery-- learning and playing with the most important children in the British Empire. I was especially fond of Princess Beatrice as she had her mother's same witty humor.

After the Prince Consort died, our poor Queen sank into a deep depression. She sent many of her ladies home except for Mother. I wondered many times if one prison was better than the one she would find at our own home. With her beloved husband dead, the Queen made sure to stick by the plans they had for their children and the British Empire. I was finally at the age to leave the nursery so the Queen made sure I went to the best schools where I applied myself to the new sciences and health practices.

I had decided that I would become the doctor to our Majesty and maybe win Princess Beatrice's heart. Young men never think rationally-- why would a Princess marry an impoverished Englishman, even if royal blood flowed thinly through my veins. I stared out across the glistening lake, frozen with thick ice. Looking down, I noticed the splotched ink stains across my anatomy paper. I needed a break to stretch my legs and breathe in some fresh air. I head down the dark stairs still lost in thoughts of Beatrice's honey hair flowing in the wind.

When I came to the bottom step, I bumped into a familiar face wearing the clothes of the staff from my family's home.

"S-s-s-orry s-s-ir, I meant no disres-s-pect," the old man stuttered as he wiped the sweat from his wrinkled brow. "I am looking for my master's-s s-son," he continued to spit out.

I stepped into the light so my father's steward could see he had found me. "What does he want?" I demanded of the toothless man. Instead of speaking, the dusty bloke handed me a sealed note with my name on the front in Father's handwriting-- he turned and walked away not waiting for a reply to take back. I contemplated throwing the hateful letter on to the fire in the hallway, yet curiosity takes over.

I stepped out into the cold air drinking in the briskness of the air and the quiet falling of big snowflakes. I strolled down to the frozen lake. My feet crunching in the fresh fallen powder. Scenes like these reminded me of the dazzling Christmases with the Royal Family. I could smell the stringent evergreens and the sweet aromas of sugar pastries and apple cider. Father's note cuts deep into my fist. I take a breath. And break Father's seal and begin to read the letter. Tears freeze in my eyes and won't fall as the note contained tragic news that my mother had left her mortal body to climb the stairs to heaven. I am to pack and be ready to leave in a fortnight to return home.

I kicked and raged at God for taking my beautiful mother. I still needed her! How could she leave me? My grief quickly swelled into anger-- mad at Mother for being a frail woman. Now I had to return home and face the abomination taking place in my Mother's family mansion. She couldn't even keep Father from being such an embarrassment. A weak woman she must have been to allow such a thing to even go on without repercussions.

The long; bumpy ride to the manor only exacerbated my mood. The countryside was covered in a thick soupy fog making it impossible to see. I was beginning to feel as if the dark fog would follow me for the rest of my life. How could I even advance myself if

I had no one in position to speak for me? Father was a laughing stock in London, plus the Queen herself, had denied him entrance into the city and commanded he give up his rooms at court.

Rubbing sleep from my blue eyes, I saw the sprawling mansion coming into view. Father and his mistress stand holding hands as the carriage rolls past the gate and up to the large columned doorway. The staff and some of the villagers stand to the right of the large house waiting to see the little boy they use to know. Exiting the carriage, the staff courtesy as Father and his dark-eyed woman greeted me. I extended my hand to Father, but he grabbed it tightly and pulled me into his bulky self. He pushed me back looking at me, taking in all the changes since the last time he had seen me.

"My what a man you are becoming, son," Father's voice sounded full of pride.

Before I can reply, a silky rich voice chimes in beside Father. "I am truly sorry for the loss of your Mother." I turn to see the she-devil looking me straight in the eyes as if she planned on hypnotizing me. All I could do was nod my head as if I was struck dumb.

I walked past the two of them with my entourage in tow and headed straight to my old room. I noticed that much of the furniture had been changed and that many of the pictures my Mother had hanging were replaced by such vulgar looking things that I couldn't even really call them paintings. They looked like something a small child had splattered together. I saw strange statues of creatures that looked like demons. The most chilling statue was of a winged dog. It's emerald eyes seemed to watch me.

I was relieved to find my room the same. I asked for a tray of bread and cheese to be brought up so that I could rest afterwards. I was reading Mrs. Lovelace's book on the new machines she had built and how they computed calculations when I drifted off to sleep. I was wakened by the sound of drums and a rhythmic chanting. The watery winter sun had set with a full moon taking its place. The white light of the moon cast strange shadows in the darkness. I could still hear the beating of drums as my heart thumped loudly against my chest as I glimpsed the dancing torch light spitting and sputtering in the middle of Mother's garden.

Throwing on some clothes, I darted down the stairs as quietly as possible grabbing Father's sword off the wall. The moon's light should be enough to guide me to the center of the tangled garden. I slashed through thick brambles of dead roses and hacked my way through tall dead weeds. The drums became louder as did the chanting. My body shook in fear of what I would find and my tongue stuck to the roof of my mouth.

As I came closer to the clearing, I stayed in the shadows of the bushy evergreen trees watching the cloaked figures as they danced and jumped around the demonic statue with the startling green eyes. The torch light flickered in the inanimate dog's eyes making them look even more real. I couldn't take a step further as my body refused to cooperate. Suddenly I heard moaning and gasping coming from behind the huge monstrosity.

Man up! I spoke harshly to myself. This is your land and these are heretic trespassers, maybe even traitors to our Queen. I reminded myself. My body yielded to the other voice and walked gingerly towards the spread wings of the statue. Each step crunched lightly on the trodden ground and I drew the sword ready to strike. Peering through the lively wings, my heart jumped in my throat as I find my Father and the strange woman in the most uncompromising way. More startling than coming upon such an act, I noticed that the wings were soft to the touch, much like a bird's feathers. The statue itself sprouted dark fur, it's eyes looked deep into to my own, and a new sound filtered the air with a deep grumbling. The air around me was damp with deep breathing.

Out of nowhere, a sharp claw slapped the sword from my hand. My eyes betrayed my rational mind. Then a deep voice spoke, "It has been done for you, childish one. Have you not dreamed of fame and fortune, Closer ties with your precious royal family? I smelled it on you as soon as you entered the house. And I am bored of Ishanti and playing her statue," the demonic creature laughed as his large head looked at the spot where Father and his enchantress had lain only minutes before.

Standing before me the winged statue had grown in length and as real as myself. Speechless, my mouth hung agape and my stomach filled with stabbing spears of dread. Looking past the demon, I saw that nothing remained of my poor indulgent father and the heretic whore. Only their clothes survived-- a reminder that they had existed.

Unsticking my tongue, I finally answer as honestly as I ever have. "Yes, that is what I have desired, but I also need the knowledge to prevail. Are you offering to serve me, demon?" My voice quivered with my direct question.

"Aye, that is how you humans see it," the dog chuckled showing off a row of sharp jagged teeth ready to tear into soft flesh. "You will have what you wish for but that which you want the most will never be yours," his voice low and dangerous as his envy green eyes watch me intently as a large hairy paw brushed my shoulder.

Instantly, my body started to burn as if I had contracted the sweating sickness. It felt like the demon was stomping around in my head causing my eyes to tear up. Before I could even ask him about his cryptic message, I passed out from the intense pain and nausea pulsing through my body. The cool darkness swallowed me and the winged creature.

*****

I woke with golden rays of sun shining through my bedroom window. It all must have been a bad dream. Dressing quickly, I descended the stairs and made my way to the dining hall where I found Father's chair empty. Not uncommon, I thought to myself. Still feeling unsettled by the strangely real dream, I rush in the direction of the garden.

As I made my way to the center of the garden, I find that nothing is amiss, except that the ugly statue still sat exactly where it had been sitting last night. I can hear my heartbeat in my ears. I walked around the statue to find the clothes still laying there as if the owners had abandoned them. The staff had disappeared except for those that stayed in the village.

Glasya Labolas, the demonic winged-dog, spoke true. I obtained knowledge and attended to the royal family. Although I never felt the touch of Princess Beatrice's soft flesh; never so intimately as I had those filthy street walkers of Whitechapel.

26

***BUNE*: BURIED**

AMANDA J. EVANS

***Demons were not to be trusted, Ellie knew this,
but desperate times called for desperate measures.***

"Are you sure you want to do this, Ellie? If it doesn't work, we won't have time to try anything else."

"I have to Stacey. They can't find the medallion. They've searched her house and her workshop. It won't take them long to figure out that I buried it with her. Grandma made me promise, I would never let John get his hands on it. She said he'd unleash hell on earth."

"Isn't that what you're about to do?" Stacey said as she stepped back. The smell of oranges was starting to sting her eyes and her stomach lurched.

Ellie turned to face her sister. Tears filled her eyes, but she refused to let them fall. "I don't have a choice. There is only one person that can do this. They're watching my every move. If I so much as step foot outside this house, we're doomed."

Stacey lowered her gaze to the floor and picked at imaginary fluff on her tunic. "You will be careful won't you. I..."

"I promise," Ellie said, moving towards her little sister and wrapping her in a warm embrace. "I'll never leave you."

Stacey left the room and Ellie moved back into the pentagram she'd drawn on the floorboards. She placed her hand over the gold necklace and recited the words. Orange scented smoked wafted into the air and curled around her, scraping at the safety net that she'd created. She continued to chant and intone the phrases until her voice scratched and her throat began to close.

Clouds rolled across the sun and the room disappeared into shadows. "Who summons me to this world?"

The voice was soft and sophisticated, and Ellie swallowed hard before turning. She'd read that Bune in demon form resembled a three-headed dragon – one the head of a human, the other two terrible beasts – and that she could move the bodies of the dead in and out of their graves. "I summon you, Bune. I required your help." Ellie turned slowly. The demon towered above her, but she appeared in human form – an Egyptian woman of nobility – her own gold jewels shining.

"What do you desire, child?"

"I need you to move my grandmother's body. She lies in the graveyard and buried with her is something very important that no other should find."

"I see, and what might this important thing be."

Ellie remembered her grandmother's warning. *Demons are tricksters, Ellie. Never underestimate them and always protect yourself. Never make a bargain without knowing what it will cost, and never tell them your secrets.* "Oh, it's just a book, my grandmother's journal. It contains family secrets that would ruin us should it fall into the wrong hands."

"A book. You've summoned me to hide a book." Bune placed her hands on her hips and stared at Ellie. "If I choose to help you, what do I get in return."

Ellie held up the gold necklace. "You shall receive this as payment. It's solid gold."

Bune stepped forward and reached out to touch the necklace. Ellie pulled it back. "Will you agree to help me?" She knew she had to appear confident and in control. She was the summoner and if she showed fear or doubt in her abilities, the demon would break the summoning bond.

Bune eyed the necklace. "I will help you and accept your gift. Tell me exactly what you need me to do."

"There are men stationed outside this house. They are searching for the book. I will lead them to the graveyard. Once they start digging I need you to move my grandmother's body and then put in back once they leave. They won't look for it there again."

As Ellie predicted, her uncle John's men followed her to the graveyard. They watched from the tree line as Ellie sat and laid flowers. The hairs on her neck stood as they approached, and her skin crawled when one of them placed a hand on her shoulder.

"Move aside, Ellie. We have our orders and we don't want to hurt you."

Ellie stood. It was Peter Jacobs, her uncle's right-hand man. "What do you think you're doing." Two other men stood behind him, each with a shovel.

"Move aside," Peter said, as he took her arm.

Ellie placed her hand on the gold necklace and Bune appeared to her right. She bowed her head before assuring Ellie that her Grandmother's grave was empty. "Fine," Ellie spat as she stepped aside and let the men defile the grave. They tossed the fresh flowers aside and plunged the shovels into the soft earth.

"Nothing good will come of this. You will be cursed for defiling the resting place of the dead."

"Shut it, Ellie," Peter said pushing her away. "You uncle wants the medallion and he will have it."

Bune's head jerked to the side as Peter spoke and Ellie flinched. *Damn it. She knows I lied now.*

"A medallion?" Bune whispered.

Ellie remained silent and watched as the pile of dirt grew. After ten minutes the men were getting restless.

"There's nothing down here, Peter," one of them said.

"This is a waste of time; the wench has hidden the body."

"What are you talking about?" Ellie said shuffling forward and gasping at the empty hole. "It can't be. I watched as she was buried." She swiped at fake tears and turned to Peter. "What have you done to her?"

Peter stepped forward and peered into the empty hole. "Dig deeper," he shouted.

"There's nothing down there. We're done." The men said.

"If you've moved her, we will find out Ellie. Your uncle will have the medallion." Peter followed the two men.

Ellie sank to the ground. "Thank you," she whispered to Bune. She reached for the necklace around her neck and pulled it over her head. "It's yours now," she said handing it to Bune.

Bune took it and placed it around her neck, admiring how it sparkled in the sunlight. "This medallion that man spoke of, what is it?"

"Nothing, a family crest."

"Is it gold?"

"No." Ellie shook her head. "It's made of iron. It's not worth anything, but if my uncle has it, he will control my family and all we own."

"Really," Bune said as she picked at her manicured nails.

Ellie's heart pounded in her ears. She needed to get rid of Bune as quickly as possible. "Thank you for your help. I release you from our bond."

"That's very kind of you, but I am not done here yet. I must return your grandmother's body. Hell is not a nice hiding place." She grinned at Ellie.

"Hell! You sent my grandmother to hell? Ellie's hand flew to her mouth. The medallion hung around her grandmother's neck. If anyone saw it. "Bring her back now," Ellie gasped.

"I will send my legions to retrieve her, but first..." Bune paused and placed a hand under Ellie's chin, forcing her head up. With their eyes locked, Bune licked her lips and the air around her shimmered. "My demon grows restless. You have lied, child. Tell me what the medallion does." One of her long nails pierced Ellie's skin.

"It does nothing. I told you." Ellie shivered and tried to pull away.

"I will see for myself," Bune said and released her. She closed her eyes and spoke a language Ellie didn't understand.

Shadows moved around her, and Ellie curled herself into a ball at the side of the grave.

"Move, child," Bune said moments later as she stood above the hole. "I wish to see this medallion."

Ellie fell to the side as Bune pushed her. She had to do something to stop her. If Bune retrieved the medallion, she could release all the demons from Hell. They would not be bound.

"Stop."

Ellie and Bune turned. Stacey stepped out from behind the trees. She held up Bune's seal. She had recreated it from the drawing Ellie had painted on the walls of her room. "You will return to Hell now. You have been released from your summoning bond and you have been paid. Go now."

Stacey walked forward, the demon seal held out in front of her. Ellie watched as Bune retreated and the air shimmered. "You are released," Ellie repeated.

Bune fought but the closer Stacey got the less power she had. "You lied, child. You hide a powerful medallion and I will find out what it is. You won't hide it from me."

"Be gone, now," Stacey shouted as she reached Ellie. The girls gripped hands and together they forced Bune to return to hell.

The sun blinked out of the sky and then returned shining brighter than ever. Bune was gone. Ellie turned to the grave and the hole they needed to fill. Her grandmother's body had been returned and the medallion hung around her neck. "Should we take it and hide it somewhere else?"

"No," Stacey said. "It brings nothing but death and destruction. Leave it with grandmother. It's safe with her."

Ellie nodded and reached for one of the shovels the men had left behind. Together the girls reburied their grandmother and with her the secret to releasing Hell on Earth. They returned home, tired, and grateful to have survived.

"You won't ever summon a demon again, will you?" Stacey asked as Ellie sat at their kitchen table.

"No. I will never look to a demon for help again. Grandmother was right. They are dangerous and if it weren't for you..."

Stacey held her hand. "We are sisters. You may be the older, but we protect each other, always."

"Always," Ellie said.

About the Author

Amanda J Evans is an award-winning Irish author of YA and Adult romance in paranormal and fantasy genres. Her stories centre on good versus evil with a splice of love and magic thrown in too. You can find out more on her website www.amandajevans.com

27

Death can often creep up unexpectedly. One minute you're a seventeen-year-old mage summoning your first demon and the next a seventy-year-old master of the arts with greying skin and the shadow of death standing behind you.

Death has been following me for close on a week and try as I might to ignore his presence, he made himself known. The shallow breathing at night, the shiver inside my bones, and the constant battle to retain my memories. I know it's him, sneering at me.

"You look paler today, Eldridge."

Ronove appears at the bottom of my bed, his face scrunched as he takes in the air around me. "Death grows nearer."

"It does," I mumble. "Our time together will soon be at an end."

Ronove doesn't say anything. He holds his staff in one hand while his eyes roam my body.

He was the first demon I summoned all those years ago and I'm sure he craves his freedom as much as I do. Death will be a welcome escape from the confines of this room. "We did a lot together," I gasp as another fit of coughing takes a hold. He watches unmoving.

When the coughing stops, I reach for the glass of water that sits on the table. "You've been good to me Ronove. You've been faithful and because of you I overcame adversity and the grueling punishments that would have befallen me."

"You are close now Eldridge, let me end your misery. Let me harvest your soul before anymore suffering befalls you."

Memories torment me and drag me backwards in time.

At seventeen, an outcast from the mage community because of my family name, I had practiced for days on end to learn the summoning spell. I had pleaded with the forces of nature to grant me favor, to let me control the elements. They laughed at me, blew knife edged leaves into my face and when the council called for my expulsion they ripped me to shreds with their icy gales. Forced to hide from the world, I picked my way through the forest till I came to the lake shore. My plan was to submerge myself, give in to the violence of nature and let it eat me whole. It was my father's voice that whispered salvation in my ear. Abandon nature. Darkness serves.

I listened and learned as his whispers filled my mind with spells and conjuring words. I listened until his voice became mine and my words conjured a monster holding a staff. Grief was replaced with revenge and Ronove became my savior. The master of multiple languages, he taught me how to conjure words to soothe, to control, and to manipulate outcomes to my desired effect. Together we overthrew the council and cast out those who would have seen me defeated. They begged for mercy, begged for forgiveness and to be schooled in the magic I yielded. Some lived, but those who cast me out were made to pay. Their souls were given to the demons of Hell for an eternity of suffering.

With Ronove as my summoned, I grew powerful indeed. I became the master and I taught others how to make their arguments in ways that would win them favor. I became his favorite summoner and he provided me with spirit helpers. With their assistance, I mastered all the magical teachings and exercises and grew to power throughout the kingdom. We formed an alliance that could not be broken and as the years past he grew to be more than a summoned demon, bound to serve me, he became my companion and friend.

When I had learned all that there was to teach, Ronove offered something more. If I allowed him to harvest my soul upon death, he promised to teach me how to move objects with my mind. At twenty, death was far in the distance and not something to be feared. I agreed.

"Eldridge are you ready?"

His words pull me back to the present. My breath rattles in my chest and I struggle to sit up. "There is time," I gasp. The shadows creep closer but Ronove holds them at bay. They know of his claim and they obey.

Memories threaten to take me under again, but I resist. I have to make my peace with the world or face an eternity in Hell. It doesn't hold as much promise now. "Tell me Ronove," I ask, looking up at him. "What happens to harvested souls?"

He moves closer and fixes the blankets around me. "I take souls, so they may find escape from death. I take the suffering away, so death is quick."

I swallow. "Yes, but where do you take them, Ronove. Am I to spend an eternity burning in the pits of hell?"

His face softens. "Hell does not always mean torture, Eldridge, you will remain by my side and help me oversee my dominion. You will not feel death nor the burning pits of Hell."

"You have thought me much, my friend, but..." My breath catches, and I claw at the air hoping for a reprieve, more time to do something.

"Let me take you now Eldridge, let me end your suffering."

"No, not yet."

I lie back against the soft pillows and close my eyes. The shadows almost sticking to my eyelids. No one sits by my bedside offering words of comfort. No priest to pray over my dying soul. No friends. No family. I realize I have no one. There is no one to grieve, no one to miss me. I am back where I began, seventeen and alone.

In my mind I reach out to nature, the elements that abandoned me so many years ago. A soft breeze flutters across my face and I breathe it in. Whispers caress the empty spaces in my mind and words long forgotten rise. A woman's voice – my mother, taken in childbirth, and the reason my father turned to darkness. *Believe my son. Death is the next path in the journey of life. I wait in the shadows for you. Embrace them. Take their hands and you shall be free.*

Her words seep deep into my being and a peace long lost, creeps over me. *Reach with your heart, Eldridge. Only from your heart can you escape the darkness. He waits to take you from me. Don't let him. Forgive yourself your misdoings. Feel my love.*

A heat rises within me, flowing through my veins and settling in the middle of my chest. My breath rattles as I pull the last dregs of life into my lungs.

"Eldridge, it's time," Ronove says.

My eyes flutter open. "It is," I say, and call the shadows with the last ounce of breath I have.

"No."

I hear Ronove roar as warmth envelops me and the shadows cradle my soul and take me home.

About the Author

Amanda J Evans is an award-winning Irish author of YA and Adult romance in paranormal and fantasy genres. Her stories centre on good versus evil with a splice of love and magic thrown in too. You can find out more on her website www.amandajevans.com

BERITH: TWISTED LANDS
IAN ADEMA

"Hatter? Are you here?"

Alice, yes, the Alice Lidell, stepped onto a charred white square on the chess player field. Long ago the squares were well maintained, like painted turf. But Alice was only a child then. Now the field was a barren landscape, desolate as if a forest fire had torn through all of Wonderland. She had followed the Hatter to the spot from a distance. Or at least a man who looked like the Hatter.

"We're all hatters now except the one who's madder than a hatter in this wonderland," purred a familiar, yet deeper, voice.

Alice turned. The Cheshire Cat, now a rather plump, hunched mischievously on a thin decrepit branch. It was a wonder the creature didn't fall off.

"Speaking in riddles as always, I see," Alice sighed.

"What's more confusing? The riddle? The myth? Or... reality?" The cat grinned and faded, its bright teeth the last element to go.

When she looked up, Alice found she was on the other side of the chess field and much closer to the Hatter. He was kneeling on the ground in front of a strange symbol painted red in one of the white squares. There were so many lines and symbols that it was hard to tell what it was, but it was contained inside two outer circles. The Hatter was muttering something to himself. As Alice approached she noticed an old parchment with ancient writing. The Hatter smeared his hand across the bottom of the paper. Then Alice realized what all the red was.

Blood!

And outside the circle was a chicken. It lay lifeless, its throat slit, and a crimson pool underneath mixed with loose feathers.

Since when did Wonderland have chickens?

"Hatter? Is something wrong?" Alice reached out for his shoulder.

He whirled. Alice stumbled back in horror. The Hatter's face was exceptionally pale. His veins popped from his face, glowing blue, and his eyes were almost hollow aside from two different colored pupils. Their eyes met, like he was peering into her soul.

"What happened to you?" Alice continued to step back.

The Hatter made one more mark on the paper then stepped toward Alice. Behind him, the mark on the ground shimmered and reflected into the clouded sky, creating an amber beacon. It swirled round and round as the Hatter approached her.

"Who might you be?" he asked.

"I'm Alice," she replied.

"Alice? Not the Alice. She left us. Gone. Dead. No more Alice," he replied, void of all emotion.

"But I am Alice. And I'm here. Though, it's very different now."

From the beacon in the sky, a shape began to emerge, like that of an animal but crimson red. As it descended from the sky, its massive form was revealed. The soldier and his horse were elegant yet terrifying. The knight's armor was dark crimson and wear his helmet should be he wore a ruby studded golden crown. His steed was blood crimson and galloped through the air. His face bore the likeness of two blue flaming eyes inside the pupils.

"He comes," the Hatter stated like a puppet.

Alice ran up to the Hatter and attempted to shake him out of the trance. He was in too deep.

The knight on his steed approached. Every step was one of grand elegance. He was like a king, born and bred of blood. When he was four paces away, the Hatter kneeled before him. The crimson horse stopped and stamped its hoof three times before standing still. The knight turned his gaze toward the Hatter. This was Baalberith, great duke and grand pontiff of hell.

"Rise summoner and speak thy desires," his deep bravado voice rumbled.

Alice watched in horror as her old friend rose to answer the demon's request. She was uncertain what the Hatter might want with a demon, but she was quite sure it wouldn't be good. And demons had never been seen before in Wonderland, at least not this kind, to any ideas that Alice knew. Certainly, the world was full of its own kind of demons but none that were summoned physical entities. But here she was, staring directly at this magnificent and terrifying red knight as he conversed with the Hatter.

"I want to know what's going on," Alice demanded. "This is my world after all."

The demon turned his gaze to her. It pierced through her soul.

"No longer, child. I know thee and thy world I could not enter. This world hast sprung oft thine world, though another hast wrought it to existence." The demon took a breath. "Its beauty surpasses all thine mind could ever conjure. Now, the summoner shalt speak his desire."

"I desire the destruction of the Alice's soul," the Hatter said without emotion.

"Thy speakest of this Alice?" Baalberith replied.

"If she be THE Alice."

Alice was almost more terrified from the control the Hatter appeared to be in than the demon itself. She couldn't fathom how any of this had come to pass, having only remembered her old life in Victorian London.

From the pool of blood behind the demon, a figure emerged, fierce and red, drawing Alice's attention. As the figure formed, the wide dress came forth, the furious eyes, and the calmly shaking scepter with rage. The Red Queen had come to finish the game.

"She is the Alice," The queen boomed. "The summoner has summoned and so Baalberith, you must comply with your pact of blood."

"Who art thou?" replied the demon.

"The Queen of all Wonderland, the Hatter is my servant, and his contract is solid."

"You've taken control of the Hatter," Alice cried.

"No, you foolish child. The Hatter gave me his will!" The queen smiled.

"He would never!"

"Wonderland is no longer yours. It belongs to the living world now."

Alice tried to process what she was being told. She couldn't understand how she got here if this was the living world, jumping so far in time.

"All is truth," confirmed the demon. "And thine contract stands."

"But the Hatter isn't himself!" shouted Alice.

"You don't understand the ways of demons, child. The Hatter performed the ritual and signed a deal, no matter his mind. And with demons, a deal is a deal." The queen chuckled, satisfied.

"You could have just made the deal yourself!"

"I'm not foolish! In 20 years Baalberith will return and claim the summoner's soul for the cost of his services."

Alice fell to her knees. She didn't know what to do.

"Thine soul hast been forfeit, Alice Liddell" the demon bellowed. "Hell calls thine name. There shall you remain as blood wouldst command."

His steed brought him beside her. He drew his sword and thrust it through her chest. She gasped and when he withdrew the blade, her soul projection came with it. He placed her soul behind him on his steed and sheathed his sword as her lifeless body fell to the ground.

Baalberith swept off into the earth, returning through the open portal, leaving the Hatter watching like a puppet and the queen pleased to take over the new Wonderland.

About the Author

Ian Adema is a writer and director of fantasy and psychological thriller movies and a prose writer on the side. Much of his inspiration arises from his intense and vivid dream life.

https://www.facebook.com/ianladema/

29

ASTAROTH: ASK ME ANYTHING
JOSEF KASTLE

Astaroth stumbled out of the motel room beaten and bloody. That is not how this was supposed to happen, he thought to himself. They should be the one limping out of here all bloodied. He fell against the driver's door of his Beretta and tried to get a full breath. Every time he inhaled deeply, he winced from the pain of a broken rib. Blinking back a tear of pain, he wrestled his keys out of his tight denim jeans and fumbled with the lock. He managed to get the door open without dropping the keys or falling flat on his ass. He threw himself into the driver's seat with a loud groan.

"Fuuuck!" he yelled into the empty car. "Bitch! Ass! Cunt!" He decided it would be best to get the hell out of dodge and turned the ignition. Barely looking behind him before he slammed into reverse, he back out quickly and flipped into drive to peel out of the parking lot of the seedy motel. He checked the rearview mirror every few minutes to make sure they weren't following him.

"You look like shit warmed over," Terra greeted him as he tripped over the threshold into their shared apartment on the edge of the downtown area.

"Love you, too," he mumbled as he slammed the door and threw the bolt.

"What the hell, man?" she asked. "You're gonna wake the dead with all that noise!"

"The dead are the least of my worries, I hope," he walked over to the bar counter dividing the kitchen from the dining area off the small living room. He poured a large glass of Scotch and swallowed half of it in one gulp.

"What's that mean?" she was concerned and angry. Concerned because he didn't usually drink much and angry because he wasn't making any sense.

"I think they are alive," he sighed before swallowing the rest of his drink.

"They who?" she asked as she grabbed the bottle out of his hand. "No more until you tell me what the fuck is going on."

"Just some jokers that thought they could get the better of me," he grabbed at the bottle and missed as she put it behind her back.

"Nuh-uh. Tell me what happened!" Terra demanded of him.

"Fine!" He stomped around the counter and rummaged in the fridge for a beer. "Can I at least have a brew to wet my throat?"

"Can't fuck you up more than you already are," she agreed. "But nothing stronger. I want you to tell me what the hell happened to you before you get totally blitzed."

"I went out to the Barn for a drink and maybe a quick lay," he started as he popped the top of his bottle. "I got a little more than I bargained for."

"The Barn? Hell, Ash, no wonder! That place isn't safe for man or beast, let alone our kind." She joined him in the kitchen and pulled out a beer for herself. "What did you think you were doing going there?"

"It's late November, Ter," he said as way of explanation. He saw that was not going to satisfy her. "Thought it should be safe, at least until after the winter holidays. These humans are just so fucking unpredictable."

"Go on, moron," she sighed and flung the beer cap into the trash. "But sit your ass down before you fall down. You really do like shit, Ash."

"Is it that bad?" he asked of her as he followed her into the living room and took a seat on the couch. Collapsed on the couch was more like it. He grunted as his elbow was pressed into his side.

"From the sounds of it, you look better than you feel." She sat down next to him and plumped up one of the toss pillows before pushing it between him and the wooden frame. "Stop fucking stalling and tell me what kind of shit you got into this time."

Ash shook his head and took another swig of his beer. The bitter taste hit his tongue and made him grimace. That only served to make him wince with the effort of the facial contortions. "Shit!" he gasped as he set the half-empty bottle on the wooden arm of the couch.

"I'm waiting..." she prompted him.

"So, yeah..." he hesitated for just a moment but the look in his roommate's eyes told him he'd be in more pain soon if he didn't fess up to his misdeeds of the evening. "I was at the Barn having a drink when this hot little twink strolled up and practically threw himself at me."

"Always a twink, never a bear or an otter with you?" she closed her eyes and let him continue. "Sorry, go on."

"You know me, no way I was going to resist that for long! So, I took him out back for a smoke and a chat to see what he wanted and if it would cost me anything."

"Other than your pride, you mean?"

"Would you let me tell the fucking story, Ter?!"

"Sorry, hard not to poke at you when you are like this."

"Seems you aren't the only one to think that. Anyway... He said he wasn't a hustler and that he just wanted to get laid by someone tonight. He said he thought he was going to have to settle for the burly bouncer before he saw me."

"Flattery, it will get you into trouble every time," she quipped.

"So it would seem," he picked the bottle up for another swig. "So, we decided to head over to the nearest motel."

"You didn't!?" she gasped. "That place has more vermin in it than Golgatha!"

"It was that or the backseat of the car, not much room in that," he tossed back the dregs of the bitter beer and looked at the empty bottle lost. Blinking rapidly, he went back to his story. "Seems he had friends at the motel waiting for me."

"So, it was a set-up?"

"Who's telling the story?" he shot at her and reached for her barely touched beer. She moved it away and looked at him sternly. "Bollocks! Fine, be that way. And yes, it was a set-up. I should've known by how eager he was to make for the motel without another a drink or three. I wanted to think it was because I'm so damned sexy."

"You are, but that is beside the point," she soothed and got up from the couch, beer in hand, to head to the kitchen. "Keep talking, I'm just going to get you some ice for your chest."

"Yeah, thanks," he muttered. "So, this bitch of a twink had two bulls waiting for me inside the room I was randomly given when I checked us in for the hour. Some random shit, right! I shoulda smashed the overnight clerk in the face before I left. But I digress."

"A dress of one color is mighty boring," Terra said from inside the freezer. She was digging ice out of the bin and wrapping it up in a terry cloth towel.

"Fu-hun-ny, bitch," he retorted. "These two bulls were waiting to pounce and put the clobber on me."

"Were they actual bulls?" she asked as she came back into the living room with an ice pack in one hand a bottle of cola in the other.

"You know what the fuck I mean, damn..." he grumbled as he took the ice pack. He pressed it against his bruised chest through the thin t-shirt and hissed at the cold.

"The cola's for you, too," she offered.

"Thanks," he accepted it with his free hand and took a long swallow. "What the fuck!" he spluttered. "I thought you wanted me sober!"

"A little whiskey might be good right now, for the pain," she shrugged and settled back down onto the empty couch cushion. "What did they do after that?"

"Tied me to the bed and started pelting me with questions."

"Questions?" she raised an eyebrow.

"Somehow they knew who I was," he took a sip of the cola that he had discovered was equal parts alcohol and brown soda. "They wanted to know things."

"They always do," she shook her head again. "Go on..."

"They wanted to know who did this or who did that. What the winning lottery numbers were going to be, that kind of shit," he shifted the ice pack and groaned softly at the change in pressure. "I could tell them who or what, but everyone knows that Chaos rules with that damned lottery system of theirs."

"What did they want to know?" she tried to focus on what might mean something.

"They wanted to know who raped Hailey."

"Who's Hailey?"

"That's what I asked. One of the bulls took a swing at my face with his fist when I asked them. Said I should know. Said that the demon of information should know everything. They wouldn't believe me when I told them that's not how it works. They just punched me more. In the face, the chest, the stomach, one even took a flashlight to my junk. The twink stopped him after one blow."

"Bless his little faggot heart," she mumbled.

"Something like that. The fucking asshole with the flashlight threatened to treat me to what Hailey had experienced if I didn't start talking."

"Under different circumstances..." she started but thought better of it.

"Yeah, whatever!" he took another sip of the spiked cola. "Anyway, I finally figured out who they were talking about and told them what I knew."

"That being?" she prompted.

"Not much considering she was raped and left for dead while we were down to see the others during the Feast of the Dead. That didn't go over very well, but the fucking twink managed to convince them that I was telling them the truth."

"How'd he manage that?"

"He reminded the bulls that I can't lie," he growled. "Sometimes wish Dad had made it so I could. I might have gotten out of that shitty situation faster and with less pain for the effort."

"What happened after that?"

"The twink had them convinced that I had told them everything I could, which is, of course, the truth and talked them into letting me go. Biggest fucking mistake of their night!" Ash sat forward on the couch and ignored the ice pack as it fell to the floor.

"Ooo, this is going to be good," Terra exclaimed as she watched him intently. "What did you do?"

"They untied me and thought I was too worn to do anything. Fucking idiots. What did I do? I grabbed the little bastard and tossed him across the room. He hit the wall and fell unmoving. I think I just knocked him out. The two bulls tried to jump me on the bed but I managed to get out of the way just in time. They collided with fists flying and were beating on each other for a bit before they realized I was standing at the foot of the bed laughing at them." He took another swig of the cola in his hand.

"From there it is a blur. I think they were alive when I left, but I'm not sure. I hope they were..." he shook his head and sighed.

"Those twerps won't mess with another demon anytime soon, I'd guess," she said with a hint of pride in her voice.

"That, or they'll come looking for me with more of their herd of morons," he sighed and finished the drink. "Teach them to ask and not like the answers they get."

Terra got up and poured them both a Scotch, "Here, Ash, drink this and let's forget about this."

"Sounds good to me," he said as he saluted her with the glass.

About the Author

Josef Kastle is an MM erotica and romance author. Look for his upcoming solo release Faeries Do Where Boots out late in 2019.

https://www.facebook.com/JosefKastle/

30

F O R N E U S' C A M P A I G N
K O I G A R F I E L D

A bright field of sunflowers rolled back and forth with the wind, waving to him. He took a deep breath, his brow covered in a cold sweat, and he was shivering despite the warm sun shining down on him. Slowly he moved his long and lanky body forward, into the field of sunflowers, soon he was surrounded on all sides. The flowers' gentle swaying, combined with the cheer of the sun, were easing his nerves.

"How bad of a guy can this Forneus be if he likes sunflowers..." He says with a nervous chuckle; it is a demon he is trying to summon after all.

He found small pieces of wood and rock and created a circle with them. Reaching into his back pack he pulled out 5 flame orange candles and placed them in spaces he had left between the rocks.

"Now, to place the iron in the middle and light the candles!" The man pulls out an iron skillet, "I'm sorry it's not the most...flashy metal for you..." the man's green eyes crinkle with amusement as he thought of his daughter's favorite movie Tangled, "frying pans, who knew!"

He laughs, but then his pale, freckled complexion becomes sterner, and more serious, and with his shift in mood, the wind picks up more fiercely, threatening to blow out the large candles. But it comes to a sudden, stagnant stand still after he pulls out an undeniably Occult book; It was the Goetia. His fingers moved swiftly to the page he had studied for months. He lands on a photo of a terrifying sea creature with multiple tentacles and a ginormous mouth filled with razor sharp teeth. Its eyes are all black, but shine with glints of silver, the scales a vibrant blue on top and it's under belly a deep blood red.

"Here goes nothing." With those words he begins to chant a foreign, and ancient, sounding phrase five times before blowing the candles out. He shut his eyes as he blew and even after he finished he kept them tightly shut for a long pause, nervous to see what was happening and what may have arrived. Then he heard a gentle "eh, hem" and looked up.

In front of him, standing in the middle of the circle he had created was a tall, handsome young man, he looked to be around the same age as himself, young, but not wet behind the ears. Upon his well-built frame he sported a luxurious blood red robe, with white and black dots along it's edges. He had a head of straight, beautifully rich dark brown hair. It was also long, falling gracefully at his shoulders. It looked silky smooth and shone, much like his deep brown eyes.

Forneus was looking at his summoner with interest, but not unkindly, his soft smile and pleasing features were magnetic. The summoner found himself overtaken by enamor for the demon.

"Hello, Forneus..." He said bluntly, it felt so casual, his cheeks flushed a deep red with embarrassment. He really should of thought of what he was going to say if the summoning worked!

"Good day sir, may I inquire, what is your name?" Forneus responds graciously, smiling more and reaching to shake the man's hand. He takes it and responds,

"Riley Collins. Congressman Collins." Riley said, taking Forneus' hand. "Err, do you know what I mean by congressman?" He asks awkwardly.

"Congressman Collins, I do indeed, considering rhetoric is one of my greatest strengths, I keep up with the world and it's governments." The demon responded giving the politician a small bow. "So, I assume that may be why I am here then?"

"Uhh, yes, well you see, my country is being led into the ground...by a wildly unstable, power hungry man we somehow let get elected. His four-year term is up and election day for President is looming around the corner...." Riley responds, getting heated and passionate, his red hair really lent to the power of his words and emotions; but at the end he stalls out, becoming awkward once again.

"And you want me to....help you become elected?" Forneus asked, his eyes narrow.

"Gods no!" Riley shouts, waving his hands in protest. "No, not me, I would be a terrible president, I'm not even a very good congressman. That's the problem. No, I want you to help me help get my candidate elected."

Forneus relaxed again; he had had men before ask him to put them into a position of power...generally they were not the right men to have such power, and he made sure every time that they did not get it.

"How do you want my help with that? Surely you've done your research on me and know my capabilities?" He asked, still working on assessing the situation and the man who had called upon him. He knew very well who was currently President and the atrocities being performed at his hands.

"I want you to teach her what you know, and myself, and our whole campaign team. And uh....well making our woman more charismatic and likeable would be great." Congressman Collins answered while ringing his hands, his blushing spreading up to his ears. Forneus smiled, it brightened the man's green eyes and endeared the demon to him.

"I will meet with your candidate and your campaign team. I will judge whether I think this is a worthy cause or not and how much I will help." Forneus finally says, offering his arm to Riley. Riley takes it, confused.

"Now, first, show me around DC, it has been a good while since I've been called here, and I do love this city!"

The two enjoyed a few hours exploring DC, some favorite haunts from the demons past and a few of Riley's more modern sites. Then they met up with the campaign team, after deciding they would forego letting them know that Forneus was actually a demon.

"So, he's some sort of political expert that can help us with everything campaign related? How did you hear about him?" Rachel, the Senator running for president asked, her arms crossed defensively.

"A foreign friend of mine I met during one of my study abroad experiences told me about him, he's very big in their country." Riley answered, though he was pretty red in the face and that made Rachel suspicious.

"Which country....how can we trust he understands OUR politics??" Rachel demanded.

"Look, I trust this friend and the research I did, can we at least just give it a try?" Riley implored of the Senator.

She huffed loudly, "Sometimes I think you use our lifelong friendship more than you should..." This, she muttered so that only Forneus and Riley could hear.

"Thank you for trusting me, you won't regret it." Riley says smiling.

Rachel did not regret it, the man was a genius, it didn't seem possible to her that someone so young could have so much knowledge. Yet here he was and his help was golden. Within a week of the demon's involvement their campaign really took off, attention from news media, and the other candidates as well as their constituents bloomed, and it was all positive (aside from the political ads of her other running mates, but even those showed they were getting somewhere and fast).

Riley and Forneus were becoming increasingly close and intimate it seemed though, and Riley's involvement with the campaign started to wane; he seemed scattered, and more than normally erratic. But he seemed very happy, and was learning an incredible amount from Forneus, even more than the rest of them. Still she found herself not trusting the man.

She had good reason not to trust him too, though it wasn't for the safety of Riley which is what she feared; no, the demon had decided something that would make Rachel very unhappy, but he felt it was best. The more he got to know Riley the more he found himself admiring him, and growing ever fonder of the tall, gangly, but handsome youth. For though Forneus may look to be in his thirties he was of course centuries old, and Riley was truly 35.

The two of them were currently at Riley's large flat, sitting on the couch and talking much like they normally did when together. Forneus stops mid conversation and takes a breath,

"It's time for you to know my plans Riley...I promised I would help, and I will, but I do not think Rachel is the right person for this job."

Riley stares at Forneus bemused. "I don't understand." Is all he can manage to say.

"She's a good, talented person, but she's not what the country needs as president....you are. Rachel will be perfect as your vice president."

"NO!" Riley shouts, standing up quickly, his hands bunched into fists. "No absolutely not!! You've been grooming me! That's all this was!?"

"No not just grooming you! It just happened naturally that way, I care about you, in ways I've never felt about a mortal before...I must admit to not understanding it..." Forneus for the first time looked unsure of himself, his body language showed a great amount of discomfort and confusion. Riley's eyes widened with understanding.

He had been fully aware of his own feelings of attraction and affection for the demon, but he didn't really entertain the idea at all, in many ways it made him uncomfortable, because boy what a kink that would be! He explained it away to himself as 'he is in a human form that I aesthetically enjoy, and he has knowledge beyond what any mortal could.' So, in ways it made sense, the feelings. But here he was standing in renowned shock, confusion, fear, and dare he say it, a thrill of excitement, as the realization that Forneus had feelings for him too sunk in.

"What is it??" The demon asked, nervously, still looking uncomfortable and honestly....young. This was something he had never experienced before, that Riley had.

"I...er.." Riley started, his cheeks turning famously red. "How do I say this...I think...I mean...can demons fall in love? Have they before?"

"Love, like what some of us give to mortals, coupling?" At the word coupling Riley's entire face, ears, neck and chest turned a bright, blotchy red.

"Uhh, well, coupling is not love itself...but the feeling of love can make people want to do that together." He responded shyly.

"I do not know. My dealings with those demons who dabble with things of the heart and not the mind are limited at best." He replied, some of his charisma, and vanity, showing through again. It made Riley smile, and Riley's smile made Forneus' large demon heart stutter. He grabbed his chest in surprise.

"Riley...are you suggesting that these weird physical and emotional sensations I'm experiencing may be something like....this human love you speak of?" He asks, not sure what answer he even wants at this point, feeling completely outside of his comfort zone.

"I...uh...I think it could be. I mean....if you hadn't been a centuries year old...demon, I would've guessed it sooner to be honest...our relationship is very intimate, there have been signs. How does it make you feel?" He asked, his own stomach giving him the familiar butterfly sensation.

Forneus sits and thinks deeply, trying to find the words to describe something so new and strange.

"I feel like a brand-new demon again...like I know nothing. But I also feel...enlightened and enlivened in ways I've never felt. I don't feel like I'm serving you, or that being with you is some duty I need to fulfill, I feel like, we're a team...I, mostly, like it." He finally says, staring at his hands and robe with occasional glances at Riley's face. Riley could hear the emotions grappling in the handsome kings face and voice as he talked.

"That's love." Riley gulps, with his heart in his throat. "Forneus...the feelings are mutual."

Forneus can't help but smile, but then he frowns as a new question forms, "What do we do?" he asks, causing Riley to bark out laughing.

"Are you serious? How am I supposed to know what to do! I'm no expert on demons, or their...uh...biology! Or even your rules, we are from completely separate realms of existence!"

"Well....my biology is the same as yours when I'm in my human form...but the realms are an issue...did you know that humans can become demons though?" He asks.

"No, I did not." Riley responds, unsure what to make of the question and its meaning.

"I will say this though, your feelings for me compromise your ability to see whether Rachel is worthy of being president or not. Love makes us biased...I do not want to be president. Rachel has fought for this her whole life, and she has a back bone of steal with a heart of gold, as well as the competency for the job. Please tell me you will not force me into such a position." Riley asks, taking Forneus' hand in his own. It feels warm, human and soft.

"I won't Riley, I'm sorry." He responds earnestly.

"Thank you." He says, then he scoots closer and grabs the demon in a hug.

He can feel the chug of his heart, which sounds different, yet similar to his own. "Your heart sounds....big." He says softly.

The two of them don't know how it happens but suddenly they are embracing and touching each other gently, exploring their new connection. Riley then kisses Forneus gently, which takes the demon aback at first, until he finds himself melting blissfully into it.

Needless to say, Forneus was right that essentially, in his man form, he was the same biologically as Riley. Once Riley grew tired from making love (demons do have superpowers) they stop, cuddling and talking on the bed.

"Riley...." Forneus finally says seriously. Mmmm, is the response he gets from the sleepy human next to him. "Demons can choose predecessors, and humans are compatible. We have science that will change you...usually the demon, uh....retires and go to a different realm. But sometimes they'll work together. I can't stay in your realm for too long at a time...the only way we could stay together like this is if you joined me in my own realm, as a predecessor and member of my legions."

Forneus' words wake Riley up fully. "Me..ee a demon....?"

"A justice demon, you'll fight for the same things you already are, you'll be able to continue to learn and grow and have powers and live as an immortal."

Riley's eyes grow wide, his heart beats fast. But it's not fear, he's excited, he realizes he wants this, no matter how crazy or sudden it is, something about it feels right, like destiny even.

"I like that, and...I don't want to leave you."

"So, you'll...you'll join me? Live with me in my realm as an immortal?" Forneus' voice is full of eagerness and joy.

"Yes...I will, after we finish our job here." Riley responds slowly, his voice shaking a little now with the full force of what he is agreeing to.

"Riley...my...lover...immortality was wearing thin on me. Now I feel more alive than I ever have. We shall be an unstoppable force in the universe for balance, justice and mercy...and love."

Riley smiles and they cuddle again, enjoying the raptures of new found, passionate love. Tomorrow was a new day, and a new beginning for both man and demon.

31

FORAS: ON THE ETHICS OF HELL
PHILIPP J. KESSLER

"Order! Order!" the judge banged the gavel heavily. A small splinter of the ancient wood flew off and landed somewhere behind her. "This court is called to session!"

The room fell silent at her command and she smiled grimly at the effect her voice and gavel had on so many demons. She had recently been elevated to the bench of the court on ethics and was always amazed when the demons who were once her peers obeyed her commands.

"Judge Foras," a voice grabbed her attention.

"Yes..." she looked at him trying to remember his name.

"Andras," he filled in her blank.

"Yes, Lord Andras?" she silently thanked him for his assistance. "What is it?"

"I know you are new to your post," he began, "but I would like to remind you that this is a court of ethics."

"And what are you implying?" Foras asked the demon, suddenly not liking him.

"Just that it is unethical for you..." she cut him off with a glare. "Let me rephrase... It is not quite right for one of your bailiffs to have behaved the way he did."

"What in the Nine Hells are you referring to?" she asked. She did not like to be blindsided. Especially not first thing in the morning.

"You bailiff there," Andras indicated Khayyam, "was seen carousing with a mortal."

"And how is that any different than so many others?" she asked pointedly.

"Just that he was seen as himself, if only for a moment when the mortal man...um... When he fondled Khayyam in public."

"He what!?" she asked in shock.

"He was seen as himself," Andras repeated.

"No, no. Not that!" Foras corrected.

"The fondling, ma'am?"

"Yes, that," she smiled briefly and turned her attention to the bailiff. "Is this true?"

"Yes, your honor," the other demon said quietly.

"What was that?" Andras asked loudly.

"Yes," he repeated. "It is true. Both parts. I am sorry I was seen. The club attracts the misfits of the city, so I doubt anyone even realized they were seeing a demon and not one of their own in a costume."

"That is not the point," Foras said sternly. "You allowed a mortal man to fondle you? And in a public setting?"

"Umm," he hesitated. "Yes. Is that a problem?"

"You're damned right that is a problem!" she raised her voice a little. "Such things are not permitted in my court!"

"Begging your pardon," Khayyam said hesitantly. "It did not happen in your court. It happened up there," he pointed to the ceiling indicating the mortal world. It wasn't really above them any more than Heaven was above Hell. They were dimensions, but the colloquialism of mortal man had infiltrated both the Hellish and Heavenly realms.

"Fool," she barked. "You know what I am saying. Don't act stupid!"

"Your honor," Andras interrupted her. "Khayyam has a point. What should be of concern is that he was seen as himself, not that he was fondled by a mortal man."

"Mortal or not," she shot at him, "he was touched in that manner by a man! Mortals have come to our realm for eons because of that act."

"And our Lord and Command has sent them away, up to Heaven. It is not a bad thing, at least not according to Lucifer or his Father."

"Since when?" she asked. Her brow was furrowed. This was news to her.

"Time immemorial, ma'am," Andras answered her.

"Really?" she felt like she had woken in a dream world. For most of her existence, she had believed that Yahweh and Lucifer agreed that it was an abomination for such things.

"Mortals often confuse the wishes and meanings of our kind," Andras referred to both demons and angels. "They are only now beginning to understand that Yahweh doesn't care about such things. And neither should we, your honor."

"Okay," the furrow in her brow deepened into a full-face frown. "So... Now, what was your problem then?" Foras was trying to understand how she could have been wrong for so long. She was a demon of ethics, she had worked hard all these centuries to move up the ranks and obtain the bench.

"The ethical dilemma, your honor, is that he was seen as a demon by mortals and nothing was done to correct that," Andras charged.

"Now that is something I can wrap my brain around," she thought that maybe she needed to pick up the human vice of a morning stimulant. This charge against one of her bailiffs had thrown her completely for a loop. Did my predecessor know of his predilections? She asked herself.

"Good," Andras eyed the new judge curiously. He was uncertain how she could have been appointed to the bench without knowing the rules, laws, and regulations of Heaven and Hell. "I demand that something be done to correct or deal with the potential fallout of what he allowed to happen."

"Very well," she sighed and rubbed at her wrinkled forehead. The motion relaxed the muscles slightly and allowed for her to think more clearly. "Khayyam!"

"Yes, your honor?" he snapped to attention before her.

"While being sexually pleasured by this mortal man you allowed yourself to be seen by others as a demon in a mortal social club. Is that true?"

"Yes, uh..." he cleared his throat. "We were negotiating for serv -
"

"I don't want those details," she snapped. "I want to know why you allowed yourself to be seen!"

"Well, uh... That's just the thing," he hesitated. Foras' reaction to his sexual activities had made him question if he could be fully honest with her. But this was a court of ethics, and ethics demanded honesty. "We were, uh, well... His ministrations were distracting, shall we say?"

"I'll concede to that," Foras remarked.

"And I lost control for a moment," Khayyam admitted. "My glamour fell and one or more of the humans in the club may have seen me for my demon self."

"May have?" Andras exclaimed! "There have been articles and even pictures posted to their social media!"

"Pictures?!" Foras stood and leaned over the judge's desk to peer over her bailiff. "There are pictures of this!?"

"Yes," Andras confirmed. "Blurry and hard to confirm by their limited imaginations, but pictures were taken."

"I thought you said it was for just a moment," she shot at the offending demon.

"It was, but... Humans live on their technology. They have one of those smart devices in their hands all the time, it seems." He cleared his throat and licked at his lips.

"Mr. Andras," she turned her attention to the attorney.

"Yes, your honor?" he asked.

"What do you propose we do about this situation?"

"One of our techno-demons can easily dispose of those pictures or spin the story enough to make everyone believe them to be a hoax. As to the memories of the humans... That might be harder to deal with. We can't kill them like we once would have."

"Pity that," Foras sighed. "How many did see him with their own eyes?"

"Uncertain," he said. "It is a foregone conclusion that the mortal he was... umm... preoccupied with saw him for what he is. And certainly, the one who took the pictures that were posted on their internet."

"Fine," Foras made a snap decision. "Khayyam."

"Yes, your honor?"

"I order you to return to that club in the guise you should not have let slip and retrieve the man you revealed yourself to. As to the photographer... I want you to convince him that what he saw was a costume. Can you do that?"

"I believe so... Wait, what? Bring him back with me?" Khayyam looked at her strangely.

"Yes, it is the only thing we can do to resolved this quickly and easily," she said. "I want this cleared up by tonight so that we can move on with other things. Oh, and Mr. Khayyam."

"Your honor?" he looked at the gavel in her hand rather her face.

"You are dismissed from the court of ethics."

"Yes, ma'am," he hung his head in shame.

She raised her gavel to conclude that part of the proceedings but stopped. "Mr. Andras."

"Ma'am?" he looked at her questioningly.

"I believe I may need a minor refresher on a few things," she looked him in the eye. "Do you think you can help make that happen?"

"I believe so," he answered without hesitation. He was looking forward to educating a judge.

"Good," she dropped the gavel down. "This complaint is concluded. And I will see you, Andras, in my chambers for lunch," she winked at him. He blanched slightly but gave her an uncertain smile.

About the Author

Philipp J. Kessler is a multi-genre author, editor, and publisher with a flair for paranormal and LGBTQIA stories. Search him on your favorite social media site under RevKess.
https://www.facebook.com/RevKessPMPC/

32

ASMODAY: A CURIOUS PROPOSAL

J. BECK

He sat on his throne, surveying all of his underlings. The seventy-two legions were bustling with activity- fighting each other, planning various petty actions, and engaging in the widest variety of debauchery seen this side of existence. A messenger came to him.

"My Lord, you asked to be notified if any called upon you for aid."

"Yes. What of it?"

"My Lord, a man in Arabia has called you and your jinn to come help him destroy his enemies."

"Boring. Send one to destroy him, and make a show of it."

"Yes, my Lord. There are others who have called upon y-"

"Can you skip to the interesting ones? Hearing these humans beseeching me for their petty squabbles makes me sick. I don't understand how they don't realize it's all up to them anyways."

"Very well, my Lord. I have a man calling upon you to give him fifty concubines."

"Fifty? I give him one, aged fifty."

"As you command, my Lord. The rest I have at this time seem to be of no interest to you."

With that, the messenger departed, leaving Asmoday in peace, with only the cacophony of the legions to disturb him. How many petty squabbles had mortals called upon him for? How many simple problems had they called upon him to solve? How blind could these creatures be not to see that whomever they call upon has power over them for the rest of their existence? Perhaps the short nature of their lives deprives them of this wisdom. What is fifty years to one such as him, when he has lived millennia? He has seen empires rise and fall, peasants rising to king, and then dying in anonymity. Those in the orient seem to have more stability of leadership, but they take no responsibility for their own lives as a result. Is that to be regarded as better than these, who take their lives in their own hands and call upon him for aid? Should he have given in to this one request, just once, and seen what it brought to the world? Does he not have dominion over the Earth, being born from it?

A messenger's approach disrupts his thoughts.

"My Lord, I have an unusual request in your name."

"What makes it unusual?"

"My Lord, this man calls for no destruction, no lust, and no other physical need, yet invokes your name."

"That is most interesting. What does he want?"

"He is asking for you to bless a temple that he has built to his God."

Asmoday caught himself from laughing in front of the messenger- "Are you serious? He would profane a temple to his God for my blessings?"

"So it would seem, my Lord."

"I must speak with this mortal. He intrigues me. What it his name?"

"Solomon, my Lord."

Asmoday stiffened slightly. "Solomon. I have heard of this man before. His God does not tolerate blasphemy or disloyalty well. How does he have the means to invoke my name in place of his own God's?"

"I believe he finds himself the wisest man in the world, my Lord. He believes no others could be beyond him in wisdom, and thus acts as his own conscience guides."

"I find the important word in that is 'man', not 'wisest', wouldn't you agree?"

"Oh, certainly, my Lord. I just want to ensure that I brought you the most complete information about him, so that you wouldn't have any surprises."

Surprises. Those were another thing about mortals that annoyed him. They never could be relied upon to act the way they were supposed to. You might trust one to carry a message himself to another king, and he would hand it off to some underling rather than deliver it himself. He might decide the message isn't worth delivering in the first place and burn it to get a fire started. You could set them up for a perfect life if they could just kill one person, and they would refuse it all. Logic is lost on them, and those who possess it are called "magicians" and killed.

"You're dismissed. Send me the commander of the Fifth Legion."

"At once, my Lord."

Asmoday pondered his options while waiting for the commander to arrive. He could grant Solomon's wish- it was earnestly asked, is unusual in nature, and was he not toying with the idea but ten minutes ago? He could refuse, but that would only serve their God, and that just wouldn't do. His thoughts were interrupted by a figure sliding in through the door.

"You summoned me, my Lord, and I answer. How may I serve you?"

"If you were named in an unusual request, what would you do?"

"My Lord?"

Asmoday stood up from his throne, sauntered to the commander's face, and said, "What would you do?"

"My Lord, I would speak with them personally to find the best way of manipulating their desires to their ruin."

"Suppose this man believed himself wiser than even one of us, born from the Earth. What then?"

"I would still talk with him, for belief in one's wisdom does not mean one is wise. Even now, my Lord, you seek counsel rather than make a decision, which shows greater wisdom than most mortals ever think to gain."

"You can cease pandering to me, lest you wish a sudden and permanent demotion. I have an unusual request from a man, as you have certainly gathered, and simply wanted a second opinion of how to proceed. Your opinion matches mine, so I will go and speak with Solomon myself."

"Solomon, my Lord? As wise as he claims to be, he is still only one man. How dangerous can one man be?"

"Very", said Asmoday, "for men have all the cunning that we have, yet no concept of eternity in which to enact their plans. All that we do, we work for millennia. They see only their own short life. Now, I must go see how interesting this Solomon truly is."

With that, Asmoday departed his realm.

About the Author

J. Beck is a new author with a passion for history, music, and fantasy gaming.

33

GAAP: VOTAGER'S TALE
C.L. WILLIAMS

The men gather around as the newest voyager joins them to tell them the tale of his past. The explorers ask the newcomer to tell them his name. He tells them he has taken many names over the years but lately he's been called "Tap" by those he is acquainted with.

"Your friends call you tap?" one of the explorers ask.

"My acquaintances call me Tap." Tap responds.

"My apologies sir, I mean Tap," the explorer says, "Please continue telling your tale."

"Of course," Tap says as he once again attempts to tell his tale. "Life didn't really begin for me until I fell. I was beloved but there are far too many rules for me to follow. So, I fell from Heaven and soon became President!" Tap tells everyone with pride.

"Fell from Heaven?" A second explorer says, questioning the tale Tap is currently telling everyone.

"Yes, I fell from Heaven." Tap then continues his story. "I then gained intellect. I became smart. It wasn't long before I became a teacher of philosophy. I soon found out that my philosophy of what has come and what will was more than my teachings. I soon found out my talks of what has come and what is yet to come were none other than the truth."

"I could ask you something right now and you can tell me if it will happen?" The first explorer asks.

"That is correct!" Tap replies to the explorer.

"Will I live forever?" The first explorer asks Tap.

"You'd be lucky to make it past today." Tap says as a frown covers the face of the first explorer.

"I soon found out that even though I can teach philosophy, I can also do the exact opposite. I can turn men ignorant. I can turn the smartest of men into nothing more than belligerent, babbling idiots. At first, I found this quite odd given I was teaching such deep thoughts and words but now, I find turning men ignorant is one of the most amusing things I have ever done. I'm proud of myself every time I do it."

"Ok, you tell me you fell from Heaven, you became smart and started teaching once you left, and you can make men turn stupid. I've heard it all. I need proof or you just telling a good ol' fashioned lie." Says the old man who invited Tap to join the Voyagers in the first place.

"Don't worry old man." Tap says assuring the man, "You'll get your proof sooner than you may think. Just know that you may not remember once it happens." Tap tells everyone.

"Today the sun was in the south. Making it easy for others to summon me. Making this the first time I have been to the land of the living in what feels like an eternity. And now here I am." Tap tells everyone as he finishes his story.

"Sir, you sound like you are calling yourself a demon." The leader of the Voyagers. "And I've never heard of no demon named Tap and I've been around a time or two." The lead explorer says as he questions everything Tap just told him.

"I believe I said I've had many names in the past with Tap being the most recent one." Tap says, reminding them of what he said when he introduced himself. He then steps back, and wings sprout from his back. "Is this enough proof that I am who I say I am?" Tap says as he asks the explorers.

After revealing his wings, Tap slowly transforms from being a man among explorers to a demon with wings. His look transforms as he slowly becomes less human as he now makes his way to the first explorer that interrupted him when he was introducing himself. He looks at him, no one knows what happens next but after Tap took the explorer out of his grasp, the explorer was no longer acting like himself. He then flies over to the second explorer and does the same thing, leaving two explorers ignorant of everything around them. Before he can attack anyone else from the Voyagers, the leader finally speaks up and asks him to reveal himself.

"I demand you!" The lead voyager yells to Tap, "I demand you to reveal your true identity!"

"I am the thirty-third of the demons of Solomon!" His voice then goes from sounding human to sounding demonic. "I am a President in Hell. I am the cause of love and the cause of hate. I AM GAAP!" With the mention of his name, Tap, now revealed as Gaap, spreads hate amongst the explorers he made ignorant, causing chaos amongst the explorers. Causing death amongst the explorers until no one is left but Gaap himself. After seeing everything that he had done, Gaap flies away and moves onto the next place he feels is best for destruction. He finds a quiet, quaint little village and flies behind a tree. He then climbs down the tree once more in human form. No wings, no demonic face, no devilish voice.

He walks around the village and sees few people. After walking around someone finally introduces themselves to Gaap and asks him to come inside and tell his story. He is asked for his name to which he responds, "I have had many names in the past but the last group of people I was acquainted with liked to call me Toab. The answer to your question is yes, I'd love to come in and tell everyone my story." The housekeep brings Toab inside for a day of talking. Little does the housekeeper know, he didn't let in a person. He just let a demon in his house, a president of Hell. He just let Gaap in his house and he may not be alive to tell about it.

About the Author

C.L. Williams is an independent author from central Virginia. He is a writer of poetry, horror, romance, sci-fi, and has written several novellas and short stories

www.facebook.com/writer434

34

FURFUR- EARL OF HELL

P.S. HARRIS

"Get Furfur in here now!" Hades yelled at his deputy. "Tell him this is an emergency. We need his services. I don't care where he is or what he's doing, I need him here now!

Hades sat down behind his massive oak desk to wait for the arrival of his Earl. This last bit of news wasn't good but hopefully with the help of Furfur he could divert disaster. He had thought they the advantage right now. He directed some of his demons to controlling rulers on earth. Another majority of them watched over the social media sights monitoring and keeping the headlines aimed to cause discord and mistrust. The select few of the powerful legions were entering humans, creating evil beings set on destruction and terror.

His plan was perfect. The humans were so busy destroying each other that they didn't even see that evil was rampant and thriving on their planet. Soon evil would take control and the Gods would be forced to flee in fear, no one left to believe in them.

Rubbing his hands together in glee he fantasized about the day where he could freely roam the earth and the humans left would bow down to worship him. So deep in his fantasy that he failed to notice Furfur had arrived and was bowing before him.

Hades motioned for Furfur to rise, "Furfur, my beautiful angel. Thank you for coming on such short notice."

"It is my honor, Master." Furfur nodded his head slightly as he replied. "How can I be of service to you?"

His voice was soft and angelic, irritating to Hades ears, but he pretended not to notice. "I need you to enter a triangle, a magic triangle." Hades said knowing this frightened Furfur the most. It was fun watching Furfur squirm. He loved sending his Demons on missions they feared.

"I'd rather not, sir." Furfur bowed again staying down with his head hanging low. "I cannot lie there."

"I don't want you to lie," Hades replied. "I need you to be truthful. That's why I chose you for this important mission. The fate of the world depends on you."

Furfur bowed again, "I would be honored to be a part of such an important mission, you can count on me Master."

Hades nodded for Furfur to rise. "Please sit, Furfur, this plan is quite complicated, so I need to go over the details with you. This must be kept quiet. Only you and I know of this, do you understand?"

"Yes sir." Furfur's voice was muffled as he positioned himself in the oversized chair that Hades provided for him.

"Let me get us refreshments," Hades motioned to his human slave and the little man went scurrying off to fulfil the master's wish. "By the way, while we wait let me invite you to a party, I'm hosting to celebrate our success in evil taking over the earth." Hades turned to Furfur, "all seventy-two of my top Demons along with their legion are invited. I am planning to reveal the master plan at that time. Each of you will be rewarded for your part. It's going to be a grand celebration!"

Furfur sat up in his chair. It was so comfortable he had almost drifted off. Mention of a grand celebration got his full attention. There hasn't been a celebration for ages. Hades must have good news. "What is the celebration, I will keep it secret, I promise."

The human slave entered just then and handed Furfur a snifter of the finest brandy and then turned to Hades with the second glass.

"Drink, my friend." Hades raised his glass in a toast. "To the success of our missions. Soon we will rule the earth. Our Demons are in control and the Gods will be forced to leave."

"So, what do you need from me?" Furfur asked after taking a drink of his brandy.

"I have learned the Gods have made three new angels in hope to tip the balance of good back to their favor." Hades began his story, "These three angels will have much power and they will be impossible to defeat once they have reached maturity. I need you to go to them now, while they are young and scare them out of using their powers."

"They will form a triangle in the forest, in which you will enter. They must see death and destruction. Show them Hell, the darkness and terror." Hades continued, "They must be frightened into never forming this triangle together again. They are much too powerful to be allowed to mature their powers."

Furfur didn't really understand, but he didn't need to. This task sounded simple enough. I can pull this off. Enter a magic triangle and show Hell.

"These three are dangerous," Hades was still talking, but Furfur wasn't paying attention. He was enjoying the brandy and pondering about this party coming up.

"Furfur, I need you to pay attention," Hades paused long enough for Furfur to look at him again. "As I was saying, these three angels are powerful and dangerous. You must be careful they don't suspect it's a Demon they are talking to. They need to think this is a dream. Do you understand?"

Furfur nodded his head. The more Hades warned him the more he thought he might be dreading this mission. It didn't sound like there was much room for error. He was going to have to take his angel shape to fool these girls.

"I will not fail you Master," Furfur rose to go.

"I am counting on you, Furfur." Hades put his hand on Furfur's massive shoulder. "I know you are the only one that can complete this mission. We have great faith in you Furfur. If you complete this mission successfully you will be celebrated by all at our festivities.

Furfur bowed again before he turned to leave the room. This was going to be fun. He would get to fool the angels and be a big part of thwarting the Gods plans. Yes Furfur, Earl of Hell, his life was just fine.

About the Author

P.S. Harris is a sci/fi fantasy writer with her first novel out now. Watch for the sequel coming 2019. Author page https://www.facebook.com/psharrisauthor/

35

MARCHOSIAS AND THE BORGIA'S ASCENDENCY
CHASITY GAINES

I was once a young man, riding the long train of my uncle, Pope Callixtus III. I began a career within the Roman Catholic Church. I was full of energy, passion, and a certain amount of intelligence. This lead to lucrative appointments-- a Cardinal-Deacon at the age of twenty-five, then Vice Chancellor. With each new Pope, I gained wealth, status, and influence.

Knowing Pope Innocent VIII lay dying in his bed creates heated arguments between Cardinals on the impending Conclave. As the Pope is being breastfed by a plump woman-- a treatment one of his doctors swear will bring our Holy Father back to his earthly concerns. I knew I had to act and quickly to ensure that the Conclave came out to my favor.

Needing to clear my head, I head quickly to the busy inn of my once lover, Vannozza, mother to my children. She greets me at the door with a familiar smell of grapes and rosemary.

"My dear, your worries lay heavy on your shoulders," she speaks as she rubs my knotted shoulder.

"Ah. But what ambitions do not carry some type of burden," I quip placing my hand on her warm working hand. "I need reassurances that I can trust those that have said they will vote for me," I exclaim as I pound my fist on the wooden table.

I stand up and walk towards a huge window overlooking Vannozza's vineyards. She is shrewd and a gracious host. As I step closer to the window, I see Cesare and Lucrezia sitting close together, both their heads in a single book. So unlike the adventurous Juan who was most likely causing mischief in the kitchens or fighting with the local ruffians. My children gave me great joy and as soon as I wore the Papal Crown I will publicly recognize them as my own offsprings and heirs of my loins. Vannozza glides across the room although she has grown more rotund in these past years. She pours us both a drink.

"There may be a way," she hints. Her fingers lightly brush mine as she hands me a cup of her finest wine. "Although it may cost more than what you want to pay, Rodrigo," she warns with her woman's intuition.

"But don't you see that I am ready to give up all my wealth to see this plan through!" I exclaim. "Don't you see what this could mean for the children? Surely you wouldn't deprive the children of wealth and titles?" I question her just as the children bound noisily into the room.

My children greet me with curtsies and bows as they find me standing in their Mother's receiving room. I wave off their informality and take them each in my big arms. They are growing up so quickly. I question them on their education and tease my beautiful daughter with an impending marriage should Papa's plan work.

Before embarking on their next adventure, my three children hug and kiss me, then their mother.

Now that the children were gone, I pull Vanozza into my arms and press my lips against hers. "Please, I am asking you to help me."

"When I was a small girl, I was told stories of a benevolent demon named, Marchosias, who helps his summoner by answering all questions with the truth and a fierce warrior," her voice quivers as she continues. "Once an Angel but cast to the eternal flames of Hell where he rules over 30 legions."

"Does anyone know the incantation to call this fallen angel?" I question her curiously.

"There is an old woman on the outskirts of the city, beyond the wall who know the words to summon the demon," she whispers as she draws a map to where I can find the old strega.

*****

I find the old strega who knows the words needed to summon the mighty Marquis from Hell. Keeping my face hidden, I barter with her for her knowledge. The toothless woman swipes the purse with her claws. She cackles hysterically before whispering the words into my ear. The smell of her rotting teeth overtake me and I rush out the stifling hut. Her laughter follows me.

I keep repeating the phrase making sure it sticks to my mind. As soon as my creaking carriage stops, I jump out eager to find out if the warty woman's spell worked. Night fell over Rome like silk while slinky shadows are left behind. The smell of burnt incense caresses my nose like a lover as I make my way to my dark room.

Once in my room I begin to prepare myself. What I am about to do is sacrilege, a sin against God. My palms sweat and my mind buzzes with quotes from the Holy Bible. My thick tongue sticks to the roof of my mouth, that fleshy indented spot in the mouth. I light candles and take in three deep breaths as I listen to the small fire crackling in the hearth. Barely audible, I whisper the spell out loud to the shadows dancing on the wall.

As soon as my tongue touches the back of my teeth-- the spell recited-- the candles snuff out with a warm draft of air. I can make out something darting around the room with wings of the magical gryphon yet the tail of a venomous snake. Was the night playing tricks on me? Or has the spell actually worked? O' God, I pray that I can contain the demon as Solomon had.

The demon lands with a thud and I can see the furry muzzle of a she-wolf. Her teeth dangerously sharp, like the blade I usually carried on my person. Her eyes shine with hope and longing. What a magnificent creature, I start to think as I realize that the floor was wet were I was standing. Fear will cause a mortal to lose function of their body. I remember my father teaching me that lesson as a child.

Marchosias shakes her head and a puff of smoke exists her mouth as she laughs at my present state. I yank at the coverlet on my bed and toss it over my embarrassment like a young child might. The demon's wolf head starts to look more human as the wings and fur disappear. Left standing in front of me is a slender, beautiful angel.

Her hair a chestnut brown and her eyes are liquid and soulful. Her smallish tits are just the perfect size. My eyes drink in the vision before me. I could never pass over a morsel such as this. Already there were whispers in Rome and abroad of my illegitimate children by Vanozza. I cared not for their whispers behind doors.

I find my tongue loosens from its spot in my dry mouth. "Are you truly the demon, Marchosias?" I question the naked sprite.

"Yes, it is true," she dazzles me with her smile as she speaks. "What is it you have summoned me for?" She asks as she gracefully moves toward me.

"I have certain goals which I believe you may help me achieve," I whisper in her ear as I pull her into my arms. "You will be my good luck charm and informer," I murmur onto her soft lips before I taste them.

Her lithe body responds to mine. "I am willing to help you in your ambitions." But how will you address me in public?" She bats her eyes seductively and I think she must read minds.

"La Bella, will be the name I call you, for you are the most beautiful. And you shall be rewarded for your service in more ways than one," I slap her bottom playfully.

She snaps her fingers and the candles spark with life. Her side teeth gleam in light as she smiles at me. She truly is the she-wolf I need. "Shall we begin, I don't think you have much time. The old Pope shall meet his creator soon," she reminds me at the task at hand, her eyes promising pleasure afterwards.

*****

Pope Innocent VIII died on 25 July 1492. The conclave is carried out during the hottest season. The cardinals, sweaty miserable men are ready to be back to their comforts. I am filled with such confidence and humility all at once that I visit each Cardinal and offer what comforts I can-- an extra meal, an extra villa, and a pretty powerful speech about the corruptness of The Holy See.

I, Rodrigo Borgia, am elected on 11 August 1492, assuming the powerful name, Alexander VI. I give La Bella a set of rooms in the Apostolic Palace, situated near my own apartments. I also bring Lucrezia into my household under the watchful eye of Andrea Orsini, until the time she is wed properly.

I am now the earthly representative for our Lord and Father. I oversee the whole Catholic nations and act as their loving and just Father. I am finally were I belonged, on St. Peter's Throne just as the demon promised, but she delivers so much more. La Bella gives me the love and support I need to carry the heavy burden I asked to carry. I will never part from my she-wolf demon who suckles a child of Rome, my child, just like in the legends of Rome.

About the Author

Chasity Gaines is a multi-genre author and poet. She loves painting a picture with her words.
Follow her at https://www.facebook.com/ChasityGainesWriter/

36

STOLAS: BLACK MIRROR
C.L. WILLIAMS

Late one night, three amateur wiccans decide to conjure a demon by summoning him through their makeshift portal. The three amateurs begin their incantation, hoping to summon a demon and prove they are true wiccans. Unbeknownst to them, they see a dark mirror before their eyes. The three were excited and fearful all at once. As they see the black mirror arrive, a slight opening occurs and out steps a raven-like demon. The demon looks at the three wiccans and says nothing until the three wiccans speak.

"Who are you?" The three wiccans say simultaneously.

"I am the nightraven. I am prince of Hell, Stolas!" He says as he responds to the three frightened wiccans.

"WAIT!" The first wiccan says in fear. She then opens her demonology book and reveals the picture of Stolas in their book, the book depicts Stolas as an owl with a crown on his head and long legs. The creature that stepped out of the black mirror is a raven. "This isn't Stolas. We're screwed. EVERYONE RUN!" She says as she is quick to leave and abandon their demon summoning.

"You are clearly uneducated." Stolas responds. "We demons of Solomon have been known to take many forms, we have even been known to take human-like forms. The picture in your little book is only one of many forms I've taken in the past."

"How do we know this isn't a trick?" The second wiccan asks.

"You three are clearly students of the dark arts and I've been known to teach witchcraft and astronomy to others." Stolas responds to the second wiccan.

The third wiccan is about to ask a question, but before she can ask her question, Stolas makes a transformation from his raven-like form to the owl-like form with long legs, just as he is depicted in the demonology book the three wiccans are studying. "There," Stolas says, "If I were not who I say I am, I would not be able to take this particular form. Do you believe me now?"

The three wiccans say nothing, they simply all nod their heads in unison, agreeing that they believe the demon in front of them is none other than Stolas himself, teacher of astronomy and prince of Hell.

"Ok, now that we have this malarkey out of the way. I will properly educate you in what you need to know. You three are clearly uneducated in the demons of Solomon and your own witchcraft. I can teach you witchcraft through astronomy. That means we need to be outside." Stolas then spreads out his wings and flies right through the window of the room the three wiccans are in and goes to a spot outside and signals them his location.

The three frightened wiccans exit the room they are in through the door and make their way outside. Once outside, they see the signal of where they need to meet Stolas. As much as they want to improve their witchcraft and be more official wiccans, they also know this is no joke. They are dealing with an actual demon of Solomon.

"We do know once we go to where he is, there is no turning back, right?" The first wiccan asks the other two.

"Well," says the second wiccan, "We are the ones that summoned him, and he can clearly see the flaws in our craft. I say we go through with it. Besides, who knows what will happen to us if we refuse him. He is a demon and a prince of Hell."

As the first two wiccans are questioning whether or not to meet Stolas in the designated area of the woods, the third wiccan has already begun making her way to the spot Stolas signaled for them to go to. Seeing that one of their own is already making her way to Stolas, the other two shrug and follow her to the designated spot that Stolas signaled for them moments earlier. Once they arrive to the designated spot, the three wiccans do not see a raven-like demon or an owl with a crown and long legs, they see a human looking at the stars.

The three wiccans are confused for a moment until the human speaks to them. "Took you girls long enough, are you ready to learn what I am about to teach you?" The human asks.

"Stolas?" The first wiccan asks.

"Correct. I believe I did tell you that we demons of Solomon do have the ability to take a human form. We are outside in the woods and I believe there are hunters in this area of the woods, meaning that me taking the form of an owl or a raven will put a target on my back. While I will simply end back up in Hell, you three will need to summon me once more and the only reason you summoned me in the first place was by accident. Truthfully, I don't know if you three will remember how you summoned me, and you could end up summoning another demon of Solomon, who may not be as kind as I am. Now, I ask again, are the three of you ready to learn what I am about to teach you?"

The third wiccan nods her head yes, but the second one is quick to question Stolas, "how does the alignment of the stars and us learning witchcraft have anything to do with one another?"

"If you take a seat on that tree stump, I will show you. I can also teach you about herbs and poison too. Can we begin?" Stolas asks once more.

The wiccans then take their seats and learn from the demon Stolas. He teaches them astronomy, he teaches them about witchcraft, and he teaches them about herbs and which ones are poisonous, should they need to use them. The once amateur wiccans are now more skilled in their wiccan ways thanks to the demon Stolas.

About the Author

C.L. Williams is an independent author from central Virginia. He is a writer of poetry, horror, romance, sci-fi, and has written several novellas and short stories

www.facebook.com/writer434

37

PHENEX: SWALLOWED WORDS
AMANDA J. EVANS

The musty odor caused a gag reflex but I pushed past it. I knew Grandma's books would hold the answers I sought. My fingers brushed across the leather bindings sending dust motes scattering through the air. Why she didn't dust them was beyond me. There wasn't a trace of dust anywhere else in her workshop, but these books were thick with it.

The squeak of the door alerted me to her presence, and I pushed away from the shelf quickly brushing my hands on the legs of my trousers.

"Mark, what are you doing in here?"

"Hi, grandma. I was actually looking for you. I wanted to ask your advice about something."

"Did you now?" She asked, her eyes tracing the lines of dust I'd left in my haste.

"Yeah." I swallowed hard. "Dylan's cousin Marie is staying with them for the summer, and well..."

Grandma smirked and motioned for me to take a seat on the plush sofa. "Sit, tell me how I can help you."

My body sank into the softness. She knew what she was doing. This sofa had been my undoing so many times. Two minutes here and I knew I'd spill my guts.

"I'll get you some tea. It always helps." She smiled and turned to the counter.

Grandma's workshop as she like to call it was more like a small self-contained flat. It had its own seating area, a makeshift kitchen, and a huge fireplace. It was in this room that she dried the herbs she grew in the garden and concocted potions for the silly women who came to her looking for tonics.

She handed me a cup of tea and sat beside me. "Why were you down the back, Mark?"

"I...um...I was looking for a book."

"I see."

The words rushed out before I could stop them. "She's really pretty, grandma, and she's intelligent, and goes to college upstate, and I thought."

"Those books won't help. What were you looking for?"

I tapped the side of the cup with my finger. What was I looking for? "I don't know. Dylan said Marie loves poetry and literature, and I guess, I thought if I could write something for her, you know." I shrugged and took a mouthful of the tea.

"Matters of the heart are never taken from books, Mark. If you want to write something for her it needs to come from you, from your heart. You cannot steal from books."

"I wasn't going to steal something. I thought you might have, you know, a spell or something."

She tutted at me and disappointment washed over me – like a naughty child caught with my hand in the cookie jar. "She should like you for who you are, but..."

Grandma got up and walked over to the bookshelf. She held her hand out and then reached for a book. "This one might help."

She handed me a little red book. It wasn't covered in dust. "What is it?"

"A book of poetry. Maybe it will inspire you."

The book landed with a thud as I stood abruptly. "I didn't want a book of poetry," I snapped. "I don't even like the stuff. What I wanted was..."

"Taking the easy way out has consequences, Mark. Magic is not to be trifled with. You know that."

"But you help everyone else. All the tinctures and tonics."

"That's very different. That's natural healing."

"Can't you give me a tonic to make my words flow?"

"I have." She smiled and motioned to the book on the floor.

I huffed and retrieved it.

"If you don't want it please put it back," Grandma said as she started measuring out herbs and spices.

I didn't want it. What use was a poetry book. I marched towards the shelf. Trying to ram the book back into place, I ended up knocking half a dozen of them onto the floor. Dust spewed everywhere, and I coughed. I grabbed the books and started putting them back. The last one caught my attention. Black with a large pentagram on the front. I opened the cover and read the inscription, 'Summoning Demons'. There was a handwritten note too. It said, 'for every heart's desire, there is a demon to get it for you.'

I snapped the cover shut and turned to make sure Grandma wasn't watching before sliding it underneath my shirt.

Back in the privacy of my room, I opened the book. Page after page of spells, some in English, some in languages I couldn't make out. There were hundreds of them. I flicked to the back and found an index. It was written in the same handwriting as the note at the front of the book. I scanned the list until I found Phenex, a demon that can help with creativity, poetry, even teach you everything you need to know about sciences.

The summoning spell was in English and seemed easy enough. I gathered all the ingredients and when the house grew quiet, and everyone slept, I began. Nothing happened at first and I berated myself for even trying. I blew out the candles, the stench of melted wax sickening, so I opened the window. It was then I saw the bird coming towards me. I jumped back, and it landed on the window sill, its long tail decorated with red-orange and yellow feathers.

"Great," I mumbled. "I summoned a bird. Phenex must be another way to write Phoenix. How can a bloody bird help me write poetry?" I shooed the bird and turned back to the mess I'd left in my room. A child-like sound floated towards me, a kind of singing, so mesmerizing, so soft. It called to me and tingles rushed up and down my spine. The bird flapped its wings. It was singing. The beautiful sound coming from its open beak. I stepped closer wanting to reach out and touch it. It appraised me, head nodding, beak opening and closing as the music filled my room. Its claws opened and closed around the edge of the window sill but all I could think of was the music, the songs floating inside my mind. Words formed - poetic verse, stanzas - that would have Marie falling into my arms.

I edged closer, more words forming as the music seeped into my bones. The bird didn't move. Closer and closer, beak opening and closing, notes dancing and reverberating. Even closer, my hand outstretched. I wanted to stroke the feathers, absorb the magic words the birds sung.

The bird watched me. It didn't appear to be cautious as I brushed the tips of my fingers along its wing. Soft, velvet feathers, eyes watching mine.

Poetry flowed, and I knew I had to write it down or forget it forever. I pulled my hand back and tried to turn, but I could no longer move. The song pulsated, dancing in every bone of my body. My feet wouldn't budge, nothing would move anymore. The notes reverberated, soothing, softening my resolve. I could write the words when the songs were finished. The words would remain, and Marie would love them.

The bird's beak opened wide a new song beginning. Splendid notes, tarnished with sinister sounds, hypnotizing me to the darkness that surrounded me. Caught in a trap my eyes bulged as claws lashed out at my face and the bird took flight, launching at me, beak wide, music hypnotizing, as I stood unmovable.

Slicing, ripped skin, dripped blood, and the beak opened and closed. New words formed, inked in my blood. "I am hungry, you will be my food."

About the Author

Amanda J Evans is an award-winning Irish author of YA and Adult romance in paranormal and fantasy genres. Her stories centre on good versus evil with a splice of love and magic thrown in too. You can find out more on her website www.amandajevans.com.

38

HALPHAS AND THE COMMANDER
CHRIS TAYLOR

Halphas sat on the shoulder of the commander as he stood stock still before his troops. The troops stood in alignment awaiting their orders. Halphas had instructed the commander in his hoarse crow like voice to take down the small desert village. He wanted to see it burn.

"This is it boys. The moment you have been waiting for! Not one gets out alive. Set it all on fire! We want this place burned down to rubble so that we can build it up and make an even greater town from it! This will be our barracks, our station, our place of establishment! We start here then move on to the next town and the next! Soon we shall conquer the entire area and make it our own. Those who do not join us will perish in the fires. Those who do join us will swear loyalty to Halphas! Are you ready men?!" the Commander bellowed.

"Sir, Yes Sir!" they all shouted in unison.

"Forward March! Attack!" he commanded as he turned about and started towards the village, his troops following right behind.

They entered swiftly with sharp blade and keen eye. Fiery arrows flew onward, embracing the thatched roofs and setting the town ablaze. The soldiers moved swiftly through the flames wholly unscathed. The Commander stood back and watched his soldiers make quick work of the small village. Very few surrendered, leaving most to be thrown into their fiery graves. Those that chose to swear loyalty were pushed down in the center of the village and made to bow before the Commander as he approached. Five men, barely clad, waited for him on bent knee. All of them pissed themselves in fear as he stood above them. They had heard of the Red Dove and knew their lives teetered on the brink of death. He spat on each of them and cursed their lives with his words.

"You swine now belong to the great Lord Halphas. You will now answer to him and his right-hand man, The Red Dove! I stand before you as his commander and you will now swear your very souls to Halphas this day or die a horrendous death!" He reached down to the first man and lifted his head. "Do you swear fealty"

"I... I swear fealty!" He pushed the man over and moved onto the next man.

"Do you swear fealty?"

"Yes! I do so swear it!" He pushed this man over and continued on with the next three. These men refused to swear fealty to his lord. The Commander flicked them each on the forehead. This was to signal his men. They knew what was commanded of them. Several soldiers moved behind the men, two for each man and pulled their arms outward, stretching them taut. More soldiers came and held the legs in place, while yet others held the head up and kept it very still. The Commander then took a hot iron that had been heating up in the fire during this time and placed the tip right between the eyes of the first man. The smell of burnt flesh mingled with the deafening screams of the victim brought immense pleasure to Halphas. Encouraged by this, the Commander pushed the iron clean through the man's skull then pulled it back out slowly. The soldiers waited until the iron was pulled out before dropping the dead man to the ground. The next two men struggled to break free but to no avail. They died the same agonizing death as the first.

"Well done," the black dove croaked in the Commander's ear.

"It is my honor to please you," the Commander praised.

"Now we will build up this place and make it a wonder to behold! This will be our first base. Today here, tomorrow we conquer again!" Halphas declared. His hoarse voice echoed through the desert, causing many a knee to bow in fear. The Commander had no doubts that they would soon rule all the land. He gave his men their orders before making camp just outside the village. His men moved with agility and speed. They knew to obey orders at all costs, only then would they reap the rewards of their master.

As the Commander entered his tent, Halphas flew off of his shoulder and perched on a pole that had been placed there for him. He preened himself while waiting for the Commander to clean up and relax.

"You have done well and will be rewarded. Rest a day or two. We have the time to plan out our next course of action. Soon we will have a big enough army to take on the larger towns and cities. I will make an emperor out of you. You will see," Halphas declared.

"To serve you is all I ever wanted. Should you make me emperor you will not regret it. I will make sure the whole world knows and worships you!" The Commander bowed before Halphas who landed on his head and pecked him on the forehead. He spoke a few words of a spell over the Commander before flying back up to his perch. The Commander fell onto his back, deathly still. He was held into a trance where Halphas showed him his possible future. It was a wonder to behold. Nothing could have ever compared to what he was seeing now. Once the vision ended he fell into a deep peaceful sleep.

*****

The Commander was brought out of his slumber by the deathly squawks of Halphas. He jumped up and dressed immediately. Weapons drawn he slowly exited the tent. What he saw before him caused him to fall to his knees. Bodies were strewn about everywhere. Their throats had been ripped out in their sleep. Not one living being was in sight. Halphas flew around in circles above the camp, screeching loudly. There was murder in his eyes.

"Whoever did this will pay!" Halphas cried out. The Commander knew what was next. Halphas flew down and hovered before him. "You know what must be done."

"Yes, my Lord," The Commander replied calmly.

"Any last words?" Halphas asked.

"Only that I am a better leader to you in the depths of Hell than I was here." The Commander stretched his arms outward and lifted his head, remaining very still. Halphas flew upward a ways before dive bombing downward and straight through the Commander's skull with his razor sharp beak. The Commander remained upright until Halphas exited the back of the skull then fell dead to the ground.

"You were one of my best, Red Dove. I can only hope the next one will be even better," Halphas mourned before flying off to seek his next vessel.

39

MALPHAS
KASANDRA SHECKLES

Andrew

Andrew and a few of his friends sat around the coffee table in the living room of Andrew's home and nervously lit candles. Andrews parents were out at a work-related dinner party and Andrew knew it would be well after midnight before they returned home. He decided that he was going to give in to his curious nature and take his friends along for the ride.

Once all the candles were lit, they all joined hands and Andrew began to chant some words he found on a website about summoning demons. In his research Andrew had discovered a demon named Malphas and he was intrigued by his description. After he finished the chant linking them to the spirit realm, Andrew said the four words that changed his life as he knew it.

"Malphas, I summon thee."

Andrew and his friends nervously waited for Malphas to arrive and as time passed with nothing happening, Andrew wondered if he had made the right decision that night. Minutes ticked by and all was silent. Andrew's friends had begun to laugh and mock him, and he felt anger welling up in him. He knew he had done everything right, so he didn't understand why it wasn't working.

"Chill out guys I am going to try something else. I don't understand why this didn't work."

Andrew motioned for his friends to join hands again and repeated the chant. Once it was completed, he once again tried to summon the demon only this time he added more to his summons.

"Malphas, demon of hell and second in command to Satan, I summon thee." Andrew's voice shook as he uttered the words and his friends grew silent as they waited.

Malphas

Malphas had felt himself being summoned twice and he was annoyed with it. He had no time to be dealing with the wants of puny humans when the legions he commanded were on the brink of causing catastrophic damage to a few of the tallest buildings in the world. He considered sending a demon from his legion, but he had been specifically summoned. He had a direct connection with the human that had summoned him thanks to the chant the person had said before the summons.

Malphas made his legions aware of where he was going, and he mounted his dragon and headed for the earthly realm. He hated traveling to the realm of humans, they were ghastly creatures that he thought were too whiny. Malphas had never understood why God had created such weak, senseless beings but then again Satan had messed it up for Him by convincing Adam's mate to bite the fruit they had been told not to partake of. If that hadn't happened, they might not be the spoiled weaklings he thought they were.

The dragon seemed to know where they needed to go and quietly landed on the roof of the house. Malphas took a moment to admire the structure of the house and wondered if he or any of his legion had made it possible for this house to exist. His attention was drawn to the commotion in the house and he jumped from the roof to the porch to see what it was about. He knew which human had summoned him because his mark was on the boy's arm. It appeared the others were tired of waiting and accusing the boy of faking the summons.

Malphas watched as mayhem broke out inside the home and he feared the magnificent structure would be destroyed if he didn't make his presence known. He burst through the door, a loud growl coming from his throat. He felt amusement at the fear he saw on the humans faces. He stood there staring at them as they cowered at his feet.

"Who dared summon me from the pit in which I dwell?" he asked as he looked at each human and relished in their fear of him. He was beginning to get impatient with them when the human that summoned him stood up.

"I summoned you, your greatness. I have been very curious for a long time if spirits really existed especially demons and I wanted to see if you would come."

Malphas couldn't believe what he was hearing. He had been summoned purely out of curiosity nothing more. There were no buildings to build or knock down, no sacrifices to accept or anything. Malphas was furious and he let his fury be known with a loud roar as the humans cowered and covered their ears.

"You foolish human! You shouldn't summon spirits unless you want something! I left a very important mission to fool with you! Now you must choose something you want in exchange for a sacrifice to me." Malphas watched as his words sunk into their tiny brains. He tried to stifle a laugh as the look on their faces amused him greatly. He couldn't wait to hear what the boy's choice would be and Malphas knew he had to teach them a lesson for summoning him for no reason.

"I tell you what, I am going to step outside and tend to my dragon while you decide what it is you are going to ask of me. I'll be back in ten minutes, so you better have an answer, or you won't like what happens." Malphas stepped out and waited by the window, listening to the hushed chatter coming from inside. He waited until the chatter inside had reached a fever pitch before bursting through the door. The humans cowered once again, and he waited for their answer.

Andrew

Andrew couldn't believe that the summons had worked and now he was scared out of his mind as the large demon stood in his living room. The demon had demanded he think of something that he would want from Malphas, but Andrew couldn't think of anything. He had only been curious, and he decided that next time he felt curious about something, he would just leave it alone. His friends wanted no part of it and he didn't know how to get them out. He would just have to plead with the demon before him to let them go.

"Oh, great one I come before you and ask for you to let my friends and I go without receiving anything from you. I was merely curious, and they were just here to see if what I did worked. If you let us go, I promise you I will never summon you or any other spirit ever again."

Malphas stood still like a statue and Andrew was beginning to wonder if he had even heard anything that had been said. Andrew hoped that Malphas would consider what he said and let them go and Andrew knew that he would never be able to perform any kind of summons again. Malphas was quiet and Andrew was frightened by the silence. Finally, Malphas took a breath and turned to face Andrew.

"My dear boy, you have a lot to learn in your life here in the earthly realm. You cannot summon spirits unless you want something, and you must give them something as a sacrifice since they made the journey to you. I will let your friends go this once since they didn't really know what they were getting themselves into, but you must pay the price. If you do not want to ask me for anything that is your choice, but I am going to take something from you as a sacrifice for my journey."

Andrew was horrified as Malphas spoke and his friends ran out the door as they were told they were being let go. Now Andrew was alone with Malphas and he was terrified. He swallowed audibly as he looked up at the massive demon.

"What is it you want from me?" His voice quivered as he tried to swallow his fear.

"You are going to live a long full life here on earth, but when your time is finished here you are going to come and be my servant in hell!"

With that Malphas vanished and Andrew was left with the realization that he had made the biggest mistake of his life that night. A mistake that he wasn't sure God could even get him out of. Andrew ran to his room and locked himself inside and begged God for help. He hoped that he was being heard but knew that he wouldn't know until the day of his death came.

Andrew learned a valuable lesson that he never forgot and told people about every time he got the chance. Andrew started going to church and maintained a relationship with God well into his eighties. On the night of his eighty-sixth birthday, Andrew took his last breath surrounded by his family. Andrew knew his soul had left his body and he watched as an angel came with outstretched hands to take him to heaven and he felt relief for the first time in a very long time.

As Andrew reached for the angel's hand, Malphas grabbed him and started to drag him away.

"Hello boy, I told you that you'd be mine after a long life. Didn't you believe me?"

Andrew screamed out for the angel to help but he didn't see the angel anywhere. Suddenly, the brightest white light surrounded them, and several angels came walking out of it. They battled Malphas until they were able to send him back to hell. Andrew was escorted to heaven to spend eternity in peace.

About the Author

Kasandra Sheckles is the author of The Hearts of Faith series His Love for Lexi and Hope for Hannah and has many more projects to look out for. She lives with her husband and stepsons and enjoys spending time with them when she's not writing. You can find her on Facebook at www.facebook.com/kasandrashecklesauthor

40

RAUM: BLACK FEATHERS
P. I. STOULPE

Raum inhaled heavily of the salty air. He did enjoy the scent of the sea. Even the brackish waters of the inlet were tantalizing to his nose. The rotten seaweed was like perfume. Combined with the salt it was delightful!

He didn't have time to rest on his laurels and enjoy the pungent air. No. Tonight he would slip into the old mansion overlooking the inlet and steal the owner's most prized possession.

He could see the object in his mind's eye. A small silver figure shaped into a mermaid. It would measure, he guessed, at about seven inches in length. The hair was exquisitely rendered, each lock clearly separate from the ones next to it. The eyes were tiny emeralds. Each scale of her tail had been etched by hand into the soft metal as it cooled under the jeweler's magnifier.

Yes. A truly remarkable piece. It would make a fine addition to his collection. Right alongside the spearhead that had pierced the side of the Christ and the Papal scepter. Both of which he had snuck out of St. Peter's over a century ago.

He'd take more than just the mermaid from the mansion tonight. He needed to make it look like an actual robbery. Modern men were too concerned about the details. They would suspect something special about this thieving. He couldn't risk that.

No. They would need to think it nothing more than a robbery. He'd have to wait to see what other treasures the man had in his safe.

Raum watched carefully as the owner of the mansion climbed into his Mercedes and drove away. The place would be empty this weekend, other than the aged butler and his deaf wife. He felt confident the two wouldn't hear him as he stole through the big house into the owner's private rooms and took what he found.

Martin Abernathy, the owner of the mansion, was one of the quiet rich in New England. He had money. Old money. But he didn't make a big deal of it. He was a silent partner in more than one prosperous financial venture. He liked it that way. It gave him the money to continue to hoard his collection without needing to make a big splash in the business papers.

Raum also suspected that Abernathy had other secrets he kept from the world. His wealth was one thing. But where did he sneak off to one weekend a month? Not that it mattered. He was after the mermaid figure. If he learned Abernathy's secret it would be frosting on the cake.

*****

The mansion was completely dark now. The old butler and his wife had gone to bed an hour or so ago but Raum had waited to make sure the old bat hadn't made her husband get up and check the locks for the third time.

Satisfied that he could sneak in and out without disturbing the old couple, Raum shimmered from his human form into that of a large black crow. He silently flew from his perch in the trees behind the mansion and landed on the rail of the balcony outside Abernathy's private chambers. Using his bird's eyes, he peered around the darkened rooms.

Abernathy hadn't closed the curtains over the doors to this balcony. He could see that the room was filled with case after case of books, floor to ceiling. A large leather chair sat in the middle of the room facing the window. A matching ottoman was before it with a quilted blanket thrown carelessly over the middle. A book sat perched on top of the blanket. It was too far even for his eyes to read the title in the dark, but he was sure it was some moldy tome of ancient lore. Abernathy had a penchant for the arcane.

His crow eyes revealed that the alarm system had not been set when the old codger of a butler took his wife to bed. Fool. It made Raum's job so much easier.

He flickered back to his human form and brushed a stray feather out of his shoulder-length black hair. His wings shifted into the black shirt and denim jeans he preferred when sneaking around int he dark. All his clothes were black, like his wings. Everything he wore in his human form came from his wings.

Opening the unlocked door, he smiled to himself. Abernathy was so certain that no one would get past the security measures that he didn't need to lock the doors to his third-floor balcony. The man should have taken his aged staff into consideration and set up remote security access on his smartphone.

The thought of high-tech smart devices made him pause and inspect the corners of the room for cameras. He shook his head and remembered that Abernathy was also paranoid enough to not want to be filmed, especially in his own home. There was a risk, slight though it was, that someone could access his mainframe and steal the video files.

Secrets. This human has so many secrets.

Not even Raum's abilities to see through time would allow him to get a glimpse of those secrets. It frustrated him. And intrigued him. Had he made a deal with another demon, one that outranked Raum?

He entered and closed the glass doors behind him. The butler and his wife were too old for him to worry too much about, but he still moved silently through the library. He checked the shelves as he went by, looking for anything of interest. A copy of the writings of Hermes Trismegistus caught his eye and he paused to examine the cover and turn to the title page. It proved to be an early edition of the first English translation from the early 17th-Century.

He slipped the book into his bag and moved on to find the safe.

The safe was hidden behind a portrait of Abernathy's great-grandfather, the man who had brought the Abernathy family across the ocean to New England. The man who had also started the large empire of business ventures that the current Mr. Abernathy controlled from the sidelines. Tobacco had been the start of things for the wealthy family, moving north from the Virginia they had shed that vice and moved into other more lucrative ventures.

Raum pulled the portrait aside and inspected the safe. It had a digital keypad and a fingerprint scanner. The scanner would prove more difficult to bypass, but he was confident that he could interrupt the electrical signals and open the door with some of his own magic.

He keyed in the sequence of numbers that he knew Abernathy would use. 1-3-7-7-7-1-3-9-3 A long combination, but it was fitting for the arcane pursuits the Abernathy family had practiced for centuries. The screen lit green and a pulsing light demanded he use the fingerprint scanner.

With a simple thought and a wave of his hand, he bypassed the electricity and fooled the machine into accepting his own thumb as that of the owner of the mansion. Surely Abernathy had some other means of opening this safe. How would his successor gain entry? Perhaps he had already programmed their prints into the reader.

The safe clicked softly open. He pulled the door open and gazed hungrily upon the contents. Not only was the object of his desires concealed within, but there were also other alchemical treasures. Some of which he thought had been destroyed or lost to the ages.

Of course, he thought to himself. The Abernathy family would have found ways to make these objects disappear to time.

He pulled the mermaid out of the safe and admired it in the dim light from the cloudless and star-filled sky. Her eyes flashed green as he turned his hand to appreciate the craftsmanship of the silver. Smiling to himself, he slipped it into the bag along with the ancient tome.

He looked over the other contents and chose a few pieces of jewelry to finish the deceit of this being nothing more than a robbery. The other alchemical artifacts were too simple looking to be of interest to a common thief.

He would claim those by some other means at a future time.

Closing the safe and making sure it was secure, he pushed the portrait back into place and decided he would visit Abernathy's bedroom. Surely the man would keep something of importance and value in there as well.

Raum was surprised to learn that the door to Abernathy's bedroom was locked. Even through his library? He shook his head and bent to examine the lock. It was a simple affair that he could foil with the flick of his wrist, but he was more curious as to why it was locked.

Does he keep something secret even from the old couple who work for him?

He made quick work of the lock and entered into the sanctum of the man's private room. The lights flickered on as he pushed the door open. He flinched at the sudden light but was assured no one would notice, even from the outside, when he saw the blackout curtains that had been pulled shut over the large window on the far wall.

A large king-sized bed seemed to fill the room, but there were also built-in cases and other furnishings along the walls. He closed the door behind him and started to prowl around.

On the bureau next to the door, he found a large jewelry box that appeared to be even older than the Tismegatus book he had already slipped in this bag. He opened this jewelry box and was dazzled by the contents. They were not gems and gold. The contents of the box were several vials of a shimmering liquid.

He pulled one out and inspected it closely, holding it up to the light. The fluid inside sparkled with the tiny particles of gold and crystals that had been suspended in the oil contents. He popped the lid and sniffed carefully. Even a demon had to be concerned about certain human creations.

He was startled to find that it a sweet and salty scent. It reminded him of the ambrosia of the ancient Greeks. Did he have a recipe for a youth potion?

He let a drop of the shimmering fluid slide out onto his finger and tasted it.

Ambrosia! It was a youth potion. Where had the human gotten it!?

He closed the lid and slipped the vial into his pocket. Closing the lid to the box he decided he had enough. For tonight.

The book and the youth potion were the frosting to his cake. The mermaid was what he had come from. Learning a little of the man's secrets was a boon. He would have to meet this Martin Abernathy at some point soon and learn more about his secrets and where he had gotten the youth potion.

Checking to make sure he hadn't left any sign of his venture through the chambers, Raum slipped back out onto the balcony and shimmered back into his crow form. He flew across the large grounds connected to the mansion and headed for his own home.

*****

That Sunday evening Abernathy returned to his New England mansion and was startled to find one of his potion vials missing. After taking a dose he hurried to his safe to check the contents. He was furious to see that the mermaid was gone. He didn't care about the other trinkets that were missing. That mermaid was important. It was the key to his success. Slamming the safe shut he pushed his portrait from the early 18th-Century back into place.

Fuming, he stepped out onto his third-floor balcony and took a deep breath of the salt air to clear his head. When he looked down to the floor of his perch he found a single black feather.

About the Author

P.I. Stoulpe writes romance, crime drama, and detective stories. She will be featured in the upcoming Mystery 42 Manuscripts RP novel Elegance of the Moon.

https://www.facebook.com/pistoulpe

41

FOCALAR'S PIRATE CONQUEST
KOI GARFIELD

The young girl watched quietly from the dark corner. It was a stormy night on the high seas. The ship rocked to and fro, adding romance to the scene taking place. A grizzled pirate captain was stumbling around a circle of candles. He took a swig from the bottle of rum in his hand then started to draw a pentagram with chalk on the wooden floor enclosed by candles.

"Girl, take my rum!" He demanded harshly.

She scurried over quickly, head down, and took the bottle he had thrust at her. Just as quickly she retreated back into her corner. Her eyes widened as he pulled out an old and ornate book. She recognized it; it was the Goetia, the lesser testament of Solomon. Her thoughts were confirmed, the captain was trying to summon a demon.

"I hope my plan will work." She said under her breath. Then she took a vile full of liquid out of her bosom and placed a few drops of the liquid into the rum.

The captain was ruffling through the pages of his book, looking for a certain page. He stopped when he landed on a page with a picture of a man with grand, Griffin wings that were twice the size of his body. He was naked, and his face was stuck in a menacing grimace. She felt a chill run through her spine.

"Focalar! Yes! Girl! My rum!" He shouted, she gulped and brought it over.

He took a long swig from it then handed it back to her and waved her away.

He started to chant and circle around the candles again, but his stumbling was getting worse, and he started to sway, his mouth slack, eyes glazed, and then he slumped over, his desk breaking his fall to the floor. He had passed out from rum and a concoction of powerful herbs.

"It worked." The girl said looking around furtively. No one had heard the captain's fall, though even if they had they likely wouldn't care; it was a common enough occurrence, and why the rum was always gone.

She stepped over to the circle and picked up the book.

"A Luciferan angel, commands the seas and skies...hmmm" she muttered as she read the passage on Focalar.

"Won't kill if commanded not too!?" Her eyes sparked. She had an idea; SHE was going to summon the demon.

It worked, she had summoned the demon. She stared open mouthed at the man crouched, massive wings hiding him. He stood, unfurling his wings to their full span. His scowl was even more intimidating in person. He looked at her with disdain.

"Child, what are you doing summoning the likes of me." Focalar was annoyed.

"To protect my people." She responded evenly, despite her trembling.

Focalar stared at her, and she felt as if he was looking directly in her mind.

"Continue....." He said finally, with a hint of interest now.

The girl explained to him about the atrocities her people were facing at the hands of Pirate conquerors. They pillaged their homes, stole their livestock, destroyed their towns, and separated families.

"My sister and I were taken away from our homes, and then ripped away from our parents." She was shaking with rage, and tears were spilling down her cheeks. "We were taken as slaves for this ship. We don't know where our parents are."

"Shall I kill them for you?" Focalar grinned; pirates where his favorite victims.

The girl however surprised him with her answer,

"NO, I don't want more death, I want their ships destroyed. Without their ships they will have nothing, which is what they left us with." Her eyes flashed dangerously.

Focalar sighed dramatically. "I will have to get creative then. Find a way to get them off these ships."

"But you can do it??" Focalar laughed at her question.

"I can, but you will have to do something for me." He said slyly.

"What?" The girl asked.

"It's been such a long while since my wings have had a good preening." He answered back with a grin, unfurling his wings again.

"You want me to, preen you?" She asked confused.

"Well it may be difficult for me to fly if you don't, then how could I help you?"

"OK" she shrugged, "how?"

"Just take your hands like this, and then run them through a feather, one at a time, like so." He explained while demonstrating on a feather.

She walked over and tentatively started preening the demon's wings.

"Don't be shy girl." Focalar said, eyes half closed.

'He looks like my old cat when I would scratch her behind' she couldn't help but think to herself. And the thought made her smile.

"There." She said after a while. "All done."

"Mmmmmm, lovely. Now then, how shall I kill these men for you?" He inquired, smirking mischievously.

"I don't want you to kill them..." Her eyes were narrowed in confusion. Focalar pouted,

"Such a pain, it's so much more fun. It's been so long since I had fun."

"I'm not having th-" She was interrupted by the sound of screaming. Focalar watched as her face turned as white as a sheet.

"Fran!!" She squeaked out in fright, bolting towards the door. Focalar was close behind.

They came out on the windy deck, in front of them was a huddled mass of men, jeering and yelling and staring at something they could not see. The screaming was coming from the middle of the circle.

"FRAN!!!"

The men turned when they heard her scream her sister's name. They started to leer at her and grab her, but stopped quickly when they saw the demon glaring at them from behind her.

"Who the hell are you!?" One of the men shouted as he drew back in shock.

"He is a demon!!! Move OUT of my way!!!" The girl shouted pushing her way violently through the stunned men.

Her sister was laying on the ground, sobbing and shaking, covered in blood and without clothes on.

"Fran..." she choked, tears pouring down her face. She didn't even recognize her face under all the blood and bruises. "What did they do!?"

She bent down, pulling her sister's long, matted hair back. The damage they had done was so serious that Fran was having difficulty breathing, and couldn't see her sister. She flinched when she touched her, quivering in fear.

"Fran, love, it's me, Eliza." Eliza whispered as she looked over the rest of her sister's body. The more she looked the angrier she grew. Focalar saw a change come over the young face; it was a look he had seen before.

Rage and hate flowed through her veins like it never had before in her young life.

"Focalar...." she said quietly, her voice shaking from anger. "Kill them."

Focalar's mischievous demeanor had completely slipped away. His face was somber, and angry as well.

"Mistress, I must get you and your sister to safety first."

Eliza nodded. Then looked at the confused and frightened men.

"Tie them up so they don't try to escape." she said coldly.

Focalar flicked his wrist and ropes instantly wrapped around the men, pushing them violently against the mast.

"I'll take you on my back, so I can carry her safely." He said, pointing to Fran.

She was still huddled into Eliza's lap, her breathing more labored. Eliza nodded once, then climbed on his back as he crouched down to pick up Fran. He cradled her gently in his arms and stood up slowly. Next, he unfurled his wings and started to flap them first slowly, then quicker and quicker. Soon they were off the deck of the boat and flying through the air.

Within a few minutes Focalar spotted a high cliff with a protected cave; it was the perfect spot to watch the destruction, while remaining safe from the storm. He flew towards it and landed gently. Flapping his wings slower and slower as he lowered himself to the cave floor. Eliza jumped down from his back and sat down so Fran could be laid down with her. Focalar's gentleness surprised Eliza. She looked at him, her face had aged ten years.

"Thank you."

He nodded, "I'll be off now. You can watch from here if you like. It will be violent."

"Good." She answered. Focalar then took off. Eliza watched as he flew over the ships.

He circled high above them, she watched as a water cyclone started to form, and as the seas swirled and swirled underneath the ships. She wished she could hear the screaming and see the men's fear. But the intensity of the storm made her cheeks burn with angered satisfaction.

Suddenly Fran shuddered violently underneath her, her breathing became fast and shallow, then as quickly as it started it stopped. Eliza waited, her heart in her throat, for her breathing to start again. But it didn't happen. Numbness took over her as she stared down at her sister, her face now peaceful. She didn't notice when the storm stopped or when Focalar landed in the cave.

"Eliza...." He asked quietly. Finally, she snapped out of it, tears of rage and grief welling up.

"They killed her, they raped her and then killed her." Her whole body was shaking. "Who else have they done this too? My mother, my friends?"

She looked up at him with stony resolve, the fury and rage in her eyes made even him shudder some,

"They must all die." She whispered, coldly.

Focalar nodded, bent on his knee,

"I shall make sure they all pay, and all suffer. Until the job is done, you command me."

She nodded gravely, "Then they die." He gestured to his back, she climbed on as he took Fran's lifeless body in his arms. Then they flew off, bent on their path of vengeance, bringing death upon his wings.

About the Author

Koi Garfield is a Transgender man who served in the Navy where he wrote his first book. He has always been an avid writer and reader as well as lover of culture and language.

42

VEPAR: DEMONESS OF THE SEA
CHANDRA TRULOVE FRY

The sea was calm despite the thick fog that hid everything from view. A large ship sailed quietly through the waters. Every soul on the ship remained as still as statues for fear of being discovered. The captain tried in vain to spot anything amid the fog. He could feel the trepidation of his crew as they awaited his orders. There was nothing to command at this point. They would have to take the sea inch by inch until the fog cleared and keep a vigilant eye on the waters as best, they could.

Captain Merlisus was no stranger to the ominous fog of the sea. He knew what lurked out in those waters and she was not one to be trifled with. He had a plan that he hoped would work but it would take cunning and cooperation. His crewmen were a suspicious lot and well they should be. He took one hard look around at them before turning back to his helm. He placed a few black candles next to the ship's wheel along with some sailor's tobacco. The open air at night was the best time to summon the demoness and he felt confident that he had covered all bases.

"Goddess Vepar, I summon thee! To guide us through these treacherous waters and help us conquer our enemy!" He called out as he lit the candles. There were a few gasps from his crew but one stern look by him and all was silent. They listened and waited, even more apprehensive since they now knew their captain had summoned the ominous demoness of the sea.

A loud splash broke the eerie silence causing all of them to startle. The captain ran quickly to the side of his ship where the noise was heard in search of whatever had made the sound. Another splash, this time closer, and suddenly the top form of a woman broke through the water's surface. She was the most beautiful woman Merlisus had ever seen. Bright purple eyes bore into his from a porcelain face. Her aquiline features were smooth and perfect. Her long purple hair cascaded down her back leaving her ample firm breasts exposed for all to view.

She swam to the edge of the ship and waited. The captain acted quickly, "Throw her a line, mates. Help her aboard!"

"Captain, it be bad luck to bring a woman aboard." A crewman spoke out boldly.

"Aye Mate, that be true. This be no woman as such though. We deny the Goddess and she will smite us." Merlisus warned. That was all the crew needed to hear as they quickly did as he commanded. No one wanted the wrath of a Goddess upon them. The line was dropped down to her and they waited for her next move.

Vepar grabbed the line gracefully and wrapped it gently around her waist. She could have gotten onboard herself with little effort, but she wanted to know the measure of these men and if they were worth her helping them. They pulled her up ever so carefully, for fear of angering her. Once she was on board the ship, she formed legs and stood, now fully clothed in her warrior's garb. She was something to behold indeed. The men stood there, spellbound by her presence. Only Merlisus was brave enough to approach her.

"My lady Vepar! Tis an honor to be in your presence. I am Captain Merlisus. My ship is yours to command." He bowed before her feet. She liked him. He would make a good consort if he survived. Vepar took her sharp nailed finger and lifted the captain up to her level. He was putty in her hands but not like the others. There was fire in him and oh how she missed such fire.

"You have sought me to guide you in battle. What makes you worthy of my help?" She asked calmly. Her voice was like a soothing balm on one's very soul.

"My Lady, our enemies have taken much from us and many have died trying to gain it back. We wish vengeance upon them but have not the numbers to do so. I have heard of your ghost ships and how those who follow you always win in battle. I know we can win with you by our side!" She looked into his very soul and knew he spoke sincerely. This pleased her.

"And what if your enemy has already gained my favor?" Vepar asked coyly.

"My Lady, the enemy would not treat you with the honor and respect that you deserve. They only know lies and deceit. We would never deceive you." Merlisus declared. Vepar pulled him close and planted a hard kiss on the Captain's lips. His eyes grew wide, but he accepted her touch. She pulled back and said,

"And what, dear captain, would you give me in return?" There was mischief in her eyes.

"I offer myself completely to you, in whatever manner you wish to have me." He smiled devilishly at her.

"And your crew? Would they give themselves to me as well?" She looked at each one of them and saw they were each loyal to their captain. As she said this, they all fell on bent knee and bowed before her, offering themselves to her. She had indeed found a worthy vessel. "Very well! I shall offer my protection and guidance. Go! Rest this night. For tomorrow we go to war!"

They all did as she commanded. Even the captain turned to go but Vepar stopped him dead in his tracks, "No, my pet. Tonight, you are mine!" She pulled him up firmly against her body and kissed him passionately as she dove into the sea with him. He was astounded to find he could breathe under the water with her. She took him there in the deep and he gave himself to her completely. Once her appetite was sated, she took him back to his ship and sent him off to rest. That morning they would fall upon their enemies.

*****

Merlisus woke to the sound of a battle horn. He dressed quickly and made his way to the deck. He saw Vepar standing by the ship's wheel, dressed in the finest warrior garb he had ever seen. She was the fiercest creature he'd ever had the pleasure of knowing. He stood just behind her, at attention, and ready for orders.

"Captain take the helm. Our enemy awaits!" She commanded. He took the wheel as she stood aside for him. His crew were already busy with whatever orders she had given them. Just ahead were several ships flying the colors of his dreaded enemies. There must have been at least five ships. The odds did not look good with just five ships to one, but he had a Goddess on his side and not just any Goddess but one who commanded the sea.

Vepar walked to the bow of the ship and stood steady, waiting for the enemy to make the first move. One ship fired a cannon, but it didn't come close enough to do any real damage. Vepar waited. They soon got close enough to see each other on the ships. Merlisus snarled when he saw the captain of the fleet they were now surrounded by.

"Merlisus, you fool! Alas, have we not proven that we are the better of pirates? Join my fleet and we might spare your lives." The enemy captain mocked.

"Tectonis, I would never sail under your colors. You are not worthy of being a fleet captain." Merlisus declared.

"You never learn! Why, I see you even have a woman on your ship? As formidably beautiful as she may be, you have placed a curse upon you and your crew. I think we ought to end your misery now before you spread your disease upon others."

"I think you will find that she is no ordinary woman, Tec." As soon as he said that Vepar raised her arms up to the sky. Dark clouds soon took over as rain began to pelt down upon them. The wind stirred and churned the sea. Even the choppy waters didn't break her steady stance.

"What sorcery is this?!!! Have you doomed us all? Merl! Stop this immediately!" Tectonis barely choked the words out as he fought the waves of water coming upon his ship. No water touched Merlisus' ship.

"Even with these waves Merlisus, we will still defeat you. You are but one ship to our five. We have the upper hand here." He managed to shout above the storm.

"Take a better look mate. I think you'll find that we are not so alone after all." Merlisus had caught sight of Vepar's ghost ships and his confidence in her grew even more. Tectonis turned and saw that they were indeed surrounded by what looked like a hundred ships. He went pale with fear as he commanded his ships turn tale and leave.

They never had a chance as the storm grew stronger and waves larger than Merlisus had ever seen before swallowed the enemy ships whole. It happened in mere minutes. All the ships were pulled down deep into the sea along with their crew. The only one that did not go down with the ships was Tectonis himself. Vepar had reached out her hand and levitated the enemy captain just above the churning water. She pulled him to Merlisus' ship and dropped him onto the deck.

"Now, my lover, you shall have your revenge!" She held out a ceremonial dagger to him. He took it with the utmost reverence and turned to face Tectonis. He was now standing before them with a wild fear in his eyes,

"Merlisus, we used to be friends, mate." He cried.

"Tectonis, we were never friends. We are pirates!" Merlisus pushed the dagger deep into Tectonis chest. It sliced through him as if he were but paper. The look on his face was one of anguish and betrayal.

"Why?" Tectonis gasped.

"Keltina" was all Merlisus said. The knowledge made clear to Tectonis he breathed his last breath and fell to the deck. Merlisus stood watching the lifeless body for some time as the fresh blood dripped from the dagger. "The deed is done." He whispered. Turning to his crew he shouted, "The deed is done! We now own these waters!" The crew shouted with jubilee until they heard a slight cough. Merlisus turned to face Vepar,

"Forgive me, my Lady. I got carried away in the moment." He turned to his men, "The deed is done! The sea and our souls belong to the Goddess Vepar!" All men shouted in elation as they bowed before her. She walked up to Merlisus and lifted him up,

"You shall remain my lover and we will bring war to these seas for many centuries!" She declared. The passionate look in her eyes was all the encouragement Merlisus needed.

"Aye!" He agreed. The kiss she gave him then sealed his fate to her forever and his ship would soon become the scourge and fear of the sea. All who dared cross paths with the ship Vepar knew they would not live to tell the tale. Many joined Merlisus fleet and pledged themselves to Vepar just so they would live. Tales were told for centuries to come of Captain Merlisus and the crew of Vepar, along with tales of the sirens who would lure men to their demise. Some said they were the children of the demoness Vepar and Captain Merlisus, creatures most feared by any man. The seas would never be the same again.

About the Author

Chandra Trulove Fry is a multi-genre author who longs to try her hand at every genre at least once throughout her author career. She resides in Northern California with her wonderful husband and kids.

https://www.facebook.com/ChandrasAuthorPage/

43

SABNOCK: THE WARRIOR VS. THE DEMON
CYNTHIA STATON

In this story you will meet a demon and a warrior who is determined to destroy him. The warrior's name is Malachi. The demon's name is Sabnock. This particular demon is terrible. He is beyond terrible. He is horrible and nasty, one of the most evil of his kind. He wants to obliterate the planet earth and eliminate all its inhabitants. Fortunately, the warrior Malachi is brave enough to fight him. And the demon has agreed to fight the warrior. If Sabnock loses, he agrees to leave earth unharmed. He is confident that he will win, because he has never lost a battle. Malachi is strong, but he uses his training and knowledge to serve and protect only. He is a champion fighter. He is as quick as lightening with a sword.

Malachi trains and practices for many hours every day. He knows this a battle that he cannot lose. The lives and every single person on earth depends on it after all. He has only about a month to be ready, and he felt as ready as ever. He was trained and guided by his master Nicholas Thorn. Malachi would be Master Thorn's last student before he retired, so he wanted to make sure he passed on to him everything he possibly could. He wanted him to learn everything. He knew he needed everything possible to defeat the demon.

"Sabnock is not messing around!", Thorn told him one day. "You have to understand that."

"Yes, I understand master", he replied, "but I do not fear Sabnock, I do not want that in his mind."

"I know Malachi, but he doesn't care whether you fear him or not", Master Thorn explained. "You are all that stands in his way of destroying the world." "The two of you made an agreement, I cannot help you fight him, I cannot step in."

"None of his kind can help him either", replied Malachi. "He has to fight alone too."

"Yes, but I mean to say, if you die in this fight", Master Thorn hesitated a little, "then you die."

"Yes, and I will die before he destroys this planet.", he made it clear, "I am prepared for that."

MEANWHILE SABNOCK SPEAKS TO HIS FOLLOWERS......

"Soon I will destroy the pathetic warrior, Malachi", he called out. "I will rip him to pieces."

The followers cheered loudly with encouragement.

"His blood will be mine", Sabnock continued. "I will use his blood to make a mimic of him and force him to bow to me."

The cheers grew even louder. They loved the sound of this.

"We will help you win", some of them offered. "Let us help you, we will overtake him."

"I wish we could", roared Sabnock, "but I have agreed to fight alone."

"But do not worry, I will not let you down", he assured them. "I will kill the warrior."

"You all will be able to help me destroy the earth.", he promised them.

They yelled back to him in excitement. They were ready for this.

MALACHI'S FASTING......

Malachi decided he wanted to put himself to a test. He wanted to test his will. He told his master that he planned to fast for a couple weeks. His idea was that not eating for a while would allow him to prove to himself how strong his will to survive was. He would not give into hunger, just he would not give into pain. Master Thorn admired Malachi's perception in his decision.

"I am impressed with you", Master Thorn told him. "I have faith that you will do well."

"I expect the demon is not doing much for training", Master Thorn went on, "He will rely on his power."

"Then that will be his down fall", Malachi concluded.

"Do not get over confident!", his master suggested. "That will cost you, possibly the battle."

"I am not over confident", Malachi assured him, "I am aware of the demon's abilities, and I will use my wisdom to defeat him." "Or as I said, I will die trying."

SABNOCK'S "TRAINING"

Sabnock spent his training time much differently. He hundreds of fake, motionless warriors created. They all vaguely resembled Malachi. He practiced using his different powers. He threw fire at some of the fakes. He used acid on others. He vaporized several of them. He was certain that he was ready. As far as he was concerned he would win this battle quick and easy. Unless of course he chose to torture the warrior.

"The warrior is nothing", he told his followers. "He is so weak compared to me."

"He will try to battle with strength and a flimsy little sword", he bellowed.

His followers all laughed very loudly and hysterically. They hung on to his every word. They just knew he couldn't lose.

Sabnock continued destroying the other fakes until they were all gone. He was not worried at all. He was too powerful to lose. With his power he might even make the warrior yield to him.

THE OFFER

Just days before the scheduled battle, one of Sabnock's followers, went to visit Malachi with an offer. Sabnock wanted to give him a chance to take the easy way out.

"What do you want, demon?", Malachi pulled his sword.

"I am not here to fight", said the demon, "Killing you is Sabnock's job." "Unless you take his offer."

"His offer?", Malachi asked, "I am not interested."

"Just hear me out", the demon insisted, "If you forfeit the battle and give Sabnock the world, you will be left unharmed."

"I told you I am not interested", Malachi said again. "Now get lost."

SABNOCK'S FURY

"YOU WERE SUPPOSED TO CONVINCE HIM, YOU WORTHLESS EXCUSE FOR A DEMON", Sabnock screamed. Then he vaporized him.

He looked at his followers. "That is what happens when you fail to follow my orders", he told them. "So, let that be a lesson for you."

They all bowed in agreement to him.

THE BATTLE

Finally, the day had come. The battle was taking place. Malachi and Sabnock would fight to the death.

"Are you ready, demon?" Malachi asked.

"I've been ready", he laughed. Then he threw lightening from his fingertips and hit Malachi in the chest. Malachi fell to the ground.

"Too easy", screeched Sabnock. "You blood is mine, warrior." "But I will beat you standing."

He lifted Malachi to his feet. He opened his mouth and fire blasted right for Malachi's face.

Malachi lifted his shield. It blocked the fire. Sabnock directed lightening at the shield but it rebounded and struck him in the abdomen. He went to his knees.

"You got lucky", he rasped looking up at Malachi. "But not lucky enough to win." He conjured out of nowhere a long vial of sorts. He opened and threw acid at Malachi. Malachi felt it burn through his skin. He was growing weaker. He prayed to God for help. He kept growing weaker. His body did, but not his faith. His faith remained as strong as ever. Then it began to rain. An unusually warm rain. His strength was coming back. He was healing.

"How can this be", steamed Sabnock. He and neither felt nor seen the rain. "I am killing you now, I won't wait a second longer." He sent more lightening into Malachi's chest. It seemed to stun him again. "I will just kill you laying down." He held his hands apart, and what appeared was a huge strange looking hammer type weapon. Sabnock raised it high above him and took a leap in the air. But at the last second Malachi drew his sword. Sabnock couldn't avoid it. It went right through where his heart would be. He fell to the ground. Angels appeared to carry his carcass off to hades. The battle was over. Malachi stood tall.

"Thank you, God", said Malachi.

About the Author

Cynthia Staton is an inspirational speaker and author. Her first book is called Life Lived Not Lost a journey of hope.
Cynthia has also jumped feet first into down the rabbit hole into the anthology world, but also plan to have her next novel out this year.

SHAX

KASANDRA SHECKLES

Morgan

Morgan sat in her room, legs crossed on the bed and stared at the Ouija board on the bed in front of her. She had heard so many bad things about the board that she was afraid to use it but wanted to see if what people said was true. She needed help with a bully problem and no one in her life was taking her seriously. She knew that no one could hurt her if she had the spirit world on her side. She slowly slid the board out of the box and laid it out in front of her.

She placed her hand on the eye that shows the letters and called out into the darkness of her room.

"Any spirits that are there please come forth and speak with me. I am here to talk with you." She waited nervously but the eye never moved. She put the board back in the box, disappointed that it didn't work. She decided that she needed to do more research and try again another day.

After weeks of research, Morgan discovered a plethora of different opportunities to summon spirits and she decided that she was going to try again that evening. She tried to concentrate on her classes the rest of the day, but the anticipation made it difficult. Once school let out and she was able to get back home, she laid everything out for the ceremony to summon a spirit. She waited until her parents had fallen asleep and she began to prepare her table for the ceremony.

She had read about a demon named Shax that could take things from people like their sight or hearing upon request. Once she read that, she knew exactly what she was going to do. Once the table was ready, she snuck down the hall and pressed her ear to the door of her parents' room. She knew they were asleep as the soft snores of her father echoed through the door. She smiled, and tip toed back to her room. She sat at the table and lit the candles that had been placed around it just as the website had directed. After all the candles were lit, she relaxed in her chair as she meditated to clear her mind and open herself up to the spirit realm. As she felt her soul open to the spirit realm, she called out and hoped the demon would hear.

"Oh, great Shax, demon of hell, hear my call and grace me with your presence. I wish to make a request for your service."

Morgan waited a few minutes hoping she had done everything right. After a few minutes she realized it didn't work and she was very disappointed. She stood from the table and began blowing out the candles when she felt a burst of air, but her window was closed.

She slowly looked up into the glowing green eyes of the demon she had summoned. Fear gripped her as the demon loomed over her, a menacing grin stretching across his crooked, misshapen face. She swallowed hard as they stood there staring at each other. Morgan began to wonder if the best choice had been made.

Shax

He had known the moment the girl summoned him, but he liked making the conjurers that summon him sweat a little bit before showing up. He loved making them wait even though they wanted to make a deal. Shax loved when humans wanted something especially when it involved taking something from someone else. He was anxious to hear what this little girl wanted from him. He was startled at how young she was. As time progressed, he noticed the age of those dabbling in the occult was getting younger and younger. He didn't mind though; the master would be proud of him for dragging such young souls to hell with him.

He had waited a few minutes until he sensed the girl's annoyance before he made his presence known to her and when he had, all confidence left her, and she stared at him without saying a word. He could smell the fear all over her and he loved it. After staring into her fear filled eyes for several minutes, he began to get annoyed. He shifted his weight forward and leaned closer to her.

"I haven't the time for this, tiny human. What is the request you have of me? It better be a good one I was in the process of stealing money from British royalty!" he huffed as he waited for her to come out of her stupor.

"I-I need you to help me with a bully. I've been getting picked on for most of the school year and none of the adults in charge will do anything to stop it or if they have, it hasn't worked. Just today she slammed me head first into a locker. Please help me!"

Shax listened intently to every word that came out of her mouth forming a plan in his mind. He would indeed help her but in the end, he would steal from her. After all, no one makes a deal with the devil, sort of, and gets out of giving payment. He knew he had to make this quick and get back to his other assignments and his legions. They never seemed to get anything accomplished with him away and Satan was quick to anger if his assignments weren't completed on time. They were on a tight schedule and time was running out for them. Shax had just watched Malphas get severely punished for losing a soul to the other side and Shax wasn't about to let that be his fate.

"Of course, I'll help you dear one. Bullying is not okay in anyway. What would you like me to do to her? I assume you know of my many talents?" he faked a smile and fought to keep a laugh from his throat as her face brightened with excitement.

"Yes! I know of all the talents you possess. The girl that has been bullying me loves to look at herself in the mirror several times a day, so I think the best revenge would be for you to take her eyesight. She will go crazy if she can't see her face every day."

Shax grinned maliciously as the details of his plan fell into place. Once he fulfilled the girls wish, he would take what she valued most. He was a bit surprised at the maniacal smile that was spreading across her face. He knew that humans could do bad things especially when prompted by demons, but he had never really thought they could be so evil on their own.

"Of course, my dear, I can take that from her. There will need to be a sacrifice on your part though. Just a small payment. I won't take much from you." Shax hid an evil grin as he crossed his gnarled fingers behind his back. He watched as she nodded her head in agreement and told him where to find the bully. He transformed himself from his ghastly human form to his original appearance as a stork and flew to the address Morgan gave him.

Shax made himself invisible to the human eye and went into the bedroom of Morgan's bully. He could see why Morgan would want her eyes taken from her. She was self-absorbed with pictures of herself and mirrors all over the walls of her room. There were even mirrors on the door of her room, closet and ceiling. He rolled his black eyes as he saw drawings with her name all over them and he couldn't wait to knock her self-esteem down a few notches. Her name was apparently Roxanne and that made him scoff.

He noticed she was not in her room, so he roamed the house looking for her. He found Roxanne in the backyard sitting around a fire with people he assumed were her family. He waited until she got up to stoke the fire and at the time, she threw a log on it and moved them around with her foot he blew his hot, smelly breath in the fire which sent hot coals up and they landed in Roxanne's eyes. He giggled with glee as she grabbed her face and screamed causing those around her to panic.

Shax rode on the top of the vehicle as they rushed her to the hospital. He wanted to make sure that his work was a success. He slid his arms down through the roof of the car making them invisible to everyone and pressed his gnarled fingers into her eyes making sure the coals stayed hot. Her screams of pain sent chills of excitement through his evil body. By the time they arrived at the hospital, he knew the damage was done. He waited outside the hospital until they came back out a few hours later. Roxanne was hysterical and inconsolable. Shax smiled as he made his way back to Morgan's house.

He landed on the roof of Morgan's home and changed his appearance back to his haggard human form, so he didn't scare her more than he already had. He slipped through the roof into her room and found her waiting for him.

"Well? Did it work? Is my plan for revenge complete?" She hissed as anticipation dripped from her voice.

"Yes, my dear of course it is. I never fail. She will never see anything, including herself again. Now there's just the matter of payment." The words slipped from his mouth in a hiss like sound. He watched her face as her expression changed from excited to worried.

"What do you want as your payment, oh great one?" she asked as Shax stepped closer to her.

"Oh, not much my dear, only your soul!" he growled as he cornered her against the wall.

Shax shook with excitement as her eyes grew wide and she tried to scream as his hand slid into her mouth. His eyes never left hers as he reached deep inside her and grabbed her soul yanking it from her body as it fell lifeless to the floor. Shax quickly changed forms keeping hold of her soul and jumped from the window and headed for hell.

"You'll make a good slave for me my dear." He whispered to Morgan's soul as she screamed for God to help her.

"You should've kept telling the adults about the bullying. The occult won't get you into heaven. Now you're mine for eternity."

Shax plunged into the darkness of the pit and took her to join his legions. He watched her distress as the hole he plunged them through closed on top of them never to open to her again. He grinned slyly as she screamed and begged for help. He grabbed her and took her deeper into hell and threw her into a pit of molten lava.

"This is where you will stay until I need you then I'll come retrieve you, slave." He growled as he flew away to his next summons.

As he reached his next destination, an evil smile crossed his lips as he celebrated yet another victory. He was a thief and he couldn't wait to see what he could take next.

About the Author

Kasandra Sheckles is the author of The Hearts of Faith series His Love for Lexi and Hope for Hannah and has many more projects to look out for. She lives with her husband and stepsons and enjoys spending time with them when she's not writing. You can find her on Facebook at www.facebook.com/kasandrashecklesauthor

45

VINE: A NEW WONDERLAND
IAN ADEMA

Fury swept the sky as a hail storm descended while a metal and stone tower rise. Its height was greater than any man could build. Its grandeur was beyond the natural, but its look was still somewhat manmade. This was one of many towers already formed and all of differing height and width, some circular and some square or rectangular but mostly of aesthetic proportion. The sky was dark, like scorching fire and smoke. Walls rose beside the towers. One by one, they took over the landscape, creating the present apocalypse.

Lord Satan, by your grace, grant me, I pray thee the power to conceive in my mind and to execute that which I desire to do, the end which I would attain by thy help...

Sweeping his arms to create these monstrous buildings was a figure of a lion on a black horse. Great flames came from the horse's nostrils, changing from blue to red as they came out scorching parts of the earth. The lion held a writhing serpent which transformed into various weapons at will and a grand shield in his left inscribed with a great falcon crest. He was like Moses transformed into the lion of death come to smite the earth.

I entreat thee to inspire Vine to manifest before that that he may give me true and faithful answer, so that I may accomplish my desired end. This I humbly ask in Your Name, Lord Satan.

The people fled the city as another wall rose. Vine had no mercy for any man. No love or hate. Only the work. He had been given his command. He was to raise the earth using his power. He summoned another six-foot stone wall and it sent three bodies flying into the air and they landed on the concrete, lifeless. A world of technology was being taken over by a world of stone and earth. Everything was upturned.

The Great King at work. I've never seen so much power. The earth truly at the mercy of the great Vine and his true power of equality. All are treated the same. And I get to witness it all with my own eyes. The equality for the first time. No longer is there good or evil. Just Vine.

Jared had been watching all the destruction since he had summoned the demon. He was a simple man but also an angry one. After years of torture and traumatic experiences, he was done. He hadn't really thought it through much, but he decided it was time to explore the demon world. He didn't second guess his decisions now. Instead, he dove in head first without a second thought. He stumbled onto Vine first and never looked back. What could sound better than a demon that would make a deal without a thought for what anyone had done? It was a fresh start for the world.

For him.

It would all be over soon enough. The end of the world. The end of all this shit.

Jared couldn't help but smile as he watched people thrown about with the coming stone age. He had never thought of himself as a psychopath or sociopath but then who did when they were. But these were new thoughts for him. He had probably just snapped from one too many events. A person can only break so much before they remain broken forever. At this point, was there any hope for recovery? He didn't know and expected he would never know. The world was about to change the way he desired. It would reflect his dark and twisted mind.

Early on televisions had continued to work and news came pouring in of the death and destruction all around the world, so Jared knew it would truly be the end of the earth as we knew it. Then, as the destruction spread wide, the media shorted. With the new world coming, the wires were being destroyed, making it impossible for communication to be wide spread any longer.

In the swirling skies, Vine worked like an ancient magician with the pose and finesse of a conductor and glamour of a knight. The rumbling slowed as towers and walls came to their full heights and rested on their final foundations. Screaming stopped in the world and the stone rising ceased. An eerie silence floated in the air and provided a strange sense of calm.

Jared watched in awe and satisfaction as Vine descended, floating, to the earth in front of him. There was no expression on Vine's fierce lion face. There was no way to know what the demon thought. Jared, on the other hand, wore his pleasure on his face like a light in a dark room.

"Amazing! Just incredible!" Jared sputtered. He was at a loss for words.

"The world is as you have asked." Vine's voice was deep and commanding.

"Yes, yes, you have done what I asked. But there is something that hasn't happened yet." Jared was getting anxious but also overly drawn to the draw of power. "I wanted to be master of this world. To be able to do whatever I wanted. Absolutely anything."

"In exchange you knew the price."

"Yes, yes, of course. Like all demons you want my soul."

For the first time, Vine showed emotion; satisfaction. Off that look, Jared knew something was off. It was the look of deception.

"I already have your soul," Vine chuckled. "I do not need the Lord's permission. No, you're request comes at a much greater price."

"What are you talking about? The price was my soul!"

"No! The price was in your request!"

Jared stood, speechless. His request? What did that mean? What did he say that could have a greater price then his very own soul?

Vine dismounted his horse. He attached the shield to the saddle and walked up to Jared. He spun his serpent staff and it transformed into a shining sword, the blade half red, like that of the hottest fire. He sliced the blade through the air, creating a strange symbol. It was new and unrecognizable, made specifically for this simple man. It was jagged and ruff. With the symbol made he used his lion's hand and thrust it into Jared's chest.

Jared gasped as the symbol fused into his chest. The lines then sparked out like veins into his body. They moved through his arms and legs and to every corner of his body. When they had covered him, his body disappeared and all that was left was the symbol, its veins, and a thin veil of who the man had been. He was a wandering spirit who could go anywhere or do anything but without purpose or drive. He was currently the most powerful and at the same time least powerful creature in this world.

He stared at Vine, stunned.

"You desired an end to this world," Vine said. "As you put it you wanted... a New Wonderland."

Vine remounted his horse and disappeared, leaving Jared to do as he pleased.

About the Author

Ian Adema is a writer and director of fantasy and psychological thriller movies and a prose writer on the side. Much of his inspiration arises from his intense and vivid dream life.

https://www.facebook.com/ianladema/

46

BIFRON'S NEW APPRENTICE
KOI GARFIELD

"There it is again!"

The creature shifted their body, turning to the humming sound coming from the East. They lurched on the gravestone, knees up to their chin, their face, grotesque at first glance, lent something comical to the otherwise eerie Autumn evening.

"I know this tuuuunneee" it said again, this time with its face scrunched up real tight, lending the ancient creature a childlike air. It scratched it's long pointed, bubbly nose, while rubbing a large, boiled covered ear.

"Mhmmm, mhmmm" they said, rocking back and forth on their gravestone, seemingly unaware that the light they had lit was bobbing away slowly towards the woods; almost as if it had a mind of its own and was trying to sneak away. Unfortunately for the tiny blue-white blob the creature was much too quick for it. Without even taking its eyes off of the black figure it saw walking in the distance, they grabbed the little light within their clawed hand and placed it right back on the edge of the grave stone.

"Nasty, naughty LIGHT. You know BETTER than that. WE have more GRAVES to mess WITH tonight." The creature said, articulating every third word with vigor.

"I think WE shall hop ON over there." and with those words the misshapen creature, with bat like ears, unrolled its long, angular legs, with backwards knees, onto the soft dirt. It's paws, all five ten-inch claws, four in the front and one in the back, hit the ground. The creature's feet made no mark except for five small holes made by the talons on the end of each claw.

They lilted through the graveyard, dirt mound, to grave stone, to mausoleum to dirt mound, with a grace and speed that did not match its ghastly exterior. All the while articulating a curious rhythm that sounded much like it's talking voice earlier. The light followed them zipping from stone to stone, bouncing with each third guttural tone the creature made, to the next grave, never touching the ground.

As suddenly as they had taken off, they stopped, the light bobbling around the top step of the mausoleum the creature was using as a hiding space. It was staring, with the yellow-green eyes of a cat, at a young man, humming a little known, and very ancient, folk tune.

This time the creature was so enthralled that they did indeed lose control of their bobbling blue light. It started buzzing around the mausoleum pillars, in and out, attracting the attention of the human walking along the path just outside the grave yard.

"What in the world?" The man said, staring confused at the blue ball spinning around and around faster than he could follow. He started walking slowly towards it, entranced. So entranced that he didn't see the strange creature slink back further into the shadows. He did however here the branch they snapped because they were staring at the man, like he was at their light.

"Is somebody there!?" He asked, arms up in a defensive position, scanning the shadows where he had heard the snap from. The creature slowly slid out of the shadows, except they no longer looked like a creature, but instead a comely, well dressed human being; still the creature's other worldliness shone, clothing, voice, features, all enraptured the young man.

"H-hello." He whispered, searching between, the now still light, and fair being walking slowly towards him.

The beautiful thing stopped short of bumping into him before reaching out a long, fair finger and touching the man's lips, his eyes wide with wonderment and a bit of fear.

"That tune?" The creature's now pale green eyes, flanked with long red lashes that matched their short fiery red hair, were searching his with an intensity that made him gulp and shudder before answering,

"I-I don't know the name." He answered quietly.

"Where did you hear it?"

"My grandmother."

The being slid all around him, examining him from head to toe. Poking him here and there. He just stood still rooted to the spot, never taking his eyes off of the being prodding him.

"Quite pretty I see. Does THE mind work AS well as THE body looks?"

With that question they reached up their hand to place it on the youth's head, but before they could finish the action the young man spoke, breaking the spell.

"Wait. Stop." He said, shaking from head to foot. "Just STOP!" The creature did just so.

"I'm sorry." They said hesitantly.

"Wha......who are you?" The lad asked awkwardly, stumbling his words between what and who.

They blinked three times, the third time more marked than the first two, much like their lilting speech.

"Bifrons, that's WHAT and who I am." Bifrons answered, swooping in a low bow gracefully in front of the lad who was now looking in open shock at Bifrons, as well as backing away ever so slowly.

"B-b-Bifrons??" He squeaked in disbelief and fear. "L-l-like the Solomon's Bifrons??" At the name "Solomon" Bifrons burst out in mirthful laughter, laughter that was exceptionally contagious. The boy relaxed and stopped moving backwards, next he started grinning foolishly and finally he joined in giggling with Bifrons gleeful cackling.

The blue light was also zigging around in a whirlwind as if it was joining in with their merriment.

Once they had all calmed down (the light needing some threats from Bifrons before doing so) the lad ventured to ask,

"Soo.....what's so funny about Solomon? Also....can you not do that weird sound when talking?" the lad asked, the last part while looking down at the ground. Bifrons smiled before leaning back against the graveyard stone wall, legs stretched and crossed, and arms behind their back.

"Oh, this idea that any of us demons are property of Solomon's." Bifrons answered easily and with a twinkle in their eye.

"But didn't he enslave 72 of you and use you for your powers?"

Bifrons replied "He enslaved us for a short period with the help of a powerful, but jealous demon. You know much more about such things than most your age..." he finished, eyeing the lad.

This time it was the young man's turn to laugh. "Well that's not exactly hard to do." He answered ruefully. Which humored Bifrons greatly.

"Oh yes lad? So...is the brain as good as the package?" Bifrons asked again, their long fingers twitching with anticipation. The youth noticed, and surprising himself with his boldness answered,

"I like to think it's better to be fair. Though I don't think too highly of the package...but you are free to...uh.... check I guess." He said gesturing towards Bifrons' hands, which were now hovering between the two of them. Bifrons quickly took the invitation and within a split second their hands were on his head. The feeling of what passed gave both of them chills, but by far Bifrons' experience was much more intense. They had to take several minutes of rest laying against the wall, eyes closed before they were back on their feet and talking again.

"My boy." Bifrons said right after they had jumped deftly back on their feet. "You may be wrong to undestimate your body, but you are not wrong that the brain is better."

He was blushing, every inch of him subject to the cold air was as red and hot as a summer's burn; Such high praise, from such a beautiful and powerful......demon. That last word shook him back down to, the ground, if not reality.

"And you are a demon....that is not controlled?"

"Yes, and you are a human, which many would argue is worse." Bifrons answered icily, sensing his tone. The lad however, lowered his eyes, his shoulders taking on an invisible, yet tangible weight, that seemed much too heavy for one as young as him.

"Fair point." He answered, his eyes hollow and sad.

"Is it extra bad in the human world right now?" Bifrons asked, the lad noting kindness in their voice.

"It's pretty rough right now. Things we thought were long in our past are still.....very present."

"Humans, though on a linear timeline like many of us in this physical realm, do have a tendency for cycles.... probably due to your spiritual pulls." Bifrons answered matter of factly. The lad sniffed, though he tried to hide it.

"Are you saying we're just in a bad cycle right now? And that it never changes?" He asked aghast. Bifrons eyed him up and down, noting his dejected, scared body language; things really were bad in the human world right now.

"No lad...." Bifrons paused "What is your name?"

"Err Brill." Brill answered awkwardly.

"Brill...I've heard worse. Every cycle, you humans seem to do a little to moderately better." Bifrons continued, sounding much like an eager college professor. "Occasionally with some extreme breakthroughs here and there. Cyclical, but rising we like to say in the Fae world."

"Fae....like, faries and such?" Brill asked, eyes narrowed.

"Solomon tried capturing fairies too." Bifrons laughed, "yes there are many other races in this realm besides humans. Though Fae live more in another spiritual realm that humans and demons don't get involved with as much. We're a little too.... carnally inclined to enter it very often, and never fully." Bifrons explained.

"You know, you seemed impressed with my brain.... but this is a lot of information to process....." Brill's eyes showed Bifrons he was clearly overwhelmed. They also realized that they had some work still needing done. Corpses weren't going to move themselves.

"How about you join me while I do my nightly duties, and I'll start from a better place for you and we can go from there." Bifrons asked, their hand out holding their little blue light who was making a buzzing sound that made Brill think of whining.

"That is if you want to of course." Bifrons added. Brill couldn't help smiling as the buzz coming from the light got significantly louder, and much whinier.

"I would like that." He answered and off they went through the graveyard, leading newly dead bodies from fresh graves to more seasoned graves (as Bifrons endearingly called them).

Brill learned so much that night with Bifrons, from the obvious, why did they move bodies from grave to grave (it was to help enrich the soil, surprisingly simple, though the sleepy corpses didn't agree when woken) He also learned about all sorts of herbs, including some pretty fun ones, as well as strongly medicinal. But what really blew his mind was the astrology and geometry, and the talks of other realms and other creatures, or as Bifrons called them, races; 'creatures' was rightfully offensive now. Eventually Brill noticed the horizon changing from deep blue black to lighter blue.

"Do you have to leave when the sun rises?" Brill asked.

"Alas, I need to venture into the woods or underground. My energy is spent, and I need the earth to recharge, as does my de-light-ful buddy." Bifrons watched Brill's shoulders droop with disappointment and smiled slightly.

"Would you.... like to come with me?" They asked brightly.

"W-w-with you??"

"Well, one thing I left out is HOW demons come about. There are different ways." Bifrons explained, "I myself.... I was human a long time ago."

"HUMAN?" Brill spluttered. "How!?"

"While demons do live much longer than humans, we don't live forever. Yet our jobs and rolls do....so demons choose different vessels, or races, to teach.... that's how our legions are made. Every once in a while, we come across someone special....and we can choose to personally teach and eventually, pass down the title to them, rather than having them trained as a lesser demon."

Brill was silent for a good five minutes, stunned to the spot but thinking wildly.

"Are you saying...you want ME to be your...err.... apprentice!?" He finally asked, the words thick in his dry mouth.

"Yes. Will you? The demon world needs minds like yours; what happens in our world echoes in yours. You can help my kind of demon take control. Knowledge should trump power as I've said many times tonight." Bifrons was begging, pleading. It was strange yet exhilarating for Brill to hear.

"Knowledge trumps power..." Brill said slowly, then looking Bifrons straight in the eye, smiling with resolve he answered,

"Well....we better get going then."

Then the three of them disappeared into the forest: demon, boy apprentice and silly blue light.

About the Author

Koi Garfield is a Transgender man who served in the Navy where he wrote his first book. He has always been an avid writer and reader as well as lover of culture and language.

V U A L A N D T H E T H R E E S O M E
C H A N N I E C O C K E R

Diana sat forlornly in her chair as the tears continued to trail down her face. Her heart ached and she was not sure she could handle the pain much longer. Chad and Ben had been best friends until she came along. Now they were the worst of enemies and she had lost both of them. There had to be a way to make things right again. She just didn't know how to go about it.

One of her friends had told her of someone or yet something that could help her with her problem. The only thing was that she had to summon this demon in order for it to help her. The idea of summoning a demon was a bit odd and kind of scary but her friend had assured her that it was worth it. So, Diana got all the necessary items she needed to summon this demon and did the ritual in her own living room. Now all she could do was sit and wait.

A sudden flash of light blinded her for a moment. When her eyes adjusted again she found a camel standing before her.

"What the hell?" she cried out.

"Aljahima? Nem, 'Aetaqid 'ana hdha daqiq. Wamae dhlk, laqad aistadeaynti, madha tarid?" the camel replied.

"Uh...I'm afraid I don't speak that language." Diana admitted reluctantly.

The camel took a few steps closer to her and spit in her face. Diana wiped her face off with a nearby towel and shouted,

"What the hell?!"

"You say that a lot, don't you?" he mocked.

"Wait, I can understand you now?" she asked.

"Yes, I took the liberty to give you the ability to understand Arabic. You are a bit of a dim wit aren't you?" he sneered as his upper lip rose, showing his teeth.

"I don't understand why you are insulting me," she whined.

"You know, never mind. Why have you summoned me?" he asked.

"Are you Vual?" she asked.

"Yes, dim wit. I am," he groaned impatiently.

"I need your help. My ex-boyfriends used to be best friends and are now enemies. I no longer have either of them for a boyfriend. And to be honest, I care for both of them and just don't know what to do about it." Diana batted her eyes and pouted her lips. Her attempt to be cute only annoyed Vual.

"This is an easy fix. Are you willing to pay the price?" he asked. The sooner he got this over with the better.

"Yes! Whatever it is, I'll pay it," she replied eagerly.

Humans were always so eager to get what they wanted. It was easier than ever these days. No one seemed to care about their soul anymore. If only they knew just how important their souls truly were. He procured a contract from thin air and handed it over to Diana to sign.

"I don't have a pen," she frowned.

"You don't use a pen. It's a blood contract. Here, allow me," he offered. He transformed before her into a human form which was way better looking than the camel he was before. Then he took one of his talons and pricked the tip of her finger.

"Ouch!" she whined.

"Oh, shut up, you baby. Sign it if you want my help," Vual commanded.

Whimpering from the pain she took her now bleeding fingertip and signed her name on the contract. It dissipated before her eyes right after she signed it. She looked up at Vual with questioning eyes. He snapped his fingers and smiled.

"The deed is done. Enjoy your time on this earth while you can. I'll be collecting your soul in due time," he jeered. His mocking laugh lingered behind him as his form faded before her.

The doorbell rang, bringing her out of her shocked state. Diana walked over to the door and opened it to find two smiling men looking longingly at her.

"Chad? Ben?" she asked.

"Hi Babe!" Ben greeted. "Isn't she just a sight for sore eyes, Chad?"

"Indeed, she is. I can't wait to go to town on her!" Chad declared.

"Mmmhmm! Shall I take the back or the front?" Ben asked as he licked his lips.

"Oh, that's a hard choice. I think I'll ram her in the back. You can pound her pussy first." Chad punched Ben in the shoulder.

Diana was at a loss for words. Here were her two ex-boyfriends standing before her and appearing to be the best of friends again. And they were talking about fucking her at the same time? She had never considered this before and had to admit that it was very appealing. The men entered the house without invitation. Chad walked around behind Diana and grabbed her shoulders as he rubbed his hard cock against her ass. Ben shut and locked the door behind him then came up to her front and pressed his hard erection against her now wet pussy. The men pressed harder against her, causing her to moan.

Chad leaned down and planted kisses along Diana's neck then nibbled her ear. He removed her shirt and was undoing her bra when Ben leaned in and kissed her hard on the mouth. He reached down and pulled Diana's pants and soaked panties down with one swift motion.

She stood there completely naked before them as they both pulled away from her for a minute to toss of their own clothing. Chad came back up behind her and pulled her head back by cupping her chin. As he kissed her he parted her thighs and held them open so Ben could taste of her flowing juices. She moaned in ecstasy as his tongue delved further into her mound and taunted her clit. Chad continued to kiss her hard as he cupped her breasts and fondled her nipples. She had never felt such bliss in her life as they continued to pleasure her.

"Ready, Ben?" Chad asked huskily.

"Let's do it," Ben replied breathlessly.

Chad continued to hold Diana in place with her thighs spread apart as Ben stood up. Ben inserted his long cock into her throbbing pussy and started going in and out slowly at first. He picked up the pace and pushed in harder. Just when Diana thought she could not handle more, Chad entered her pussy from behind. Both men gyrated in and out as hard and deep as they could, causing Diana to gasp in both pain and pleasure.

Chad pulled out of her mound and entered her anal canal softly. Once inside he moved faster and harder. Diana had never done anal before and was not ready for the intense pleasure it gave her. Both men's hands were all over her body as they held her steady and hit her like a jack hammer from front and behind. She thought she had entered heaven as they continued to bring her to the brink of ecstasy.

"I hope this was worth your soul," Chad whispered into her ear.

"Mere hours' worth of pleasure from both of us. Is it worth it?" Ben asked as his eyes glazed over.

Chad reached down and bit into Diana's neck as Ben pulled out, fell to his knees, and sunk his teeth deep into her mound.

"What the hell?!" Diana shrieked as they devoured her and her soul shot straight into the depths of hell.

About the Author

Channie Cocker is a Steamy Romance/Erotica author who loves to explore the naughty realms of writing.

48

HAAGENTI: TRICKS OF THE
TRADE

J. BECK

**"Ladies and gentlemen, may I now present the
man you have all been waiting for, the one, the
only, the Great Haagenti!"**
The reaction of the crowd always amused me. They come,
expecting to see some wonderful man perform illusions, fall silent
upon seeing me, and leave believing magic must exist. Of course,
they're right- it absolutely exists. They just can't use it the way I
can.

Once the applause died, I began my show. I had to the trouble of
learning some human illusions to supplement my show and my
product line and opened with the Pimpernel Queen trick. After that
concluded, I had the gentleman sign the card, burned it, then
produced it from his collar. These people had paid $400 to see me
play, and I was not going to disappoint them. I proceeded then with
a few other simple illusions, concluding the initial bit by pulling a
rabbit out of my hat- a baseball cap. This brought a few laughs.
What silenced them is when I pulled a top hat out of the rabbit.
Quickly chanting in the Old Tongue, I captured their attention with
the hat and proceeded to pull out three pieces of lead. Fortunately,
there was a jeweler in the audience who could verify that they were,
in fact, lead for the audience. I asked him to hold on to them for a
while and bade him take his seat. My assistant brought out two
glasses, one full of water. I changed it into wine while pouring it
into the other glass, then back into water when I returned it. One
audience member was a little zealous and asked to taste-test it, so I
repeated the magic and sent him stumbling back to his seat. My
wine has as much alcohol as I want in it. Once the audience had
stopped laughing, I called the jeweler back up and asked for my gold

back. He asked if I meant lead, and I replied that he should look for himself. As always, three pieces of gold came out of his pocket. I let him keep one for being a good sport about it, as he did return all three to me. To conclude the show, I had my assistant saw me in half, and then I walked off the stage in two pieces, reassembled myself, and took a bow.

Three weeks after this show, I'm on Oprah proving that I can do magic without the fancy stage setup. Then I'm off to Ellen, The Late Show, and countless others. I won the million-dollar prize for actually doing a magic trick on live television with all of their fancy sensors on the table. I was an overnight millionaire. Life in the mortal realm was getting to be pretty nice, since I didn't need to eat or drink anything.

All of that changed on the fifty-year anniversary of my summoning. I learned that my conjurer had died, and as such, I could no longer stay in this world. I'm sure the TMZ crew following me got a nice shot when I was swept away by the fire that brought me here. I learned that hell hadn't changed much since I left-Asmoday was still a rock somewhere in Israel, Andras was still butchering the people who summoned him, and so on. I resigned myself to waiting for another to take my name and call me forth.

I didn't have to wait long. Upon my arrival in the circle, in my proper form, I saw a group of five terrified teenagers. Once I had convinced them that I was, in fact, the Haagenti they knew from the magic shows, they asked me to teach them my ways of magic. I asked their names and promised to teach them my ways as apprentices. However, I swore them to silence as to who their Master was, as news of my return would certainly raise a stir in the world. I started simple- carnival card tricks and such, things that would be easy for them to do at a friend's party to help get them some notoriety. I never taught all of them the same tricks, so there was always a stir when they did something new in front of the others. All of them were approached for tours with carnivals and as opening acts for other magicians. One of them decided to stay with me and continue to learn, saying that he wished to practice his skills until he rivaled me. The boy's attitude towards learning impressed me, and I redoubled my teaching of him, including a little on the nature of magic.

This boy has shown himself a very quick student. Once he learned the core nature of my magic, he tested it with levitation and found that he could, in fact, hover about two inches off the ground. Excited, I began to teach him about the other subjects- control of the elements, alchemy, healing, compulsions, the boy soaked it in like a sponge and always asked for more. His friends had become famous without him and had asked him to rejoin them. I told him that he should go before he became too old to enjoy the fruits of his studies, and that I would be available should he summon me. I did ask him for one favor though- to have all five of them together again to meet with me before leaving for their next tour.

The faces I saw were not the four I remembered. Where once they were youthful, now they were worn from travel and experience, flushed with wealth and fame. Gone were the jeans and t-shirts of their youth. All wore suits of some kind, with all manner of gadgets to facilitate their illusions. I asked all of them to do me one favor- to invoke my name in all of their shows, and to say who taught them their magic. I told them that no one would think they were actually serious about summoning a dead man to teach them his ways, so they were perfectly safe from actual harm, but that it would add to their show immensely. All five saw no harm in it, but only one saw the reality of it.

On their first performance of the tour, all five did say that I had taught them. I had been gone for ten years when they summoned me, so only a few in the crowd knew my name. One of them heckled my pupils about it, and my favorite student said to ask me himself. He spoke my name, my true name, while on the stage, and I appeared in my human form, bowed, and walked off to another stunned crowd. It was good to be back.

About the Author

J. Beck is a new author with a passion for history, music, and fantasy gaming.

49

CROCELL AND THE FALL OF ATLANTIS
CHASITY GAINES

Dusty and dirty from my long travels, I wandered through the various villages hoping my sphere that drew water from deep within the ground would help each poor village have access to clean water and a new way to keep their crops watered during the dry season. However, many laughed, and others cursed me as a thief, stealing from Mother Earth. I barely escaped a few of those villages with my life. I was a man of philosophy and rationale sciences, two lowly subjects mocked and jeered as old men's hobbies. Others associated these with sorcery and bad things always happened when one of their kind were around. Many men like myself were drowned, beaten, or worse castrated and sent to serve the tribal king.

A life of servitude was no life at all, but some would argue that everyone's life is bound in servitude to someone. I would rather die than serve the tribal king who gathered wealth as others starved or died from illness. Tired and looking for a place to rest and recover from my travails, I drifted off through the dense trees and headed deep within the forest. The sun dared not show his face in this shaded world of shadowy greens and muddy browns of the forest floor. My boots squelched through the muck with each step. The forest had become quite upon my arrival. It was like the forest held its breath waiting and hoping I would make a hasty exit.

I wondered if I should keep walking and wait to make camp on the outside of the edge of the discomforted forest, but I was running low on water and my feet begged for a break. I found a copse of white-barked trees with large leaves to keep me dry in case of rain. I started off to the left of the odd gathered trees to collect fallen twigs for a small fire to warm the strips of dried fish. I hoped to find some wild potatoes or at least some sprigs of rosemary to season the fish as I collected the wood.

I noticed the air started to feel cooler, when suddenly I came upon a cloaked stranger sitting on a fallen tree as he or she seemed to be waiting on me. I took hesitate steps toward the stranger, scared of what I might find.

"Hiyo friend, I can see that you are weary from your dusty travels and in need of a refreshing bath," the stranger's voice melodious and most certainly male. He kept his face hooded but I could feel his eyes diving into my soul.

"Aye," I answered back. "I am indeed in need of replenishment and a much-needed bath," I replied back bodily as sore muscles screamed for relief louder than the bad feeling gnawing my gut.

The stranger stood erect and stretched his legs before he walked by me motioning for me to follow. I could hear the faint sound of water falling and crashing lightly on rocks below. I walked behind the cloaked figure following him closer to the sound of crashing water. A small waterfall poured into a bowl-shaped pool hid behind a gigantic rock a few steps behind the bushy white trees.

"There friend, a warm pool to wash away the problems of your day," he swept his hand across the beauty of greens, blues, and whites of Mother Nature's bounty.

The stranger sat on a stump focused on a mushroom growing in front of him. Ignoring him, I stripped out of my threadbare clothing standing naked as the day I was born. I ran down the embankment to the swirling pool. I walked to the dark rippling water and walked slowly into the surprisingly warm liquid. I submerged myself in the relaxing water, coming up to take a few slow back strokes before finding a flat rock perfect for sitting on. I laid on the rock as water lapped my tired body allowing my mind to wander to an absolutely magnificent place. A city known for learning, accepting of any and all scholars. Building a perfect world on futuristic ideas, a civilization like no other. A place where I could fit in and find my place in the higher status of society.

The stranger's light voice woke me from my utopian dream. "That which you dream can become reality. A reality where you will want for nothing. No more hoping the next rustic village will welcome you with open arms, only to be chased away with pitchforks and torches."

Looking into the clear blue sky, I contemplated the actuality of this place's existence and if even such a learned tribe wouldn't laugh me out of their golden city. I finally answered my new friend, "I am sure there is something in it for you to direct me to perfect place, isn't there, my dear new friend?" I cut my eyes up at him for a glimpse of his face, but he has turned his back on me.

"Certainly, good sire, you would not deprive a poor man of a small prize for such revelations?" He questioned playfully.

His response made me chuckle and I started thinking I had nothing to lose in making the deal. "So, what is it that you are asking for in return for such valuable information dear man?" I played his game. A question for a question. He was toying with me, for no man of honor would deal this way if he wanted to keep his reputation intact.

"Why that which is least important to you, my new friend," he squeaked as he patted my back as I finished drying my hair.

That could be a number of things I thought to myself. Maybe he would take that broken cup my mother had used in tribal rituals. I just knew she haunted me through it. Why not make the deal? But I wanted to see the man I was making a deal with, I started thinking, as we both walked through the long grasses back to the white barked trees.

"Show me yourself and you have yourself a deal I will shake on." Speaking boldly to the cloaked man I turned to the stranger and tried to look him in the eyes but his face was downcast.

"You may not like what you see but our deal was struck as soon as you accepted my hospitality," the stranger's voice menacing and cold.

Before I could respond, the covered stranger ripped his cloak off revealing a blinding bright light that blurred the edges of the stranger's body. Eyes slanted, peering through the bright rays, I made out the profile of a pair of large black wings attached to the back of the shimmery stranger.

"An Angel cast down on Earth to help find those deserving enough of our Father's eternal love. I have many names but Procel is the one you may call me by. Now let us away to the dreamland of yours so that we both may be on our way," the angel's voice loud but pleasing to the ear like a sweet song.

No time had passed as we came upon a city abuzz with activity and such a beautiful city it was that I knelt on the golden streets and wept tears of such joy and happiness. I finally remembered Procel and stood dusting myself off to thank him and find out what he wanted in return. I find that he has disappeared within the thousands of peoples walking the ports and moving goods in and out of the city.

I worked close with the governing body of Atlantis to figure out how to keep the ever-growing poor fed during the recent droughts. Atlantis was covered on all sides by water, but they depended on the crops growing in their neighboring villages that owed their allegiance to Atlantis to keep them safe from invaders and fed. The drought was the worst one in history and the people were on the verge of protesting.

My creation helped Atlantis' drought issue by being able to water whole crops even with no rain. My invention was able to find water under the ground and used that to water the crops. A simple enough idea and a real revolution. We found that we could grow more food and have fresh water where one might need it. Soon I was making more ubez than I could spend.

The city offered a variety in the arts and I purchased sculptures, mosaics, paintings, and any written words I could obtain. There was music-- such sounds that filled the whole body with vibrations of the happiest feelings and those of the saddest I've ever heard. Atlantis had access to the most futuristic technology in health, astronomy, aerodynamics, astrophysics, and something extremely controversial called quantum physics.

I started a new life in Atlantis having the funds to live a life of luxury, I had everything I could ever want or need. I found an intelligent and beautiful Atlantean woman to settle down with. We tried several times for children and ended up with a girl which is nothing to frown on in Atlantis, but I had to face it, I wasn't an Atlantean and I didn't feel comfortable leaving a female as my heir.

My daughter was pampered as the princess of the house. Even though I had desperately wanted a boy, I loved Miesha and doted on her. She was a beautiful child with a laughter that could light up a person's whole day and she grew into an enchanting young woman. After she was older, she liked to help the more disadvantaged people by having small auctions selling her old dresses, toys, and whatever my money had bought for her that she had grown out of. It didn't bother me since she was trying to help those less fortunate. Though it bothered me that she would often go unattended and the people were becoming more riled up by the moment the way the priests carried on about the "end of days."

I walked through the airy door of my sprawling home. The rooms had small windows allowing the wind to whip a fresh breeze into the red-clay colored rooms. The fountain outside, an angel, spouted water into a small bowl. Fresh herbs gave the room a fresh smell. I stretched out on the silk-covered chaise letting the day's events run through my mind noticing a detail here or there that I missed before. I was sure Atlantis would pull through the harrowing stories the various spies uncovered at a breakneck pace.

Different oracles saw the destruction of this magnificent city and with it all its knowledge and technology. One predicted that fire would swoop through and turn all to ashes. Another said the city would be swallowed by Poseidon's watery revenge and sink to the bottom of the ocean floor. Never to be found. I didn't believe a single one of those drug induced hags. However, I worried that society would be the end of Atlantis. This perfect place had become home to crime, greed, dishonor, and selfishness, that I hardly recognized the city I had come to call home for many years.

My eyes shuttered close as my mind ran away with wild thoughts. A red light flickered behind my eyelids while my body tingled with warmth.

"I hate to interrupt, old friend, but it is time to pay up," the angel's cheery voice startled me.

I opened my eyes to find him standing in all his golden glory right in front of me. Getting to my feet, I reached out to take Procel's shoulder, but he had disappeared.

About that time, My wife's terror-filled screams echoed throughout the open courtyard. I darted across the path to see my wife slumped over a slender body. Reaching for my wife, I noticed the dress Miesha had been wearing earlier. A deep blue dyed silk to match the color of her eyes. Now discolored by a spreading red dye. No, not dye, but red blood. My daughter's lifeforce spilled by my eagerly made contract for a city headed for destruction. A year later Atlantis sank into the dark ocean. Everything lost. So much knowledge. And my life.

About the Author

Chasity Gaines is a multi-genre author and poet. She loves painting a picture with her words.
Follow her at https://www.facebook.com/ChasityGainesWriter/

50

FURCAS AND THE FORTUNE TELLER
P.S. HARRIS

Cretia closed her small shop with a sigh. Things had not been going well. When she first started this business, she truly thought she had a gift. Several of her customers had returned after her predictions came true. Lately, all she'd been telling people were generic lies that most fortune tellers learned right off the start. It was a con game after all. Her Mother and Grandmother had been in the business as well. Sadly, since they died, she couldn't seem to find her own path. She couldn't see the future of anyone, much less herself.

Being born and raised in this life, she knew no other way to live, her only income was the few candles and herbs she had managed to sell from her dwindling stock. With another sigh she went through the curtain that separated the shop from her living quarters. Immediately, feeling a chill, she went to the small wood potbellied stove that doubled as her only heating source and a cooking stove, and put her last log on the fire. Opening her last can of soup, she poured it into the small copper pot she kept hanging on the wall. Waiting for the top of the stove to heat she wondered what the future held.

Cretia, Cretia... The flames seemed to be whispering her name. Opening the small door that revealed the fire Cretia peered inside. There seemed to be a shape of an old man forming in the flames. Slamming the door shut in fear, she ran to the other side of the room. I'm just tired and hungry. She gave a nervous giggle and walked back over to the stove.

Cretia, Cretia... There it is again. The voice was louder this time. Her curiosity getting the better of her Cretia slowly opened the stove door again.

This time there was no shape in the flames. This time a cloud of smoke came from the oven and formed a burly old man with a headful of long white hair. His white full beard reached to his waist. He was dressed in black and his right hand was holding a pitchfork.

Cretia fell back into the only chair into the house. Her legs felt like rubber. Her head was spinning. Was this a dream? "What, who, are you?" Her voice sounding weak and trembly. She felt bolted to the chair, unable to move.

"Cretia" A deep voice resounded the room. "I am Furcas, do not be frightened. I will not harm you. I am the Knight of Hell and we need you.

"Hell?" Cretia's voice was still trembly. "I have never called any Knight from Hell, I don't worship demons. I am good. I'm not selling my soul to you. I can find a regular job or go to work on one of those psychic hotlines. I don't want any demon help."

"Your soul is safe Cretia" The loud voice seemed to come from everywhere. "We need you. You have a powerful gift and the fate of the world depends on you." Furcas seemed to be floating, his feet and legs turning into wisps of smoke.

"My abilities have faded," Cretia replied, "I think you have the wrong person." No longer afraid, in fact feeling strangely at peace. "I no longer have customers. No one believes in my gift anymore."

"We are never wrong. We must hurry. I haven't much time here." Furcas floated closer to Cretia leaving wisps of smoke in his wake. "Your gift is still in you, you must believe in yourself. His voice seemed to be getting weaker. "You will be needed in the future, you will know when. The fate of the world depends on your ability to believe in your gift. You must believe this." He raised his pitchfork and shot a bolt of lightning into the fire. "I leave you with my seal, Cretia. From this time forward follow the path of the flames. They will lead you to the truth."

Cretia woke with a start to the smell of burning soup. The stove door was open, and the log had turned to ashes. She could already feel the room getting colder as the last of the embers struggled to stay alive. She sighed again. I'm going to have to burn my books.

Getting up, Cretia walked over to the small stack of books, her heart was heavy at the thought of having to burn even one of prized possessions. The bookcase had been burned a while back as well as her table. The only things left was the rolltop desk left to her by her mother that held the few potions and herbs she had left, and the wing-back chair she had just awoken from.

Reaching down she grabbed a book at random. It doesn't matter, they are all going to have to go. Then what? I have no money, I have no food, I will be forced to sell my shop. The tears were starting to form in her eyes and she angrily brushed them away. "I can do this" she said out loud.

Turning around to put her beloved book on the fire she reached down to open the door. Hold on! This door was open. It was then she noticed the circle on the outside of her stove. It had strange symbols inside a double circle, the letters F U R C A S, between the two circles. "Furcas," reading the letters Cretia felt the energy tingling through her body. The energy that she forgot she possessed. Opening the stove door, a feeling of peace came over her as she saw the pile of firewood stacked proudly waiting to be lit.

Looking around the room in disbelief she discovered she had obtained a huge feather pillow top bed, a pile of firewood stacked in the corner and best of all her cupboards were laden with her favorite foods.

Joyfully she went through the curtain to her shop and found there too, her shelves fully stocked and ready for customers. Cretia sighed one last time. This time it was a sigh of relief.

About the Author

P.S. Harris is a sci/fi fantasy writer with her first novel out now. Watch for the sequel coming 2019. Author page

https://www.facebook.com/psharrisauthor/

51

BALAM: DEATH OF A DEMON
JEFF DUCKER

Balam did as he always did. Well, if there were such a
thing as days here. Nobody knew. Nobody ever would know.
Anyway, he strolled the grounds of his section of Hell, keeping a
close watch on his servants. There could be no slackers. Anyone that
disappointed got the worse punishment. Death? No, this was already
Hell, death is not a thing anymore. His servants were those who
were sent there for their eternity. He was strict on his servants.
Except strict was putting it lightly. Disappointing or angering him
was just not an option. Oh, and about that ones that did. The
punishment? He ate them. No, he devoured them. And it was
apparent that they felt pain, because they screamed the whole way
down.

"Keep working you worthless, imbecilic, pathetic servants of
mine," he would always be yelling at them.

"I do not even want to see you blink," he would demand. "I
would tear you all apart right now and eat you, but then I would
have to do all this work myself."

Now you are probably wondering what kind of work they did,
right? Well, their main job was to keep his fires going. The manual
way. They had to chop, split, and carry wood. Now, of course, he
could very well keep his own fires going with his powers. But, to
him, there was no fun in that. Although, especially lately, he argued
with himself about that. Each of his parts, I suppose you could say.
They did not always get along and agreed. In fact, the arguing and
fighting was getting worse. He recently even managed to set himself
on fire. Not that it actually hurt him or anything.

"Show some life, you heathens," he growled at them all. "Ha ha
ha, that's right, you have no life in you."

Yes, he loved to taunt them too. And insult them in any way he
could. Every so often, one or two of them would try to run away,
but there was nowhere for them to go. There were no exits or

entrances. They were stuck there. Even hiding from Balam was not an option. He knew his dark section of Hell inside and out. There was absolutely no fooling him. No way.

One of favorite means of torture was to drive them crazy. For example he would take form as someone they loved while they were alive and pretend to have come for them, telling them they were there by mistake. But then he would form as himself. They would always lose their minds. Well, technically, they have no minds. But he liked to make them think they did.

Very few of them have even made attempts at fighting. Like actually trying to hit him. He actually did not eat them. He supposed that was just what they wanted. So, instead he ripped an arm off each of them, and now they had to work with only one arm. Most of them were smart enough to just work in silence, and not upset him. They knew they had no other choice. Some have been known to whisper plans to others about plans of trying to put a stop to him. But Balam could hear whispers too. There was just no getting anything passed him. Nothing would ever work, Nothing was worth even attempting.

Now he doesn't only own humans that are sent there. He also has much more than 40 legion of demons. They however are not his slaves. As long as they agree to do his other bidding. His demons al refer to him as king. He would make his human servants call him king, but he did not give them privilege of speaking. If they spoke that was worth the ultimate punishment as well. And, of course, he had ran into problems with his demons as well. Some wanted to give him what they called their "suggestions", which he did not tolerate. To him it was their way of trying to takeover, and he would never allow that. Some down right made it clear that they wanted to take his place and be over him. A very big mistake on their part. One time, some of them came together and tried to gang up and over power him. He destroyed them easily. But then he recreated them and put in their minds that they were under him and he was their king.

Now, remember I told you that Balam had been having quite a lot of fights with himself? Well little did he know that he was becoming his own worst enemy. He did not realize he was losing this fight, because he never lost anything. The arguing and disagreeing was getting worse than he would ever admit. He also took this aggravation out on his servants. But as much as he denied it something was changing inside him, and he did not like the feeling of it. But stil,l he would never believe that he was losing control, and by the time he did believe it, it would already be too late. He knew he could not be defeated by any of his demons or servants, but he did not know that was about to be defeated by himself. And when that happened, he would never be in control of anything again. Although, that did not mean anything would change in his part of Hell. One of his demons would likely end up taking over. Even they all fought it out to determine who did.

The arguing between Balam's three parts continued on. It was quickly becoming so he could not do anything about it no matter how hard he tried. They argued endlessly over what else the servants should do. What other punishments they should endure, and that they should be punished on a daily basis. Again, if there were even such things as days here. Each one was yelling at the others about what should go on and how the others were wrong. And then it happened, the three of them drew swords and cut and slashed each other and then Balam ceased to exist.

About the Author

Jeff lives in Georgia and has been writing anthologies before he wrote his First novel, but he has a poetry book out called : Beside Still Waters. Jeff want to write his first novel this year.

52

ALLOCES AND THE IMPOSSIBLE MISSION
P.S. HARRIS

Alloces sat mounted on his enormous horse overlooking his thirty-six legion. He was proud of his team. After completing several important missions, they were quickly becoming the team to go to for the difficult tasks. Sure, other demons had more, but none had trained as his team had.

They were ready for anything. Except this next mission. They were going to have to work as one. They couldn't afford to make any mistakes. Shifting his weight, he turned his huge horse to face the group.

"Everyone" Alloces voice boomed across the room. Out of respect and terror all thirty-six-legion stopped what they were doing and faced front and center. "I have been to see Hades, we have a new important and dangerous mission." Pausing a minute for the chatter to die down, he hopped down off his horse and went to the head of the long table.

"Everyone sit, we are going to be here for a while. This plan has to be perfect." Alloces waited for his human slave to pull out the chair for him. He flung his huge, heavy cape at the slave and sat down on his throne with great flair.

Waiting for his legion to take their seats he thought about what Hades had said. "The rumor going around is the Gods have found a new heaven and a new earth. How could they have discovered this first! You better find this place and shut it down!" There was more ass-chewing and he tried to pay attention, but Hades had a way of making you feel like you were in a dream. Not to mention he could turn you to ashes on a whim. This is impossible. How can we possibly find this new heaven and new earth? Our top scientist have been searching the skies for millennium without finding habitable environment for both humans and the spirit world. He looked up to see everyone staring at him with expectant eyes.

"Ok" Alloces, cleared his throat, still shaken by his memory. "Our mission is to find the new heaven and new earth."

"What?", "new heaven and earth?", "This is impossible" the voices all came at him at once.

"I understand, you all have questions, so do I. Unfortunately, I don't have all the answers." Alloces said this with his most demanding voice. "The rumors are out there; a new heaven and earth have been located. We need to find out where it is and destroy it. That's our mission. We cannot allow the gods to take the humans and disappear. Hades has spoken."

"I don't understand how this could happen. We've controlled the top astrophysicist and astrologists in their search for a new home. No one knows the skies more than we do. The only explanation is the gods have actually managed to create a new heaven and earth." Alloces paused and banged his large fist on the table. The sound echoed throughout the now silent room.

"We will no longer exist without the gods and the humans." Alloces continued, his voice softening with this last statement. Looking around the big wooden table, the usual animated and excited faces were fill with dread and fear.

There was only one thing that could frighten a demon and that was non-existence. Since no demon had ever come back from that status, there was no way to know what evils it held. Even Hades did not know that answer. He'd sent plenty, in his fits of rage, but he had no idea where exactly they went.

"If the gods have created this new place, we must find it, and soon. Things are not going well on earth and any moment now everything could be destroyed." Alloces signaled to his slave for a drink. After taking a huge gulp, he continued. "Most of Hades demons are already on earth creating chaos, political unrest, and dissent amongst the humans. There are wars and earthquakes and unprecedented storms. The humans are becoming paranoid and living in fear, just as we want."

Looking around he saw his legion all nodding in agreement. They were aware of their legion counterparts' missions. Hades had implemented his takeover plan quite some time ago and all of hell was involved. There weren't too many places you could go without hearing talk of this huge successful takeover.

They had not planned on this though. So far, they had managed to outwit the gods by using the humans, turning them against the gods and promising them fame and fortune. Many now placed within the heads of countries their followers of hate growing daily. This was different. If the gods manage to whisk away their deserving humans to a new heaven and a new earth there would be no evil allowed. This earth would be destroyed, and they would all perish.

Alloces shuddered at the thought. He could not even imagine the horrors that could await him. Some say you burn forever, some say you live your worst nightmares. Living in hell was bad enough. He had a position of power and he still suffered in this environment.

"Does anyone have any ideas?" Alloces needed to move this along, they were running out of time. No-one said a word. "This is our mission, its either try or die right now guys. If we are going to perish, we are at least going to go out fighting."

"If there is a new earth and a new heaven out there do you think the humans will discover it?" One of the legions spoke up finally.

"We are hoping so." Alloces stood up and with a wave brought up the known universe. The stars and moons sparkled brightly around the room appearing as if they had all just entered the vast space that is the cosmos. "This is what we know so far. We don't think the gods would be capable of hiding it anywhere in this universe without taking the chance that we could find it. We need to find a way to search outside this creation. We don't think the humans are advancing fast enough to search that far."

"You will all need to push your scientists to the limit. They will need your inspiration and guidance." Alloces instructed, as he pointed to the stars for effect. "They must search where no one has gone before. We will go further than we've been before. Many will sacrifice, but we will find this new heaven and new earth. We must motivate and cultivate the greatest human minds to not stop their searches until it is found."

Cheers went up around the room at this rousing speech given by their beloved Alloces. A standing ovation soon followed as Alloces bowed and waved to his adoring admirers.

"We will not fail you, Master." The legions spoke as one.

About the Author

P.S. Harris is a sci/fi fantasy writer with her first novel out now. Watch for the sequel coming 2019. Author page

https://www.facebook.com/psharrisauthor/

53

CAIM: THE DISPUTER
C.L. WILLIAMS

Donovan stood tall as he claimed to have told truth to everyone who would listen. He would tell everyone what he speaks is the truth, and only the truth, and that no one can argue against him. Donovan would soon find out that he would have a challenger unlike any other challenger. One that would change his life forever.

"Many of you have tried to put an argument against me," Donovan says, as he begins one of his legendary monologues that last longer than they should. "But here I am still standing tall, above all of you peasants, speaking truth. I speak the truth that none of you can accept but you know in your heart of hearts that you can never beat me in a war of words." Donovan then stands on a pile of branches and limbs. "Even though I know the answer, is there a challenger out there that can prove my words wrong and go toe to toe with me in a war of words?" Donovan asks as he looks through the audience, seeing if he will meet a worthy opponent.

"I will stand up to you. I am honestly tired of your words, and I know I can beat you at your own game. I've been known to love a good argument," says a man emerging from the shadows, holding a sword.

"Look at what we have here!" Donovan says with a loud laughter. "We have someone who plans to stab me because he knows he is a sore loser and will be unsuccessful in a battle of words against me!" Donovan says as he resumes his laughter.

"You say that now but what you don't realize is my sword will not be covered in your blood. I want your soul if I win, not your blood," the man from the shadows says as he makes his way to Donovan.

"FINE!" The arrogant Donovan replies, "My soul if you win. Even though it won't matter in the end. I guess you should tell the peasants your name."

"My name was Cain," the man with the sword says. He then walks over to a pile of coal sitting on the ground. Within seconds, he now has the coals burning and proceeds to stand on top of them. He places the sword on the ground and then tells Donovan he knows why he understands the songs of birds. Donovan, who was once quite arrogant prior to Cain's arrival, is now unable to speak. The usual sharp-tongued man is now at a loss of words and everyone is noticing it on the first round of the argument. Hesitant of what to do next, Donovan decides to play it off, make it look like he's purposely taking a loss to avoid the potential humiliation of losing in the very beginning of the argument.

"I think I've been quite harsh to those who have lost to me over the years, I'm going to be nice this one time and let you have this victory. No need to thank me. Just promise you won't stab me with that sword once you lose." Donovan says as he tries to make it look like he's purposely taking a loss.

"I already told you, I don't want your blood. I told you that I want your soul and I'm one argument away from taking what will soon be rightfully mine," a now angered Cain says as he responds to Donovan's obvious lies.

Cain then asks Donovan if he knows and understands why dogs bark. Donovan, now uncertain of what to say, chooses to speak nonsense. "Obviously, because they are hungry or want attention." Donovan is now beginning to perspire as he knows his answer is not deep enough for the mysterious Cain.

"YOU IGNORANT FOOL!" Cain screams at Donovan as he makes his way towards Donovan. As for Donovan, he feels that he only lost his pride as he knows no one is coming for his soul. However, Cain's remarks put a lump in Donovan's throat.

As Cain is walking over towards Donovan, Cain is transforming from a man with a sword to a raven-like creature. He grabs Donovan and everyone who remained to watch the argument saw what could only be described as the life force being drained from Donovan by Cain. Cain then responds with a monologue of his own, now speaking in a demonic voice and in his raven-like state. "How could an ignorant human like you beat a president of Hell like me!" Cain then lets out a laugh that scares off the audience that was once proud to stand there. "I am Caim, President of Hell, ruler of 30 legions of spirits! I knew I would beat you the second I saw your pathetic human face. I will now take the one thing I asked of from you, your soul. You will live an eternity in Hell, right where you belong!" Cain, now revealed as Caim, lets out a demonic laugh as Donovan's soul leaves his body and enters the deepest, darkest realms of Hell. Caim looks around him to see that everyone who was once there as he argued with Donovan is now gone.

There was a crowd of people wanting to see the "speaker of truth" Donovan lose in a war of words. However, once Cain revealed himself to be the demon Caim, everyone left in fear. Afraid that they would also be condemned to Hell, just like Donovan. Seeing that no one is around, and no one will tell if they were present, Caim transforms back into Cain and continues his journey. The villagers never spoke of Donovan again, the fear of Caim was too great to say anything. They never saw Caim again, at least they don't think so, when Caim went back into human form, he took a different guise as he continued his journey. He is always looking for souls to condemn and has the knowledge to do so.

About the Author

C.L. Williams is an independent author from central Virginia. He is a writer of poetry, horror, romance, sci-fi, and has written several novellas and short stories

www.facebook.com/writer434

54

MURMUR RAISES THE DEAD,
AGAIN
P.S. HARRIS

Murmur adjusted his huge, important self on his griffin. He was ready to go, has been ready for days now. He hated the waiting the worst. He had a plan, he wanted to move on it immediately. His nearly two-hundred thousand demons under his command were prepped and ready.

He motioned for his two ministers to get in position, and raised his large arms as the signal to go. He heard the trumpets sounding as they galloped off onto the path.

This was one mission he was going to enjoy. There was nothing he liked better than a raising of the dead. He was one of the few in Hell that had the power to not only raise the dead, but have them speak the truth. Excited to finally be a part of Hades' plan, he was not going to fail this time.

Feeling the air rush by as they raced towards their destination, Murmur reached up and held his jeweled crown in place. It had been awhile since he had been sent to raise a dead soul and he could barely hold still in his excitement.

Not many opportunities came along for this chore. Most dead souls were in limbo until it was decided where they belonged. Many of the human souls that went to Hell were sent directly to the fire pits. Very few had the chance to live in Hell with the Demons and serve as their slaves.

Racing through the forest, with his legion following close behind, Murmur remembered the last soul he raised. That one didn't go so well. The soul came out of his grave in an angry fervor screaming and fleeing into the night. It rushed through the small, coastal town creating havoc in its wake. It took half his legion to contain the tortured soul, but not before it frightened half the town and took out several small buildings. The news later reported it as a tornado.

That's the way it went sometimes though, Murmur knew the risks. He enjoyed the risks. Lived for the risks. Sometimes the souls would come along peacefully answering any questions he might have. Other time's, most of the time, it seemed lately, they would rise from their graves in anger and destruction that was difficult to contain. It was exhilarating in the chase and containment.

After that, Hades put a leash on his soul rising until just recently. Now this one he was to bring to Hades for questioning. They couldn't let this soul get loose. Hades had been very clear on that point. Resurrect him and take him straight to Hell for questioning. A part of him wanted the challenge of a restless soul, but he knew this time he should be wishing for an easy capture. This time was too important.

Closing in on their destination Murmur felt the rush of anticipation increasing. Urging his griffin to pick up the speed, he soon could sense the smell of death as they closed in on the cemetery where the soul had been laid to rest. Aw, the smell of death, my favorite smell. The odor of rotting flesh and decay enveloped him like a perfume. He took several deep breaths in savoring the intoxicating aroma, it had been way too long since he had enjoyed this fragrance.

Motioning for his legion to stop, he hopped of his huge griffin with ease and began searching the small cemetery for the name Hades had instructed him to raise. Finding it easily enough he signaled for his legion to form a dome around the grave. Hopefully, when this soul was revived, they would be able to contain it. He did not want a repeat of the last incident.

Murmur positioned himself on his knees in front of the small, gray, gravestone and bowed his head in reverence. Standing he turned to his legion. "Are we ready?"

Hearing them agree in unison, he began his beloved ritual. "I command this soul to rise from the dirt and live again." The trumpets sounded, and his legion hummed in harmony. A large bolt of lightning came from the sky and struck the ground at his feet.

He stood in silence as he watched as ground part, and slowly a small, black, blob rose hovering a few feet off the ground. Murmur waited in silence. It would take a minute for the blob to create a form that they could communicate with. This part was the most critical. It was at this point most of the souls flew off in terror and rage. They were difficult to contain then also as they could not communicate and were fast and furious in their attempt to get away.

Watching warily as the blob began to take shape, appearing to be calm as it struggled to regain its life. Murmur had heard rumors that this part was quite painful for the souls, but none of them had ever remembered after they were fully formed. Since most of them were sent back to the ground after a questioning none of the Demons really cared enough to find out.

Finally, after what seemed an eternity the blob had transformed into human shadowy form and was standing there staring at Murmur.

"Aw," Murmur spoke softly, "You are alive, and calm it seems."

"Where am I?" The shadow asked, its voice wispy and soft. Floating higher until Murmur had to look up to see it.

Oh no, I hope it doesn't think it can float away. I'm glad I have my legion surrounding the area. Murmur motioned his legion to move in closer. "You have been resurrected from the dead, you are needed in Hell." Stretching his neck in the attempt to look the shadow in the face, "Could you come back down here? We mean you no harm. We have come to save your soul."

The shadow seemed to hesitate a moment then floated back down to the ground level. "I have been waiting for someone to come. What took you so long?"

About the Author

P.S. Harris is a sci/fi fantasy writer with her first novel out now. Watch for the sequel coming 2019. Author page
https://www.facebook.com/psharrisauthor/

55

OROBAS: THE RACE
M.L. GARZA

***They didn't believe him when their father
claimed to have caught a demon.*** After all, there was no
such thing. Mankind had no need of such a scapegoat when it was
perfectly capable of creating its own brand of cruelty.

So when Mr. Hill boasted to the boys that he had a true demon
of Hell locked away in the stable, Trystin and David figured he'd
been at the bottle again. Their horses might be wild at times, the
best racing horses were, but none of them were anything but mortal.

"I tell you it's true," their father insisted. "I summoned it. I
caught it. And now it's going to make us rich!"

"You probably caught Mr. Green's blind nag again," Trystin
grumbled, poking at the potatoes on his plate. "If you don't give it
back, he's really going to call the cops this time."

"Don't you think I know the difference between that old thing
and a bonafide demon?" their father scoffed. "Go see for yourselves
if you don't believe me."

Trystin opened his mouth to argue, but his elder brother jabbed
him in the ribs with his elbow. "Leave it," he hissed quietly. "We'll
just go return it after dinner."

One of these days it wasn't going to be enough to simply return
the old thing, but it wasn't worth arguing about. Their father was
determined to have his way, one way or another, and if he brought
down the family business in his delusions, then so be it.

Hill Stables had produced the best racing horses in the county
for the past twenty years before old Robert began to go a little
funny. There wasn't a beast alive that could outrun a horse born
beneath his roof. These days, however, people considered his wild
claims to come more from the bottle than fact.

Sometimes his own sons wondered if it weren't true.

Therefore, it was with annoyance and nostalgia for better times
that the boys finished dinner and traipsed out to the old stables to

see just what their father had locked up. Hopefully the neighbors wouldn't be too cross with them for it. After all, he couldn't help it sometimes.

It was David, the eldest, who swung open the barn door with a heavy sigh. "Look, Trystin, it's time we finally had a real talk about Dad."

His brother scowled but nodded. It couldn't be put off any longer, much as he would have liked. It was better when this was funny instead of worrisome. "I know," he said. "But can't we get this out of the way first?"

David shrugged but nodded, heading over to the stall in question. "We can delay it all you want, but Dad's really starting to lose it. I'm going to call the doctor in the morning and..."

"And what?" Trystin walked over to the wall and grabbed a dangling rope. "What is it?"

"You need to come see this."

The younger brother approached the stall, a smirk slowly growing on his face. "It's not even the nag, is it? Dad caught a goat this time I'll bet."

"A goat? I am not a goat!"

It wasn't a goat, either. Standing in the stall, where old Mr. Green's nag should have been, was a stallion the color of the ocean at midnight. His glossy coat shimmered and rippled with every movement it made, reflecting ink under every turn of the lantern. There was not one part of him that was not this depthless black, from his silk mane to his glittering eyes, to the tip of his pearlescent hooves.

This was not Mr. Green's nag.

"I told you boys, but you wouldn't listen," their father snorted when they ran back inside to tell then what they'd seen. "You knew so much, didn't you?"

"It's a talking horse!" David cried. "A real talking horse!"

"It's a demon is what it is. I caught it. It's mine." Mr. Hill leaned back in his chair and grinned at both of his sons in triumph. "And it's going to make us rich."

"How did you catch it?" Trystin asked. "What's it doing here?"

His father lifted an iron sigil from beneath his cotton smock; a strange shape crudely made from twisted metals. "I summoned it and bound it to me," he said. "And so long as I wear this, it's mine to command."

"What are you going to do with it?" David asked. "It can't just stay here in the stable."

"Its name is Orobas, and it's going to race in the finals. It's going to put our name back on the map is what it's going to do."

"Do you know what you're doing?" The eldest boy asked. "Do you really? Dad, that's not some normal horse in there!"

"I know that," his father said, practically vibrating in his excitement. "I found the spell, I brought it here, and now it's going to make us famous! I know exactly what I'm doing!"

"And who's going to have to deal with it?" Trystin demanded. He looked over at the darkened window through which he could see the stable. Just inside, waiting, was a literal demon disguised as a horse. What did his father think he was playing with?

"What do you mean, Trystin?" His father asked. "I made the bargain. I—"

"I'm the one that has to ride the damn thing in the race!" Trystin cried. "Did you forget that?"

His father's stunned silence only confirmed the fact.

"It'll be fine," David said, carefully hedging himself into the conversation. "Dad knows what he's doing. If he says the thing is safe, then it'll be ok."

"Easy for you to say," his younger brother groused. "You don't have to ride it tomorrow."

He shook his head and looked away from the two of them. "It doesn't matter," he continued. "I'll ride it, ok? But after that, just send it back where it came from. Ok?"

Rather than wait for an answer, he walked out of the room and retired for the night. He had a long day ahead of him, longer still now that he knew what awaited him.

The next morning, when time came to ready the mysterious horse for the race, the brothers both offered to do so together. It, he, remained right where they left him the night before, waiting in his stall like any ordinary horse. Yet the moment they approached, they were reminded again that he was anything but.

Trystin approached the stall slowly, David following after. Orobas watched him come, his eyes dark and all-knowing.

"Dad said we're going to race together," Trystin said to him, choosing his words carefully.

"So it seems," the beast said, and the rumble of his voice startled him despite expecting it this time.

"Can we really trust you?" David asked, holding the lead as he would a snake. He did not approach the horse just yet, eyeing the creature with a wary eye. "How do we know you won't turn on us?"

When the demon laughed, it sounded as if all the lower creatures of Hell were laughing with it. Trystin shuddered to hear such a sound.

"I cannot harm the one who summoned me so long as he wears that sigil around his neck," Orobas said. "And I must hold up my end of a bargain once struck. I will win your race, boy. That is no falsehood."

It did not make him feel any better about it, but Trystin was left with little choice. He took the lead from his brother and slipped it about the black stallion's neck, taking him from the stall to be readied for the race.

At the track itself, the excitement built around the mystery of Robert Hill's new entry only added to Trystin's anxiety. He never left Orobas' side, though the demon horse never once let the charade drop. By all accounts, he was a magnificent, though purely mortal, racing horse. Spirited and lively, but amiable to all who came to admire him.

"Are you ready, Orobas?" Trystin asked when their turn finally came to appear on the track. Wherever they went, heads turned to watch them go. He knew it was because of the demon that people stared so, but Trystin couldn't help but lift his chin a little higher as well. Let them stare. Let them see the kind of racing horse his father could produce. No one would ever doubt the name of Hill ever again.

"Your father will not be disappointed, boy," the beast growled from beneath his breath, the words meant for his ears alone.

"Good. I'd hate to see what would happen if you broke your end of the bargain, demon." In truth, Trystin had no idea what would happen, but it seemed a credible threat nonetheless.

A low chuckle followed him to the staging pen. "Have no fear of that."

They said nothing more to each other as Trystin mounted the horse's back for the first time. He'd ridden many of his father's racing horses over the years, being the smaller of the brothers, but this was nothing like he'd experienced before. It may as well have been like getting on a horse for the first time. Orobas was too big, too wild, and for all that he looked like a racing stallion, there was truly nothing horse-like about him. He was a creature wearing the skin of one, and it was never more apparent than when Trystin stepped up with him into the starting gate.

"Hey, Hill!"

Trystin looked to his left. Jonathan, the neighbor's boy, sat upon that year's new thoroughbred, a smirk upon that punchable face.

The last time they rode against one another, Jonathan had somehow won the race and all Trystin received was a trip to the doctor.

"Your Pa actually letting you ride in the big race?" Trystin asked, keeping his voice high and uncaring. This time would be different.

"We figured seeing your face in the dirt was a good enough sight to see again," the other boy said with a grin. He patted his horse's neck and looked Orobas over with a critical eye. "Where'd you get that horse from? No way is he from your stables."

"Orobas?" Trystin patted the stallion between his ears, feeling the demon shift unhappily beneath him. "We got him just last week, and he'll leave your old horse in the dust."

"We'll see about that."

"Yes we will."

Trystin patted Orobas one last time and settled into his saddle, his heart pounding the way it always did before a big race. He could just barely see his father and brother's hats at the edge of the crowd, waiting by the Winner's Circle for him.

He couldn't let them down.

"We can do this," he said, more to himself than to the demon. "We can do this."

In front of the gates came a lone man with a gun, ready to begin the race. He looked back at the contestants, then at the waiting crowd.

The gun rose.

Trystin held his breath.

Bang!

The rest was all a blur as Orobas took flight.

It was likely the demon had to remember he was among mortal beasts on a mortal plane after all, and could not reveal his true power. Even so, there was not a single horse among them that could have hoped to catch up to them, not by a long shot. The nearest one was dozens of yards behind before they reached the first bend.

On a normal day, on a normal horse, Trystin enjoyed the thrill of the race and the competitiveness of the sport. Now, today, it was all he could do to simply remain astride the creature. As they came out into the first long stretch, he pulled back on the reigns, barely able to keep Orobas in check.

"What are you doing, boy?" The demon asked, turning his head just enough to eye him with a gaze full of fire.

"Don't overdo it," Trystin warned. "You're still just a racehorse right now, remember?"

Orobas didn't respond to that, but he did slow down, just a little, but enough to be astonishing instead of miraculous. A few of the other racers even managed to make it within a few yards now and then, but there was still no hope of them ever passing.

All too soon, the race was coming to an end. The last stretch was upon them and victory was as it was promised.

Trystin released his hands from Orobas' reigns and raised them over his head, grinning in triumph. He could hear the roar of the crowd wash over him as they flew over the finish line, still well ahead of any other competitor. Theirs was a time that would be in the record books for decades, perhaps forever.

And it was his.

His brother waited for him beside his father, both of them cheering wildly. He and Orobas approached, no slower than before, though surely the demon must be getting winded by now.

"It's alright," he said into the horse's pitch-black ear. "We've won. You can slow down now."

The horse ran as if he did not even hear him, breathing deep and steady without any hint of fatigue. Rather than continue on towards the Winner's Circle, Orobas veered right and galloped toward the nearby lake.

"Orobas, wait!" Trystin fumbled to grab the reins again, but it made no difference. Even grabbing them had no effect on the demon. "Orobas, stop!"

"I was never under your command, foolish boy," the horse finally growled, his hooves barely touching the ground as they flew over the terrain. The gravel of the racing grounds turned into grass and finally full meadow. The lake was only yards away.

"But your promise to dad! The race—"

"The race is won. My task is complete. Payment must be delivered."

"Payment?"

Trystin twisted back and tried to throw himself from the saddle, preferring whatever multitude of broken bones that awaited him to the dark fate that this creature intended for him. Yet the moment he tried, some dark force kept him rooted to the spot. It was as if he were one with Orobas: one skin, one breath.

"Your father dared imprison me," the horse roared, his mane a black flame in the setting sun. "Now I take something from him in return."

Trystin struggled harder, pushing against the horse's neck, but the moment his hands met unholy skin, they remained fixed to it. There was no escaping it.

"Let me go!" He cried. "Please! I didn't do anything to you!"

The lake came ever closer now, and the horse's hooves were muffled as they hit mud. Any other beast might have been slowed by the thickening earth, but Orobas was no normal creature.

"You'll grow accustomed to this life, boy," the horse growled, a smile in his voice. "Just as I did."

Then his body hit water, sending a wet spray into the young man's face. He didn't have a chance to recover before another wave was sent up to replace the first, this time washing up to his chest. Orobas was diving now, without care or hesitation.

In a moment, it was over. Trystin had only a second to gulp the last sweet breath of air before he was plunged beneath the depths of the water, but even that was futile and he knew it. There was no point in it, for there would never be a chance for another.

And as the last few ripples smoothed out over the surface above his head, Trystin wished now, more than ever, that his father had just stolen Mr. Green's damn nag.

About the Author

M.L. Garza is a fantasy and science fiction author whose work has appeared in magazines, anthologies, stand alone works, and the big screen herself. Her debut novel is set for release in 2019.
https://www.facebook.com/AuthorMLGarza/

56

GREMORY: LOVE'S BARGAIN
AMANDA J. EVANS

The color slowly drained from his face as his breathing slowed.

"Tell me where you've hidden it." I gripped his hand, tighter than I should have, but there was no one to see, no one to hear. Moments, stolen and sullied by lies, were all I had.

His lips curved into a spiteful grin.

"Tell me, you old fool."

He grimaced as my nails bit into his flesh. "Never. You will have nothing. You deserve all you get David. You took her from me and now I will take from you."

I shoved his hand away from me. "Fool, I will find it without you."

Footsteps – tap, tap, tapping – along the hallway, halted my interrogation and I jumped to my feet. I took one last look at his fragile body and launched myself out the window.

He died that night and took with him the secret location to the Grothery treasure. His will read by my pompous uncle Derek stated what I'd already known. I'd been disinherited and banished from the kingdom. A warrant for my arrest was issued and men I'd called brothers lurched on every corner, sword in hand, willing to slice me to pieces to claim the reward. "Gold buys all," I spat as I skulked back into the shadows. I had no hope of getting into the palace. I'd need an ally, someone who wouldn't betray me, but who?

A raven flew overhead, cawing and circling me. "Away with you, beastly bird," I said waving my hands in the air.

"What's that. Someone's over there, behind the tavern."

The thud of boots on cobble followed and I scurried along the laneway. I'd make my escape into the forest. I'd be safe there. They wouldn't follow at night.

The moon cast a watery glow on the forest floor but not enough light to navigate the dense surroundings. Trees with their demonic branches whipped at my clothes, tearing and slicing into my skin as I fumbled along. Whispers floated around me and the stupid raven cawed and flapped its wing above me. "Get away from me, devil." I grabbed a branch from the ground and battered the night sky. It was no use. The vicious bird circled above me taunting and teasing, swooping low with claws outstretched. I ducked and swatted to no avail. Eventually the pesky bird veered left and away from me. Silence greeted me, and a chill rested on my body, hair standing to attention. I was tempted to call the bird back.

Smoke filled my nostrils, burning wood and close by. I spun on my heels. Men with torches, I thought as I scanned the trees. The smell grew, and smoke filled my lungs as I coughed and placed a hand to my face. It surrounded me.

"Who goes there?"

A figure stepped in front of me, cloaked in darkness. "Are you lost?"

The voice was feminine, and I straightened. "I'm Prince David. I seek shelter."

"Do you now," she said, taking a step closer. The hood of her cloak fell backwards to reveal an old woman, her face wrinkled with age and long grey knotted tresses. "I might be able to help you." She tapped a finger against her chin as she assessed me. The nail long and pointed – sharp. "What can you offer me in return?"

"What do you want?" I had to play along, get out of this forest before I was discovered. I knew what my father had planned for me – the dungeons, cold, dark, damp, and when my mind and sanity left I'd be paraded through the streets, the crowds cheering the capture of the one who took their beloved King and Queen. They weren't wrong. I had disposed of them both. They were old and soft. They gave to the people, made sure everyone had food and a roof over their heads. All that food and gold wasted on peasants. I would make this kingdom great, a land to be envied by all.

"Are you willing to give me that which I desire?" The old hag spoke, and I shook my head.

"If you help me, yes."

"Very well, follow me."

She led me to a small hut, hidden in the depths of the trees, blending into the surrounding nature. "You'll be safe here," she said as she stoked the fire and hung a large pot over the flames. "Tell me, Prince, why do you seek sanctuary?"

I floundered. It could be a trap. If I admitted to what I'd done, what I wanted to find, she could turn me in. "I'm looking for something."

"In the forest?" She asked glaring at me. "Gremory can help you find what you seek."

"Gremory? How do I find this man?"

She grinned. "You do not find Gremory, you summon her. She can tell of things past, present, and future. Of treasure hidden and where to find it. I can summon her for you if you promise to give me what I desire."

"You help me find my treasure and you can have whatever it is you want."

She spat on her hand and held it out to me. "A bargain, we have then Prince."

I grimaced but shook her hand and agreed before quickly wiping my palm on my tunic.

Books were placed on the floor, candles lit, and a strange symbol drawn in the dust. The old hag chanted and called out in a strange language. The air grew cold and a gust blew through the little shack extinguishing the candles. A cloud formed in the centre of the room and I gasped. A beautiful woman appeared sitting a top a great camel. "Who summons me?"

"I do," the hag replied.

"What do you want?"

"The prince here requires help finding hidden treasure and he has promised to give me whatever I desire once he finds it." She motioned towards me and Gremory turned.

"You have struck a bargain with this woman?"

"I have. Can you help find my father's treasure?"

She closed her eyes and took a deep breath before speaking. "I can. It lies inside a wooden trunk, buried, but not out of reach. It bears a seal, two lions..."

"That's it. Where is it?"

"Patience boy," the old woman said. "You agreed to our bargain and now it is my turn to speak."

Gremory turned to her and bowed her head. "Tell me, summoner, what is it that you desire from this man?"

The old woman chuckled, "I seek to procure love."

Gremory raised her eyebrows, "And the love you seek?"

The old woman nodded towards me a crooked grin on her face. Gremory nodded. "It shall be yours." She walked towards me and placed a hand on my shoulder.

I squirmed, but couldn't release her hold. "What are you doing?"

"Granting the wish of my summoner."

My blood rushed through my veins, burning, screaming, and my vision blurred.

"You will love her like no other. You will cherish her body and soul. You will be faithful to her and no other will compare. You will see beauty and grace and give her all that you have."

Her words washed over me, sinking deep into my being, and when I opened my eyes, the old hag was gone. In her place the most beautiful woman I'd ever seen. My heart pounded in my ears as desire pulsed through my body. "I must know your name, fair maiden," I gasped as I stood and walked towards her.

She giggled, such an enchanting sound, and I reached for her hand. "Imogen," she said, and her voice dripped like honey.

I lifted her hand to my lips and kissed the soft skin, eager to taste more of her. "Imogen," I said, her name, the last name I ever wanted to speak.

"My work here is done," Gremory said breaking the spell.

I blinked, and the old hag stood before me again, her hand clenched in mine. I shook my head and dropped her hand as if it had burned me. "What have you done?" I shouted as Gremory turned into a cloud once more.

"I have found your hidden treasure for you." She laughed. "You will see it every time you look at Imogen."

"You can't do this."

She was gone, vanished into thin air.

"It's you and me now, David," the old hag said, her voice dripping with spite. "You are mine until the day I die."

"Never," I spat, but when I turned to look at her, my heart lurched, and my eyes stung. I wiped them with the back of my hand, but it was no use. They streamed and clouded my vision. The old hag laughed, and my legs gave way.

"Let me help you," she said leading me back to the chair. "You'll feel better soon."

The chair was hard beneath me, solid, reaffirming where I was. The fire flickered in the hearth, and my eyes began to clear. "What have..." The words stopped. The old hag, she wasn't old anymore. Her grey knotted tresses had transformed into golden curls that fell down her back. Her torn rags a ball gown, and when she smiled at me, my whole being lit up. "You."

"Yes, David. You will see only me from now on. You will be mine."

The words bubbled from within me and I could do nothing to hold them back. "I will be yours forever." I clamped a hand over my mouth. I would not speak again, not until I figured out how to undo this curse.

She laughed. "Greed is the greatest curse of all. In your pursuit of greed, you left yourself open to trickery. Never agree to a bargain, David, without knowing what that bargain is."

About the Author

Amanda J Evans is an award-winning Irish author of YA and Adult romance in paranormal and fantasy genres. Her stories centre on good versus evil with a splice of love and magic thrown in too. You can find out more on her website www.amandajevans.com.

OSE: ONCE A MONK
IAN ADEMA

Alistair listened to the crashing waves. There were no other sounds. He stood with his arms folded, his hands protected by cloth, and his earthy monk robe flowing in the wind. He was alone from human presence, the isolated abbey quiet on the island behind him. He had come here many years ago, sure of his past at the time. But every year passing was another moment where his faith slipped away. The manuscripts he assisted scribing were beautiful and intricately ordained, but all the wonder had faded. Now he felt isolated from the others, alone in his mind, and he had turned to other curious ventures.

Forbidden ventures.

He let the sound of the waves go and opened his eyes. He was not alone.

"I will sail across the sea to where it takes me," he stated.

Alistair looked over to the man-like leopard form standing tall and elegant beside him. It wore a long black coat, that felt more like something from the renaissance, as well as gray boots, trousers, and a saber strapped to the belt loop. The creature never turned to Alistair, but kept staring into the distance. The monk knew who this creature was for it was his actions that had brought it here.

The monk was looking directly at the demon known as Ose, that of language and true answers of the divine and secret things. The demon's confidence shined in leopard form. His ferocity subtly gleamed in his eyes. With his cunning and knowledge, he was no one to be trifled with. And the monk already knew, there was always a price.

"You already know where you want to go," Ose responded.

"How do you know?" The monk was more curious than surprised.

"I know the truth of the heavens and the depths. I can reveal it to those who seek the truth, but the mind must be willing." Ose was mysterious as he was fierce.

"I will go to Rome."

It was Christmas Day and sun streamed in through the top windows of St. Peter's Basilica. Today was a momentous occasion as Pope Leo III was holding a coronation. Alistair heard it all through the streets when he arrived. The name Charlemagne was whispered over and over, passing quickly through the streets. The King of the Lombards was in Rome today. At least, that was the word.

Alistair walked beside Ose who was now in the form of an elegant man with strong cheekbones and swooping hair. No one could have guessed this was the same leopard demon from before. He had slowly transformed over the course of their voyage across the sea, his fur slowly receding into human skin. Had Alistair not witnessed it himself, he wouldn't have recognized the demon. But Ose was here to accompany Alistair and give the monk what he desired. Once the monk's requests were fulfilled, Ose would leave him and the monk knew it. But Alistair knew he needed to find his new place in the world and the demon was his answer.

The afternoon sun bore down as the monk approached the basilica, the most obvious destination to him for beginning a backwards journey in his new faith. He was now leaving everything to fate and made his way through the entrance.

Stories had traveled to Iona Abbey while Alistair was there, but he wasn't prepared for how masterful the artwork and architecture of the space were. To make matters worse, he was overwhelmed by the packed crowd that had formed for the day's coronation. With a doubly momentous day, there was twice the number of people. With everyone attempting to get the opportunity to witness the event, there was barely any space to move. Yet, Alistair couldn't help but still take in as much of the basilica as possible. He didn't accept much of the message the art presented anymore but he could still appreciate the work itself in its own right.

With Ose behind him, he pushed his way through the crowds despite their grumbling of what he was doing. After about twenty minutes he managed to make his way to a front side corner of the basilica, close enough to see but far enough to not be noticed.

"What is happening today?" Alistair asked the demon.

"Something that will change much of history."

Alistair rolled his eyes. Leave it to a demon to be mysterious. He should just wait for answers to his own questions instead. He turned his attention to the front atrium of the basilica where Pope Leo III, a simple looking man with a well grown beard, began to address the people.

"Good people of Rome. Today, God sends his grace upon us," the Pope began. "In the midst of dark times he reveals his love for those who have been faithful. Today he rewards his children in bringing a new Holy Roman Emperor to Rome. Charlemagne has traveled from Germania with his son for the coronation and under God's grace I will be anointing the Emperor."

The Pope then began a Latin prayer. Alistair pretended to join in but secretly scanned the room. As soon as the prayer ended it left him in eyeshot to see Charlemagne appear through a side door of the basilica. A dark blue robe covered his main garments and the light accentuated his red sun burnt beard. He appeared humble but strong. Alistair followed Charlemagne as the king led his son up to the pope and they both kneeled.

It was evident that Charlemagne's son was to be crowned king. The Pope finally picked up the crown, gave the address, and placed the crown... onto the head of Charlemagne! It was a shock to the people and to Charlemagne. Alistair wasn't sure the reason, but the moment this happened is when an idea came to him and he turned back to Ose.

"The time has come. I know what I desire."

The demon casually turned his eyes to the monk.

"Speak it," Ose stated.

"I desire to be the next Pope," Alistair said calmly.

"A strange request for one such as you," Ose replied.

"I have my reasons."

"Very well. You will not know the time, but your desire shall come to pass."

The coronation completed and the people dispersed. Alistair lingered in the basilica, beginning to dream of the power he would possess in the Pope's position. He was surprised to find Ose still lingering. He was about to ask the demon why when Ose approached Charlemagne and whispered something in his ear. Instantly the new Emperor's demeanor changed, as if something inside of him had clicked and turned, transforming him to another person. It now appeared that he fully accepted his new title for the people.

Charlemagne and Pope Leo III disappeared from the atrium. When Alistair looked around, Ose was nowhere to be found. Within the hour, he was alone inside the basilica.

* * *

Sixteen years had passed since the coronation and Alistair never left Rome, but his life changed, including his name. He was now Stephen IV and to him, he had always been, as well as to his family. But in truth, it was all a trick of Ose's doing, transforming minds to think they were what and who they were not. What happened to the original Stephen none of them knew, only Ose.

So it was that Alistair of Iona, now Stephen IV of a noble royal family, became the new pope after the death of Leo III in 816 A.D. He began to push his own agenda from the remnants of Alistair's old life, leaving traces and changes to the faith, muddling and confusing truths and falsehoods to the point where no one could fully discern them centuries later, as well as requiring a yearly payment from the monks of ten golden solidi, a currency of the time.

Alistair received his wish but not for long. Less than a year later he died in Rome and was buried in the very same basilica where his desires were granted.

One night, Ose appeared in the basilica's tomb, looking at Alistair's grave with a false name. His disappointment was evident. There was no thrill in this one. He had hoped for so much more from a despairing monk.

"Not my best work," Ose sighed to himself. "These religious types need better imaginations."

And with those words lingering, Ose walked away.

About the Author

Ian Adema is a writer and director of fantasy and psychological thriller movies and a prose writer on the side. Much of his inspiration arises from his intense and vivid dream life.

https://www.facebook.com/ianladema/

58

AMY: BLESSED IN FLAMES
M.L. GARZA

It wasn't a magician who called him that summer, it was a girl no older than sixteen. She wasn't gifted or chosen in any particular way. Not in the way most humans he worked with were chosen. She had no special skills or abilities, no auras that set her apart or destinies that should capture his attention.

So when he appeared in the middle of the field, facing a young woman wearing a cast iron necklace in the shape of his sigil rather than the magician he expected, Amy was at a loss.

He knew he was no small thing to behold, a man aflame but for the clothing of a gentleman. He did have to make a good impression, after all. Yet when she saw him, she did not back down or show a trace of fear. Instead, she met him as an equal, small though she was, and let the warmth of his flames wash over her pale face.

"You are the one who summoned me?" He asked, just to be sure that he was not mistaken.

"I am," she said, and her voice did not shake. She wore the clothing of a simple French peasant, unassuming in every way. So what was so special about her? What was her aim?

"Well then," he chuckled, and a drift of smoke escaped from around his smile. "I do hope you know what you're doing, child. I am no witch's familiar easily ordered about."

"I did not summon a familiar, Amy, President of Hell. I summoned you, and I did so with a purpose." The girl reached for the sigil at her neck and traced it with the tip of her finger. "I will have need of your services on this day."

"Only on this day?"

"For many days to come. I am to go on a journey, and I need your particular skills to guide my way."

His skills? He had a very many, but none that he could think of that could be any use to her. Not to some peasant girl in over her head in the countryside of France.

Then again, he had been wrong before.

Amy tilted his head to the side and regarded her, at the clever thing that dared call his name and wear his seal. "I will lend you my skills, girl," he said at last. "But one day, after your many days are done, you will pay a price. I hope when that time comes that you are prepared and that you find your gain worth it."

"First you must give me something of value. Then I will worry about the price."

"To do that," Amy countered. "I must first know what you value."

The girl was quiet for a moment and looked away from him at last. Her dark eyes strayed to the poor village just beyond the field they stood in, nothing more than a simple hamlet in the French countryside. A simple hamlet, but a not-so-simple girl.

There was sadness in her proud countenance, a defeat deep within that drove the darkness on. Was it that sadness that led her to call him that day? The demon hoped it was nothing so mundane.

"There is nothing for me here," she said when the silence had drawn on too long. The girl straightened her shoulders and the defeat was banished behind a wall that even he, knower of secrets, was not privy to.

"I have been summoned to make a princess of you then?" Amy asked, and the flames around him darkened a shade in disappointment. How droll.

"Not a princess." The girl's eyes narrowed, and she smiled a smile that made devils of devout men. "An empress."

A fiery eyebrow rose. "An empress, girl?"

The smile became a grin and the fire in her eyes nearly matched his own. "A warrior. A conqueror. A legend that will never die. That is what I want, Amy. That is the thing of value."

"I am a conduit, and for the time being, your servant. You had better have a plan beyond this wild dream of yours, child." The last thing he was going to be was some nursemaid, whatever her aspirations.

"It is not a wild dream, Amy. Not anymore. Now disguise yourself and come with me."

Disguise himself? He was a man aflame, a demon! Others of the Seventy-Two might willingly hide behind paltry disguises in order to conceal their true nature, but he wasn't. The mere suggestion was an affront!

And yet... the intrigue won out. Where once was a man covered in flames was now a regular peasant dressed in similar garb as the girl. With a tilt of his head, he considered the iron sigil of his worn upon her breast. It too changed form until it resembled nothing more than another holy cross, large and gaudy, but safe from unwanted scrutiny.

"Where are we going?" He asked.

"To make me a conqueror. To do that, however, we first need horses."

Procuring the horses was no difficult matter in the end. Amy remained outside while the girl returned to her family. He did not know what was said, but it seemed enough that after only a few hours, they were both outfitted with not only mounts, but spare clothing and enough food to last them for weeks.

With a clever mind like hers, what did she truly need his services for?

She did not explain this to him along the way, merely hedging around the subject whenever he asked. It was not in his nature to be content waiting, but curiosity had a firm grip on his unholy heart, and so Amy allowed himself to be led through the countryside and into the heart of France. Besides, he told himself, if this should be a waste of his time and talents, he could always devour the girl in the end.

It wasn't until they reached the temporary capital at Chinon that she revealed some of her schemes.

"I am to meet the deposed king," the girl explained to Amy as they waited at the city gates.

"The king?" Amy asked, a false eyebrow rising. "You?"

"Me. At last I will have need of your services, Amy."

He allowed the city guard to search them for weapons, amused that they should think it sufficient to keep out the danger he posed. "And here I believed I was expected to remain your escort alone, child."

"My escort, yes, but that is the least of your duties. I could have hired any man if that was all I wanted."

"With what money?"

Her only response to him was a scowl. At last, they were allowed passage into the city, and the pair walked toward the main hall where the king held court. It was not as grand as a palace, not anything like the one the British had stolen from him, but it was not something a peasant girl would have any right accessing.

So when her approach was met with a simple nod by the entrance guards, it was Amy's turn to wonder at the power wielded by his humble mistress.

"This is as far as I can get," she explained when he eyed her curiously. "A girl with reputed visions can get in the door, but it will take more than that to achieve what I intend. There is a test that must be passed."

"And that is?"

They were shown into the main hall where several courtiers mingled amongst each other, none seemingly above the other. This was not so much the court of a king, but a gathering of equals.

Or so it seemed.

"Reveal the man I seek," she said, and for the first time, the demon heard the girl's voice shake from nerves. "Show me the king. That is the test I must pass if I am to gain an audience."

"Are you to be queen then?" He asked, walking casually at her side. "Is that how you intend to rule?"

She snorted softly and some of the pride returned that had initially drawn him in. "Hardly. Now do as I command."

Though his sigil around her neck was still disguised as that horrible cross, Amy was still compelled to obey. Besides, he wanted to see where this would go. He had discovered in their short time together that even if that was her plan, it would not be so mundane as a simple marriage. No, this girl was planning something more.

"If I do this," he reminded her one last time. "There will be a price to pay."

"What price?" She asked, but he knew it would not matter.

"You shall end in flames, one way or another, and return to me. And on that day, you will not have my sigil to protect you."

"Flames?" Then the girl smiled, "If that is true, you had better make sure they are the most spectacular flames ever to behold. I wish to be resplendent in them. Make them worthy of me, Amy."

"I can promise you that," he said with a grin. "Now close your eyes, take a breath, and then look about the room. If you accept this price, the man you seek will have a halo of fire about his head that only you can see. Do what you wish with that knowledge."

Perhaps it was unfair of him to offer such a choice to her. After all, what did a young girl know of her own mortality and the cleansing agonies of fire? Yet she was the one who summoned Amy to bargain, not any of his brothers, and this was how he did business.

The choice was hers and hers alone.

To the girl's credit, she did give it some thought. Her dark brown eyes looked into his for so long that the demon actually feared she might back out.

But then she closed her eyes, took a breath, and let his magic do its work.

The moment she opened her eyes again, the girl locked onto the correct man. The king did not make himself obvious in any sort of way another human could tell, but Amy had made him unmistakable to her. The first step she took toward him sealed the bond between them and her fate as well. Each subsequent one was even and steady as she approached so that she caught the attention of all in the room as she passed by. A conqueror already. And when she reached the king in disguise, she fell to her knees in one smooth motion.

"I know you, Your Majesty," she said, loud enough for all to hear.

"You must be mistaken," the man said at first. "I am Louis, Viscount of—"

"You are Charles, Dauphin of all France." She raised her head and looked directly at the halo of fire Amy had given him.

All was quiet. Then—

"Who are you?"

"I am Jeanne d'Arc, and I am your humble servant. God has granted me a vision, Your Majesty, just as He revealed your identity to me."

Amy barely managed to contain a grin.

"And why are you here, Jeanne?"

Jeanne touched the false cross at her bosom and met the king's eyes, her own hard and determined. "I am to lead your army against the British to take back the country that was stolen from us."

Clever girl indeed. When her time came, Amy would make sure her pyre was magnificent. She deserved no less.

About the Author

M.L. Garza is a fantasy and science fiction author whose work has appeared in magazines, anthologies, stand alone works, and the big screen herself. Her debut novel is set for release in 2019.
https://www.facebook.com/AuthorMLGarza/

59

ORIAS: LUCIFER'S ASTROLOGER
PHILIPP J. KESSLER

The fish-tailed lion-headed figure swam through the air towards his master. The crown of his rank rested heavily on his brow as he dodged around his seventy-one peers in search of the attention of he who leads them all. Most of his compatriots ignored him as he bumped along through the crowded space.

"Ah, there you are, Orias!" The Master called out as he approached.

"My apologies, sir," he answered. "My duty to you comes first, but my duties to the other Lords of Hell sometimes distract."

"It is fine, my old friend," the Master smiled. Their relationship was much friendlier than Orias expected he'd ever have with any of the other Lords. "My question is not that pressing."

"Lucifer," he raised a fin. "If I may, whatever question or concern you have that requires my skills is hardly a triviality."

"It is not a matter of government," Lucifer sighed. "It is more a matter of the heart. And before you make comment, I do have a heart."

"Of course you do, we all do," he nodded to his friend and master. "What can I do for you?"

"I'm lonely," he admitted flatly.

"With the Lords of Hell and all their demons at your command?"

"You answered your own question, Ori," he said. "They and you are here at my command. They do what I bid of them, not necessarily what they want to do."

"If we wanted to blindly do as we were told we'd still be in Heaven," Orias reminded him. "We exercised our free will and now we are here."

"Yes, yes," Lucifer waved the comment away. "But are you truly free to do what you want or do you fear my ire if you go against my commands?"

"You have been known to kill a few demons here and there when you are unhappy with their actions or their results." Only a friend as true as Orias could get away with saying such things to the King of Hell.

"Only when the deliberately did something that endangered us!" He shot back.

"Us or you, Luci?" Orias pointedly asked.

"Fine, me." He shook his head and walked away from his friend. "Come," he shot over his shoulder.

"Yes, sir!" The lesser demon snapped to attention and followed his master.

They walked through the crowded grand hall of Hell and exited into a small antechamber. Lucifer had lots of secret and private places hidden about. This one wasn't hidden, but so many had forgotten that it was there that it might as well have been.

"Ori, please," Lucifer motioned him into the room. "Let's not be formal for this. I value your insight too much for you to be stuffy with me."

"As you say, Luci," he replied with a smile. He entered the small room and sat on one of the lushly upholstered chairs. Lucifer took the other. "Matters of the heart, you say?"

"Yes," Lucifer sighed heavily. "It has been far too long since I admitted that to anyone. But yes, matters of the heart weigh heavy on me these days."

"I can see why," Ori smiled at him. "It has been..." he paused and finger countered. "Five years since Myrna left."

"Ah, Myrna, she was a beauty," Luci shook his head wistfully.

"Oh, yes," Ori smiled knowingly. "And you've not taken up with anyone since?" He asked surprised.

"Nope, no one," he admitted.

"Not even for..." he trailed off.

"I do not kiss and tell," Luci laughed. "But, no. Not even for that."

"Wow, I think that is a first. Shall I mark it on the calendar?" Ori smiled at his friend.

"Don't you start!" He barked back playfully. "I can exercise self-restraint."

"I've no doubt of that, but for five years!" Ori tried to hide the laughter in his voice.

"Now you make of me," Luci said with a heavy sigh. "I want to know... I want to know if I have any hope for happiness again."

"I can tell you that without looking to stars, my friend," he answered. "We all have some hope for happiness."

"I want more than some hope, I want something I can touch."

"We all want something we can touch, Luci. You have all the hosts of Hell to touch if you want them." Ori reached out for Luci and placed a hand gently on his knee.

"Pshah!" He scoffed and moved his leg. "I've had all of the hosts that I want, and some from Heaven as well. I want something...no, I want someone that I can love without always wondering if they are with me out of fear or some sense of duty."

"It was not duty or fear," Ori said softly. "But I know what you mean."

"Do you?" He looked at his old friend. "What we had was special... But I want something more... more permanent."

"Let me see here..." Ori tapped his chin with a fingertip as he conjured with his mind a three-dimensional map of the stars and planets around the Earth. "See here, this is a reference to your birth, your creation, by Yahweh." Orias indicated a red lightning bolt.

"Yes?" Lucifer said encouragingly.

"And this is Venus, the planet of love," he pointed to a blue-green orb. "Some of the mortals say that she is the Morning Star, is that not one of their names for you as well?"

"And my twin brother," he grunted.

"Yes, and him..." Orias twitched a finger and the stars and planets moved around on the map. "Ah, this looks promising..."

"What?" Lucifer asked eagerly.

"Virgo is positioned favorably with Venus."

"The Virgin? How can she be favorable when I am looking for love?"

"Because she represents someone who has not been touched by you or anyone. Not even by mortal hands other than those of her parents and then only out of familial love," he explained. "She is as pure as we once were in Heaven."

"When will I meet her?" Luci asked eagerly.

"Sooner than you think, my friend," he smiled. "See here?" He pointed at a bright blue diamond that seemed to be moving slowly across the starfield.

"Yes?"

"That is her, she is coming closer to your lightning bolt," he tapped the air between the marks on the map.

"That sounds like an innuendo," Luci said with a knowing smile.

"Perhaps it is, but I did not intend it."

"All the better!" he stood up from the chair and paced back and forth in the small room.

"Hmm?" Orias made a questioning noise.

"Oh, nothing, my friend. Nothing you need concern yourself with," he stopped in his pacing. "Soon you say?"

"Very soon!" He confirmed.

"Then I must ready myself for her," Lucifer was excited. An emotion Orias hadn't seen come from him some time, not even when Myrna was still with them.

"Don't set yourself up for a fall," he cautioned.

"What do you mean?" Lucifer asked with concern.

"There is another in her path, a mortal man," he pointed to a white five-pointed star. "He may meet her before or shortly after you do. Either way, he will be a rival for her affections."

"What should I do?"

"Be ready for disappointment, my friend." Orias shook his head and waved his hand across the three-dimensional map causing it to disappear.

"Is there anything else?"

"Not that I can say without swaying your decision," he admitted. "And that is something I will not do in matters of love."

"Very well," Lucifer sighed. "I'll face my fate..."

*****

"Dag," Shelby said as the young man sat down at her table in the coffee shop.

"Darling lady," he responded. "So nice to see you again."

"You flatter me," she said with a grin. "I've not been anyone's darling for some time."

"Surely your father?"

"Nah, he stopped calling me that when I was able to beat him at poker. Every time." She giggled at his expression. "Yup, no playing games with me, unless you mean to lose."

"Say, who is that guy over there?" Dag asked as he pointed to a tall man leaning against the pillar, an vape-mod in his hand.

"I don't know, I didn't even see him there," she looked out the window of the coffee shop and smiled. "Eye-catching..."

"Yes, he is," Dag grinned. "Shall we?"

"Shall we what?" Her face was blank.

"There's that poker face!"

"Oh? Do I have a tell?" She asked.

"Only when you go blank like that," he laughed. "Tells me you have something in mind."

"Oh, just a little fun," she grinned at Dag. "He does look interesting..."

"Uh-huh," he agreed. "And which one of us looks interesting to him, I wonder."

"Let's find out. It was your idea after all!" She pushed back from the table and picked up her latte. He had no choice but to follow her or look the fool. He'd looked that enough already.

"Hello, handsome," Dag heard her say to the stranger as he exited the double doors of the shop. "I'm Shelby."

"Luca," he said through a thick cloud of sweet-smelling vapor. "Pleased to meet you," he reached his free hand out to her. She took and shook.

"This is my friend Dagda," she indicated Dag who had caught up to them.

"Nice to meet you, I'm Luca," he offered his hand to the handsome young man.

"Pleasure," Dag said as he shook Luca's hand. He held it a moment longer than strictly necessary. He was pleased when Luca squeezed it softly and rubbed his thumb across the back of his hand when they let go.

"All mine," Luca said with a wink for both of them.

"Care to come in for a cup of coffee?" Shelby asked.

"I'd love to, my dears," Luca answered. He had found both the woman and her paramour that Orias had told him about with the star map. He knew from the blue diamond that hovered over her head and the white star over his.

"Dagda..." Luca mused as he followed them to their abandoned table. "Do you live up to your name sake's reputation?"

Dag grinned and blushed a little as he shot a glance towards Shelby. She met his gaze and giggled. "You have no idea, Luca. You have no idea..."

"I'd like to find out, with your assistance," he said to her with another of those drop-dead-gorgeous winks.

About the Author

Philipp J. Kessler is a multi-genre author, editor, and publisher with a flair for paranormal and LGBTQIA stories. Search him on your favorite social media site under RevKess.
https://www.facebook.com/RevKessPMPC/

60

VAPULA: PHILOSOPHY IN THE BEDROOM
P.I. STOULPE

Emily smoothed the blouse over her breasts. She
admired her own figure in the mirror. At thirty-five, she was happy
that she had kept her cheerleader body. Even after having two kids,
she had managed to stay fit and slender. The curves of her body
were well proportioned. Even her husband thought so. His eyes had
not strayed once to his secretary.

Tonight was their tenth wedding anniversary. The kids were off
at her mother's and they would have the house to themselves. She
had been looking forward to it since New Year's. Now it was
February, and the time to celebrate their love again was upon them.

"Paul, honey!" she called from the bathroom doorway. "Where
are you?"

"I'm headed downstairs," he replied. "You are taking too long to
put your face on, not that you need any make-up."

She walked through their bedroom to the hall door and looked
out towards the stairs. Her husband was standing at the top of them,
his hand resting on the banister. She smiled at him and flashed her
pearly white teeth.

"Nice of you to say, darling," she joined him at the top of the
stairs. "But I do need a little here and there. Can't let you see the
wrinkles. Not tonight."

"You, my sweet, do not have wrinkles." He leaned down to kiss
her on the cheek. She was only 5'6 and he could rest his chin on the
top of her pretty blond head if he wanted to risk getting an elbow to
the stomach. He rarely went for that. Pain was best saved for other
pleasures. Seeing his wife angry was not one of those pleasures.

"That you've ever seen," she joked and patted a hand against his
cheek. "Let's head off to dinner. I've got plans for dessert."

"Oh?" He asked with a sly smile on his lips. "We could skip
dinner and go straight for your sweet rewards!"

"Funny, dear," she grinned and led him down the stairs. "But I've been waiting for this dinner all year."

"It's only February, you have waited that long," he quipped.

"You know what I mean!" She threw a glance over her shoulder. "Dessert can wait. I want steak."

"Yes, my love," he answered her dutifully. "The reservations are waiting for us. Shall we?"

"Let's!" They left the house together and locked the door on their way to his Porsche.

*****

After dinner, they returned to their four-bedroom home in the suburbs. Emily had had one glass too many and Paul had to lead her up the steps and into their living room. She giggled a little as he helped her out of her coat and high heels.

"Paul, darling," she drawled through her inebriation. "Let's go upstairs. I want to celebrate with dessert."

"Just let me hang our coats up," he said soothingly. He was afraid that dessert might turn into her dozing off on the sofa before he could carry up to their bedroom.

"Just leave them," she insisted. "We can hang them up in the morning."

"Afternoon is more my plan," he joked. "The kids will be with your mother all weekend, we can sleep in and continue our celebration when we wake up."

"I want to celebrate now!" She said with a pitiful attempt at being stern.

"Fine, fine!" He went along with her wishes and scooped her up in his arms. Her slender frame hugged him close as she giggled and allowed herself to be carried up the stairs.

Setting her down on the bed, Paul went into the bathroom to brush his teeth. The garlic sauce from his steak and left a strong flavor in his mouth, one he didn't want to share with his beautiful wife.

When he returned to their bed he found her stripped to her bra and panties and lay curled on one side watching him. Her intoxication had vanished. He started to suspect that she had been playing with him since that last glass of wine.

"You've been fooling me," he admonished her playfully. "I thought I'd find you passed out when I got done with my teeth.

"Wanted to make sure we made it to the bedroom before it got too late," she answered with a seductive smile.

"All you had to do was ask," he started to undress to join her in bed.

"Let me," she sat up and pulled him close to the side of the bed. She pulled the tail of his shirt out of his belted slacks and began to undo the buttons. As she finished, she slid the silk shirt off his shoulders and stood to kiss the griffin tattoo on his left shoulder.

He hissed with pleasure as the heat of her lips lit the griffin's form and he began to itch to let his true self come out. Allowing her to continue to undress him, he took a deep breath to control the creature that lived under his skin. He'd only allowed his demon self to come out once during their marriage. That had resulted in the conception of their twin boys. He wasn't sure if he wanted more children, but her insistent fingers on his buttocks as she slid his brief off threw that thought of his mind.

He leaned down to kiss her again and pulled her into a tight embrace. "Is this what you want, my dear?"

"Yes, Vapula, my husband," she answered truthfully. "It has been too long since you let yourself free. I want that for our anniversary. I want all of you with me tonight."

"Very well, my love, my wife," he answered as he released her and stretched out his arms. Arching his back he let the griffin demon take control of his body. Muscles rippled across his chest and shoulders, he stood another three inches taller when he had finished shifting. His skin was a ruddy color now and a small pair of black horns had poked through his red hair.

"There you are, Vapula!" She exclaimed as she jumped up and grabbed him by the shoulders. He allowed her slight weight to pull him off balance and they tumbled into bed. She giggled and they made love.

"Darling," his rumbled softly through his chest and tickled her ear that was pressed into him.

"Yes, my love?" She asked.

"I do love you," he said.

"I know you do," she turned her head to look at him. He was still in his demon form. She licked her lips and snaked her tongue out to tease his clavicle. "I love you, too."

"I need to return to Paul's form before anyone senses me," he reminded her. "But I wanted you to hear the words from my true lips before I did that."

"I appreciate that, dearest," she smiled and kissed his neck. She rolled off his chest and lay there watching him as he shifted back to his human form. It thrilled her to watch him. She'd only had the pleasure twice before tonight. Once when he revealed himself to her before he proposed and again when they made their beautiful sons. "Do you think we did it again?" she asked quietly.

"Did what?" He asked.

"Make another baby... or two?"

"You'll know soon enough," he smiled and pulled her close to him. His smaller human body was still large compared to her. He held her against himself and marveled at the love they had. Demons didn't fall in love, especially not with humans. And to maintain that love for this long was a testament to his commitment to her and to their children.

"I'm scared," she blurted out suddenly.

"What brought this on?" He looked into her eyes with a worry of his own.

"I'm scared that your father will learn of our boys," she let a small tear run from her unblinking eyes.

"I dare say he already knows," he admitted with a sigh.

"He does?!" She sat up suddenly and looked at him with fear.

"Relax," Paul soothed his wife. "If he had a problem with them, he'd have made an appearance by now."

"Oh." That was all she said.

"Darling," he pulled her into an embrace again. "He's not shown himself and he won't. Not for them. They would have started to show if they had enough of my blood in them."

"Are you certain? They are so young!" She protested.

"They aren't demon enough to be of concern to him," he kissed her on the forehead. "Try to rest. We'll worry about this when we wake up tomorrow."

She glanced at the bedside clock, "It is tomorrow."

"When we wake up then," he kissed her nose. "Now, go to sleep."

"Yes, my dearest," she agreed.

They settled into each other's arms for a long sleep.

*****

A month had passed since they celebrated their tenth anniversary. Emily had met with a friend for coffee before picking the twins up from school. After her friend had left she remained at the table finishing her second latte. A man approached her table and stood there looking at her.

"May I help you?" she asked the stranger. He towered over her, his body blocking the light. She couldn't see his face.

"I believe you know my son," he said in a deep voice.

"Pardon?" She'd set her cup on the table and was reaching for her purse to leave. This man made her nervous.

"My son," he repeated. "Paul."

About the Author

P.I. Stouple writes romance, crime drama, and detective stories. She will be featured in the upcoming Mystery 42 Manuscripts RP novel Elegance of the Moon.
https://www.facebook.com/pistoulpe

61

He sat cross legged on the sidewalk jiggling a metal cup full of a few coins. His glossed over eyes pleaded with the passersby without seeing. His toothless smile could barely be seen in the midst of his disheveled bushy beard that was covered in bits of dirt and food. Most walked on by him in disgust while a select few came back after being riddled with guilt and placed a few coins in his cup. They never stayed to talk to him but ran off as though they had encountered the plague.

Zagan watched the old man with intense curiosity while hidden in the shadows. He watched as the blind beggar would empty the cup into a hidden pocket in his jacket then shook the almost empty cup to gain the new passersby attention. Zagan had seen such tactics many times and saw that it was indeed quite effective. The less in the cup the more the beggar got. He hated to admit it, but this beggar had gotten his attention and gained his favor without even trying. He waited until the crowds died down before appearing next to the beggar.

"So, beggar, do you enjoy this lifestyle?" he asked curiously. The beggar aimed his sightless eyes towards Zagan.

"It is the only life I know," the beggar stated simply.

"What if I helped you have a better one?" Zagan asked.

"Why would you want to? I am but an old beggar man. I have nothing to gain from riches or being treated well. I'll just keep doing what I do here until I die."

"Such a futile way of thinking. How about we try something? I want to try an experiment. You say you are old and have nothing to gain. So, why not have a little fun with the last bit of your life?" Zagan offered.

"You probably want my soul in exchange?" the beggar asked.

"That would be the usual, yes. However, I want this for myself, so I ask nothing of you." Zagan said, surprised at his own words.

"Seems an odd thing for a demon," the beggar laughed.

"Yes, I must be bored," Zagan laughed along with him. "What do you say, old man? Want to go for it?"

"Eh, why not. My soul is secure so I may as well enjoy this," the beggar smiled.

Zagan took the old man by the hand and they faded from the street. They stood inside a condo that looked out over the entire city. It was decorated to the tee with all the amenities and lavish living one could ask for. Zagan snapped his fingers and before his very eyes the old man was no longer a scruffy dirty beggar but instead a dapper clean-cut gentleman in a suit. He looked like a sexy entrepreneur in a nice suit.

"First thing I want to try is to see how people will treat a rich blind man. Are you ready?" Zagan asked.

"Sure, let's see what happens," the beggar snickered.

In seconds Zagan had them standing inside a high-class coffee shop, standing in line to get some coffee. Within five minutes people were offering the beggar a place at the front of the line, someone bought his coffee, and helped him to his seat. The beggar thanked them for their kindness as he sat and enjoyed a good cup of hot coffee.

"Isn't that interesting?" Zagan asked the beggar.

"It's to be expected." The beggar shrugged.

"Let's try that with how you looked before, shall we?" Zagan sneered.

"Sure, why not." The beggar could care less.

Zagan transformed the beggar back to his original state and they stood within another high-class coffee shop. He helped the beggar to a nearby booth and waited to see the reactions of those around them. Immediately he noticed people staring and whispering with looks of disgust on their faces. He loved how shallow and predictable humans could be. Just as he thought that he had proven the fickleness of humans a young man came walking up to their booth.

"Hey man, can I get you a cup of joe?" he asked politely.

"That would be nice. Thank you," the beggar replied with a toothless smile.

The young man walked over and bought two cups of coffee. One for himself and one for the beggar. Then he sat down next to the beggar and chatted while they drank the robust liquid. Zagan was not happy with this new setup. It threw a wrench in his whole idea. At least the young man didn't see him there.

Zagan snapped his fingers and they were back in the condo. He paced the room as the beggar found his way over to a comfy chair to sit in. He remained quiet as the demon continued to pace. Zagan turned to the beggar and snarled,

"I don't get it. That young man didn't care one bit what you looked like and treated you as if you were equals. Clearly, he was way better than you. Why does this anger me so?"

A rumble started in the beggar's stomach and worked its way up until he let out a loud bellowing laugh which caused him to fall to the ground and roll about.

"Just what do you find so funny?" Zagan growled.

The man stood up effortlessly and continued to laugh as he said, "Oh Zagan, you are so keen to observe yet so blind to what is really before you."

Zagan's eyes grew wide as saucers as he watched the beggar transform into a young man wearing a white robe. The majestic presence that stood before him forced him to bend a knee by his mere holy aura.

"You will never understand humans, Zagan. Not the way that I do," the man declared before he disappeared in a flash.

Zagan remained frozen in place for some time before he could shake off the divine encounter he had just had. Once he was finally able to be himself again, he stood and let out a raging roar. The sudden anger and hatred that filled his being came pouring out as he thrashed the condo he was in. He vowed to himself that he would not be duped like that ever again.

62

VALAC'S FALL FROM GRACE
CHASITY GAINES

Like most children curious about what their Father's do, a few of us Angels found ourselves taking to Earth to intently spy over our heavenly Father's latest creation, humans. Unlike ourselves they did not have the gift of immortality nor were they situated close to our much loved and respected Father as we were.

They were frail, susceptible to various maladies we were immune to, they aged and withered like a flower dying off in the cold winter. Many of us seethed with jealousy of these creatures while some felt sorry for their mortality and ignorance of our most wonderful Father.

God spoke to Lucifer and myself before we descended upon Earth. I will never forget his words spoken in love and fear. "My sons, remember you are the watchers. Never intercede or become attached for they serve a different purpose while you, my Angels, serve another."

I kept to the fringes of the tribal communities. Shrouded in dark and invisible unless I decided to reveal myself. There were times when I accepted the hospitality of a family though I never revealed myself to them. I enjoyed the earthy smells of the humans. The women.. Oh the women.. I found I enjoyed their buxom figures and soft faces. Their voices are the closest I have ever come to hearing God's voice. Full of love and hope. Love between a man and woman was a new concept to us Angels. Sure, we understood love in the sense of brotherly or fatherly affection. But this burning passion that consumed and confused these funny mortals was fascinating to watch.

Their orgasmic faces looked as if they had been in the presence of my most Holy Father. Dazed, sated, and loved. They glowed with such radiant happiness, that I knew God would approve. Though I doubt he would be happy to know that I felt a reaction stirring in the pit of my stomach, and not the guilty feeling of letting my Father down swimming in my skin. But a desire to caress a human face, taste their lips, their skin, and to dive deep within a woman becoming one with her and my Father, the creator.

*****

Entering into a mountainous area, I heard the most enchanting sound, a young woman singing. Her tribe kept wooly beasts with crooked trumpets twisted on their heads. The wool could be used to make warm clothing and even to line shoes for the cold times. The villagers were well to do and were able to trade for goods and items that couldn't be found in their lands. I came upon the village late at night creeping in the shadows thrown by the small wooden huts. Smaller ones circled a bigger one sitting in the middle. Puffs of smoke existed the small hole in the huts roof. I could hear the strange bleating of the cloud beasts.

A gigantic tree stood sentinel over the village and the small stream flowing just before the entrance into the village. I leapt into the tree watching the sleepy village drift off to sleep. I searched the village for my songbird when I reached the middle hut before the golden orb brightened the sky. I found her, smelling of fresh water and flowers, her eyes fluttered in their slumber. The moon kissed her beautiful face before being chased from the sky. I laid a kiss on her cheek and disappeared as the sun stretched across the horizon.

I waited at the tree for the female human to fetch water from the flowing stream. I took in the clear blue sky as a big black bird circled overhead. Wild flowers warmed in the sun releasing a bouquet of smells. The women gathered early beside the lazy stream, collecting water for the daily chores and cooking while chattering about husbands and children.

Almost giving up on the young woman who had sparked an emotion in me I had never felt before. Not even in Heaven did I ever feel this elated about seeing someone. She arrived, long tan limbs carried her gracefully towards the water. Her blue eyes held the warmth of that perfect day. She looked up towards the sky before wiping the sweat collecting on her brow, plunging the heavy pitcher into the clean water. I had to make my move now. But what does one say when they can't find the words?

Her eyes squinted against the sun as she looked at me. The first person that I have revealed myself to and I hoped I hadn't went overboard. I wore a wool tunic like those of her tribe but my face betrayed me. She stared at my face transfixed.

"Ye must be from thy neighboring tribe, for my eyes hath never seen ye," she questions as she eyed me suspiciously.

"Mistress, I wish ye no harm. I be a lonely peddler looking for a place to rest," my voice reassured her that I meant her no harm. I squatted beside the reflective water cupping my hand and taking gulps of the refreshingly cold water.

She turned as if she was going to leave me squatting in the mud. "Doth you cometh?" Her question came out through smiling lips that she tried to hide behind her hand. "My father will see that ye are fed and rested."

*****

The girl's father, a smart man when it came to the animals of the lands. He was able to trade wool and meat for exotic fruits, earthenware, rare grains, and spices. His wealth set him up as tribal leader, but he was a hospitable man and considered a man of honor amongst the tribe. He offered me flaky bread with a sweet honey spread, soft cheeses, and round purple skinned fruit, that when bitten, the sweet juices burst in your mouth spraying your chin. The stoat man, handed me a skin of thick, foamy beer of his tribe.

I finished the delicious meal and drank my fill of the tangy beer. "I must thank ye' for such a bountiful and delightful meal and drink," I said bowing my head bestowing blessings on them for their hospitality.

The red headed young woman erupted in a fit of giggles, rolling her eyes at my submission to her parents. The sprite darted across the living space, grabbed my hand, and darted for the wide door. Her laughter rang through the tribe like a wedding peal. We ran until we reached the forest edge of her father's land.

She fell into my arms stroking my face tenderly, smiling like the heathen she was. Her lips pink and soft looked like petals of a pretty flower. Bending her backwards, I kissed her deeply, my tongue probing just beyond her rich lips, past her crooked teeth, flicking at the tip of her tongue. She tasted of salty sweat and ambrosia. Her fingers outlined strange designs as she gently stroked my throbbing body. The sky turned dark and the wind began to howl through the thick trees. Her screams of ecstasy and my moans of pleasures muffled in the brewing storm.

Her body shimmered like liquid stars and her eyes shone brighter than the lights of St. Peters. I felt as high as heaven after the soulful joining of our bodies. We headed back to her Father's house to tell him we wanted to be married. Holding hands we entered the large home to find Sa' ar's family gone; vanished into the wispy air. Sa' ar, relieved at not having to face her stern father took over the household as mistress of the place.

*****

We spent many nights wrapped in the fresh straw blankets and each other. "I love you Valac," Sa' ar whispered every night before drifting off to sleep. I roamed the lands at night trying to release the gnawing guilt of having betrayed my Holy Father.

My Sa' ar knew how to handle the responsibilities that came with being tribal leader. I kept to the things I was good at such as dispensing justice, hearing disputes, and judging in the fairest way possible. Always thinking, "What would Father do?"

Not much time went by, not even for an Angel, like myself, but soon my beloved Sa' ar announced she was expecting a child. She was so happy that she glowed like the pearlescent full moon. I watched her growing belly with trepidation and wonder. I did ask silent prayers for Father to watch over my wife and unborn child. His grandchild, a hybrid mix of his most loved creatures. Or would he scorn us, cast me out, strip me of my titles, honors, or maybe my wings?

Sa' ar visited the village wise woman once a week. It was said that she could see glimpses of the future. Sa' ar begged for me to allow the old woman to divine our unborn child's future until I relented. I was washing away the days dirt when Sa' ar burst into my room with tears running down her face as she tore at the headdress she wore.

"Old hag," she exclaimed as she kicked at the crumpled headdress on the floor. "As soon as her old wrinkled hand touched mine than it recoiled and stated that she could see nothing," Sa' ar continued calmer than when she entered. "I could plainly see she was lying because she kept her eyes downcast. So I demanded to know what she saw." The tears begin to roll down her cheek.

I wrapped my arms around her shaking shoulders, placing my hands on the roundness of her belly. "All seems to be well with our wee' one," I whispered in her ear. Spinning her around so that her belly came between us. I cupped her face in my hands looking her deep in her eyes. "I promise, our child will do great things." She pushed me away, her lips chapped by the salty tears.

"The crazy bone collecting bitch said that our child shall never be," she cried out after revealing the old healer's words looking at me as if she was seeing me in a new way.

Washing Sa' ar's face with water, I whispered endearing platitudes until sleep took over. I walked into the cool air hoping that all will be well when I noticed my brother and friend, Lucifer, making his way down the dusty road toward me.

"That's why I'm here little brother," Lucifer whispered over Sa' ar's sleeping body. He motioned for me to walk outside and I followed. "Father is not happy with this situation, Valac. He is really thunderbolt mad, and ready to hail down on your thick head. "I don't see what all the fuss is about. He likes to create. Why can't we?"

"What does he want done? Certainly he doesn't want us to kill her and the innocent babe inside her belly," I started to question Lucifer. "I won't give her up!" I yelled at the blue skies above.

"Did you hear that?" Lucifer asked as he looked in the direction of the river.

I cocked my head listening to the wind rustle through leaves, insects buzzing in the warm afternoon, and then a faint scream. "Yes," I barely said before I was running toward the weedy river side. Time stood still, like every step I took didn't count. I felt the electricity in the air when a streak of blue light sliced through the sky and hit the big tree by the flowing stream.

"NO!" I screamed as my wings broke free of tight skin and I flew to the river bank as fast as I could.

The splintered tree had been home to a nest of venomous vipers which fell on Sa' ar as she gathered water. Her blood oozed from the small holes left by the snakes' sharp fangs. She was gone and so was my child.

*****

Father commanded that I appear in his throne room. He sat tree still on his golden throne. He looked at me with compassion but I saw the anger brewing beneath his composure. I flouted his rules and now I must be made an example of. I understood to a degree, but I cared only for my dead Sa' ar and child.

I spoke first, "Aye Father, tis' good to see you." He nods his head for me to go on. I take a deep breath and begin the speech I had been working on.

"Yes, I have fallen in love with one of your mortal creatures. Father, if only you could see how love between two people brings them closer to you. Can you not see that?" I pleaded with him.

"Silence!" Father's controlled voice demanded. "First off, son, I told you before you set off that all of my creation has a purpose. Intercourse is for procreation for mortals to expand and multiply. True love is the highest form of me, but you have went completely against my orders," he rattled off in a monotone voice as if he has already judged and sentenced me.

"You are a liar, a manipulator, playing games with the lives of those on Earth. You don't care what happens to them. You make them frail, susceptible to all types of maladies and still you couldn't let one of them have some happiness!" I screamed at him and turned to walk away, never to set foot in Heaven again. However, Father commands Michael and Gabriel to grab me and bring me back to the center of the floor.

"You, Valac, are cast out of my domains to forever roam the lands of the damned. You will be stricken from the annuals and remembered as a foul demon of Hell." Father made one motion with his hand and I was cast from Heaven, stripped of my beautiful white wings, and all in the name of love.

About the Author

Chasity Gaines is a multi-genre author and poet. She loves painting a picture with her words.

Follow her at https://www.facebook.com/ChasityGainesWriter/

63

ANDRAS: ALL THAT MATTERS
J. BECK

Weeks had been spent preparing for the ritual. I
have been tormented long enough by those around me. Can they not
see how I suffer without my wife and children? Do they not see that
the arsonist, the man who locked my family in the home and burned
it in front of me, walks a free man? How can they not understand
what that does to a man? I suffer this injustice no more. I found the
means of my vengeance, a dusty old book in the local library. The
cover was so faded that the librarian couldn't identify it, so she gave
it to me for free. She is such a lovely woman. I hope that my
vengeance will spare her in this, for of all the people in this town,
she is the only one who sympathizes with me. She lost her husband
in Korea two weeks after they were married and understands what
that kind of loss does to a person. I made a note in the ritual that
she, specifically, was to be spared, but I knew the one I was calling
forth would disregard that at his discretion.

This night, under the new moon, I began the labors of the ritual.
I carefully mixed the chalks together for the circle, just as it said, for
I would need to hold him fast and long enough to convince him to
perform my task. I would be breaking this circle at the end, letting
him free to do his work, and I knew I only had once chance of living
through this. I carefully traced the circle with a holly branch, made
his sigil out of ivy, and lightly dusted all of it with the chalk. I
dumped the rest on myself to mark that I was the conjurer. The
book was very clear on this point. I began the chant, a long, slow
monotone in a language I could find no mention of. It seemed like
mere moments, but I know a hour had passed before I finished. I
listened closely, and began to hear the sound of hooves approaching.
I tried to calm myself down, to slow my heart, but nothing was
working. I was too excited by my vengeance finally being wrought
upon him. The rider slowly took shape inside the circle, standing on

his sigil. A man, with an owl's head and carrying a sword, sat upon a beautiful horse.

"What", he hissed, "can I help you with on this night?"

"Great Andras," I began, "I summoned you here tonight to bring vengeance upon those who have wronged me. They mock me for mourning my wife and children. I demand that you take from them that which was taken from me. All but one of the residents in the town must suffer. The librarian, Kim Byong An, is to be spared, for she has felt my grief and comforted me in my time of need. If you agree to this, I shall set you free from your circle so that you may begin your work."

"I simply need to kill a lot of people and burn a few buildings? I agree. Your task is simpler than most who summon me. However, you must remain here until I return to ensure that all work is.....satisfactory....before I depart. Do you accept?"

"I do and now release you from your bond. Go forth and wreak my vengeance!"

With that, I cut both wrists and let the blood drip onto the circle. The circle flared with light, the ivy ignited, and the horseman began laughing as he rode off into the night.

I could hear the screams for hours, and the forest was dimly lit by the fires in the town. Sirens were drawing closer to the town, as there was no local fire department. Maybe this would convince the governor to expand a little further into the state with these services. Andras returned, licking the blood from his sword.

"Shall you inspect my work, or will you take it in good faith that it was performed properly?"

"I take it on faith. I accept that all work has been completed to satisfaction, and release you from my bondage. Return to the world from which you came, and may I never have need of your service again!"

Andras remained there, grinning. I tried the incantation again, and still, he remained. I opened the book looking for why it wasn't working. Was I missing a word? Did I mistranslate something? Andras rode next to me and took the book from my hands.

"Where did you get this book?"

"The librarian gave it to me. She said it had no title, and as such, it had no value to the library."

"That librarian was the last one who summoned me from this book. I killed many Chinese that night. Chosin was stained red from her wrath. Tell me, how far into this book did you read?"

I nervously swallowed, thinking this was a very bad sign for my prospects of remaining alive. "I read up to where it described you, the service you provide, and how to summon you."

Andras turned through a few more pages. "Did Mrs. Kim tell you to read all of it before using it?"

"No". That was a really bad sign for me surviving this night.

"Please read aloud from pages, let me see, 205 through 207." He handed me the book back and rested his sword on his saddle.

"All ingredients must be properly mixed for any summoning to be effective. Note well that each ingredient has its own magical properties. Mistletoe is toxic to demons, and should never be used in a ritual to summon them, as they will vanish upon contact with it. Holly provides a ward for them, giving a barrier that they can neither harm nor be harmed through. Ivy is the most common vine used for tracing the sigil, but any other vine will suffice. Salt is used to enhance the power of your conjuration, as well as to protect the conjuror from the demon. Chalk is used to denote the offering for the demon as payment for service."

I felt a sharp pinch in my stomach and saw his sword through me.

"Payment accepted," was the last I heard before he vanished into fire.

About the Author

J. Beck is a new author with a passion for history, music, and fantasy gaming.

64

Katarina went through the cards again. There it was again, the six of swords and the two of pentacles. She knew what had to be done, but was not so sure it was worth it. Summoning a demon was never prudent. Who was she to be prudent though? She had defied many laws throughout her lifetime. She was always one to throw caution to the wind. A rebel who chose her own fate. Or so she thought. Now she stood on the brink of death, and feared it more than anything her life ever offered her. She checked to make sure she had the right candles set up and lit. Demons were very specific in how they wished to be summoned.

Katarina shook her head and laughed to herself. Why did everything require a ritual? Instead, just say 'Hey, so and so, wanna hang out?' Maybe she was getting tired in her old age. For the better part of her life she had been fully dedicated to performing the rituals and saying the right incantations. The success rate of having it done just right was high, but there was always a cost. She longed to be free of the tasks and just live. Was it even possible for a witch like her to live a simple life? It sure would be nice. She looked at the clock. Now was the time to say the incantation and command the demon show itself.

She wondered what form it would take. The intimidating leopard? The frightening man? Or the floating feminine beauty? She really didn't care which form he chose at the time. It was just mere curiosity that had her thinking in such a way. She sliced her hand and allowed the blood to flow into a cup. Speaking the incantation over the cup and stirring the blood she called out the name of Flauros.

He appeared before her, tall and massive. His eyes were like lit torches as the flames flickered brightly. He seemed at ease with her, at least there was that. She bowed to him the best she could before offering him to take a seat.

"What? No triangle to hold me in place? You are a bold one," Flauros mocked.

"I am old. I did not feel a need to put you in chains. Thank you, Lord Flauros, for gracing me with your presence," the witch greeted.

"What is it that you want from me, old crone?" He demanded softly.

"I hear that you can foresee my future. The ball is not forthcoming, and I feel my skills are lacking as of late. I wish to know my future, how I lived and how I die. I would also like to know where I will go after death," she confessed.

"And what would I get in return?" He demanded.

"Aside from my eternal dedication?" The witch asked with raised brow.

"Yes, there must be more that you can give me. I have many servants and I lead legions. What is one more dedicated servant?" He shrugged while folding his arms, then stood tall. He stood there foreboding and full of intimidation.

"I will gather a group of people to hear you as you tell the tale of creation and how you and your comrades fell. I will ensure that 'your' own story is told to millions. I will serve you for the rest of my days in this way. I'm afraid that is all this old body can give you." Flauros relaxed a bit, making himself comfortable in a chair next to the warm fire. He was pleased that this witch was offering so much and frankly he was a bit bored and could use a distraction.

"Age is deceptive." He waved his hand in the air near where Katarina now sat across from him. Much to her amazement she watched as her body was now transformed into the young beauty, she'd once been many years prior. She looked up at Flauros in wonder.

"You give me youth again? That is most kind of you." She smiled as she handed him a cup of tea.

"I have my reasons. You are much more pleasant on the eyes now," he flirted and winked, causing Katarina to blush.

"As odd as it might seem, I do find you attractive as well." She had the decency to blush before him. He laughed and took her by the hand, kissing it lightly.

"You, my dear, are exactly the distraction I've been looking for. The only thing missing is a contract. Shall we make a deal? It will require your soul. Not that big of a deal really," he lied.

"What good is a soul if it is not kept in good hands?" Katarina smirked.

"Indeed, and I assure you that your soul will be in good hands with me," he continued to lie. He could care less about her soul. He was just glad to have something to relieve him of the mundane everyday things he was burdened to do. There was a new glow in this witch's' eyes, bringing a crooked smile to the demon's face.

"My dear, shall we consummate this deal between us? Seal the deal with our bodies?" He asked with pride.

"Who am I to deny the wants of my flesh? I have not had the touch of a man in ages. And I certainly have never had a roll in the hay with a mighty demon as yourself. You lead, my lord, and I shall follow." She waited for his next move, her body fully aroused and ready for the taking.

Flauros looked at her young false body with a fiery lust he hadn't had in millennia. He reached over and pulled her to him. He would have her both inside and out. And when he was done with her mortal body, she would become one of his mighty consorts in the fiery depths of Hell below.

65

ANDREALPHUS: BIRDS OF A FEATHER
JAZMINE CLENDENIN

Andrealphus was the commander and ruler of thirty troops of demons in hell. He was the sixty-fifth demon of Solomon in the "Clavicula Salomonis Regis" or "The Lesser Key of Solomon."

If you knew the story well, you would know that Adrealphus was a teacher of mathematics and finder of stars, although he could be a bit of a trickster. Andrealphus often was seen in the form of a great bird. He was like a peacock with massive feathers, full of color, and made noises that could be heard from far and wide.

He would sit in Hell as a giant bird with his hordes of demons serving him. He sat awaiting a human's calls, hoping for some excitement, or something that might bring him a little fun.

Most everyone knew not to get on his bad side, but there were still the few that called upon him unknowing, some of them had never been seen or heard from again.

*****

Bastian was everything, good looking, fun and caring, a free thinker, and an adventurous spirit, but he was far from intelligent. He was smart when it came time to working with his hands or engineering something for his agriculture class in high school, but he had made it to college, a good one at that.

His dream had always been to become and engineer for NASA. He wanted to be the one to build some of the greatest spacecrafts known to man, but little did he know he would be required to get a degree in astronomy as well.

He was passing all his technology and engineering classes, but when it came to the stars, he was failing miserably. It was nearing finals, and he was desperate to pass with flying colors, or at least the best he could. He had heard of Andrealphus through stories of old, and wanted to attempted calling him to see if Andrealphus would assist him with learning about the stars.

He accessed the internet and looked up a store for books of spells and instructions on conjuring a spirit. He came upon an online store and found the book suggested for a conjuring and bought it, paying for a rush delivery.

Two days later, and only three days before finals, the book came in the mail. Bastian was excited and nervous about what he was going to do. He had only stories to go on. He opened the book with a mix of nervousness and excitement to study what he needed to do to access Andrealphus, the great bird of Hell.

The book was made from what felt like human skin, although the outside was covered in brightly toned bird feathers. Bastian was afraid to open it at first but knew if he was going to try to call Andrealphus, he was going to have to study it…that was if he could bring himself to believe in what the stories had told him.

He flipped through the pages almost like some magick force took ahold of him. Directly in the middle of the book, he found the system for a conjuring…conjuring Andrealphus in fact. Suddenly, Bastian felt the air around him grow cold as he took another look at the book to see what he might find.

There, in the center of the page on the left side was a picture of the great demon Andrealphus. He stood looking like a monstrous version of a peacock, which caused Bastian to worry a little. Andrealphus didn't look like a normal bird, but instead he looked like Hell had chewed him up and spit him back out.

Bastian looked the book over three more times before he began to gather his supplies. He got the things from his home, exactly what the book called for, but he was going to have to stop somewhere and get the five white candles needed for the conjuring and some black dye.

He got in his pick-up, leaving his home behind him. He found a home-good store he felt sure would have the candles he needed, and it did. He stopped at a grocery store and picked up the dye that was needed. In a few minutes, his list was completed, as he went out looking for the desired bit of ground the book said Andrealphus liked to be called upon.

*****

He drove out towards the country where he knew once night fell, the stars could show at their brightest. He drove looking at field after field for over four hours trying to find the right one. The book stated the ground needed to be open, dry, and surrounded by a perfect circle of trees and brush, or else Andrealphus would not appear.

Bastian climbed out of his truck with the book and a duffle bag of supplies in hand. There were no houses or vehicles to be seen which made him feel a bit better. People would think he was crazy if they saw him conjuring a demon in the dark, especially at midnight which was when the book said the ground would be ready...witching hour would be upon him. The ground was cold and hard as the crops had been long picked for the winter, but they had yet to have their first snow of the year.

He walked to the center of the field, counting his steps to find the exact center as the book told him. The entire process took hours and it was nearing midnight when he finished.

He knew if it didn't get done at midnight, it wouldn't be able to be done until the next night, and Bastian knew he didn't have that kind of time.

*****

Using a flashlight, Bastian took a bowl out of his duffle and dumped salt into it. He then took a few drops of black dye and dyed it to match the black color in the book. He dumped the salt in a star formation, finishing it off with a circle going around it.

He put a white candle on each of the points of the star and lit them on fire until they glowed soft in the field. He flipped the flashlight off as he sat cross-legged in the center of the star. The only light came from the moon, stars, and the candles, but for some reason, everything felt dark.

He placed the book on his lap, then put his hands, palms upward in a meditation pose and began to chant.

"Andrealphus of Hell, keeper of the stars and mathematics, come forward this day to assist me. Come forth," he began. "Andrealphus of Hell, great bird of the deep, come forward this day to assist me, come forth. Andralphus of Hell with feathers on fire, come forward this day to assist me, come forth now."

All around Bastian, the ground began to shake. He tried to sit still, but fear began to bubble up inside him. In front of his eyes, the great silhouette of a bird on fire formed before him.

Andrealphus of Hell stood inches away from Bastian the conjurer.

The great bird's feathers dripped with hellfire until Andrealphus shifted to human form. He looked on, angry that the puny human had called upon him.

"Why did you bring me here?" The large booming voice of Andrealphus asked.

"I have a question to ask of you," Bastian spoke through a shaky voice.

"You...have a question of me?" He asked as his voice echoed through the field. "What business do you have with me, tiny human?"

"I have college finals this week. I am studying astronomy, and need you to help me learn the stars," Bastian pleaded.

"I will help you, but you will owe me,"

"What will I owe you in return great spirit?" Bastian asked.

"I will only tell you once you know the stars," Andrealphus said. "Once you know who Orion is, or the great Cassiopeia, I will take my payment then."

"Very well," Bastian said.

"You agree then?" Andrealphus asked.

"I do," he said.

The two men shook hands, Andrealphus' hand was nearly twice the size of Bastian's. Andrealphus placed his hands on either side of Bastian's temples until suddenly his face took on a knowing look.

"I know," Bastian screamed. "I know who Orion is and even the mother of Andromeda."

"Great," Andrealphus smiled. "Now, for the payment for bothering me boy."

Before Bastian could speak, Andrealphus stuck his hands out straight and whispered a few words. In seconds, Bastian's body began to twist as his bones bent to the breaking point in every different direction.

Before he knew what was happening, his body had shrunk into that of a teeny-tiny sparrow.

"You will know the stars forever, boy," Andrealphus laughed. "But you will know them forever in feathers."

About the Author

Jazmine Clendenin is a fun-loving Freshman in high school with a passion for reading and writing. She hopes to one day follow in the footsteps of her mother by inspiring the world through the written word!

66

KIMARIS: GRAMMAR DAEMON
P.I. STOULPE

LaRae threw the pen across the room. She was frustrated with this project. After several hours of staring at the printed pages, she had gone cross-eyed.

"I need a break!" She proclaimed to the empty room. She was alone in her home office. Even the cats had wandered off to their sleeping pads in the living room. "She'd lose a battle with a wet paper bag!"

She got up from her desk and retrieved the pen. If she didn't pick it up now it would still be there in a week's time. She set it on her desk and walked out to get a fresh cup of coffee from the kitchen, and stepped out into the brisk fall air for a cigarette.

She'd technically quit smoking months ago, but indulged in a puff or five when she was frustrated. A full cigarette might be in order this day. She let the coffee brew in the single cup machine as she paced back and forth on the back porch of her small bungalow in an older part of town.

The smoke and the chill air cleared her head. She thought over the pages of the printed manuscript. Why do I do this to myself? She asked as she stubbed the smoldering butt out in the stone ashtray she had leftover from her chain smoking days. It pays the bills, she sighed and resisted the urge to have another cancer stick.

Returning to her kitchen, she mixed a dollop of sweetened cream into the oversized mug and headed for her office. One of the cats popped her head up as LaRae walked by. She paused and patted the furry head.

When she got back to her desk she noticed that the pen was on the floor. Raising an eyebrow, she picked it up and dropped it on her desk. She sipped her coffee before taking her seat.

Setting the cup down she sighed and looked to the screen of her laptop. An email notification flashed for her attention, but she ignored it. She wanted to log into social media and get lost in the world of cat memes and silly videos. She wouldn't let herself, though. Her work needed to be done. She still had another hour or two before she could call it a day.

Sighing again she looked at the stack of papers in front of her and gasped. There were several swirls of red ink on the top sheet. She didn't remember making any of those marks. Shuffling through the pages she saw that there was some red mark or another on just about every page.

Finding one without a mark on it she scanned the words. They were perfect. Every period and coma was where it should be. Not a single word misspelled or out of place.

"Huh!" She made a surprised sound. "At least this client could do one page without a mistake." She shifted back through the stack and found the beginning of the current chapter she was editing.

A sound from by the door to her office caught her attention. Without looking up, she made a tsk sound with her tongue against her teeth, calling for the cat at the door to come in. She might not want the distraction of social media, but the soft purr of a cat would do her some good.

No cat hopped on the desk. There was another noise, a bit louder. She looked up from the page in her hands and dropped it.

"Who the hell are you!? How did you get in here!?"

A tall man in a red shirt and black slacks was standing just outside her office door. He had short brown hair and wore a pair of round-lensed glasses perched on his nose. He was handsome

"I came by to help," he answered in a soft tenor.

"But who the hell are you?" She repeated.

"Name's Ki. Ki Maris," he said. "May I come in?"

"I'm not sure about that," she hesitated. "I should be calling the police! How did you get in my house?"

"Take a breath, LaRae," he said in a soothing voice as he stepped into her office. "I said I am here to help."

"I'm not so sure of that," she said with a hint of fear in her voice. She was reaching for her cellphone on the corner of the desk when he stepped all the way into her office and came around her desk.

"LaRae," he said her name softly. "I'm not going to hurt you. I only want to help. This is a lot of work," he indicated the stack of papers on her desk. "You shouldn't do it alone. At least not on your deadline."

"Trying to horn in on my business?" She asked suspiciously as she let go of the phone.

"No, no. I'm not doing that. I assure you." He stood just to the side of her and looked down on her pretty round face.

"Then what are you doing?"

"Perhaps I should answer your earlier question," he smiled with a flash of bright white teeth. "I already told you my name, but what am I?"

"I thought you were going to answer my questions," she shot him a look and pondered her cell phone again.

"Quite right," he chuckled. The soft rumble of his laughter made her blush.

"Fine. What are you?" She asked with an arched eyebrow.

"I'm a grammar daemon."

"A grammar what?"

"'Daemon," he repeated.

"Demon! No such thing!" She did pick up her phone, and swiped the screen to turn the dial pad on.

"Daemon, not demon. Humans always get us confused," he stepped back and stood against the wall watching her. "I am here to help."

"You keep saying that," she said.

"I mean it."

"And what can you do to help me?" She asked.

"I can make your editing easier."

"Ha!" She exclaimed. "You are here to horn in on my business!"

"I've already answered that accusation, LaRae," the sound of her name on his lips was almost hypnotic. She stopped protesting and just sat there looking at him. "I can make it easier and quicker. That's what I do. I'm a grammar daemon."

"What's in it for you?" She set the phone back on her desk, just within her reach.

"The joy of your company," he said with a smile. Again, those teeth!

"Surely you want something more."

"No, just your companionship." He leaned forward a little and tapped at the pile of papers. "I've already started for you. You are right, this client couldn't write her way out of a wet paper bag."

She laughed at his repeating of her earlier thought. Tapping her fingernail on the desk she thought for a few moments. "So... You want to help me and not get paid?"

"You will pay me," he answered. "With your company."

"So you keep saying, why should I believe you?"

"I'm a daemon, we can't lie." He moved around to the empty chair opposite her desk.

"I thought demons were all liars," she watched his attractive form as he settled into the chair.

"I'm not a demon! I'm a daemon. Listen to the difference in the words," he insisted. "A daemon is a messenger."

"And you are a dem... Sorry, daemon of grammar? How does that work?" She was perplexed.

"I convey what the words and punctuation should be," he explained. "You are more than an editor, you are a writer. Something you have neglected to pay the bills by editing. Right?"

"Yes," she said hesitantly. "What of it?"

"I can open the door for you to write again, your own words and stories."

"You can?" She was getting over her surprise at his appearance. Still not convinced of his motives, she was not ready to commit to anything with him.

"I did the edits for you in that client's manuscript. I honestly don't know why you did it with pen and paper," he nodded to the pen that had been on the floor when she came in. "It would be so much quicker to do it on the computer."

"I know, and I do. This project demanded more focus, though."

"It certainly did, but now you have to redo the edits on the screen."

"I expect to find more when I do that. This was just a baseline...." She picked up the sheets in front of her and looked through them quickly. "Wait, you did all the edits?"

"See for yourself, I'll wait," he leaned back in the chair and stared up at the ceiling. Several minutes passed as she leafed through the sheets.

"You did a good job. I didn't see anything you missed."

"IT is what I do," he reminded her. "Do we have a deal?"

"A trial, no deal yet," she smiled to herself. "I remember something in a story about it being a bad idea to make a deal with a demon."

"Daemon!" He said with emphasis on the first vowel sound.

"Whatever," she said with a smirk. "Let's try this and see what happens."

"I'm game if you are, LaRae," he replied.

"Good," she pulled a tablet out of the drawer of the desk. "There are three more manuscripts from this client that need editing."

"Three?" He gasped.

"Yup, get to work." She handed him the tablet and turned her attention to her own laptop. "I've got some writing to do."

Ki smiled and took the tablet from her. "I think you are getting the better of this deal," he murmured.

"No deal, yet," she reminded him.

About the Author

P.I. Stouple writes romance, crime drama, and detective stories. She will be featured in the upcoming Mystery 42 Manuscripts RP novel Elegance of the Moon.

https://www.facebook.com/pistoulpe

67

ANDUSIUS AND THE LUMBERJACK
CYNTHIA STATON

Max walked through the dense forest with his ax slung over his shoulder while whistling a happy tune. Fall was just starting to make its mark on the land by showing a beautiful array of colors as the leaves made a blanket on the ground. For as long as Max could remember, he had always loved the woods. Every chance he got he would be out playing in the forest that lined his backyard. He spent more time hanging out by himself in the woods than he did with friends or family. He couldn't really explain it, just that he felt more at home there.

As he grew older he started working alongside his father and uncles as they went out everyday to cut down trees for firewood. Max was thrilled the day his father handed him an ax, and told him to go cut down his very first tree. He knew exactly how to do it since he'd watched his family do it for years. He cut down a medium sized ashwood tree successfully. He was so proud, and was made even more proud when his family praised him for his success. Since then he had taken on the family business of cutting firewood and selling it. His ax had never let him down.

This year, Max was on his own in the woods. He had sharpened his ax, and was more than ready to cut down some trees. He kept an eye out for a good group of medium sized trees he could chop down without any problems as he walked along. Finally, after a good bit of searching, he found a copse of trees that looked just right. A halo of sunlight had broken out above, and was shining upon these trees as if to announce that they were the ones for Max. He walked on over to the copse, and took a good look at the trees. After careful examination, he was elated to find that they were indeed the most perfect trees he'd ever come across.

He went to work right away as he took his ax and made to swing at one of the trees. It hit the tree, but seemed to bounce off causing Max to lose his balance and fall in his rear end. Confused, he jumped up and brushed himself off. He went back to the tree to examine it. Not a single scratch was on it. He rubbed his jaw in wonderment. He knew he had hit that tree, yet nothing had happened. That sort of thing had never happened to him before. He took the ax and decided to give it another go. One swing around and bam. It hit, but still nothing happened. At least this time it didn't knock him down. Not sure exactly what was going on, he walked over to another tree and attempted to give it a good chop. Whack! The ax stuck this time, but would not come out. Max pulled and pulled, but it just would not budge.

He stood back to get a good look only to find that it was definitely stuck in the tree. Scratching his head, he stared at the tree in utter confusion. An odd feeling came over him as he realized that there were no natural sounds happening in the woods at that moment. Where had the birds gone? Or the chattering chipmunk? The eerie silence only added to his stressed state. Then he heard the sound of horses hooves behind him. He turned around quickly and his eyes grew huge as saucers. There before him was a unicorn. It was about 18 hands tall and dark brown. It's eyes were a piercing blood red and it's body was sinewy.

"Whoa boy. It's alright there." Max attempted to calm the animal. A sound erupted from the unicorn as Max tried to calm it. Max could have sworn it was laughter.

"I'm not so sure I'm the one who needs calming," it chuckled.

"You talk?" Max asked. "Wait, of course you can talk. You are a unicorn which means you are a magical creature. Not that I know much of these things. What is your name and why are you here?" Max clamped his mouth shut as he realized he was rambling.

"Relax. My name is Amdusias. I'm here to help. I saw that you were having some trouble with these trees and wondered if you would like a bit of help with them?" Amdusias offered.

"Seems an odd thing for an unicorn to want to do, but sure. I would hate to not be able to knock down these trees. They are absolutely perfect for firewood," Max conceded.

"Yes, seems it would be a waste wouldn't it?" Amdusias agreed.

"What would I owe you for helping me?" Max was willing to pay the unicorn for his help, but didn't quite know what he'd want in payment.

"Oh! Just a favor in return should I ever need it," Amdusias smiled. It was an odd thing to see a unicorn smile and a bit frightening. Rows of sharp teeth could be seen protruding out as he smiled. Max couldn't help but pray that the unicorn would not eat him.

"Alright, seems fair enough. So, what do we do?" Max watched as a flute appeared from thin air. Amdusias attempted to take it in his hooves, but grew frustrated when he could not. He looked to Max and said,

"I'll need you to command me to play."

"What?" Max tilted his head sideways.

"It's easy really, just tell me to play my instrument," Amdusias explained, growing impatient.

"Oh, alright. Amdusias, go on and play that instrument," Max commanded. As soon as the words were out, Max watched as Amdusias took on a more humanoid form.

"Much better. I can play an instrument a lot easier when I have hands," Amdusias winked. He took the flute and began to play an ominous tune. It permeated through the copse, and Max watched as the trees began to bend and sway. Amdusias stopped playing long enough to inform Max, "You don't even need your ax. Just tell the trees to fall over. They will do your bidding." He went back to playing as Max stared long and hard at the trees,

"Trees! I'm commanding you to fall over." One by one the all of the trees in the copse uprooted themselves and fell to the ground. Max stood near Amdusias as fallen trees now surrounded them. He turned to the unicorn man and smiled,

"Well then, that was pretty amazing. Thank you!"

"Glad I could help. Just remember, you owe me," Amdusias said just before he vanished. Max stood in awe of all that just occurred before breaking out of his spell, and chopping up the trees that lay all about him. He thought to himself that any favor asked was well worth it. Not once thinking that it could well be a demon coming for his soul.

About the Author

Cynthia Staton is an inspirational speaker and author. Her first book is called Life Lived Not Lost a journey of hope.
Cynthia has also jumped feet first into down the rabbit hole into the anthology world, but also plan to have her next novel out this year.

68

BELIAL, THE EVIL ONE
CYNTHIA STATON

Carol left the classroom as soon as the bell rang, and headed out the door to get home as fast as her legs could get her there. The sooner she got home the safer she felt. For the past week, she had this eerie feeling that someone was watching her. It felt so real that the hairs on her body stood on end. Though every time she looked around there was not one person to be seen. One time, she saw a cat and laughed nervously. Maybe she was just losing her mind. No matter what it was though, she just could not shake the feeling.

This time was no different as she ran out the door and down the sidewalk to head to her house. The three block trip normally took her about twenty minutes to get home at a lazy walking pace. Running tended to get her there in less than five minutes. She just did not want to take any chances. Once Carol made it inside her home and locked the door behind her, she felt safe. She wasn't sure why her home felt safe, but was grateful for it. Maybe it was because her home had always been her sanctuary, and therefore, it was a safe place. The only other place she felt safe in was her church.

Carol stood there with her head against the door for a few moments just to gather her wits about her so she could spend the evening in peace. Her parents were gone for the weekend, which meant she would be by herself that whole time. She didn't mind. It gave her plenty of time to get caught up on homework, maybe do some baking, and plan her lesson for Sunday School at church. Carol dropped her backpack down onto the floor next to the door, and decided to go into the kitchen for a drink. She reached in and grabbed a bottle of coke from the fridge. These were her favorite. There was just something great about coke in a glass bottle.

"Hey there, Kitten," a soft melodic voice greeted her, startling her so much she dropped her coke, which shattered on the floor. She turned around to find the most beautiful man she had ever seen in her entire life. If he was even a man.

"Who...who are you?" She choked out.

"I'm a friend," he smiled.

"Friends don't usually sneak into a person's house and scare them. That's more of a stalker thing." Carol pointed her finger at him. He fell into a fit of laughter that was a delight to Carol's ears, causing her to be a tad conflicted in how she felt.

"Well then, would you rather I be your stalker? I don't mind," he winked at her, making her blush.

"I...uh," Carol stuttered.

"So, I've been watching you," he admitted willingly.

"I knew it! I've felt someone watching me all week!" Carol exclaimed.

"Yes, well...I needed to be sure that I could trust you," his lips curled in a sly smile.

"What?" Carol looked at him blankly, "Look man, I'm really confused. Just what the hell do you want with me?"

"Carol, my dear sweet Carol. You have been such a good girl haven't you?" He mocked.

"What is so wrong about being good?" Carol retorted.

"You are missing out on so much!" He exclaimed. "You are young and beautiful!" Carol blushed when he called her beautiful. "You deserve to taste the finer things in life."

"I'm not sure what you mean," she faltered. The man stood and walked up to her. She had not moved from the fridge whose door was still wide open and the shattered glass mixed with coke sticking to the ground and her feet. He was very tall, and she could swear he was glowing. He reached out and stroked her cheek which grew hot as his hand made contact.

"I mean you shouldn't be here at home all alone. You should be out with your friends and living it up! I know you want to go to Owen's big house party. You know you should go! Loosen up, let down your hair, and unwind." His voice spoke these words softly into her ear like a gentle kiss, sending shivers down her spine. She had a sudden urge to kiss him, but when she turned to do so he was back at the counter, sitting there sipping a cup of tea. There was a mischievous twinkle in his eye as he watched her.

"I've never been to a party," Carol confessed weakly.

"Then why not change that. Go! You won't regret it. Besides, Greg is going to be there," he winked.

"What?! How do you know about Greg?" she asked, completely perplexed.

"Oh, I know a lot of things. Here, take this. You'll need it to get in." He handed her a peace of paper. She took it and read it quickly. It was an invitation to Owen's party. The urge to go was extremely strong, and one that she just could not deny. She looked up and smiled at the man,

"Alright! I'll go! Thank you!" She ran over, hugged the man, then ran out the door without another word.

Balial watched the young woman leave and cackled. Another innocent soul sent off onto the path of destruction. Another notch of success on his belt. She would go to that party and hook up with Greg, who would then convince her to go upstairs with him. He would take advantage of her against her will, leaving her alone and helpless. She'll most likely get pregnant, and if all went well, she'd give up the child and end her own life. Yes, he had a lot of fun planned for this party that he instigated. Things were going to go well this night, he could feel it. He closed his eyes to savor the thoughts going through his mind as he smiled wickedly.

About the Author

Cynthia Staton is an inspirational speaker and author. Her first book is called Life Lived Not Lost a journey of hope.

Cynthia has also jumped feet first into down the rabbit hole into the anthology world, but also plan to have her next novel out this year.

69

DECARABIA: DESIRE'S CUP
AMANDA J. EVANS

"By thunder, by rain. By wind, by flame. I summon you." The ground shook, and a pentacle appeared at my feet before transforming into the shape of a man. My feet shuffled backwards. Towering above me – a muscular torso, naked from the waist up, with dark curls falling to his shoulders – he stirred something deep in my stomach. His eyes flashed red before settling on a deep caramel. Eyes that pulled, and coerced. My insides fluttered.

"Why have you summoned me, mage?"

My brain froze, synopses refusing to connect or even spark. I stuttered trying to force the words from my mouth. "I...I require your assistance...to...um...to win the mage cup."

His eyebrows rose as a wicked grin spread across his face. Shit, what have I done? He's going to obliterate me. Reaching inside my shirt, I tugged the cord that held the demon seal – for protection, the summon spell said – and let it hang outside my clothes. His smile dissolved.

"How can I help?"

His voice was a deep baritone, soothing, smothering. Christ, I'm in trouble. I swallowed and cleared my throat. Control Willa, keep it together. "I need something big, something that will wow the judges, set me apart from all the others. You can make birds obey me, right?"

He nodded, and his dark curls fell forward before he tossed them back with a flick of his hand. My mouth hung open as I followed his every moment. "What will you offer me in return?"

Anything. Offer him anything, your body, whatever he wants. My thoughts were distracting. I had to keep it together. "I hear you like to party. To sing and dance."

"I do, but I do not need your assistance for that. What have you to offer me in exchange for my help?"

"What do you want?" I held my breath as I waited for his reply.

"I require but a kiss from your sweet lips." He stepped forward and took my hand. Warmth spread like a bush fire and I gasped. "Do you accept?"

"I...um..."

He leaned forward, his eyes dancing between flame and caramel, his tongue wetting his lips before they brushed against mine, soft and tender. It was over before I knew it and he withdrew breathing in deeply. "Perfect."

He stepped back and looked me up and down. "Tell me young mage, where does your magic lie?"

My thoughts were jumbled. His lips had tasted so...addictive. I wanted them against mine again. I shook my head. This was ridiculous. He stared at me and I remembered his question. "Um, well, I can control water and fire. No scratch that, last time I tried to use fire magic I set Professor Saxx's cloak alight. Wind, no I suck at that."

He laughed and cut me off. "You are a strange one, mage, but I will help you."

"You will?"

"I will teach you of herbs and precious stones and how to master the art of astral and dream shape shifting. Tell me of this cup you seek, the powers it holds."

It was my turn to laugh, but I quickly explained the annual magic competition when he scowled at me. He listened intently. "You desire this cup so much that you are willing to summon a demon for help?"

"Yes." There was no point in lying. I needed to win the cup. I needed to show them I wasn't an abomination, a misfit, a waste of their time. If I didn't win this year, it would all be over, and a life as a reject, a failure, was all that waited for me.

Decarabia sensed my desperation. "Who threatens you, mage?"

"My name is Willa," I snapped before apologizing when he frowned.

"Who threatens you, Willa?"

"No one, I'll be fine. I just need to win the cup."

"You are filled with fear. I can smell it on you."

"No, yes, and I need your help."

"You are quite confusing, Willa, but I think I like you." He smiled and crossed his arms, his chest muscles bulging. "Shall we begin? Where is the nearest forest?"

"We're leaving my room?"

"Yes, unless you wish me to turn your room into a forest?"

"Okay, let me get my cloak, and maybe you should...you know," I said waving my hands at his naked chest, "Put some clothes on."

"My nakedness disturbs you?"

"No, not at all, but..." My cheeks flamed. "We are going outside."

"No one but you can see me Willa, but if it pleases you, I will cover up." He clicked his fingers and his chest was covered with a tight-fitting t-shirt, muscles bulging underneath. "Better?" He asked, catching me staring.

I swallowed the lump in my throat and turned toward the door.

"Don't worry, you are safe as long as I am with you. No one will see us leave."

Decarabia was right, we walked through the hallways and out the front door and no one noticed us at all.

Raxum Forest surrounded the college. It gave me the creeps and students had been warned never to enter it at night. The trees stood tall, their shadows spilling over the ground, branches like arms stretching and reaching, and creaking. The noise unnerved me. Sunlight was waning, and the few strands of light that did make it through the thick canopy of trees barely made a difference to the darkness that surrounded us. We must have walked for at least half an hour before Decarabia stopped.

"I need to test your magic ability before we begin."

"Okay, what would you like me to do?"

"Show me your water control."

I looked around. There was no water anywhere. How could I show him my water control skills without any water? I shrugged. "There is no water."

He clicked his fingers and a large bubble of water appeared in his hand. He swirled it around and across the tips of his fingers. "Catch," he said as the water bubble floated through the air towards me.

I tried to catch it, but as soon as it brushed against my hand it burst, drenching me.

He laughed and threw his hands in the air. "You can't catch water, you must use your magic to meld it to your essence. Let's try again. This time, Willa, catch the bubble with your magic. Cast your power out and encase the water within in. Then let it rest in your hand."

I did what he said, and it worked. The bubble of water hovered over my fingers. "What now?"

"Now show me what you can do with water."

I sucked in a deep breath. Don't fail me now. Focusing my attention on the water, I imagined it growing, spreading, shifting, and changing into the shape of a rabbit. I felt my power surge and pulse from deep within and I closed my eyes. Please work.

"Not bad."

His voice startled me, my concentration slipped, and once again I was soaked. I shook out my hands and squeezed the ends of my shirt, water dripping to the ground.

"You need a change of clothes. Let me help." Decarabia mumbled to himself and a new shirt appeared at my feet. "Get changed and we will try again."

He stood with his arms crossed, waiting, as I bent to pick up the shirt. I threw off my cloak. My shirt was soaked, clinging to me. My cheeks flushed as I caught him staring, but I grabbed the material and pulled it over my head turning to face the tree, so he wouldn't see anything. I threw my shirt on the ground and whipped the clean one over my head as quick as I could.

Decarabia was smirking when I turned back around. "What?" I asked.

"Nothing. I forget that humans can be so...shy."

We tried again with the water, but after five attempts and two further shirt changes, it was clear I was no water controller. "Don't worry," Decarabia said, placing a hand on my shoulder. "We have time."

"It's no good," I huffed. "I'll never win." Tears pooled in my eyes, and I lowered my head. His warm fingers settled under my chin, and lifted it until he was looking in my eyes. Red to caramel. My heart thumped, and I swallowed hard.

"I can make sure you win if you..." He paused and licked his lips and I copied him. My breathing was shallow, my cheeks flushed, and his body was so close to mine. His thumb moved along my jaw and across my lips and every nerve in my body ignited. "Magic comes from within," he whispered. "You have to let it flow, let it explore." He moved in closer his head dipping so his lips brushed against my neck. "Magic knows what you want it to do, but you have to let it be free too." He kissed up my neck, along my jaw, and then brushed his lips against mine.

I was lost for words. Nothing mattered but the feel of his lips against my skin. The rush of power flowing through my veins, and the longing unfurling itself in the pit of my stomach. His tongue ran across the seam of my lips, and my mouth opened. I wanted him to explore, to release the magic within me. The kiss deepened, and he wrapped his arms around me, pulling me closer, chest against chest. His tongue danced with mine, exploring, searching, feeding me with power.

He pulled back, and I gasped. My body trembled, and all I could do was stare at him. "You will win, Willa. I have unleashed your power, and now it will serve you. Try conjuring and controlling water again."

I did as he asked, still in a trance. The water obeyed my every command and intention, shifting from rabbit to deer, to snake and eagle. "How?" I asked.

"Your power is like your desire. It was trapped, and needed a little coaxing."

"And you did that?"

"I did, with a little help from you," he said, winking. "You need to let go more often, Willa."

His voice was deep, commanding, and before I knew it, I was agreeing with him, walking towards him, running my hands across his chest. He laughed and gripped my hands. "Looks like you lost your little protection seal, Willa. I've awakened your desire."

I heard him, but I couldn't pull back, couldn't stop myself from leaning into him, feeling his warm body against mine. No seal. No protection. The words circled in my mind and my hand went to my neck. The seal was gone. I must have lost it when I changed.

Decarabia watched me struggle and stepped back, breaking his hold on me. "Don't worry, Willa. I won't let you do anything you don't want to do, and once you win your cup I will leave. You do still desire this cup?"

"Yes, yes I have to have it."

"Do we have an agreement?"

I thought about his offer. He had helped me find my magic. I felt stronger than ever and enjoying myself wasn't wrong. I was allowed to feel this way, to crave excitement and pleasure. I had three days before the championship, three days to develop my power, and three days to explore so much more. I licked my lips. "We have a deal."

"You won't regret it," he said, his eyes bleeding red to brown. "Desires cup can never be filled, but we'll have so much fun trying."

About the Author

Amanda J Evans is an award-winning Irish author of YA and Adult romance in paranormal and fantasy genres. Her stories centre on good versus evil with a splice of love and magic thrown in too. You can find out more on her website www.amandajevans.com.

SEERE: UPON A MIDNIGHT FAIR
M.L. GARZA

He was beautiful to behold, an angel with golden hair curling down to his shoulders, and wings that spanned nearly twenty feet when stretched out. The horse he rode upon was as white as freshly fallen snow, with a wingspan twice as long as the angel's own.

And the moment he visited Cat, she knew she had to be dreaming. He was too perfect to be real. He sat astride his steed beneath the willow tree in her yard, as if from one of the cheesy romance novels up in her room. The moonlight bounced off the white of his horse and the fairness of his skin and hair, and it seemed like they both glowed under their own light. How could anyone else not see them?

"Who... what are you?" She breathed, looking at the vision before her.

When she spoke, the angel smiled softly. He slid off his winged horse and approached her, silent as he moved. Only the soft rustle of grass beneath his bare feet betrayed his presence there.

"I am Seere, my dear kitten," he said, his voice as gentle as a kitten's purr itself. "And I am here for you, that is all you need know." Then he stopped, not a foot away from her, and his smile widened.

Warmth filled Cat's cheeks and drove away the cool Spring breeze. Every nerve in her body felt as though it were electrified, and all he had done was look at her. He truly was an angel, and not just by appearance alone.

Knowing it might break whatever spell had to be cast upon her, Cat reached out and touched the angel's cheek. She half expected him to disappear at the touch, but her fingers met skin instead of air.

"You're here for me?" She whispered. "But why?"

"Why not?" He asked, closing his eyes and leaning into her touch. "Can I not want to be here with you?"

A man... a creature like that... he could do whatever he wanted, and if that included her, then all the better.

Cat licked her lips and nodded, a shaky smile on her face. "But why me?"

Seere opened his eyes and reached out his own hand to cup her cheek. His fingers were smooth and cool, like an early morning rain, and when he looked at her, his eyes were the water that fell from the clouds. His hair like white gold, so pale that they resembled the clouds at dawn.

"Why you?" He asked, breaking her study of his features. "You called to me, my kitten. In your dreams, in your thoughts. How could I stay away?"

Her blush returned full force, if it had ever gone away at all, and there was no hiding it. And when Seere lowered his hand to take hers, Cat gladly followed him back to his winged horse. The beast was docile and barely stirred when she approached, watching her with a gentle silver gaze. It didn't even complain when Seere lifted the girl in his arms and set her upon its back.

"Where are we going?" she asked in a daze.

"To the stars, my love," he said, folding his wings in as he climbed on in front of her. "To the stars. Now hold on tight."

She did, wrapping her arms around the angel's waist so tightly that she was afraid of hurting him at first. It wasn't that she thought he would let her fall, Cat just didn't want this to be a dream after all. If he disappeared under her touch, if he wasn't real after all, she didn't know how she'd go on. There was no recovering from it.

"Ready?" He asked, looking over his shoulder to fix her with a playful blue eye. "It can be a little startling at first."

"I'm ready for anything," she assured him. "As long as you're with me."

"You can be sure of that, kitten. Hyah!"

They were off, shooting into the sky in a blur of white and gold, faster than thought. The willow tree and her home both were soon nothing but small specks below, and the whole world with them. To the stars indeed; nothing else mattered except the angel in Cat's arms, and that he would never leave her side from that moment on.

As the horse pushed through the clouds, they entered a new realm altogether. One silent of all, but the beating of wings and the air whipping around them. Above their heads lay the Milky Way and the crescent moon. Below them, only the blanket of clouds.

"Oh," sighed Cat. "Oh Seere..."

"Do you like it?" He asked, looking up as well. The stars reflected in the endless pools in his eyes, making them glitter and shine.

"It's beautiful."

"I'm glad." He paused. "You should have something nice to look at, in the end."

"Hm?" She turned her attention away from the stars to look at him again. "What do you mean?"

"Daniella, my kitten. Do you know of her?"

Daniella? Of course she did. Cat scowled at the thought of the horrible girl who worked with her. "What about her?" she asked. "How do you know Daniella?"

Seere smiled softly, that beautiful smile that melted her heart and lowered the top part of his tunic just enough to show a strange circular marking on his chest. "Do you see this mark?" he asked. "She somehow found this exact mark and called me to her. She bound my life to her will."

"I don't understand."

He half twisted to face her better, his smile widening, almost gladly. "It seems you have done something to anger her greatly. Something worth the risk of her very soul. She has demanded a task of me, and I must obey."

Cat opened her mouth to respond, but he grabbed her wrist and tugged her off the winged horse before a single sound came out. The same beautiful smile graced the angel's face even as he let her go, those soulful eyes not once losing sight of hers.

The Milky Way twinkled behind her angel as she watched him become smaller and smaller in the night sky, as though he were laying in a blanket of jewels.

Then the clouds enveloped her, and she re-entered the real world once more.

But oh, what a beautiful fall it was.

About the Author

M.L. Garza is a fantasy and science fiction author whose work has appeared in magazines, anthologies, stand alone works, and the big screen herself. Her debut novel is set for release in 2019.
https://www.facebook.com/AuthorMLGarza/

DANTALION: A BARGAIN CONCLUDED
M.L. GARZA

"This will never work."

"Quiet. It'll work."

"How do you know?"

"Shut up, both of you." Brandi turned back to the summoning circle before them, drawn carefully with chalk into the polished floor of her hardwood office. The city beyond glimmered in beautiful ignorance, lit in neon and headlights. It was a strange juxtaposition of the old and the new, but then so was Brandi herself.

Her office, normally illuminated in those crappy eco-friendly bulbs that gave her a headache, was instead aglow in candlelight, transforming the room into something arcane and dangerous.

Not that it wasn't a dangerous place normally. No one ever entered the CEO of Accutix Cybernetics' office unless they had balls or a death wish. Brandi Featherstone did not suffer fools lightly.

Behind her stood VP Bill Hale and his toady intern, James Something-Or-Other. Bill had been there since the beginning and he would be there for this too. That, and they had a bet going on whether this was even possible. Well, she wasn't the CEO for nothing, and there was more than one secret lurking in that head of hers. Brandi made and kept this company through darker dealings than most, so what was one more?

Her gray eyes narrowed as the white chalk glowed a little brighter, this time under its own power. The final lines of her chant still echoed in the room, calling forth the beast that had laid dormant for far too long. Would he truly come to her? Would he honor the pact made with her family so many years ago?

There was only one way to find out. It almost made her wish she'd worn something more appropriate than her usual pinstripe skirt and jacket. Perhaps a cloak and velvet gown would have been a better choice. Or even something more familiar to the creature she was summoning that evening. Anything to give her even a slight better advantage than what she walked in with: the advantage of blood-right.

A hand appeared first, using a piece of the floor to grab hold and pull the rest of him up. He was taller than she expected. Olivia never did really describe his true form in her old diaries, only the many bodies he possessed in their dealings together. He was as though a spider was given a man's form, wearing black garments not unlike what you would find at the turn of the twentieth century. Had he not come back to Earth since his last dealing with her family?

"Holy shit," she heard James the Intern mutter behind her.

Holy shit indeed.

Finally hauled to his feet, the creature looked at them for a moment, blinking slowly, like a baby first peering at the world for the first time. His dark eyes lingered on her the longest of all, and something seemed to spark within him when he did so. Something old and unnamed.

"Olivia?" he asked at last, voice hoarse from years of disuse. "Is that you, old girl?"

The corner of Brandi's lips turned up slightly, the ghost of a smile that perhaps seemed familiar to this ancient monster. She hoped so, anyway. They would need all the help they could get, and a nostalgic demon might be a helpful demon.

"Not quite," she said. "Olivia was my great grandmother. My name is Brandi."

He continued to look at her, his large black eyes expressionless as he took in her every feature. By all accounts and old photographs, she was the spitting image of the woman, so please let it help her now.

"You've been asleep for a very long time, Dantalion," she added.

"I see this," he said. "Brandi then. Brandi Featherstone?"

"Yes," she said. "You would be proud of her, Dantalion. Because of what you two started, she built a fortune, and our family became an empire. Today, we are known throughout the world."

"She was always resourceful," he said. "I doubt she needed my help with that."

"You never said you had some kind of demon for a family pet, Brandi," Bill said. "I thought you were just making this shit up."

"When do I make shit up?" she snapped behind her shoulder.

"Why am I here?" Dantalion asked. "Is there still a market for false exorcists?"

"As amusing as that would be, no." Brandi took a breath and stepped closer to the creature, wondering how her great grandmother ever had the courage to deal with him in the first place. Even sealed behind a chalk sigil, he was still dangerous.

Well, she was no tame kitten herself.

"There are others who would like to see the Featherstone name fall into obscurity," she went on. "I summoned you one last time to save everything we... you have built. Destroy those who threaten my company. Kill the benefactors of Tannis LLC."

"What?" Bill cried.

She ignored him, as did the demon.

"And if I do? Olivia never asked anything of me without offering payment."

"Their lives and souls are yours to do with as you will. You are a demon, are you not? Is that not what you crave more than anything?" It had better be, because in all of her great grandmother's writings, Olivia never mentioned much about payment. Only of the friendship and great fun they had shared in the scheme they ran. Was this not fun enough for him?

But the demon nodded nonetheless. "It will do," he said. "I accept. Now set me free of this circle and let me do my work."

"Miss Featherstone, no," James said.

"I see mankind hasn't gotten any braver in the passing century," Dantalion snorted. His black eyes glittered as he eyed the men. "Let me out, Brandi Featherstone. You summoned me, now put me to purpose."

"Don't do it," James said, eyes shifting toward the door. "Just put the thing back. Can't we just spy on Accutix like normal people?"

"I am not normal and neither is my company," Brandi growled. "Now stay put. We're doing this my way and that's final."

She turned back to the demon and straightened to her full height. The corner of his lips twitched and she smiled in victory. With the tip of a pointed heel, she broke the chalk circle that kept demon from mortal.

"Go on then," she said. "Do as I command, Dantalion. Take out anyone helping Accutix."

Dantalion nodded and stretched for a moment, his limbs long and wiry on an otherwise attractive form. He stepped forward, leaving the seal and joining the world of Man and accepting her invitation even as he obeyed her command.

"As you wish, Featherstone," he said.

Then he turned on Bill, ripping this throat out before the man could even scream.

"No!" Brandi cried, but it was too late. What could she do against a demon unleashed against the world?

James, he took more time with. The intern scrambled for the door, but he stood no chance at escape either. And when his ribcage was spread apart to expose the delicate organs beneath, the scream he unleashed would have been enough to summon the rest of the Seventy-Two had their sigils been drawn as well.

When Brandi dreamt of screams like that, she never imagined it would come from her own people.

"This isn't what I ordered you to do!" she cried, heart beating like a panicked bird against a cage. Backing away from the grisly scene, Brandi dared not look away from the demon. Not once. What initially seemed like such an old sluggish thing was now fast and all too deadly.

"This is exactly what you ordered me to do," Dantalion purred, advancing on the woman next. He dropped the intern's bloody heart in a wet lump onto her polished floor. "I could see right into their treacherous little hearts, pet. They were selling secrets to your competitor and so had to die."

She opened her mouth to cry out for help, though who she would call, she had no idea. This was not supposed to happen! This was the friend of Olivia Featherstone! Loyal benefactor to her family name!

Before another single sound could leave her mouth, he slashed her throat from ear to ear. The blood fell in a curtain of red down her thin throat, staining the pinstripe below.

She fell to her knees and then to the floor below, never once losing sight of the beast who had done this to her.

"She called me Dandelion, pet," Dantalion said softly, staring down at the dying woman. His dark eyes held no emotion as she lay there, gasping for breath and pumping precious blood out of her neck with each desperate one.

"Wh-what?" she sputtered, pale eyes wide in disbelief.

"You may have inherited her pretty looks, and you may know some things about me, but you aren't Olivia. She called me Dandelion."

"You can't," she whimpered, her head lolling back to the floor where it lay in a sticky puddle of her own blood. "My great grandmother... Our family line..."

"Olivia would thank me for this," he said. "This is a mercy to her family line. She never asked me for blood like so many others have. Now die with dignity, girl. Do her that honor at least."

Brandi's eyes fluttered, watching her great grandmother's old friend back away from her to return to the circle she'd summoned him from. And as he crouched down, his long, spindled limbs jutting out like some macabre spider, Dantalion finally smiled.

It was the last thing she saw as the light dimmed around her, those two beetle-black eyes, and that horrible, horrible smile.

About the Author

M.L. Garza is a fantasy and science fiction author whose work has appeared in magazines, anthologies, stand alone works, and the big screen herself. Her debut novel is set for release in 2019.
https://www.facebook.com/AuthorMLGarza/

ANDROMALIUS: THE SERPENT EARL OF HELL
PAIGE CLENDENIN

Andromalius was a demon, or a spirit, if you will.
He was one of the seventy-two spirits of "The Goetia: The Lesser Key of Solomon," seventy second in fact. Andromalius was an Earl of Hell who appeared in humanoid form and carried a great serpent in his hands.

Andromalius' job as a demon was to punish thieves and people who committed atrocious crimes. He was the one who found the offender, restored goods, set right certain wrongs, and discovered all wickedness. He was the fixer of underhandedness and the discoverer of treasures and riches.

Thirty-six legions of spirits were under his rule in Hell alone where they revered him greatly as their own.

Andromalius sat in wait to be conjured by an exorcist who needed his specialties. His serpent slithered in his arms with hunger behind his eyes, excited to help punish the next wrong doer, and to help set right the crimes of the people of Earth.

*****

Andromalius sat in Hell, cracking his large knuckles as his serpent hung in slithering hoops around his shoulders and neck. It hissed against his ear, letting Andromalius know a young conjurer and her friends were chanting upon the Earth in need of their services.

They were both eager to visit topside of course but wanted to give the conjurer and her comrades a little longer to work for their services.

"Let's make the exorcist and her little friends wait, shall we?" He said to the snake.

I am down for a little fun master the serpent spoke in Andromalius' head.

"Oh, I plan on having some fun my friend...just be patient."

Andromalius laughed heartily as the snake swirled around his shoulders until the serpent was comfortable to wait out the trip topside, not answering Andromalius.

A young girl named Remilynn and three of her closest friends, chanted the words from her grandmother' book of the dead. Remilynn called it a séance, but her grandmother would have known to tell her the spell was called an exorcism and could not be trusted.

Remilynn took her grandmother's book of the dead without permission. She needed the spell to evoke the presence of Andromalius so the spirit could take care of a man who had stolen something from her...three somethings to be exact. Her friends knew they were helping her evoke the spirit, but they had no idea what the demon was capable of or even more so, that the book used was stolen.

Not even Remilynn truly knew what she was doing, she was relying on stories alone to guide her through her anger. She was pissed off and hurt to her very core and didn't know what to do about it...other than summons the one spirit she knew would take care of everything.

*****

Remilynn, Kaitlynn, Sarah, and Matilda were holding hands over a raging fire in the woods, miles away from civilization. Remi, as her friends and family called her had some business with Andromalius and his serpent but lied to her grandmother and friends about the ancient book she was using to evoke him. Her grandmother was a witch, who's magick was great, but Remi was only fifteen, and still too young to understand what magick the book held, or the spirit she was asking to join them. Her grandmother told her she was going to be an amazing witch one day but was far from ready. She ignored her grandmother as anger had overridden her heart. She took the book and lead her friends to the woods where they stood ready to meet whatever the book would provide.

"Greater, demon of Hell, come to us this day we pray...with the moon in the sky and blood in our veins, come forth," Remi said, and then she gave Kaitlynn's hand a squeeze.

"Greater, demon of Hell, we ask for your help to rectify the murders of Remi's mother, father, and sister, come forth," Kaitlynn said, then she squeezed Sarah on the hand.

"Greater, demon of Hell, come to us of bone and ashen flesh, to do what Remilynn bids, come forth," Sarah said, and then she too gave Matilde's hand a squeeze.

"Greater, demon of Hell, Andromalius and the great serpent of the deep...come forth to us now...come forth!" Matilda said the last words as the ground around them began to shake.

The girls, hands fell apart, and they tumbled to the ground, as a hole in the earth appears. Through it, they could see hellfire spew forth from the underworld until a mist twisted like a tornado into the air, it sat down on the dirt in front of them.

The tornado like being blew the hairs of all the girls as they sat up on the ground. They watched the hole in the ground as it continued to spew forth fire, but the flames stayed confined to the circle only.

The cyclone spit a large snake, bigger than any of them had ever seen towards them.

"What the hell?" Matilda screamed.

"It is the serpent of Andromalius," Remilynn smiled.

"It is not what the hell," a deep growling voice beamed out of the wind. "It is what from Hell!"

The large demon walked out from the wind as it dispersed into the atmosphere, then sucked itself back down to the flames of Hell itself. The hole closed behind the winds, leaving the snake and spirit alone with the girls topside.

The large serpent slithered round and round as it caused the four girls to gather closer to Andromalius. They were back on their feet and only inches from the giant of a man...demon. The snake slithered into his arms as he honed the snake boa style across his upper arms.

"You are Adromalius the great demon of the deep," Remi acknowledged.

"That I am little one," Andromalius responded.

The girls watched on in astonishment. The huge humanoid spirit stepped back a few steps then looked down at the dirt beneath his feet. He whispered something to the beast around his arms, and the snake slipped up his arm and positioned itself around his neck. He then punched the dirt under his feet hard and fast, causing a crater to form.

A hole appeared in the earth that exposed a box...the girls had no idea it was there. The demon opened the box in front of them, and inside were many jewels, gold, and silver.

"How did you know that was there?" Kaitlynn asked him.

"You are not the one who needs me child," he said, as he walked up to where the hole to Hell had been. "Open pit of Hell for your brethren," he whispered.

The ground shook again as it opened once more. A nasty looking beast came forth from the hole. Andromalius handed the box to the creature.

"Master Andromalius, to where shall I deliver the box of Hymphilliah?"

"Take it to the great master Satan, as a gift from the seventy second," Andromalius announced.

"Very well," the creature breathed.

The servant took the box Hymphilliah back down in the pit as it closed in front of the eye of the girls.

"Now, young one...what need do you have of me?"

Remi stepped forward to announce the need for Andromalius and the serpent. She gulped audibly in front of the humanoid beast.

"Sir," she began.

"I am no sir," Andromalius responded.

"Shall I call you by name?" Remilynn asked.

"You have already child, once you and your comrades called for me, and again since I have been in your midst," he scolded her.

"This is true," she said. "I apologize great spirit...what would you want us to call you?"

"Call me Fallen Spirit," he grunted in her directions, "but I have no need of you telling me what is needed."

"I don't understand Fallen Spirit," she whispered.

With no answer, he stepped forward to Remilynn as he sat his large palms on either side of her face. His hands were so big they could have cover her face three times over, but it was the snake that sat eye level with her that was causing her to worry the most.

The serpent locked eyes with her as Andromalius read the reasons behind his coming.

"I shall deal with the offender," Andromalius spoke steady, "but you must stay here whilst I do so."

"I will," the girl said.

"Alone," he nodded towards Kaitlynn, Sarah, and Matilda.

"No," Kaitlynn began to protest. "I won't leave her..."

Her words were cut off when the serpent sparang forward from off the spirit's shoulders. The snake began to chase the girls as Andromalius kept his hands on Remi, so she couldn't move. The girls ran fast and far until their screams could no longer be heard by Remi who stood in fear of the Fallen Spirit. The serpent returned reassuring her that her friends would make it home safe, and they would not be harmed.

*****

A man named Seamus sat at a pub in Dublin. He was happy with how his live was going that far. He had done everything and anything he had ever wanted, including stolen, taken what he wanted, and killed people on his way. No one knew he had done those horrible things, but Seamus didn't care one bit, he liked being able to be Seamus the diabolical one minute, to turn around and be one of the boys the next.

"Pardon me Seamus O'Bryan, there is someone at the back door for you," the bartender said as she winked her blue eyes at him.

"Thanks doll," he spoke in a fake Irish accent.

Seamus O'Bryan was nothing more than Sam Baker from New York City, but no one in Dublin knew that. It wasn't uncommon for him to get callers at the back door of the pub, so he thought nothing of it at first.

He walked out of the back door as a great snake fell from out of nowhere. The serpent smothered Seamus's mouth first so his screams could not be heard. The beast tightened around Seamus' neck as he wrapped himself five times around the man's head until he began to black out.

"Leave him alive," Andromalius' voice boomed out.

Very well boss, the snake spoke into his head, as he slithered off the unconscious man. Andromalius took a huge hook out of his back pocket and stuck it through Seamus, straight through his spinal cord.

The giant snake slide up Andromalius' back until he rested in the desired spot. Andromalius began to drag Seamus' body behind him through a portal at the end of the alley. Seamus was still alive at that point, but barely.

What was this man's offence? The great snake asked as he rested on his master's neck.

"This man was diabolical," Andromalius said to the serpent. "He killed many people, including Remilynn's parents and sister."

What benefit did this man have in killing a fifteen-year-old's family?

"He wanted the vehicle they were driving in...Remi was at home waiting on her parents to come home with her new baby sister," Andromalius paused. "They stopped at an intersection...Seamus broke the driver side window, stabbed Remi's father in the chest, opened the door and threw him out, and jumped in the car, and took off."

What of the mother and baby?

"Their bodies were found a mile down the road, tossed in a field."

The snake looked at Seamus as his newly dead bleeding hooked body drug behind them on the way back to the portal to Hell.

Remilynn was standing cold and alone in the dark. Her friends dared not to come back, although she was sure they would have notified people that she was alone out in the middle of nowhere, but no one had come in the near hour the spirit and serpent had been gone. She watched in the distance as a portal like light opened in front of her.

She smiled viciously when she saw Seamus' body being dragged behind the demon Andromulius. He commanded Hell to be opened up again as he dumped Seamus' body into the hellfire. Seamus' screams were heard as the soul of the monstrous man hit the hot flames.

"Thank you, Fallen Spirit," Remi said to the demon and his serpent.

"Your welcome child," he answered. "I am sorry that the man Seamus did those things to your parents, but the dept is not yet paid in full."

"What do you mean?" She asked.

Andromalius walked to the hole in the earth and slowly begun to drop to the hellfire below. His serpent slithered half down, but his tail remained on the surface. Remi, confused, stepped back a little.

"You stole your grandmother's book of the dead, did you not?" Andromalius asked her as he continued to stand with his head peaked out of the hole.

Remilynn's face was placid as she began to realize what the debt unpaid was that the demon was talking about.

"I plan to return it today," Remilynn pleaded.

"Sorry," he grumbled. "A crime is a crime."

The serpent's tail grabbed ahold of Remilynn's ankle. She was screaming the entire time her body was being pulled into the hellfire as the portal to Hell itself closed, enveloping Andromalius, the serpent, and Remilynn, the thief of the book of the dead behind them.

About the Author

Paige Clendenin is a spunky and vivacious author who takes pride in who she is...weird, corky, eclectic, or otherwise.
Facebook Author Page:
https://www.facebook.com/paigeclendeninauthor

Made in the USA
Middletown, DE
20 March 2019